copy

Copyright © 2025 by Sara Ney

All rights reserved.

No part of this book may be reproduced in any form or by any electronic or mechanical means, including information storage and retrieval systems, without written permission from the author, except for the use of brief quotations in a book review.

Editing by Author Services by Emma

Proofreading Virginia Tesi Carey

Cover Design by Okay Creations

Formatting by Casey Formatting

This book contains material protected under International and Federal Copyright Laws and Treaties. Any unauthorized reprint or use of this material is prohibited. No part of this book may be reproduced in any form or by any means, electronic or mechanical, including photocopying, recording, or by any information storage and retrieval systems without "express " written permission from the author, except for the use of brief quotations in a book review.

This is a work of fiction. Names, characters, places, and incidents either are the product of the authors imagination or are used fictitiously. Any resemblance to any actual persons, living or dead is entirely coincidental.

License Notes

This ebook is licensed for your personal enjoyment only. This book may not be resold or shared with other people. If you would like to share with another person, please purchase an additional copy for each recipient.

Thank you for respecting the hard work of this author.

No part of this book may be reproduced in any form or by any electronic or mechanical means, including information storage and retrieval systems, without written permission from the "author, except for the use of brief quotations in a book review.

HIT ME WITH YOUR BEST SHOT

USA TODAY BESTSELLING AUTHOR
SARA NEY

For Logan.
Hot girls read and you're the hottest.

Obviously.

1
austin

*They thought I was a nice, nerdy, bookish girl—
then hockey season started...*

If you would've told me I'd have to miss going to this hockey game, I would've laughed/cried in your face. Seriously.

Hockey isn't just a sport to me—it's a *religion*.

The thing you should know about me (because we're still strangers, you and I) is that I'm a *Super* Fan.

Capital S, capital F.

I'm talking: custom jerseys, face paint, cardboard signs to hold up—*the whole nine yards*.

It must be genetic because my dad? He loved hockey, too. And since he's up in heaven looking down on me, watching makes it feel like he's still here. So, yeah.

I'll probably never stop loving the game.

When Dad passed, I was gifted his season passes to the Houston Blaze and I haven't missed a game since.

Until tonight.

Missing the game feels sacrilegious somehow; like the universe is playing a cruel trick on me. But here I am, out of the arena, with my heart in the rink, watching the game from a screen instead of my usual seat.

But hey, I did a good thing, right?

Letting my friend Paul—*also* a die-hard fan—use the seats. He's planning to propose to his boyfriend during the third period, and it's going to be on the freaking Jumbotron.

Super romantic.

Super public.

So extra—exactly like Paul and Emilio.

Giving him the seats felt like the perfect engagement gift. If missing the game means they'll have a night to remember, it's worth it.

So here I am, at a bar called Five Alarm near my condo, watching from a plasma screen like a mere mortal instead of the superfan I am.

Love trumps hockey.

Sometimes.

"Come on!" I shout at the wall of monitors in front of me. "Let's go!"

The Baddies aren't going to win the way they're playing tonight.

Like complete shit.

A groan escapes me as one of the forwards fumbles a pass, turning over the puck. Again.

"It's like they've forgotten they're on ice!" I complain to no one in particular, throwing my hands in the air. A couple of heads turn my way from the far end of the bar, but I'm not bothered.

If I can't be in the arena, I'll be the loudest Blaze fan this place has ever seen, my eyes never leaving the television set.

And just like that, they miss another goal.

How hard is it to shoot the puck *into* the net?

"You have *got* to be kidding me!" I practically levitate off the stool in frustration, smacking at the bar top as I screech, "Come on!"

HIT ME WITH YOUR BEST SHOT

The handsome bartender chuckles as he wipes down the counter.

"Rough night?"

"You could say that," I huff, crossing my arms. "I should be there. You do one nice deed for a friend and look where it lands you."

I wave a hand at the screen, clearly unimpressed by my team's lackluster performance.

"Tell me how you really feel." He grins, sliding another drink my way.

"Maybe they're losing because I'm not there," I theorize, narrowing my eyes as if I could somehow will the team to score by force of disappointment.

The bartender snorts. "For sure. I'm sure you're the missing piece."

"I'm serious!" I exclaim, leaning forward. "I haven't missed a game in years, and now this? There is no such thing as a coincidence."

He raises an eyebrow. "They play better when you're screaming from the stands?"

"Exactly!" I'm oddly validated by his sentiment. "My energy fuels them. They *need* me. And I'm stuck here, drinking this sad little beer while Paul is out there making *romantic history* on the Jumbotron."

Bastard.

"Paul?" The bartender looks intrigued, wiping down another glass and lingering nearby. "Is he your boyfriend?"

"My boyfriend?" I snort. *Please.* "No—platonic friends from elementary school."

He stops wiping and leans forward. "And you're only here because you let him have your seats."

I nod, sipping the beer. "Indeed."

"So you're a giver?"

Eh?

Is that some sort of sexual innuendo or is he genuinely asking if I'm a kind person?

"Uh. *Sure*," I reply cautiously, giving him a half-smile, unsure where this is going. I don't love it when guys make snarky comments—it makes me uneasy and off-kilter.

My eyes flicker back to the monitor and I realize I missed the last few minutes of the game because of the bartender's chatter.

Damn.

"Shit, what did I miss?" I ask, sitting up straighter, but the bartender grins wider as if pleased he was a distraction.

"You sure are cute when you're riled up."

I ignore him as I fixate back on the screen, trying to catch up on the action. I need him to stop talking to me and go away—not flirt.

He is not my type.

I hope he doesn't try and pass me his phone number because there's another number I'm obsessed with, and player thirty, the goalie, who is letting one shot after another slide right through his legs like a rookie on open skate night.

Houston is struggling and it's getting harder to stay calm.

"Block it, number thirty! Block it!" I shout, voice escalating. "It's called being a goalie! Maybe try it sometime!"

I slam my fist onto the bar, making my beer glass rattle.

At this point, I'm fully invested in my meltdown.

God it feels good, hands gesturing wildly, legs are bouncing in frustration. Brows in my hairline. Angry mouth agape.

"I think number thirty should buy you a drink after this," the bartender teases.

I think you should stop talking to me, I want to retort.

Seriously. This guy is so annoying.

"Maybe thirty should go home and take a nap!" I grind out, frustrated. "GET IT!" I shout, leaning forward as if my glare could get these boys into action. "You've got this! One good shot! One!"

The bar goes quiet around me, but I'm too caught up in the game to notice.

"Move your feet!" I raise up out of my barstool again. "*Oh my God*, Montagalo, this is hockey, not a freaking stroll through the park! What are you doing?!"

I rise to my feet, ready to throw myself into the game as if I could magically teleport onto the ice. Then I sit back down.

Then I stand again.

I want to pull my hair out.

The bartender laughs like he's watching the best comedy show of his life, but I ignore him, too focused on the screen to give him my attention. My body sways left, then right—then left again—mimicking the movement of the puck.

I'm completely absorbed in the play.

"Dang," a new voice chimes in, commenting on my hockey-fueled dramatics, and I glance over at a young woman who's pulled herself up to the bar right next to me. Her hair is down but she's wearing a ball cap and hoodie. "Good game?"

"Depends on your definition of good. Gio Montagalo has literally shit the bed."

She laughs and taps on the bar top to get the bartender's attention, giving him her order.

"I take it you're a fan?" she asks once she's settled, setting her cell on the bar top in front of her.

I give her a half smile. "Oh, you know, a casual observer who's one missed block from losing her shit."

The girl grins. "I think I'd pay to see that."

"Trust me," the bartender interjects himself into our conversation. "So would I."

The newcomer smiles at him, lifting her glass before taking a sip.

"Has she been like this the entire time?" She nods toward me and they proceed to discuss me as if I weren't sitting two feet away with a perfectly good set of ears.

"Absolutely," he says, grinning as he rests his elbows on the counter. "In fact, she'd be there in person but gave up her seats for true love."

I roll my eyes. "Please. It's not that deep. I'm a decent friend."

The girl raises an eyebrow. "True love? Do tell."

"Okay, fine. I gave up my season tickets tonight so my friend could propose on the Jumbotron. That's it." I take a sip from my glass and continue ranting. "Meanwhile, Montagalo is single-handedly ruining my night. Does he know he's supposed to stop pucks? Or is this some avant-garde performance art where defense doesn't exist?"

She chuckles and raises her glass. "Here's to being a good friend. And to that rat bastard Montagalo pulling his head out of his ass and doing his job."

"Amen!" I clink my glass with hers. "I'll drink to that—but I'm going to need something stronger if I'm going to survive this game."

The clock ticks closer to the third period. Closer to the proposal.

She takes another sip from her glass, eyes fastened to my face. "At least you're not doomed to suffer through an entire season watching at home."

"No, *thank God*. I'm back in my rightful spot for the next game." I shake my head. "Seriously though—if Montagalo continues to play like crap, I'll storm the locker room and give him a piece of my mind."

The girl bursts into an evil laugh, tipping her head. "I can totally picture you barging into the locker room while they're all half naked."

Half naked?

Had not considered that.

I nod solemnly. "I'd be like, 'Listen, Montagalo, your job is *simple*: stop the bloody effing puck. I don't care if you have to grow extra hands–you have one job and that job is to get after it." *Clap.* "Do." *Clap.* "Your." *Clap.* "Job!'"

She nearly chokes on her drink, laughing harder. "I'd pay good money to see you versus Montagalo. He looks like the kind of guy who needs to be brought down a peg or two."

"Damn straight." I take another sip, feeling validated and righteous. "He's way too cocky for someone who's spent the past two games playing with his head shoved firmly up his ass."

Granted, it's a good-looking ass. Not the point.

She agrees easily. "Yeah. He looks like he's a giant asshole, doesn't he?"

Tall. Dark.

So handsome if he walked through those doors I would retract everything I said about him, fall to my knees and—

"Have you seen his social media?" she asks, yanking me from my dangerous train of thought. "It's all pictures of him volunteering. The whole page! Like, is anyone buying the 'nice guy' act? He's probably totally banging every girl who so much as breathes near him."

I snort, leaning in conspiratorially. "Oh, 100%. The pictures of 'him with his buddy's dog' thing? Classic bait. And have you seen the comments? Barf. *'Oh, Gio, you're so amazing,'* and he laps it up."

She smirks. "You know what would make my night? If the man himself showed up here and overheard us dragging his entire existence."

I raise my glass. "If that happens, drinks are on me."

"My name is Nova, by the way," she says, finally letting a giggle slip.

"Oh—oh my gosh, I'm so sorry," I say, suddenly realizing how much I've been ranting. "I'm Austin—like the city. Nice to meet you."

"I'm Kyle," the bartender chimes in, completely unprompted.

Nova and I both freeze for a second, glancing at each other before bursting into full-on laughter.

Not to be rude but no one asked for his name.

Certainly not us.

Kyle shrugs, smirking like he's somehow part of the conversation and in on the jokes. "What? Figured I'd introduce myself, too."

I tilt my head, giving Kyle a look. "Well, Kyle, now that we're on a first-name basis, do you have any thoughts on Montagalo's tragic inability to stop a puck?"

Kyle doesn't miss a beat. "Guy's got butterfingers, for sure. But at least he's consistent."

Nova snorts into her drink, her shoulders shaking. "Consistently terrible."

Kyle shrugs, grabbing a rag to wipe the counter. "Consistent is consistent. Besides, I'm a Bruins fan, so, you know…" He shrugs again, like this confession is supposed to mean something profound.

I clutch my chest, pretending to be mortally offended. "A Bruins fan? Here I thought we were starting to bond."

Kyle waves his rag at us like he's shooing a couple of flies. "Oh, don't mind me. Doing my job here." He claps twice. "Do. Your. Job!"

He's mocking me.

"Dude!" Nova absolutely loses it, clutching her stomach as she laughs. "Kyle's got jokes!"

I roll my eyes, but can't stop the smile from widening on my face. "You two are the worst."

Kyle winks. "Cheers to that."

2
gio

We didn't lose the game. We ran out of time...

The locker room is a mess—towels draped over benches, water bottles knocked on their sides, and the faint hum of the overhead lights buzzing like they're mocking us. The air is heavy, thick with sweat and disappointment, clinging to everything like a second skin. Dirty socks are strewn across the floor, mingling with drenched, musty pads that have been thrown aside in frustration.

It smells like defeat.

Mine.

Ours.

A unique, sour stench that's somehow worse than the usual hockey funk. Defeat has a scent all its own, one that seeps into your pores and lingers long enough to remind you how badly you've failed.

I sit on the bench, staring at the scuffed tile floor as if it holds the answers I'm looking for. It doesn't. My mask dangles from my hand, the plastic still damp, still sticky, like it's absorbed every bad decision I made out there tonight.

The chatter is subdued, voices muffled by exhaustion and bruised egos.

No one wants to talk about it, but everyone's thinking the same thing: we blew it.

Or worse—they're thinking *I* blew it.

You let them down, Montagalo. Again.

What are they paying you for?

"Montagalo," Coach's gruff voice snaps through the haze, and I look up instinctively, my heart sinking further at the sight of his expression.

Stern.

Tired.

Disappointed.

"You good?" he asks, but it's not really a question. It's a subtle demand for an explanation—one I don't have. Not yet, my brain is too tired to come up with excuses. Too tired to explain why I bit it.

"Yeah, I'm good," I reply, voice sounding hollow. "Sitting here thinking."

I sound like a pussy. A wuss.

Coach narrows his eyes; for a second, I think he might start screaming in my face—the way he was screaming during the game. Instead, he shakes his head.

Frustrated.

He wants better from me. Hell, *I* want better from me.

No one is more disappointed in my performance than I am.

"Think less," he demands shrewdly. "React more."

With that, he's gone, moving on to someone else to give cold advice to; it won't make us feel better or add goals to the scoreboard.

Sure, our defense didn't exactly show up tonight, but I'm the goalie.

The last line of defense.

The one who's supposed to clean up everyone else's messes.

And I didn't.

I sit for several more moments, letting Coach's words settle.

Think *less*. *React* more.

Easier said than done, yeah? Out on the ice, there's no room for hesitation. No space for second-guessing. But tonight, all I could do was think—and every thought led to another mistake.

I put my mask into my bag, the action mechanical. Automatic.

I've packed my shit thousands of times.

Around me, the guys move, talking in low tones that sound distant—I feel like I'm watching through a fogged-up window.

The locker room remains weighed down by our failure and unmet expectations.

"Gee," Dominic Gagnon calls my nickname from across the room, his toothless grin annoyingly wide for a dude who lost his third game in a row. "You coming to Blanco?"

Of course Dom is in a good mood.

He always is, win or lose. Some people are built differently and not necessarily in a good way—not him though. Life of the party, shoulder to lean on, hype beast all the way.

And normally, I'm always down for a good time.

Blanco's is a chic steakhouse with a dark, moody bar. The owner keeps it closed for the team after home games so it doesn't get overrun by fans looking for autographs or selfies. The food is great, the drinks are better, and the atmosphere is perfect for blowing off steam without being watched like a zoo exhibit.

Tonight? The last thing I need is to get drunk and stew in my own mediocrity.

I sucked.

"Nah. No thanks," I mutter, standing up and slinging my massive bag over my shoulder. The weight of it feels good—a reminder I still exist in the real world, even if I'm walking out of it with my tail between my legs. "Not tonight."

Dom frowns. "Aw, come on. You're not gonna leave me stuck

with LeBlanc and Petrov, are you? Those two can't hold a conversation to save their lives."

I roll my eyes, halfway to the door. "Sounds like a *you* problem."

His laughter follows me out, light and easy in a way that makes me want to turn around and punch him square in his stupid, gap-toothed grin.

I'm not in the mood for his good mood.

The cold air hits me as soon as I step outside, biting at my skin and cutting through the lingering haze of sweat and frustration. The parking lot is nearly empty, shadows stretching long under the flickering overhead lights.

My car sits alone near the far end, a beacon of solitude I can't decide if I'm grateful for or resentful of. I toss my bag into the trunk with more force than necessary, the satisfying thud echoing in the still night air.

Blanco's would be easy. A couple of drinks, some laughs, and I could've pretended, for a little while, I'm not the reason we're on a losing streak. But that's the problem, isn't it?

Pretending only gets you so far.

I climb into the driver's seat and sit there for a moment, staring at the dashboard. The silence feels heavier out here, away from the team, the locker room, the noise.

For a split second, I consider texting someone—anyone—to avoid going home and being alone with my negative thoughts. But I shake my head, shoving the idea aside.

This is the third game in a row I've played like shit—the weight of the entire team on my shoulders—and tonight the realization I may not be strong enough to carry it hits me square between the eyes.

I don't deserve distraction tonight.

I deserve to be miserable.

I need to be home.

Soak in the hot tub.

Sleep it off.

If I can't figure out how to get my act together soon, I'm not only letting the team down—I'm letting myself down, too.

No sooner am I throwing my bag down in the front entry of my penthouse than my phone buzzes in my pocket. I don't have to look to know who it is. Only one other person besides my teammates would bug me.

Nova.

My twin sister has a sixth sense when it comes to me being in a funky mood. Like clockwork, she knows the exact moment I step through my front door.

> **Nova:** Hey loser. How you holding up?

I sigh, regretting I haven't muted her notifications by now.

> **Me:** Define 'holding up.'

The response is almost instant, as if she's been waiting with her thumbs poised over the keyboard.

> **Nova:** Yikes. That bad?

I don't reply straight away. Instead, I toss my car keys on the counter, grab a water from the fridge, and let the cool condensation roll over my palm as I lean against the counter.

I flex the hand that has been stuffed in my goalie glove for the past few hours.

> **Nova:** Wanna talk about it?

I smirk humorlessly at the screen. Nova always wants to talk about it—as if me spilling my guts is the answer to all my problems.

Talking.

Ha. Good luck.

> Me: Not really.

I take a long drink of water, anticipating her next message.

> Nova: Too bad. I'm coming over.

I almost spit out the water.

> Me: NO. Don't.

> Nova: I'm already in the elevator.

Of course she is. Why do I bother anymore?

I groan, glancing toward the door as if I can will her to stay in the elevator and take it back down to her floor. Pfft. No chance of happening. Nova isn't persistent—she's relentless.

Have I mentioned my sister lives in the same building? In a swanky little apartment I purchased several floors below mine. It's not the penthouse—*that* is all mine—but it's too big for a petite girl like her, with panoramic windows and a skyline view.

She calls it "our building" as if she's got some kind of equity stake in the place.

She does not.

Try telling her though, when she strolls through the lobby in sweatpants and demands the concierge carry her grocery bags.

Brat.

It wasn't entirely selfless, buying her the apartment. Sure, I wanted to make sure she had somewhere safe and comfortable to live—but it came with the added bonus of keeping her close.

Too close since she can storm into my life unannounced with a key and food and zero respect for my boundaries.

> Me: Go home. I DO NOT WANT COMPANY.

I am not in the mood.

HIT ME WITH YOUR BEST SHOT

> Nova: You never want company.

> Me: Yeah but this time I mean it.

She's impossible. Guess this is what happens though when you lose your parents as teenagers and only have your sibling for support. You learn to lean on each other, *sometimes a little too much*. Nova has always been the one to show up, whether I wanted her to or not, with unyielding energy and the annoying ability to make me feel better without actually solving *any* of my problems.

When Mom and Dad died, it was the two of us.

Nova dealt with the loss by pretending nothing could touch her—bulldozing through life like she was invincible. I dealt with it by throwing myself into hockey. Practice. Games. Working out.

She says I use the game to avoid using emotions. She's probably not wrong. But she avoids her emotions by pretending everything's hunky-dory, so who's winning here?

Neither of us.

When the elevator dings I hear the faint sound of her sneakers squeaking across the cold, marble tile of the hallway. She's not in a hurry—she never is—but there's something deliberate in her stride, like she's preparing to pounce on me.

"Open up, loser!" she calls out cheerfully. Knocks a few times. "I brought snacks!"

Snacks. Nothing says *'Sorry you're failing at life'* like a bag of chips, gummy bears—and unsolicited advice.

I take my time walking to the door, letting her knock again, harder this time—cause that's what brothers do. Live to irritate their sisters…

"Come on! It's freezing out here! Don't make me eat all these snacks myself!"

Snacks?

I love those.

Still, when I yank the door open, it's with a scowl. "You do realize it's not actually freezing, right? You're in a hallway and live three floors down."

She ignores me and breezes past, heading straight for the kitchen.

"No hello?" I complain. "No 'How are you, Gio?'" I close the door behind her.

"You look like crap, by the way," she says, glancing over her shoulder with a grin.

"Thanks," I deadpan, following her. "Exactly what I needed to hear."

She ignores me, of course, wandering to the fridge like she's searching for something to critique. "Ooh, nice. You bought the fancy sparkling water again."

I roll my eyes. "It's water."

"Correction: it's rich-people water," she says, twisting off the cap and taking a long swig. "*Ahhh.* So refreshing." Nova plops down at a barstool and surveys my giant kitchen. "Seriously, you could use some plants or something. It's like a robot lives here."

So she's always reminding me.

"A robot who likes his privacy." I groan, running a hand through my hair. "Why are you like this?"

"Because I'm your sister," she says with a shrug. "And you'd be totally lost without me."

As much as I want to argue, I know she's right; I would be lost without her.

Nova's smirk softens as she reaches across the counter and slides a bag of gummy bears toward me.

"Eat one," she demands, her tone leaving no room for negotiation.

I shake my head. "No thanks."

"Eat a gummy bear." She wiggles the bag. "Trust me, it helps."

I stare at her, then at the bag, before reluctantly grabbing one. I pop it into my mouth to shut her up, the chewy sweetness hitting my taste buds as she watches me with an annoyingly smug expression.

"See?" she says, leaning back in her chair with a satisfied grin.

"I feel *so* much better," I deadpan.

"You're welcome." She ignores the sarcasm entirely, plucking another gummy bear out of the bag and biting its head off. "Now, tell me what's going on with you."

"It's nothing," I say finally, my voice quieter than I meant it to be. "One bad game."

Nova snorts. "You've had bad games before, and you didn't look this miserable. What gives?"

"It's not just tonight," I admit, the words slipping out before I can stop them. "It's been three games, Nova. Three. Everyone's counting on me, and I can't—I—"

I trail off, not sure how to finish the sentence.

She doesn't say anything at first, watches me with those sharp, calculating eyes. Somehow they always see right through me.

My sister sighs and gets up, walking around the counter to stand next to me, sliding her arm around my waist and giving me a squeeze.

"Know what your problem is?" she says, crossing her arms.

I glance at her.

"No, but I bet you're going to tell me."

She laughs. "You take everything too seriously. You're allowed to screw up sometimes, Gio. You're human. Mostly."

"Not for the amount of money they're paying me," I mutter, leaning back against the counter.

Nova rolls her eyes, hopping up to sit on the edge of the counter like she owns the place.

"Boo-hoo, Mr. Million-Dollar Contract. Poor you, with your fancy penthouse and fancy sparkling water. The world must be so hard."

"It's not about the money," I snap. "It's about the team. They're counting on me to deliver, and I'm—"

"—*Human*," she interrupts. "You said it's not about the money, but you're acting like the weight of the world is on your shoulders. Gio—it's a game. You're not curing cancer."

"Not the point," I say through gritted teeth, but she cuts me off *again*.

"No, you're missing the point," she says, leaning forward. "You can't carry the team on your own. That's not how hockey works. You're one guy, and last time I checked, there are five other dudes on the ice with you at all times. Maybe let them share some of the load, huh?"

I hate that she's right.

She sees the look on my face and grins. "There it is. The face of someone realizing his brilliant sister knows what she's talking about."

I shake my head, but a reluctant smile tugs at the corner of my mouth. "Brilliant might be pushing it."

"Admit it," she teases, kicking her legs playfully then hops down from the counter. "You'd be a total mess without me."

"Debatable," I say, grabbing the bag of gummy bears and tossing it at her. She catches it with ease, ripping it open like it's her reward for a job well done.

She chews on a gummy bear, grabs several more, then heads toward my living room.

"Not to make you feel shittier," she singsongs. "But I met one of your fans tonight—she wasn't exactly thrilled with your performance."

I freeze, halfway to grabbing the remote. "Shocker. Someone is pissed I shit the bed."

"This girl was roasting you so hard I thought about ordering marshmallows," Nova fires back, her grin stretching ear to ear.

That actually makes me laugh, despite myself.

I sink onto one end of the sofa, stretching my legs out as Nova clicks on the television, amused by her own joke.

"She had the whole bar laughing," she continues, scrolling through streaming options as if her words weren't making my nostrils flare. "During the third period she did an impression of you flailing in the goal and I almost fell off the barstool."

"Which bar?" I sit up straighter.

"The one on the corner," she says nonchalantly, still not looking up from the screen. "I think it's called Five Alarm."

Ahh. That bar.

Nova's answer only makes me more suspicious. "What were you doing at a bar on a *game* night?"

She pauses, peeking at me with an innocent smile that's anything but innocent. "Watching the game, obviously."

"Nova." My tone is heavy with warning.

"What?" she says, feigning confusion. "I like to support my brother. Is that a crime?"

"It is when you're doing it from a bar instead of the arena?" I ask tersely. "You have family tickets, Nova. Expensive ones."

As a matter-of-fact, the seats she usually sits in are against the glass and the most sought after seats in the arena. So the nights she doesn't show up, they remain empty and could be sold for hundreds of dollars.

More so when the team is on a winning streak, or those years we're in the finals.

She shrugs, her attention drifting back to the television. "I wasn't in the mood to be at the arena tonight. Too many people, too much noise. You know how it is."

"That's it?"

Another shrug. "Maybe?"

I pause.

Wait.

Something's off and I know her well enough to sense it.

"Fine!" she bursts out, throwing her hands in the air. "If you must know, I was there to meet a date, but he stood me up."

I blink back my surprise.

"You're kidding."

"Nope," she says with exaggerated cheerfulness. "The guy bailed, without bothering to text. So I ended up at the bar alone, which was more entertaining than the date probably would've been."

"Nova…" I trail off, not sure what to say.

My sister doesn't *do* vulnerability.

She's the type to brush everything off with a joke, and hearing her admit to something like this feels weirdly…*raw*.

"Don't." She holds up a hand to stop me. "I don't need your pity, Gio. It's not a big deal."

"Not a big deal?" I repeat, my voice rising. "The guy didn't even show up! Who the hell does that?"

Cocksucking loser.

"Apparently he does." I see the flicker of hurt in her eyes before she looks away.

My hands clench into fists, the protective older brother in me roaring to the surface.

"What's his name? I want to beat his ass!" Give me something to do with this pent-up aggression.

She snorts, shaking her head. "Like I'm going to tell you. I don't need you going full hockey enforcer on some guy who's not worth my time. I know Gio, you don't have to lecture me."

I open my mouth.

Close it.

"Sorry it didn't work out." I want to argue with her so bad.

My sister grunts. "I'm not. Everything happens for a reason."

"Surprisingly zen of you," I remark, leaning back against the couch.

She smirks, grabbing another gummy bear. "What can I say? I'm a fountain of wisdom."

"Or denial," I mutter, earning a playful shove from her.

"Shut up," she says, laughing. "Seriously, though, I dodged a bullet. If a guy can't even text to say he's not showing up for a date, he's not someone I want in my life."

HIT ME WITH YOUR BEST SHOT

"Fair point," I admit, though the idea of someone treating my sister like an afterthought makes my blood boil.

"Exactly." Nova pops another gummy bear into her mouth. "Besides, I had more fun pretending not to know you and roasting you at the bar than I would have on a date."

"Gee, thanks." I groan, dragging a hand down my face. "Are you ever gonna let that go?"

"Absolutely not," she replies, grinning. "The girl was hilarious, Gio. Like—brutally honest in the best way. We need people like that in your life."

We?

"People who insult me in public?" I ask, raising an eyebrow. "I have you for that."

"Eh. We can always use one more."

3
austin

I'm all yours until a hockey player falls in love with me. Then you're on your own...

*W*hy *does the guy at the end of the bar look familiar?*

I give him another glance, squinting slightly as if it'll help my memory. Nope. Still can't place him.

Sliding onto a stool in the center of the bar (luckily, it's one that doesn't wobble), the worn leather creaks under me as I cross my legs and settle in, propping my elbow on the bar.

And before you go asking what the heck I'm doing at the bar for the *second* time this week, the answer is simple: grabbing dinner. I've had a long day and don't feel like cooking, and this place makes a burger so good it should probably be illegal.

I open the menu, even though I already know what I'm ordering. The bacon cheeseburger is a no-brainer, and their fries? Life-changing. I skim the options anyway, stealing another quick glance at the broody guy down the bar.

The guy at the bar.

His broad shoulders.

He sure is good-looking.

Something about him keeps pulling my attention.

There's something about him—something familiar. It's not the way he's hunched over his drink—which looks like ice water—as if it personally offended him. It's the jawline, the dark, messy hair, and unmistakable energy of someone who's mentally replaying every bad decision they've ever made.

Like the universe has wronged him recently and he's still debating how to retaliate.

Huh.

I tap my fingers on the edge of the bar, debating. Curiosity isn't a good enough reason to talk to a stranger, is it? Then again, *what's the harm in striking up a little conversation?*

Before I can overthink it, the words are out of my mouth.

"Rough day?"

He doesn't react at first; stares at the ice cubes floating in his glass. For a moment, I don't think he heard me—or worse, he's ignoring me.

But then he turns, locking his eyes onto mine.

Oh.

Oh…

Okay. Wow.

Did I say good-looking?

I take it back.

He's…

Wow.

So stunningly similar to Gio Montagalo that I am taken aback.

But. With the ball cap he has on, it's hard to see his eyes–the bar is way too dim, the lighting throwing too many shadows over his face.

I blink three more times before realizing I've been staring. LIKE A WEIRDO.

I swear the corner of his mouth twitches like he knows exactly the effect he's having on me.

"Rough day," he repeats, voice low and gravelly. "Something like that." Pause. "Rough *week*, actually."

I raise an eyebrow, leaning slightly toward him. "Well. Whatever's in that glass doesn't look like it's helping."

Ha ha.

His lips twitch, *but barely*. "It's water."

Ding, ding, ding—I was right!

"Let me guess," I continue, gesturing toward his glass. "You're one of those people who think water solves everything. Bad day? *Water.* Hangover? *Water.* Life falling apart? *Water.*"

He shrugs, his dark eyes flicking back to mine. "I'm not a big drinker."

"Valid," I concede, grabbing my Sprite with lime and raising my glass in a toast. "You know what helps more?"

He arches an eyebrow, waiting.

"Bacon. *Cheese*burger," I declare victoriously. "Guaranteed to fix any bad mood."

"Now you sound like my sister." He laughs.

"Why? Does she like burgers?"

"No—she's always pushing gummy bears on me like those are a cure for any ailment."

Interesting. "Gummy bears?" I repeat, tilting my head. "That's oddly specific. Is she a doctor or something? Is this her medical opinion?"

He chuckles, shaking his head. "Nope."

"Does it help?"

He pauses, considering. "Sometimes."

At that exact moment, my burger arrives. It's in a to-go bag, packed neatly in a white Styrofoam container doing nothing to disguise the mouthwatering smells wafting out of it.

My mouth waters as I untie the knot and lift the lid, taking a deep whiff.

"Mmm." I sigh contentedly, then glance at him. "Want one?"

I lift a fry and hold it in his direction, wiggling it slightly to tempt him with it.

He eyes the fry like it's some kind of foreign object, then

looks back at me, one eyebrow raised. "You offering me pity fries?"

I grin at him. "Yup."

He hesitates for a moment, then leans forward, plucking the fry from my hand with an almost begrudging smile.

"Thanks."

To keep myself busy I eat a fry, too.

Swallow.

"You live around here?" he asks, chewing.

I push the container closer, so it's between us now, an unspoken invitation for him to grab another.

"Yeah, not far. A couple blocks over."

He nods, reaching for another fry. "Nice area."

"It's alright," I say casually. Nice isn't the word for this area; expensive. Waspy. High-end. Those are better words to describe it, but I won't get into that. "What about you? You a regular around here?"

Never seen him here before, not that I come here often.

In the shadows beneath the brim of his cap, I watch his lips twitch, almost forming a smile. "Not really. Thought I could use a change of scenery."

"Sure, sure." I gesture toward his glass. "Because the water at home wasn't cutting it?" I chuckle. "You like their Sonic ice better?"

The quip earns me a soft laugh and I feel an odd sense of victory. I pause to grab another handful of fries—three at a time, naturally—and take a bite before continuing my banter.

"I was here the other night for the Baddies game—what I love about this place is it doesn't get crowded so I can watch games in peace."

His expression shifts enough to make me pause.

"The Baddies game?" He goes still, one fry suspended halfway to his lips.

"Yeah," I say, nodding. "Talk about a letdown, hey? Goalie seriously screwed the pooch on Thursday. Ugh."

He's silent for a moment, dark eyes watching me intently.

"What?" I chew and talk at the same time now that we found a topic I feel passionately about. "Am I *wrong*? 'Cause I'm *pretty* sure I saw that puck fly past him at least three times, and he wasn't even close."

His lips twitch, but it doesn't quite reach his eyes. More like…

A restrained smile.

He looks constipated.

"Everyone has off nights," he says finally, studying his water glass, pushing it forward so the bartender can refill it. "Including goalies."

"True—but three nights?" I pop yet another fry into my mouth. "This wasn't an off night though. This was a train wreck. Like, they should check the poor guy for whiplash."

Poor bastard.

He exhales a quiet laugh through his nose, finally setting the fry down on the napkin beside his glass. "At least you're honest."

"The good news is, he's not around to hear me rant about how horrible he's been playing." I hesitate. "I mean, I love the guy, but lately I have no idea what his deal is."

His countenance doesn't change—no smirk, no frown—just a stillness that suddenly feels heavier than it should.

"Right?" I ask again, my voice faltering, confidence waning.

One second passes.

Then another.

Then,

"Right." The guy clears his throat. "You sound like you know what you're talking about. Huge fan?"

I nod enthusiastically. "I am. My dad passed away a few years ago and I inherited his season tickets; I've been coming to games since I was little. What about you?"

"Yup. Big fan." He also nods. "Where are your seats?"

"Upper level, center ice," I say. "They're great. You can see the whole rink, every play, every bad call from the refs."

He smiles faintly. "Good seats. But..."

"But?" I prompt, reaching for a knife so I can cut my cheeseburger in half. Might as well eat it now since we're sitting here chatting. I hate reheating food.

"They're not at the glass." He says it nonchalantly—as if those seats weren't a big deal.

I laugh, shaking my head as I finish cutting the burger. "No. I'm not made of money, so nosebleeds will have to do until I win the lottery."

The guy raises an eyebrow and leans toward me. "What if I told you I could get you seats at the glass?"

I laugh at him again, picking up one half of my sandwich and manhandling it as I say, "I'd say you're either delusional or you know someone important."

"My sister," he confesses. "She has great seats and hasn't been going—if you want two tickets for the next home game, they're yours."

I feel a slice of pickle slide out the corner of my mouth.

It lands with a slimey *splat* on the bar top.

"Wait, you're serious?" I do not care that I probably have ketchup on my chin! This man is offering me tickets against the glass? Say what?!

"Totally serious," he says, leaning back in his chair and taking another sip of water, like he didn't drop an insane offer on me.

"Why though?" I ask, still trying to process what happened. "Those tickets cost a fortune and I am a total stranger."

"A *cute* stranger."

"Excuse me?" I manage, my voice pitching up a little too high. Is he flirting with me or am I imagining things?

He shrugs his broad shoulders, completely unbothered, lips quirking into the faintest smirk. "I can't call you cute?"

I blink at him, feeling a flush creep up my neck. "That's not the point! You don't give people tickets based on appearances. I could be a lunatic. Or a crazy stalker fan."

"Are you?"

"No."

"Then it's settled. Fans should get good seats. And cute fans? Even *better* seats."

Did I just fall in love?

Is this love at first sight?

No. Absolutely not.

That would be ridiculous!

I do not *believe* in love at first sight.

No.

That's what happens in movies and my life has never been picture perfect—not even close. Not even a little. My love life? An even bigger mess. My last date ended with a guy who "forgot" his wallet, ordered the most expensive thing on the menu—then ghosted me when I asked if he could Venmo me the money.

I'm still waiting for that $120, by the way.

So, no.

I'm not falling for the stranger with the toothy grin and the absurdly good hair and deliciously broad shoulders who's offering me *free*, outrageously expensive VIP tickets to see my absolute favorite sports team.

Pfft.

As if.

"Are you okay?" His voice cuts through my mental spiral, pulling me back to the present. He's watching me with one eyebrow raised.

"Huh?" I blink as I come to. "Oh, yeah. Totally fine." Never been better. "Why?"

"You went quiet," he says, smirking again. "I thought I broke you for a second."

My head shakes. "Honestly, it's because I don't know what to say."

My heart wants to burst with excitement and I bite down on my bottom lip to stop any word vomit.

"Don't take this the wrong way, but—can I get your number?" the guy says. "I'll have to message you the QR code."

"Oh," I say, surprised, but not in a bad way. "Yeah, of course."

I rattle off my cell, and stare at his hands as his fingers deftly type my numbers into his phone. Big. Strong hands.

Rough looking.

Man hands…

A moment later, my phone buzzes.

"There." He slips his phone back into the back pocket of his jeans. "Tickets should be there."

I glance down at my phone, the confirmation text lighting up the screen. My eyes widen, and I can't help the soft gasp that escapes my lips.

"Wow," I murmur, feeling a mix of awe and unease settle in my chest. "Thank you, seriously. This is so—"

"Generous? Thoughtful? Too good to be true?" he cuts in, smirking.

"Yes." I squint at him as he stands, digs into his back pocket for his wallet. From it, he pulls out several crisp bills and places them on the bar, tipping the bartender generously. Too generously, in my opinion because he was only drinking water, but who am I to judge? "Unless your plan is to murder me."

It's meant to be a joke, but even as the words leave my mouth, a tiny voice in the back of my head wonders if I should be more cautious. After all, no one is this perfect without a catch.

"Too late for take-backs," the guy announces. "Already have your number."

Oh shit. That's right.

My stomach dips at how easily I handed over my phone without much thought, and now I'm suddenly regretting it.

"Well if you're going to murder me, shouldn't I at least have your name?"

He glances over his shoulder, his smirk back in full force as he pulls on a leather jacket. "My friends and sister sometimes call me Gee."

"G. Like the *letter*?"

He nods. "Yup—like the letter."

I tilt my head, trying to make sense of it. "Is that your real name, or are you trying to make yourself harder to track when you inevitably end up on the evening news?"

He is in no rush to defend himself. "Stick around long enough, and you'll find out. What's yours?"

"Austin," I feel oddly self-conscious under his gaze.

He seems to mull it over for a moment, his head tilting slightly, and I brace myself for whatever witty remark he's about to throw my way. Trust me, I've heard the jokes before; stupid comments about Texas, the song with the same title—you name it.

Instead, he watches me several moments before saying, "That's pretty," and I blush from the roots of my hair down to the tips of my toes.

He steps closer, closing the small distance between us, and for a moment, I think he's going to say something else. Instead, he reaches out and gently tugs at the sleeve of my jacket, almost like a reflex.

"Take care, Austin." The guy winks and I suppress a shiver. "I'll be in touch."

I stand frozen for a beat, staring at the space he's vacated. My mind races, half tempted to chase him down and demand more answers. Who even *was* this guy? Gee? G? What's his real name? And what was his deal, swooping in and leaving like some kind of mysterious knight in shining tinfoil?

I let out a labored sigh and force myself to look down at my phone and swipe on the screen to look at my new message: *"Let me know if you need anything else for the game."*

It's so simple, yet it somehow makes my heart skip a beat. Gah, I love it! Can't help but grin from ear to ear, biting my lip to keep from giggling to myself. What was I even smiling about? I didn't know anything about him, yet here I was, giddy like a dang teenager.

Well.

This whole evening just got a whole lot more interesting.

Glancing toward the exit, I half hope he'll come back, already knowing he won't. The moment is over—fleeting but electrifying — like a spark in the dark.

4

the one where they flirt via text...

G: Hey you—just circling back around to make sure the QR code for the tickets uploaded for you....

Austin: Hey! YES! Worked perfectly. Looked them up earlier to make sure this wasn't a scam, ha ha. These seats are INSANE. Are you sure this isn't a mistake?????

G: Not a mistake—just damn good seats, yeah? You excited?

Austin: Excited? I'm over the moon. Thank you SO SO much. Seriously, you didn't have to do this—and just so you know, these badass seats are going to ruin my original seats for me. It's like going from economy to first class—then back to economy.

G: Sorry in advance LOL

Austin: You're like the hockey version of Santa Claus

G: If Santa didn't wear red, sure.

HIT ME WITH YOUR BEST SHOT

> Austin: And if Santa wasn't in such good shape….

G: Ohhhhh…you noticed I was in good shape, eh?

> Austin: I wasn't staring at you if that's what you mean. Besides, everyone is in better shape than Santa and you seem…active?

G: "Active" LOL

> Austin: Oh my God. Stop laughing at me

G: Why? This is fun.

> Austin: Fun for YOU, maybe. I'm over here contemplating deleting my number—I called you active and hot and compared you to Santa in the same breath.

G: Wait. You think I'm hot?

> Austin: Please don't do this to me. I'm melting…

G: Fine. I'll stop. Lame, though, but I'll be nice.

> Austin: Thank you. I can only handle so much embarrassment in one night.

> G: You're welcome. And just so you know, I won't be forgetting this conversation anytime soon and will probably look back at this text at the Santa part and HOT part.

Austin: I deserve this roasting.

> G: Ha ha. Don't we all deserve to be roasted?? But switching gears back to hockey—who are you going to be cheering for? Don't tell me it'll be the goalie.

Austin: Okay, first of all, he shit the bed. Spectacularly. For the past few games. I have secondhand embarrassment for the poor bastard.

G: Bastard? Wow. Tell me how you really feel.

Austin: BUT—

G: Oh boy, here she goes....

Austin: BUT he's NOT a terrible goalie. Everyone has bad games. He had an off night. 3 nights in a row, but still. This is not his month.

G: You're still cheering for him after he fucked the team over?

Austin: Of course! He's my guy. He needs to get his head back in the game.

G: Interesting. How will you be cheering him on now that you're sitting SO CLOSE. Signs? Chants? A strongly worded DM?

Austin: Don't tempt me. I'd slide into his DM if I thought he'd see the message, ha ha. And I'm not above standing at the glass with a big sign that says, "Get it together!"

G: DO IT. I'm sure he could use the motivation.

Austin: Or the humiliation??

G: Sometimes humiliation is the best motivator. Tough love and all that...

Austin: Exactly. Tough love. Coz nothing says "I believe in you" like public shaming.

G: I'm sure he'd appreciate the sentiment.

HIT ME WITH YOUR BEST SHOT

Austin: You think? Maybe I'll add stickers and glitter to the sign.

G: Glitter says "GET YOUR SHIT TOGETHER but also: I'm fabulous"

Austin: "Stop pucks + Stop killing my dreams."

G: Wow.

Austin: What? Too much? Or too subtle?

G: Subtle? You told the man to stop killing your dreams.

Austin: Sometimes the truth hurts.

G: If that doesn't light a fire under his ass NOTHING will.

Austin: Honestly, I'm practically doing the coach's job at this point.

G: You're a hero—truly.

Austin: Finally, someone who gets it!!!!

G: Don't let it go to your head.

Austin: TOO LATE. I'm unbearable now.

G: LOL Will you be cheering for the whole team, then?

Austin: Obviously. I'm not one of those people who only goes to games to watch the fights.

G: Fights do make things interesting, don't you think?

Austin: Oh, for sure. A good fight is like the cherry on top of a great game. But I'm here for the plays—NOT the punches.

> G: Respectable. You're there for the art of the game.

Austin: Absolutely.

Austin: Are you sure I can't convince you to join me tomorrow?

> G: I'm sure you have someone else you were planning to bring as your plus one, and not the dude you met in a bar.

Austin: I was planning on asking my friend Dolly to come along, but if you change your mind, you have until 10 PM tonight before I turn into a pumpkin. She's not a superfan like I am, but she doesn't mind eye-candy.

> G: Eye-candy?

Austin: Hockey players tend to be ridiculously good-looking. Don't tell me you haven't noticed.

> G: Can't say I have.

Austin: Have you told your sister you gave her tickets away to some random woman you met at a bar?

> G: Yup. She totally approves. And they're her tickets by proxy...

Austin: I have no idea what that means but I'll take your word for it. Did she ask you a million questions about me??

> G: Of course she did—she's my sister. Asking a million questions is practically her job.

Austin: And? What did you tell her?

> G: The truth.

HIT ME WITH YOUR BEST SHOT

Austin: Which is…? (this is like pulling teeth, my God)

G: I told her I gave the tickets to a random woman I met at a bar because she seems like a nice person who REALLY loves hockey.

Austin: Oh.

G: LOL why do you sound disappointed???

Austin: I don't sound disappointed! I'm processing my feelings about that sad, basic description of myself.

G: How is that basic?

Austin: The fact that "nice person who really loves hockey" is apparently my entire personality now.

G: Would you rather I told her you're a glitter enthusiast who plans on savagely roasting a goalie who sucks at his job?

Austin: You know what? YES DEAR GOD YES. It's entirely more accurate.

Austin: Also. I'm still stuck on the fact that your sister was cool with this. Mine would've interrogated me for hours.

G: Mine tried. I told her not to push her luck.

Austin: Ah, classic. Is she older or younger?

G: Neither. We're twins

Austin: WHAT?! Twins? That's awesome. Are you the good one or the evil one?

G: Depends who you ask.

Austin: I'm asking YOU.

G: In that case, yes—I am the good one. My sister is way more diabolical than I am, as most sisters are...

Austin: Oh, come on. What's the most diabolical thing she's ever done?

G: Once when we were teenagers, she hid under my bed for an hour while I was reading. And then when I shut off my light, she scared the shit out of me.

Austin: Did you scream?

G: Like a damn banshee.

Austin: So—like a girl?

G: Totally.

Austin: I'm dying. That's incredible. Did she at least feel bad afterward?

G: Nope. She laughed so hard she fell and hit her head on my nightstand.

Austin: Karma.

G: You'd think so. But then she blamed me for it and got out of trouble.

Austin: I want to be her when I grow up.

G: You're uninvited from sibling stories now.

Austin: Fair. But for real, thanks again for the ticket—please tell her I appreciate it. I feel like I owe you a favor.

G: You don't owe me anything. Just enjoy the game.

HIT ME WITH YOUR BEST SHOT

Austin: That's too easy. There's gotta be something I can do to repay you.

G: You already promised to make a glitter sign, remember???

Austin: I'm serious, though.

G: So am I. The glitter sign will be legendary. If I were a player, I'd skate right up to it and kiss the glass to show my appreciation.

Austin: You'd kiss the glass? What if I made a sign that said, "STOP PUCKS + STOP BREAKING MY HEART" or something equally dramatic?

G: If you actually did that, I would find you and kiss you on the lips.

Austin: STOP! I'm blushing. Seriously.

G: If you're going to go that hard with a sign like that, it deserves a proper thank you.

Austin: Well it's too bad you won't be there.

5
austin

*H*oly.
Crap.

These seats. Are. Ah-*mazing*.

Armed with a sign that says **BETTER LUCK THIS TIME, GIO**—and one of my best friends, Dolly—the arena is buzzing.

"These seats," I say, sinking into the plush cushion of my chair, "are the most incredible thing to ever happen to me."

Dolly rolls her eyes, her lips curling into a smirk as she unwraps a pretzel. "I mean, other than me, obviously."

"Obviously," I echo, not even bothering to argue.

"You know," she says, waving her pretzel at the ice, "if you scream loud enough, Gio might actually notice your sign. Then again, I doubt he'll be able to read it with how fast you'll be waving it."

I laugh, holding up the bright blue poster board for emphasis.

"That's the plan." I lift it from the spot where I've tucked it. "I want him to know the fans haven't forgotten about his last game. Better luck this time, buddy!" I shout, lifting it.

Bright yellow paper.

Bold lettering.

HIT ME WITH YOUR BEST SHOT

Blue glitter.

Team colors.

There isn't a chance Montagalo will miss this sign.

Dolly snickers as I wave it over my head like a maniac, even though the players haven't taken the ice yet.

"You're going to throw out your shoulder before the game even starts," she says, biting into her pretzel.

"Worth it," I say, lowering it cause she's right; my arm is beginning to hurt and I need to save my energy. The team will be out soon— after the lights dim and the Jumbotron explodes with graphics and loud music, of course.

It's all part of the show, and I am HERE FOR IT!

Hell yeah!

The pregame video begins to play; the highlight reel illuminates the arena, displaying Houston's best plays from the season. Every goal, every hat trick, every save—it's a montage designed to rile us up, and it works.

The crowd's energy builds with every second, and I can feel the vibration of their cheers in my chest.

The lights go out.

Swirling blue and yellow spotlights sweep across the ice.

Smoke machines crank out thick billowing clouds along the player tunnel, and the first strains of Houston's anthem blare through the speakers.

Dolly jumps beside me, clutching my arm as she screams along with the crowd and I grip my sign tightly as the announcer's voice booms through the arena.

"Ladies *adies* and gentlemen...*entleman*," the announcer's voice booms out an echo. "Please stand *and and*. For your Houston *ouston*. Baddiessss!"

The team bursts onto the ice, one by one, to thunderous applause and my eyes seek out Montagalo. He skates out last—the goalie always does—name echoing through the arena as the crowd roars and a few boos.

Yikes.

He skates in circles around the rink, his movements smooth and confident, and I tremble, excited, as I clutch this ridiculous sign.

Waiting.

"Think he sees me?"

"Not yet." Dolly squints in his direction, chewing on her snack. "But give it time. You're hard to miss with that obnoxious sign."

I laugh, nudging her. "You're jealous you didn't make one."

"Not jealous," she says, holding up her pretzel like it's the trophy of the night. "I know my priorities."

Pucks fly in every direction as they pass, shoot, and slap them against the boards. The arena buzzes with anticipation, but my eyes are glued to one person—Montagalo.

He skates slowly. Deliberately.

Does laps around his crease, stretching and settling into his rhythm.

Every few laps, he veers out, circling past the blue line before coasting back, movements smooth, confident, and mesmerizing.

I sit frozen, gripping the sign in my fingers, holding my breath every time he gets closer to the place where we're sitting.

Closer to the glass.

Close enough to…

"Relax." Dolly laughs, nudging me with her elbow. "He's some dude on skates."

He's not just a dude on skates.

My heart thuds in my chest as I lean forward, gripping the edge of my seat.

Literally on the edge of my seat.

I stand.

Dolly grabs the sign and thrusts it forward, glitter catching beneath the lights.

BETTER LUCK THIS TIME.

It beckons him.

On his next lap, he slows as he approaches our section,

gloved hand pushing at his helmet and I swear he's looking right at me.

My breath catches. For a moment—the briefest of moments—I think I'm imagining it. But then...he coasts closer still...stopping inside the blue line, and lifts his mask.

Oh my God.

It's him.

I'm literally frozen, caught somewhere between awe and disbelief. How did I not piece it together before? The easy smile, the confident swagger—it all makes sense now.

The realization hits me like a slapshot to the chest.

I insulted him. I told him he shit the bed.

That he was going through it.

To his face.

I mean—not to his face—I didn't know at the time it was him, but you get what I'm saying!

My heart pounds as memories of that night at the bar flood back—the teasing remarks, the sarcastic comments, the way I scoffed at his "generous" offer of tickets because I didn't think he'd follow through.

Oh, he followed through all right.

"I'm going to puke."

I roasted him and he gave me the tickets anyway.

Oh he's grinning at me alright, coming to a stop in front of our seats.

"Hey." I see him mouth. "You made the sign."

He points to it with his gloved hand and I want to die.

I...

I...

My mouth drops open and I watch as he leans forward, pursing his lips and presses them against the glass in a wet kiss.

Did he—did he *just kiss it*?

Yes he did.

There are lip prints to prove it.

The roar of the crowd around us barely registers because all I can focus on is him. The smirk as he winks, his gloved hand resting on the edge of the boards like this is the most normal, natural thing to do.

As if we were the only people here.

Dolly grabs my arm, shaking me. "Oh my God! Did that just happen? Did he seriously just do that?"

"I—" *Words fail me.* My mouth opens and closes like I'm a fish, brain scrambling to process what the hell happened.

I can't move.

Can't breathe.

All I can do is sit there, holding this *ridiculous* glitter-covered sign, while Gio Montagalo—the man I roasted within an inch of his life—stares me down like I'm the most entertaining thing he's seen all night.

And maybe it is.

I'm shook.

In *shock*.

I'm…

As Gio skates away, blending back into the flow of warm-ups, I finally let out the breath. My heart is pounding, my grip on the glitter-covered sign so tight it's a wonder I haven't crushed it yet.

I let it fall to the ground.

Dolly nudges me hard enough to jolt me back to reality. "Okay, seriously. *What* the hell was that? What on earth is going on?"

I shake my head, still staring at the ice like it's going to give me answers.

"I have no idea." Actually, that is not true. "That's the guy who gave me the tickets."

"Him?" Dolly's brow is furrowed, confused. I'd told her about our exchange at the bar but clearly there are details neither of us could have predicted.

"Dolly." I put my hand on her arm. "The horrible things I said to that man. What's the protocol for apologizing to the

HIT ME WITH YOUR BEST SHOT

professional athlete you were talking shit about?" My groan is loud enough for her to hear. "Look at him! He's down there skating laps like it's no big deal, and I'm over here contemplating faking my own death."

"Don't you *dare*." Dolly laughs. "This is amazing. You insulted the star goalie of the Baddies and not only does he not hate you, but he's out here putting on a show for you. It's like—foreplay."

Foreplay.

Sounds fucked up.

"Do *not* call it that."

She grins, unbothered. "What else would you call it? That man is *flirting*, and you're sitting here having a *crisis*."

"I *am* having a crisis!" I hiss, gesturing toward the ice. "I can't handle this! It's too much! I'm so embarrassed, Dolly. I roasted the man—like, I was so freaking rude—and instead of being *offended* like a normal human he's out here acting like I'm the most fascinating person in the room!"

Who does that!?

Is this his sick way of getting revenge?

"Guys eat that up," she says matter-of-factly. "Maybe he's into bitchy women."

"I didn't say I was being a bitch," I protest. "I was merely lobbing insults at him."

"Oh, is that different?" She smirks, motioning to the concession guy with the oversized tote of beers. "You clearly need a drink."

"I don't want a beer! I'm too mortified," I counter, burying my face in my hands. "I'm going to crawl under these seats and live there forever. Tell my family I love them."

"Stop being so dramatic." Dolly rolls her eyes and grabs my wrists, pulling my hands away from my face. "You're going to sit right here, enjoy this game, and figure out what you're going to say to him after."

I blink at her, panic rising in my chest. "After?"

"Yes, after," she says firmly. "You think he's not going to find you?"

God, I hope not.

"Please." Dolly snorts, taking two beers from the concession guy, handing me one despite my protests. "You're so hopeless. The man kissed you in front of an entire arena."

"He did not kiss me," I mutter, clutching the beer in my lap. "He kissed the glass."

"Same thing," she says, sipping the foam from the blue cup. "You're the one he was looking at. Everyone saw it. He's putting on a show. So cute."

The puck drops, and the game begins in a blur of movement and sound. The Baddies are fast, aggressive, and relentless, immediately taking control of the puck and charging down the ice. The crowd erupts as one of their forwards sends a slapshot flying toward the net, only to be deflected by the opposing goalie.

I clutch the edge of my seat, my eyes darting to Gio as he skates to his crease, effortlessly blocking a shot from the blue line. The sound of the puck ricocheting off his pads echoes through the arena, and I can't help the way my stomach flips.

He's completely in his element, sharp and focused, moving like he's choreographed every second of this game.

"You should see your face right now." My friend chuckles, nudging me.

"Please stop talking."

But she's not wrong.

My eyes are glued to him, drawn to the way he moves with such precision, the way he commands his space on the ice. It's infuriating how good he is—at hockey, at smirking, at making me question every life choice that brought me here tonight.

Houston scores halfway through the first period, and the arena erupts in cheers. Dolly jumps to her feet, screaming, while I clap politely, my heart racing for an entirely different reason.

Gio skates toward the bench for the line change, but not before glancing toward our section.

It's brief, almost imperceptible—but *enough to make me grip my beer tighter and my lower parts tingle.*

"Did you see that?" Dolly announces to everyone sitting around us. "He's looking at you!"

"You're imagining things," I mumble, taking a sip of my beer to hide my face.

Shit.

I'm smiling—like a damn fool, too!

Ugh!

"Imagining it my ass—he's not even being subtle about it."

I roll my eyes, desperate to hide the blush creeping up my neck. "He's scanning the crowd. They always do that; it doesn't mean anything."

"Gio freaking Montagalo," Dolly repeats, shaking her head like she's witnessing a miracle. "Goddamn, I'm jealous. If a man like that looked at me the way he's looking at you, I'd be planning the wedding."

Before I can reply, the Baddies light up the scoreboard again and the arena explodes with noise.

Dolly jumps up, screaming and clapping, while I try to focus on anything other than the six-foot-four goalie who's been living rent-free in my head since the second I saw him sitting at the bar on my corner.

Tonight Gio is sharp and unrelenting, blocking every shot being blasted his way, and the crowd is

Eating.

It.

Up.

"See? Just doin' his job," I say, gesturing toward him. "Nothing to be jealous of."

Dolly whirls around to face me, her grin so wide it could rival the arena lights.

"Nothing to be jealous of? Are you *blind?* The man is out

there single-handedly shutting down the other team, and I swear he keeps checking to make sure you're still watching."

I had noticed that, but I'm not about to admit it.

"He is not," I argue, crossing my arms. "He's literally focused on the puck. You know, like a *professional*."

Dolly snickers, leaning closer. "Oh, sweetie, the only thing he's more focused on than that puck is you. I mean, look at him! He's putting on a clinic while you sit here pretending your stomach isn't doing flips."

"It's not doing flips," I say, immediately betraying myself with a deep breath to calm the chaos in my chest. "It's nerves. And the beer—you know what it does to me."

Lies.

All lies.

Despite my best efforts to play it cool, I can't help but let my eyes trail after him, drawn to the precision in every movement.

The buzzer sounds, signaling the end of the period, and the players begin their slow glide toward the benches. The crowd cheers and claps, a sea of energy that doesn't let up for a second.

"Last chance to admit you're into him before he comes over here and proves me right."

"He's not coming over," I say, my voice firm but my resolve shaky.

"Why would he? He has a game to play."

Dolly grins, a knowing glint in her eye. "Oh, honey. He's playing a different game now."

She shrugs, unconvinced. "Suit yourself. But I'm telling you right now—if he skates over again, I'm taking a video. The internet deserves to see this."

I glare at her, but the intermission show starting on the ice pulls her attention away before I can argue.

For a moment, I let myself relax, the noise and lights of the arena dulling the chaos in my head. But it doesn't last long. Because no matter how hard I try, I can't stop thinking about him.

I am a nobody.

With a smart mouth.

There is no way I'm ever going to see him again.

That thought should be comforting—it really should—but instead, it twists in my chest, leaving me feeling hollow as young kids in Blaze jerseys race oversized, inflatable pucks toward the goal while the crowd roots for them.

It's adorable, really, but it does nothing to settle the storm in my head.

But just like that, the ice clears and players start filing back onto the ice. The fans roar, the energy climbing higher and higher, and for a split second, I let myself get swept up in it. Cheer along with them.

Houston is up by one, and the second period promises to be as chaotic as the first.

And then he skates out.

Moves with purpose, every motion fluid and precise, and then—he looks directly at me. Not toward the crowd.

Not at our section.

At *me.*

Gio Montagalo is not just playing hockey tonight.

He's playing *me.*

6

Austin: You kissed the glass.

Gio: You made the sign! We had a deal.

Austin: For HIM not for you!

Gio: Okay that makes no sense—because I am him. Ha ha.

Austin: This isn't funny. I'm horrified. The entire place was staring at me like I was part of the halftime show.

Gio: You're welcome! Don't think I didn't see you smiling.

Austin: Why were you watching me, you had a GAME TO PLAY!

Gio: Obviously you're good luck. I didn't play like total shit this time. Coach thanks you.

Austin: You're not funny.

Gio: You're overthinking this. Besides, you're texting me, so I can't be that bad.

HIT ME WITH YOUR BEST SHOT

Austin: I'm texting you because I need answers.

Gio: Answers about what?

Austin: YOU LIED TO ME ABOUT WHO YOU WERE!

Gio: Not technically. I told you my name and you have my phone number—not many people can say that.

Austin: Not the point.

Gio: Actually that IS the point.

Austin: The point is, you conveniently left out the part where I'd been insulting you to your face.

Gio: Didn't think it was relevant.

Austin: Not relevant? Are you kidding me right now????

Gio: What—you wouldn't have insulted me if you knew?

Austin: Of course not! I'm not an asshole!

Gio: I liked that you don't hold back. It was... refreshing.

Austin: Refreshing?

Gio: Yes. Most people kiss my ass. You didn't. It was a nice change.

Austin: I can't tell if this is some twisted ego thing or if you're insane???

Gio: Why can't it be both?

Austin: Oh my od! You are twisted.

Gio: Some call it twisted, I call it flirting.

Austin: Is this how you pick up ALL women?

Gio: No. LOL. It's been a long time since I tried to hit on someone.

Austin: Oh REALLY? And why is that? Enlighten me.

Gio: My relationship with my sister sometimes suffers—I've chosen the wrong women in the past. Or they've chosen me I should say. And I told myself I wouldn't date women who see dollar signs when they look at me…

Gio: Hence, it's been a long fucking time since I've dated.

Austin: I… am so sorry. I don't know what to say. I…

Gio: There's a reason I was at the bar—that wasn't a coincidence.

Austin: What do you mean?

Gio: Nova told me about you.

Austin: Nova? Your sister? I don't understand.

Gio: Yeah. She met you last week, during the game you watched at the bar.

Austin: Last week at the bar….

Gio: The dark haired chick who was laughing at everything you said? We live in your neighborhood. I've gotten pretty good at spotting the red flags but every once in a while, Nova likes to play matchmaker and I'm keen to let her.

Austin: So, she scouted me for you?

HIT ME WITH YOUR BEST SHOT

Gio: More like gave me a heads-up. I'm not on any dating apps. You impressed her.

Austin: I can't tell if I should be flattered—or if this is stalking.

Gio: Flattered. Definitely flattered. NOT STALKING good god.

Austin: Easy for YOU to say that's not what this is—you had all the info going in. I was taken off guard.

Gio: It's not like I knew your life story. All Nova said was "She's funny and unrelenting and doesn't put up with crap. Maybe you need someone like that."

Austin: ... Still deciding how I feel about this.

Gio: Well. Take your time. My goal was to make you happy with the tickets and I did, so—maybe I'll see you around. You know, since we're mostly in the same neighborhood.

Austin: Wait. Are you breaking up with me??

Gio: I'm giving you space LOL

7
gio

*S*pace?

Turns out I didn't have to give her space because the media wouldn't let me.

My photo was plastered all over sports television—front and center, lips pressed against the plexi during our game against the Ravens.

I scroll through my phone, headline after headline taunting me like a bad breakup song: "MONTAGALO'S MYSTERY GIRL: WHO IS SHE?" and "HOCKEY'S HEARTTHROB BREAKS FUNK."

Fantastic.

Just what the world needs—my face, every damn where.

The good news?

Apparently I'm out of my funk, the credit for breaking it bestowed on Austin—though the media doesn't have a name to go with the face, which was artfully captured in high-def.

Her expression? Absolutely priceless.

So damn funny I laughed the first time I saw it, replaying on a loop in several *Top Plays of the Week* segments on the sports apps. Except this time, the play in question wasn't my save.

Nope.

It was me—one of the league's favorite bachelors—blasted for flirting with a hockey fan. Or girlfriend?

No one knows.

The memes are relentless.

"PUCK BUNNY OR TRUE LOVE?"

"WHEN HOCKEY IS YOUR FIRST LOVE BUT SHE'S A CLOSE SECOND."

By the time I reached the rest of them—my face photoshopped onto a cheesy romance novel cover titled *Skates of Passion*—I'd had enough.

I toss my phone to the kitchen counter and rub my temples, trying to figure out how my life spiraled into internet fodder overnight.

Then my phone buzzes. Again.

Not a text this time—an actual call. I groan when I see the name flashing on the screen.

Except this is the third time she's called this morning and if I don't eventually answer, she's going to assume I'm avoiding her. Which I am.

Or dead.

Which I'm not.

"What?" I say, already pacing the kitchen.

"Gio, we need a statement," she says without a greeting, drawling the sentence out in a southern accent.

"A statement?" I repeat, pressing a finger against my temple. "What am I supposed to say?"

She sighs. "Gio the media's digging. They're trying to figure out who she is and if we don't get ahead of it, they're going to be camping outside her door by lunch."

"False." I run a hand through my hair. "They're going to be camped out no matter what."

"Good. You agree." Danica clicks her tongue, the familiar sound of her keyboard clattering faintly in the background. I picture her sitting at her desk, glasses perched on her nose, fingers flying over her laptop as she plots my damage control.

"So this is what I was thinking—wait. You *do* know this woman, correct? She's not some fan you decided to indulge?"

I shake my head, even though she can't see it. "No, not a fan. She's actually, uh, a neighbor."

Sort of.

Danica goes silent for a moment, and I know that pause isn't good. "How long have you known her?"

"Uh." I do the mental math, from the time I sat my ass down on that barstool on the corner, to this very second. "About forty-nine hours?"

"Oh, Jesus Christ," she mutters under her breath.

"I said she's kind of a neighbor!" I defend myself.

"You said she was a neighbor!"

"It's the same thing!"

"Does she live in the same building?" Danica fires back before I can finish my protest. She doesn't give me a chance to respond before barreling on. "What's her occupation?"

I shrug, pulling open the fridge and staring blankly inside. "Don't know."

"You *don't know*?" Her disbelief is palpable through the phone, as if she isn't listening to a single thing I've said. "Great. Okay. Fantastic. So, we'll go with: She's someone you've been seeing, and it's not serious."

"Yes. I see her with my eyes," I joke, grabbing a bottle of water.

Danica groans. "Gio, I swear to God, if you keep making jokes—"

"What do you want me to say?" I interrupt impatiently, leaning against the counter. "Should we lie and say she's the love of my life and we're planning our wedding for next summer?"

"That might actually help," she mutters, typing.

I laugh. "Yeah, until they start following her to the grocery store and asking her how many kids we're going to have."

There's a beat of silence, and for once, Danica doesn't have a snappy comeback. "You're right, that's exactly what's going to happen thanks to your impulsiveness." There's another pause. "That's why we need to control the narrative before it controls you—or her."

I rub the back of my neck, staring at the floor. This isn't my first rodeo. Ever since I went pro, I've been stuck in this endless song and dance with the media—and I have the bad choices in women to thank for most of it.

Not this time. I will not let my past come back to haunt me.

"Fine," I mutter. "What do you need me to do?"

"First, you're going to text her and let her know what's happening," Danica dictates, her businesslike tone snapping into place. "Then, we're going to draft a statement together. Something vague, but clear so we can all move on with our lives. Got it?"

"Got it," I reply. "You're the boss."

I can hear Danica smile. "Thanks."

She laughs, unbothered. Danica reminds me of a barracuda, but with glasses and adult braces. Ruthless and polished. The kind of person who smiles while she sinks her teeth into you.

"Look," she says, her voice softening slightly. "I know this sucks, but if we play our cards right, this will all blow over in a few days. Just follow my lead."

"Yeah, yeah," I mutter, already pulling up my messages. "I've got it under control."

"Good. And Gio?"

"What?"

"Try not to make it worse."

I stare down at my phone as the call ends, the screen still lit with Danica's contact photo—a stock image of a shark, which felt fitting when I saved her number. My thumb hovers over the screen, hesitating, as I debate how the hell I'm supposed to explain this to Austin. A girl I've only met in person once. And under a guise, no less.

I drop my phone onto the counter with a sigh, already

dreading the conversation. If this situation isn't awkward enough, I know my sister is bound to have an opinion about it. She always does. Honestly, I'm shocked she hasn't already barged through my front door, armed with iced coffee and unsolicited advice, ready to insert herself into the mess.

Mess? Nah.

Not really. This isn't a mess.

It's just gossip.

Gossip is standard, part of the job. Lucky for me, I'm not usually the target—there are plenty of higher-profile players for the media to hound. Just so happens, though, that I'm single. Rich. Good-looking (I'm not going to argue with them on that point).

Toss in the fact that we'd lost three games in a row— then I mysteriously turn it around last night only *after kissing the glass where she was standing?*

Boom.

News.

It's the perfect storm: a struggling team, a dramatic comeback, and a handsome bachelor "inspired" by a mystery woman. The media's eating it up like it's their last meal. And honestly? I can't blame them. If I were in their shoes, I'd probably run with it too.

My ass is against the counter and I'm drumming my fingers as I think about Austin. What the hell am I supposed to say to her? What to say, what to say…

She's a Blaze fan. Surely, she's seen the headlines by now. If she's even glanced at her phone today, she's probably been bombarded with pictures, memes, and analysis dissecting every second of last night's game.

I open our text thread, my thumbs hovering over the keyboard. How do you even start this kind of conversation?

> Gio: Mornin. Not sure if you start your day off with local sporting stats, but

HIT ME WITH YOUR BEST SHOT

I stop, deleting the message before I send it. Too casual. Too cheeky. She might not be amused if she has seen the news.

I try again.

> Gio: You've probably seen the news...

I delete that too, groaning under my breath. Why is this so hard? I'm a grown man. A professional athlete. I can handle a text message.

Finally, I type:

> Hey you—good morning. Not sure if you have seen the news but the media is having a field day with photos of us from last night. Wanna chat about it?

> Austin: I was wondering when you were going to reach out ha ha. I wasn't about to start whining about it first.

> Gio: I just ended a call with my publicist—she said to sit tight. She's going to issue a statement and then we're going to let the story die down.

> Austin: It's that simple?

No, not always. But fingers crossed...

> Gio: Usually? Should blow over in a day or two as long as I don't do more stupid shit.

> Austin: What are our options? I mean, obviously I'm not famous but it's not like my face was blurred out. I'm so visible it's horrifying! I look SO FUGLY lol

> Gio: What's fugly??

> Austin: Fucking ugly.

Gio: Oh LOL. Did not know that, and no you do not.

Austin: Oh, I do. It's a fact. I've looked at the photos. The camera caught me mid-blink, and my mouth was hanging open like I'm getting ready to give a blow job.

I ignore that last comment—though I'm dying to respond to it.

Gio: I don't know what pictures you're looking at, but the ones I've seen you look fine. BETTER than fine.

Adorable. Cute. Fun.

Austin: Lies. But thank you for saying so.

Gio: Not lies. Just facts.

Austin: Yeah, well, tell that to the people on Twitter. I made the mistake of reading the comments, and now I'm emotionally scarred for life.

Gio: Rule number one: NEVER READ THE COMMENTS. Rookie mistake.

Austin: I'm so seriously butt-hurt right now and never want to leave my house. One woman said I look like your "dorky cousin" who is so far beneath you it's laughable.

Gio: My dorky cousin? Wow. Harsh.

Austin: Like, not just a cousin. The DORKY one.

Gio: First of all, I don't even have a dorky cousin. I have three cousins total and all of them are male.

HIT ME WITH YOUR BEST SHOT

> Austin: That's what you're focusing on? The cousin part—not the part where I'm so far beneath you?? Shit.

> Gio: Yes, Yes, because the cousin thing is ridiculous. You're not "beneath" anyone. Especially not me.

At least not yet…

> Austin: You say that, but Twitter begs to differ.

> Gio: STAY OFF TWITTER. It thinks the moon landing was fake and pineapple on pizza is a crime. Not a reliable source.

> Austin: You're really defending pineapple on pizza at a time like this?

> Gio: I'm just saying, Twitter's full of bad takes!!!! FOCUS.

> Austin: I mean, pineapple pizza is a crime against humanity but whatever….

> Gio: I regret nothing. You're awesome, Twitter is trash, and I will die on this hill. WE RIDE AT DAWN.

> Austin: Are you going to come hide out with me now? Is that the next step?

> Gio: Er. I doubt we have to hide out…

> Austin: I mean. It sounds fun though, doesn't it?

> Gio: Maybe we meet at Five Alarm and plan our course of action.

> Austin: Hmm. I guess I could eat.

> Austin: Is your sister coming?

> Gio: Fuck no!

Two hours later I'm walking into the bar.

She's standing at the counter, waiting for someone—waiting for me—and for the second time this week, I stroll into an establishment I've only set foot in once in the three years I've lived at the end of the block. The place is busy, a low hum of conversations blending with the faint sound of the playlist over the speakers.

It's dimly lit; the kind of place where you don't come to be seen.

You come for privacy. Good drinks.

Better food.

I observe her a few moments before walking over.

Austin is facing the counter, back to most of the room, chatting with the same bartender that was here the other night. Her posture is relaxed—but I notice the subtle shift of her weight, the way her hand fidgets slightly against the counter.

She's nervous? Or maybe I'm imagining it.

She shifts her weight again, glancing over her shoulder like she knows I'm here. Her face is calm, but I catch a flicker of something in her expression—relief? Annoyance? Maybe both. Her lips curve into a faint smile, enough to let me know she's spotted me.

I take a breath and start walking toward her, weaving between tables and barstools. With every step, I tell myself to play it cool, to act like I'm not ridiculously aware of how every guy in this bar is probably noticing her too.

By the time I reach her, she's turned fully to face me, her hand tucked into the pocket of her jacket.

"Hey you." She greets me with a big smile. "Man of the hour has arrived."

"You forgot to roll out the red carpet." I smirk.

She tilts her head slightly, glancing up at me. "You seem

surprisingly calm for someone whose face is all over the internet right now."

"I am," I say with a shrug. "You get used to it."

"That sucks." Her eyebrows raise slightly, glancing up at me again, smile a tad snarky. "I didn't realize how tall you are."

"Six four," I inform her, feeling the corners of my own mouth twitch as I watch her process the new information.

"Well." Austin clears her throat. "I'm not used to looking this far up. Congratulations on making me feel short."

She is short, *but I don't hate it.*

In fact, there's something oddly endearing about the way she has to tilt her head to look up at me.

"Booth okay?" I ask, glancing down at her.

"Works for me," she says with a small shrug, falling into step beside me as we follow the hostess toward the back of the bar.

I can feel the weight of her gaze as we walk, like she's sizing me up in more ways than one. Normally, that kind of scrutiny would bother me, but with Austin, it doesn't. It's not judgment—it's curiosity. Like she's trying to figure out what makes me tick.

Not that there's much to figure out.

Honestly? I'm a pretty simple guy.

Ha ha.

Still, I can't help but wonder what she sees when she looks at me like that. Does she see the guy plastered all over the internet right now? The guy who can't seem to avoid turning his personal life into a public spectacle?

Or does she see something else—something quieter, something closer to the person I used to be before all of this?

Before I can spiral into overthinking everything, we reach the booth and I step aside to let Austin choose which side to slide in first, eyes sliding down her backside as she scoots in.

Nice ass.

She catches me looking, but doesn't comment; just arches a brow as if she knows *exactly* what I was thinking.

We settle in. Remove our coats.

"Alright," she says, flipping the menu open like we're not here to strategize our way out of a PR nightmare. "What's the plan?"

I lean back in the booth, crossing my arms as I study her, in no hurry at all. "Plan for what?"

Her eyes widen as she lowers the menu enough to shoot me a pointed look.

"Maybe the fact that your face—and mine, by association—is currently trending on every social media platform? Is this us laying low?" She lifts the menu again, her eyes scanning as she chatters on. "By the way, I *love* the part in your press release where you describe me as a 'family friend.' So thoughtful."

Oh, yeah.

That part.

"I didn't write it—I only approved it," I mumble, leaning back in the booth. "Mostly." I sigh. "Okay fine I didn't actually read it 'coz I trust Danica to do her job."

Her head bobs up and down in exaggerated agreement, her expression impossible to read behind the menu.

"Nothing screams 'family friend' like a guy smushing his face against the glass for a woman he's supposedly not interested in."

I scratch the back of my neck, trying to come up with a rebuttal that doesn't sound like total bullshit.

"We didn't have a ton of options—I told Danica we were neighbors, and you've met my sister, so…" I trail off, watching for her reaction.

"Uh-huh," she says without looking up, focused on finding something to eat.

I lean forward, resting my elbows on the table. "Look, the press needed something—something that wouldn't make your life harder."

She finally sets the menu down, her gaze locking onto mine with the kind of intensity that makes me sit up straighter.

"And you think calling me a 'family friend' makes my life easier?"

"Would you have preferred 'mystery woman'?" I counter, raising a brow.

Her face scrunches up in mock disgust. "Ew, that's horrid. Like something they'd say fifty years ago, back when people still wrote letters instead and didn't have the internet."

I laugh, relieved the mood is lightening. "Exactly. I was doing you a favor."

"Oh, yeah. *Huge* favor," she snorts dryly, picking up her glass of water. "What on Earth would I do without you?"

"Probably live a much quieter life," I admit with a grin.

"Eh. I don't mind the excitement. My life is pretty boring."

I lean forward, resting my arms on the table. "Alright, enlighten me. What is it you do, anyway? Danica was asking."

"Oh, *Danica* wants to know, does she?"

"Hey, I'm just the messenger," I reply, raising my hands in mock defense. "You've got her all curious. She's trying to figure out if you're a threat to my public image or, you know, just a regular person."

Austin rolls her eyes, her lips quirking in amusement. "Wow. A threat to your public image. Little me?"

Yes, little you.

"Are you secretly plotting my downfall, or do you have a boring day job like the rest of us mortals?"

She tilts her head, pretending to think. "Let's see. I do own a black hoodie and sunglasses, which are basically prerequisites for an evil mastermind. But no—no secret plotting. Sorry to disappoint."

I motion impatiently for her to go on. "And when you're *not* preparing for world domination?"

"I'm a professor."

I pause.

Blink.

Blink at her some more. "What?"

She is so full of shit—there is no way.
She's not old enough to be a professor.
"You're fucking kidding," I blurt out leaning forward as if that will somehow make her confession make more sense. "Right? Please tell me you're joking."

She is enjoying my confusion. "Why would I joke about that?"

I study her, trying to reconcile the quick-witted woman sitting across from me with the image of a *professor*.

Impossible.

"You're not old enough to be a professor."

"Okay. *Rude,*" she says, though her lips twitch like she's trying not to laugh.

"No, I mean you look—" I stop, realizing this is a minefield I'm about to step into. "You don't look old enough for that job. What do you teach, anyway?"

"For your information, I teach sociology. At a university. With real adults." Her chin tilts and her expression smug. "You can google it if you'd like. I'll wait."

My brain cannot compute.

"Like…*college* sociology?" I continue to sound stupid, unable to wrap my brain around this.

"Yes. Like—the college here. It's a university, technically." Austin crosses her arms. "Monday and Wednesdays at 9 a.m. to 11:30. Tuesday and Thursdays at 1. My office hours are on Fridays at 2. I even have a nameplate on my door."

The only university I know of is State, about a thirty-minute drive out of the city. It's huge—twenty-five thousand students, nationally ranked programs, and a football team they televise like it's the Super Bowl.

A big fucking school.

I lean back, still trying to wrap my head around it. "This is blowing my mind right now." I feel my face melting off as I squint across the table at her. "How old are you?"

She laughs again. "Twenty-nine. How old are you?"

"Twenty-six," I say automatically, still stuck on the fact that she's *twenty-nine* and a *professor*.

"Aw, you're a baby," she teases, resting her chin in her hand, fluttering her lashes at me.

I glare at her, though I can't help but grin. "You don't get to call

me a baby when you've not even cracked thirty."

"But it's still older than you, and I'm your elder, so show some respect."

I find her smart mouth so…

Goddamn sexy.

Sexier now that I know her sharp tongue comes equipped with an even sharper brain. She's confident, quick, and completely unapologetic about it. It's a lethal combination—one I wasn't prepared for when I walked into this bar.

Inside my pants, my dick twitches.

Of course, it does.

Because apparently, my body has zero chill when it comes to her.

I shift slightly in my seat, forcing myself to focus on something else—anything else. But it's hard when she's sitting across from me, her eyes daring me to keep up with her.

Her lips are moving but I'm no longer listening to a word she's saying.

Blah blah *"…my students love me, I'll have you know."*

Oh I *bet* they fucking do.

My gaze dips to her mouth as she talks, the curve of her lips pulling me in. Glossy. Full. Pale pink tongue darting out to lick them. Every word out of her mouth is designed to knock me off balance and it's working…

"Are you even listening to me?" she asks suddenly, chin tilting as her voice cuts through the fog in my brain.

"What? Yeah, of course. Your students love you."

She narrows her eyes. Doesn't believe me. "Uh-huh. What else did I say?"

"Uh…" I scramble, frantically replaying the last ten seconds until I come up with, "Something about office hours."

Her lips press together as she tries to hold back a laugh. "All I have to say is, *wow*."

"In my defense, as soon as you said professor, I started objectifying you."

Austin's eyes widen.

"You've gotta admit," I continue. "It's not every day a guy meets someone as gorgeous as you *and* finds out she's brilliant."

Her cheeks flush, a deep pink that she tries to hide by dipping her chin and brushing a stray strand of hair behind her ear.

"I'm not brilliant," she mutters, though her lips are curving into a reluctant smile.

"You definitely are," I counter, gaze fixed on her. She can't convince me otherwise. "Brilliant, beautiful, and apparently modest."

Which is more than I can say for myself.

She lets out a soft laugh, finally looking up at me, her eyes narrowing. "You're ridiculous."

Maybe.

"Can we change the subject?" she asks, the blush still lingering on her cheeks.

Before I can respond, a voice interrupts from behind me. "*Oh my God, are you Gio Montagalo?*"

I glance over my shoulder, already bracing myself. A guy in his early twenties, wearing a Blaze hoodie and a baseball cap, is standing a few feet away, staring at me like he's just won the lottery.

"Yup," I say, offering a polite smile. "That's me."

"No fucking way!" he says, his voice rising in excitement. He pulls out his phone, fumbling with it as he steps closer. "Holy shit, man—I'm such a huge fan. Can I, uh, get an autograph or something?"

HIT ME WITH YOUR BEST SHOT

"Sure," I say, reaching for the napkin on the table. "You got a pen?"

The guy practically throws one at me, and I scribble my name across the napkin before handing it back.

"Thanks, man," he says, grinning from ear to ear. Then his gaze shifts to Austin, and his eyebrows shoot up. "Wait—is this her?"

"Her who?" Austin joins the conversation, glancing around to discover who the *her* is though we all know what he's referring to. He's clearly seen the news.

"You know," the guy says, snapping his fingers and loudly whispering, "The girl from last night's game. Holy balls, dude—the story is true. I thought it was a load of crap."

"Because they usually *are* loads of crap," I tell him, keeping my tone casual. Flippant. "Don't believe everything you see on the internet."

He blinks, taken off guard by my rebuttal.

"Right. Totally. But, uh…" His gaze darts to Austin again, and the curiosity is practically radiating off him. "So, are you two—"

"Nope," I cut him off before he can finish that sentence. "She's actually my cousin. My very dorky cousin who loves pineapple pizza and thinks the moon landing was fake."

Austin's head snaps toward me so fast, I'm surprised she doesn't pull something. Her jaw drops, her eyes wide with disbelief.

The guy's face drops into a mask of confusion.

"Wait… *seriously?*"

"Absolutely," I say with a completely straight face, leaning back in the booth. "Loves frat parties at the college."

Austin narrows her eyes at me, clearly unimpressed. Then she turns to the guy with an exaggeratedly sweet smile. "Actually, it's the opposite. Don't tell anyone, but I'm in the process of becoming a nun. I've been considering a vow of chastity lately. A lot lately. Real recent."

The guy blinks, his brain clearly short-circuiting as he processes her words, the same way my brain did learning she's a prof.

"A nun?"

"Yup," she says, making the sign of the cross on her chest. "Just me, my prayer beads, and a whole lot of spiritual reflection."

I bite back a laugh, folding my arms across my chest as I watch her babble with a straight face.

"Looks great in black and white, by the way," I add, unable to resist. "Super sexy."

Austin's head snaps toward me, and the glare she shoots me is so sharp, I almost flinch.

Almost.

"Thank you for your input, *cousin*," she says through gritted teeth, her voice dripping with sarcasm.

Oh shit.

That's right.

I just told him we're cousins and three seconds later I called her sexy.

Whoops.

The guy stares at us for a moment longer before shaking his head.

"Man, you guys are wild." He takes a step back, looking like he's ready to escape. "Anyway, good luck with, uh, the nun thing."

"Bless you my child," Austin says sweetly, her expression pure innocence—but as soon as he's out of earshot, she turns back to me, her eyes blazing. "Super sexy? *Really*? You're terrible at ad-libbing."

I shrug, grinning unapologetically. "I panicked."

"No shit you *panicked*." She crosses her arms and glares at me like I've committed some kind of cardinal sin. "What if that guy goes to the press and tells him you're dating your cousin?"

HIT ME WITH YOUR BEST SHOT

 I laugh, gesturing for the server. Order two beers when she takes our order—and a pineapple pizza.

8
austin

I can't stop thinking about Gio Montagalo and it's affecting my work.

Alone in my office, I stare at the wall and do my best not to Google him—but it's hard. It's like trying not to scratch an itch. He's everywhere, and yet the moment I close my eyes, he's still there, taking up space in my brain like he's paying rent.

Since our meeting this weekend—if you can even call it a meeting—he's been the only thing I can think about, and it's beginning to show.

Case in point: the half-written grant proposal sitting on my laptop screen. Deadline tomorrow.

Words? Completely gone.

Focus? Nonexistent.

Not good.

This is ridiculous!

I've had crushes before; fleeting distractions that barely register in the grand scheme of things. But Gio? He's a category all his own. It's not just because he is a famous athlete. Or because he's good-looking—*though, let's be honest, the man could model for a cologne ad and no one would bat an eye.*

Nope. It's his presence.

The way he's so damn sure of himself, yet somehow manages to make me laugh even when I'm trying to be mad at him because we're in a media frenzy I never asked to be part of.

I glance at my phone sitting on the desk, face down like it's a temptation I can't afford to indulge. He hasn't texted me since we met Friday at Five Alarm, which should be a relief.

It means he's probably moved on, forgotten about me entirely. Right?

Right.

So why does that thought make me feel like shit?

Because. You have the hots for him. You think he's funny, charming, and he's a great conversationalist. He's not boring. Plus, he's tall.

So.

Tall.

My office door creaks open, and I nearly jump out of my chair.

"Professor Adams?" A student who works in this department peeks her head through the crack. "You have a meeting scheduled with the department chair in five minutes. I thought you might need a reminder since you're normally early to those?"

Crap.

I plaster on a smile, hoping I don't look as flustered as I feel.

"Thanks, Logan. I'll be there in a minute."

She nods and disappears, leaving me alone with my racing thoughts.

I take a deep breath, forcing myself to stand and grab my planner. Work. *Focus on work.* Gio Montagalo does not belong in this office, he does not belong in my head, he does not belong anywhere near my carefully constructed life.

Period.

You are in academia.

His face almost blew off when you said the word professor.

The memory makes me laugh, despite the serious tone of my thoughts. The way his jaw dropped, the way he blinked like I'd just told him I was an astronaut—it's almost enough to distract me from how off-balance he makes me feel.

Almost.

I step into the hallway, adjusting the strap of my bag on my shoulder as I head toward the department chair's office. The sound of low chatter drifts through the corridor, and at first, I don't pay much attention. But then I hear it—*that* voice.

I stop in my tracks, my heart skipping a beat.

No. Can't be.

He wouldn't.

I round the corner, and there he is, leaning on the reception desk like he owns the place. Elbows propped up, his signature smirk firmly in place, Gio Montagalo is chatting it up with the other student aide, who looks about two seconds away from swooning.

My brain short-circuits for a moment, caught somewhere between shock and disbelief. What is he doing here?

Gio looks up just then, and our eyes meet. His smirk grows wider, like he's been caught but doesn't mind one bit.

"Professor." He winks at me, his booming voice carrying down the hallway. "Fancy running into you here."

I blink, my feet frozen to the floor. *What the hell is he doing here?* "What are you doing here?"

The student aide—Paul—looks between us, his eyes wide with fandom.

Gio straightens his stance, shoving his hands into his jacket pockets as he steps toward me. "I thought I'd surprise you."

Surprise me? My pulse kicks up, but I do my best to keep my expression neutral. "I have a meeting in, like, two minutes."

"It's not an important meeting," Paul interrupts, eager to help. "I can tell Professor Casey you have a fever."

"A fever?" I repeat, my head snapping toward him. "We are *not* going to lie to Professor Casey!"

Gio chuckles softly, clearly enjoying every second of this. "I like that plan," he says, nodding toward the aide. "Thanks for having her back."

"Oh my God," I mutter, pinching the bridge of my nose. "This is not happening."

Paul looks genuinely disappointed as he glances between us. "Are you sure you don't want to bail? I can make it really convincing."

"I'm sure we are not going to cancel on the department head one minute before the meeting," I say firmly, though the corners of my mouth twitch despite myself.

Paul sighs, deflated—but Gio is undeterred. The man loves a challenge, it's in his DNA.

"I can wait," he announces, his voice too loud for someone who just invited himself into an academic building where people typically speak just above a whisper. He gestures to Paul. "He can show me to your office—I'll occupy myself until you're done."

Occupy himself?! By doing what?!

"That's not how this works," I snap, turning my glare on him.

"It's fine!" Paul says eagerly, perking up at the suggestion. "I'll make sure he doesn't touch anything!"

I want to smack them both.

"*Paul*," I warn to no avail.

He's already gesturing for Gio to follow him down the hall, like a student ambassador tasked with showing the new kid around campus.

I feel my defenses weakening.

"Babe, don't worry," Gio says, flashing me a grin that's equal parts charming and infuriating. "I'll be on my best behavior."

Babe?

He's calling me babe now?

What parallel universe am I living in!

"You don't have a best behavior, I'm sure of it," I complain under my breath, even though they're already halfway down the corridor, in the direction of my tiny office.

I stand there for a moment, frozen in place, watching them disappear around the corner. Then, as if on cue, I let out the longest, most exasperated sigh of my life. Of course, this is happening. Of course, Gio has decided to insert himself into my Monday morning!

Why wouldn't he?

By the time I drag myself to the department head's office, my brain is spinning with all the possibilities of what kind of chaos he might be stirring up back in my workspace. *Is he rifling through my desk drawers?*

Rearranging my bookshelves?

Chatting up every passing student because he's a pseudo celebrity?

The thought is equal parts horrifying and absurdly distracting.

Professor Casey is mid-sentence when I take a seat at his desk —exactly on time, no less—but I barely catch a word of it. Something about new policies? Budget cuts? It all blurs together as my thoughts spiral.

I force myself to nod at the appropriate times, jotting down nonsense in my planner to make it look like I'm engaged.

My mind refuses to cooperate.

Instead, it cosplays images of Gio sitting in my desk chair, playing with my pens, tapping on my keyboard, his cocky smirk plastered across his face as he says something that makes Paul laugh like they're friends.

What does the man want?!

"Professor Adams?"

I blink, snapping back to the present to find Professor Casey staring at me expectantly.

"Uh, yes?" I say, hoping my voice doesn't sound as guilty as I feel. "Sorry."

"Do you have any thoughts on the matter?" the department

head asks, his tone suggesting he's losing patience with me for my lack of attentiveness.

Crap.

"Could you repeat that last part?" I ask, offering my most professional smile.

His eyes narrow slightly, but he obliges—thank God—launching into another explanation about departmental priorities and some vague mention of student engagement initiatives.

I do my best to appear focused on his words.

All the while, my mind keeps drifting back to the man currently occupying my office—and the undeniable chaos he's brought with him.

I glance at my watch. We've been in this meeting for sixteen minutes, though it feels like an eternity. I tap my pen against the page, willing myself to focus.

"And as for the faculty workshop," Professor Casey continues, his tone dry as he flips through his notes. "We'll need all hands on deck to ensure its success."

"Mmhmm," I murmur, nodding in agreement, though I couldn't tell you what workshop he's referring to if my life depended on it.

I glance at my watch again.

Seventeen minutes.

"Professor Adams." Professor Casey stares at me. "Are you with us?"

"Yes, of course," I reply too quickly, straightening in my seat. "The workshop. Hands on deck. Got it."

My boss stares at me for a moment longer, unconvinced, before continuing his droning monologue about the department workshop, blah blah blah.

Blah.

I tap my paper with the tip of my pen. Let out a quiet breath of relief, my mind once again drifting back to my office.

Is this some kind of prank? Or worse, does Gio think

showing up unannounced is *romantic*? Some grand gesture? Is he trying to impress me?

I click my pen, gripping it tighter, ignoring the way my heart skips at the idea.

This isn't a rom-com! I'm not a quirky heroine, and Gio Montagalo is definitely not the charming lead.

He's a disruption.

A distraction.

And yet…

The thought of him waiting for me at my desk…flashing me a smile when I walk back in… sends an uninvited spark of warmth through me.

Professor Casey clears his throat, pulling my attention back to the present.

"Adams," he says. "I trust you'll handle your end of the workshop preparations?"

"Absolutely." I nod briskly. *I have no idea what I've just agreed to, but I'll figure it out later.*

As our meeting finally wraps up, I gather my things and make a beeline for the door, managing to mutter a polite goodbye to him and the other colleague who had been in the room.

The moment I step into the hallway, my feet quicken their pace toward my office.

Red face.

Beating heart.

As I grow closer, I hear his voice.

His laugh echoes down the hallway, rich and deep, like he doesn't have a care in the world. Because he probably doesn't!

When I turn the corner, the scene that greets me makes me stop dead in my tracks.

Gio is sitting on the edge of my desk, leaning back on his hands with the kind of cool confidence that should be illegal. Paul is standing to his right, doubled over laughing, and another student—Rachel from my Tuesday morning seminar—has joined the audience, leaning against the doorframe, wide-eyed and completely captivated.

"I'm telling you, it's true!" Gio is gesturing animatedly with his hands as he tells the story. "Third period, Coach loses his mind. We all get stuck running suicides for an hour because Parker Fiffe decides to tape his water bottle to the ceiling in the team room. To this day, none of us know how he got it up there."

Paul rasps, tears practically forming in his eyes as he stares at his new hero. "No way!"

"My lips to God's ears." Gio kisses his fingers and holds them up like he's delivering the gospel. "And the worst part? Parker blamed it on me!"

Rachel is in love. "That is insane."

"It was," Gio says, his grin widening. "But hey, those were the good old days when I was your age."

Oh lord.

Time to break up the party.

I clear my throat loudly, and all three of them turn toward me.

"Am I interrupting?" I ask, my voice sharper than I intended.

"No, no—come in," Gio says smoothly, gesturing like he's the one who owns the place.

Rachel giggles, and Paul tries to hide his smile.

I roll my eyes and step into my office, setting my bag down on the chair with a little more force than necessary.

"I didn't realize you were going to make yourself so at home. I've been gone thirty minutes."

"Just filling in," Gio says, completely unfazed. Clueless. "I'm a natural. In fact, hook me up with a lecture hall and I'll give a speech."

"Don't doubt it," I deadpan, shooing him out of my seat so I can sit.

Rachel clears her throat, clearly sensing the shift in the room. "Um, Professor Adams, I stopped by to ask about the extra credit assignment for next week? Uh. I was wondering if you were willing to extend the deadline?"

She knows my policy on making exceptions: there are none.

"Put that in an email and I'll get back to you by the end of the day," I tell her, cutting her off so she can't linger.

Rachel steals another lovesick glance at Gio.

"Oh. Okay." She glances at him one last time, her curiosity evident, before scurrying out the door.

Paul, however, remains, torn between staying and leaving.

"*Paul*," I say pointedly, raising my brows.

"Right, yep, I'm going," he says, holding up his hands in mock surrender. But just as he reaches the doorway, he pauses, turning back to grin at me. "For the record, Gio is awesome. You should give him a chance."

I'm startled, caught completely off guard as Paul finally steps out and the door clicks shut behind him.

What on Earth were they yapping about while I was stuck in my meeting?

The door clicks shut.

I turn my attention back to Gio, who's now lounging in the chair opposite my desk, looking completely at ease—as if he belongs here, as if he hadn't just derailed my entire day.

"Give you a chance?" I repeat, narrowing my eyes at him. "Care to explain what that's supposed to mean?"

Gio leans back, his grin widening as he stretches his arms behind his head. "We were just talking. Paul asked some questions, I answered. Nothing scandalous."

His eyes are practically sparkling as he watches me cross my arms over my chest.

"I doubt that."

He raises a brow, his expression one of mock innocence.

"What? You think I was out here spreading lies?"

"I think," I say slowly, "you were probably out here charming the pants off my students—and have not tried explaining to me what you're doing here."

He shrugs, completely unbothered. "Seemed like the best way to see you."

I stare, dumbfounded. "Have you ever heard of texting? Or calling? Or literally any other normal method of communication?"

"Sure," he says easily. "But where's the fun in that?"

"You're not supposed to show up at a person's office unannounced—I wouldn't do that to *you*."

"Right. You were given *tickets* to my office."

My mouth gapes. "That is not the same thing and you know it!"

"Isn't it?"

"No!" I practically shout, eyes darting to the closed door. I lower my voice, pointing a finger at him. "This is *completely* different."

He tilts his head, pretending to consider. "Different how? Because I didn't bring a sign?"

Wow. He thinks he is so cute and clever.

I let out a frustrated sigh, trying to ignore the heat creeping up my neck. It would help if he wasn't so damn adorable and clueless.

"Gio, I have a *job*. A very serious, professional job. You can't just waltz in here and act like...like—"

"Like I want to *see* you?" he interjects, his tone soft enough to have me blinking at him.

I'm speechless.

He leans back in the chair, crossing his legs, grinning as he watches me struggle to form a response.

"You know, for someone who spends her days lecturing people about sociology, you're not very good at reading between the lines."

"What's that supposed to mean?" I ask, though my voice comes out quieter than I'd like.

His shoulders move up and down as he regards me. "It means I'm here because I wanted to see you. No ulterior motives, no grand plan. It is what it is."

The sincerity in his tone throws me.

My emotions are a tangled mess, and I can't seem to settle on one long enough to form a coherent response.

I'm dismayed.

Pleased.

Confused.

Delighted.

He's watching me, expression calm but curious, like he's waiting for me to say something—anything.

I clear my throat, forcing myself to regain some semblance of composure. "You can't just show up like this, Gio. It's disruptive."

"There's that word again," he teases. "What am I disruptive to? Your work?"

"Yes," I say firmly, though the slight waver in my voice betrays me.

He untangles his legs and arms and leans forward, resting those beefy forearms on the desk, closing the distance between us.

"And here I thought professors were supposed to thrive under pressure."

The way he says it causes me to tingle.

"Pressure is one thing," I retort, trying to ignore the way his proximity is making my pulse race. "You're something else entirely."

"Good 'something else' or bad?" he asks, his grin widening.

I narrow my eyes at him, refusing to dignify the question with an answer.

I shiver again.

"If you're going to stay, you need to behave."

"Define *'behave,'*" he says, the teasing edge in his voice making it clear he has no intention of doing so.

His eyes say it all and eyes don't lie.

He likes me.

Likes me likes me.

Never in a million years would you have been able to say to me, "Austin Adams—in one week, Gio Montagalo, your favorite hockey goalie—is going to give you tickets to his hockey game and chase you down at your office because he wants to date you."

I would have bet money on it.

A ton of money.

The idea is so far-fetched that even now—with him sitting right in front of me—I have trouble wrapping my head around it.

And yet...

Here he is. In the flesh.

"You're staring," Gio says, stating a fact.

"I'm not," I lie, shaking my head as I force myself to look at the papers on my desk. I shuffle them to avert my gaze and give my hands something to do.

"It's okay. I get it, this is a lot to take in." He sighs so long and loud as if he had the weight of the world on his shoulders. "Trust me, I'm struggling with it too."

Say what now?

I glance up, narrowing my eyes. "Struggling with what?"

"This. Us."

Us.

The word hangs in the air like a challenge, and for a moment, I'm sure I misheard him.

"It's been a long time since I've dated anyone," he continues, completely oblivious to the mini heart attack he's just caused inside my body. "And honestly, I didn't think I'd ever get back into it, you know?"

"No," I say quickly, my voice sharp as I sit up straighter. "I don't know. There is no 'us.'"

Gio tilts his head. "Not yet."

He sounds so convinced. So sure.

"Gio." His name on my lips causes me to pause, the weight

of it heavy in the air. Suddenly, my best friend's voice pops into my head, loud and clear, like some kind of guardian angel.

"*Do not tell him there is no us. What the hell are you doing? You're going to turn this man down? Why? YOU ARE SINGLE. We literally talked about dating last week! You said you were lonely! You said you wanted a steady lay and didn't want to sleep around! You said you wanted a boyfriend! And HERE HE IS! And he's famous, and hot, and funny! Do not shove this man out of your office.*"

My inner monologue spirals, her words playing on a loop like a broken record.

But that's the problem, isn't it?

He's hot. And famous.

Two things that do *not* add up in my brain.

I cross my arms tighter over my chest, trying to ground myself in the present moment, but Gio doesn't miss a beat. He leans forward slightly, his elbows resting on the desk, his gaze steady and unwavering.

"You're overthinking it," he says, his tone soft but sure, like he's reading my mind.

"I am *not* overthinking it," I reply, though the crack in my voice betrays me. Overthinking it is what I do best. In fact, as a smile tugs at his lips, my eyes go to the small, framed sign on my wall. "*Overthink it later.*"

How ironic.

"You are," he tells me matter-of-factly. "You're going to make this more complicated than it needs to be."

"It *is* complicated," I argue, though my conviction feels shaky. "You're you. And I'm not."

"You're not me?" He raises a brow, clearly unimpressed with my logic. "What does that even mean?"

"I meant—you're you and I'm me." I fumble for the right words. "This doesn't make sense. *We* don't make sense."

"Says who?" he asks, leaning back in his chair like he's completely at ease.

"Says reality," I snap, overwhelmed with the conversation. I did not wake up planning for this.

I did not plan for him.

Obviously.

"Reality is overrated," he quips, his grin widening. "Haven't you learned that by now? The internet says so."

"Oh shut up." I laugh.

He seizes the opening, shifting tactics. "Did you read the article about yourself this morning on *Sports Center*?"

My head shakes. No I have not.

"You should," he says casually, leaning back in his chair. "It makes you look like the better, smarter part of this partnership."

"Partnership?" I echo, arching a brow.

"Yeah," he says, grinning. "You're the one with the Ivy League degree—I went to a Podunk college in Canada and used pancakes to make sandwiches when we ran out of bread."

I blink at him, my lips twitching as I try to suppress a smile.

"Pancakes? Really?"

"Hey, they're versatile," he says, completely serious. "And don't knock it till you've tried it. They're so fluffy."

That does sound delicious.

"Anyway. The media loves you. They also love the fact that you were roasting me at the game."

I snort.

"It's what any sports loving enthusiast would do, given your recent stats."

He clutches his chest like I've just mortally wounded him. "Wow. Straight for the jugular, huh?"

"Some would say I helped you win this last game."

"That's exactly what they're saying. You're my good luck charm."

Good luck charm?

"Please don't tell me you believe in superstitions." Although if I'm being fair, most athletes have some kind of pre-game superstitious ritual.

"Are you out of your mind? Of course I do!" he replies, looking genuinely offended by the suggestion that he *wouldn't*.

I can't help but laugh. "You're kidding."

"Dead serious," he says, leaning forward like he's about to let me in on some life-altering secret. "Do you have any idea how many rituals go into being a hockey player? It's practically a religion."

"Let me guess," I say, crossing my arms. "You have a pair of lucky socks that you've worn twenty games in a row."

"Not socks," he says, his eyes gleaming with amusement. "But I do have a routine. And now I have a lucky charm." He pauses. "You."

"I need you at every game."

"Every game?" I repeat, staring at him like he's lost his mind. "Do you realize how insane that sounds?"

"Not insane," he corrects, holding up a finger. "Committed to the cause."

"What cause? Driving me crazy?"

"If that's what it takes," he says, smirking.

I open my mouth to argue, but he cuts me off.

"Think about it," he says, his tone turning thoughtful. "You come to my games, I win more often, the media gets to keep their feel-good story about my 'brilliant, beautiful good luck charm.' Everyone wins."

Everyone wins.

"What's in it for me?" I blurt out. "Besides the fact that my team will become champions." Which is the ultimate goal, yeah?

"Well. You get me." He spreads his arms wide like he's presenting himself as a prize on a game show. "Whatever you want."

Whatever I want...

My eyes trail down his torso.

Broad chest.

His is a body roughened by years of hockey, with hands

you'd expect to see gripping a stick or wrapping around a big, thick—

"Uh-huh," I say, forcing my focus back to his face. His stupid, cheeky grin is firmly in place. "I have a job, you know. A full-time one."

I'm a Big Kid! My tone says.

"And?" He shrugs like this is the most minor inconvenience in the world. "My games are mostly at night. Doesn't conflict with your office hours, Professor Adams."

"How generous of you," I lament dryly.

"I know."

"You seriously think I'm going to drop everything and become your personal good luck charm? That's ridiculous."

"It's not ridiculous," he counters, his grin softening into something closer to sincerity. "It's practical."

"Practical?" I repeat, my voice rising slightly. "For who? You?"

"Sure." The giant oaf leans back in his chair like he doesn't have a care in the world. "But also for you. Think about it—this is your chance to be part of something bigger than yourself."

"I am part of something bigger than myself," I say, gesturing around my office. At my diplomas—Bachelors, Masters, and Doctorate degrees, *thankyouverymuch*. "It's called *academia*."

He snorts. "Does academia have championship trophies and screaming fans?"

"No," I admit reluctantly. "But it includes tenure and health insurance."

Ha!

"Touché," he allows. "But it also doesn't have *me*. And for the record, I don't half ass anything."

He is giving me a pointed look so intense, I squirm uncomfortably.

"Right," I reply dryly. "Because it's not like I have papers to grade or meetings to attend or, you know, a life outside of work."

"You'll make time," he says confidently, like it's a foregone conclusion.

"Wow." I blink at him. "You're unbelievable."

"Thank you." He flashes me a smile so bright it should be illegal and for a brief moment, I catch myself wondering if he's had any teeth knocked out and if so, which ones.

"That wasn't a compliment," I snap, unconvincing even to my own ears. He is turning me into a liar!

"Sure it was," he says easily. "You don't want to admit it."

I roll my eyes, but Gio only laughs, the sound warm and entirely too charming. Intoxicating, even.

"Okay," I say, holding up a hand. "Let's say, *hypothetically*, I agree to this madness. What exactly would this…*arrangement* entail?"

His grin widens, like he's been waiting for me to ask. "You'd come to my games, obviously. Cheer for me. Maybe throw a few good-natured insults at the opposing team."

"Duh." I toss my hair. "What else?"

"Well." He sits forward, getting excited. "We'd probably have to hang out a bit outside of games, you know, to keep up appearances. Make it believable for the media."

"Believable?" I echo, raising an eyebrow. "You mean you'd want me to fake-date you?"

"Who said anything about fake?" he says, his grin turning mischievous.

My stomach flips, and I hate how easily he gets under my skin.

"Dude," I start, my tone holding warning.

"Relax, relax." He stands. I track him with my eyes as he rounds the desk, his presence so commanding that it feels like the entire room shrinks. "I'm not asking you to marry me. Just to think about it."

I'm not asking you to marry me…

Marry me.

He stops right next to my chair, towering over me, and every logical part of my brain is screaming at me to stand up, too. Or wheel my chair away. The massive lunk crouches so we're eye level, his face impossibly close to mine.

My heart pounds so loudly I'm certain he can hear it.

"I-I don't think this is appropriate."

"What's not appropriate?" he whispers, closing the space further by gripping my chair by the arms and pulling it forward.

Not aggressive.

Just deliberate.

Purposeful.

"I'm working. It's not appropriate to…"

"To do what?" He leans forward, mouth brushing the side of my neck where my pulse beats erratically.

He kisses it again.

"That."

"Why?"

Cause.

Just…cause.

He is giving me every chance to stop him. To turn my head. Shove him away. *Resist him like a good girl because I AM AT WORK. THIS IS NOT PROFESSIONAL!*

But I don't push him away.

I don't resist.

As much as I hate to admit it, I want him to keep kissing me.

I want him.

Not because he's Gio Montagalo but because he's so fucking sexy and sure of himself.

And so, when his lips brush against mine, tentatively to test the waters, I let him. In fact, my breath hitches with excitement and before I know it, I'm kissing him hungrily, hands instinctively reaching up to touch his face.

Stroke his cheeks.

My fingertips trail along the curve of his jaw, feeling the roughness of his stubble against my smooth skin—a contrast between us that sends a shiver racing down my spine.

Yum...

His lips, soft yet demanding, press against mine with increasing fervor, coaxing me to respond in kind.

I tilt my head, giving in completely, and the world narrows to just this: the heat of his mouth, the gentle scrape of his stubble, the intoxicating taste of him.

Sweet, like candy.

My candy—the kind I keep on my desk for students to take.

The air between us is charged—electric—and I feel like I'm floating and free-falling both at the same time. My senses are flooded—his scent, the warmth of his body, the rhythm of his breathing mingling with mine.

Hot tongue.

Full lips.

When we break apart, gasping for air, I feel lightheaded, my lips tingling and swollen from the force of our connection. My chest rises and falls in uneven bursts, heart pounding so hard it's a miracle it hasn't leapt out of my rib cage.

The whole thing gives me butterflies.

"Whew," I let out, doing my best to smile. As if I make out in my office on the daily, like—no big deal.

Gio straightens to his full height, his presence still commanding even as he steps back, and the wheels of my chair roll me gently into place.

"Think about it," he murmurs, his voice low and teasing, his lips curling into a grin.

"Mmm?" I manage, voice shaky. I have betrayed myself and judging by the look he's giving me, he is well aware.

Gio stands slowly, the absence of his warmth making me feel unmoored. Makes me want to yank him back and kiss him all over again...

"You know—*us*."

"Us?" My head tilts to look *up, up, up* at him, brows furrowing.

He grins down at me, that maddening, cocky smile that has my knees going weak even though I'm sitting.

"Yeah, you goof. Us. I'd love to see you at my next game."

I roll my eyes. It's impossible not to. "Yeah—so you win."

"That's not the only reason I want you there, but if it gets you to the arena, I'll take it."

Gio Montagalo is still sniffing after me to be his good luck charm and the thought still blows my mind. Of all the things...

"You'll come around to my way of thinking."

Arrogant bastard.

I open my mouth to argue—tell him how ridiculous he sounds. Unfortunately the words get stuck somewhere between my brain and my lips and before I can untangle the mess of thoughts swirling in my head, he steps back, hands sliding into his pockets.

"I'll see you later, Professor," he says, giving me a wink that manages to feel both playful and arrogant. Like he knows I'm putty in his big, strong hands.

Then.

He turns and walks out of my office, leaving me staring after him like a freaking idiot.

When the door closes behind him, my hand drifts to my lips, still tingling from the kiss; my brain struggles to catch up with what just happened.

What *did* just happen?

I blink at the door, half-expecting him to come back, to say something else, to explain himself. But he doesn't. He's gone, and I'm left alone in my office, my thoughts racing and my heart still pounding.

Think about it.

As if I'll be able to think about anything else.

9
gio

I whistle while I skate to the center of the goal, the tune for my ears only.

It's one that's been stuck in my head all morning; a melody with no name and something to keep my nerves steady.

As I settle into position, the familiar rhythm of practice takes over. The ice is my sanctuary, the only place where everything else fades away—except maybe for her.

I smile at the thought of Austin.

Coach blows the whistle, signaling the next round of shots, and I drop into my stance, stick ready, eyes sharp. Charlie barrels toward me first, puck on his blade, trying to deke left.

Rookie beyotch.

I slide smoothly to cut him off, my pads swallowing the puck with a satisfying *thud*.

"Nice try."

Not.

I flick the puck out of my crease and back toward the blue line.

I hear him groan.

"Come on, bro. Can't you let one through? For morale?"

HIT ME WITH YOUR BEST SHOT

"Not my job," I reply, grinning behind my mask.

The next shooter is Liam, one of the wingers who never stops chirping, even during drills. He skates in fast, snapping the puck toward the top corner. I react on instinct, my glove shooting up to snatch it out of the air.

"Denied!" I shout, tossing the puck lazily to the ice.

I am in the fucking zone.

Liam flips me the bird—I can't see it because of his mitt, but I translate the gesture as: *Fuck you, dude.*

It's all banter. Lighthearted, easy. Beneath the facade, I feel my focus sharpening with every save. Every blocked shot is another reminder of why I'm here, why I love this game, why I'm good at it.

But then, like an annoying little whisper, her face creeps into my mind. Austin. Sitting at her desk, rolling her eyes at me.

She's so damn sexy.

A professor—who would have imagined that!

The mental image of her standing in front of a classroom, commanding the room with her wit and intelligence, does something to my dick that I can't explain.

She's fucking thrilling.

Never met a woman like her.

I'm standing in the box though my mind is back in her little office, imagining her in the glasses that were resting on her desk. Imagining her *naked* on her desk...wearing heels. I imagine what her tits might look like. If they'd spill out of my hands, or if they're small—like her.

Her sassy mouth gets me so hot and bothered.

The thoughts are so vivid my cock twitches inside my gear.

Coach's whistle pierces the air, dragging me back to the present. Another drill. Another shot to block. I drop into position, but my mind is half a step behind, lingering on Austin's sharp tongue and her softer side—both of which I've gotten glimpses of.

Another sharp whistle.

Get it together, Gio. *This is practice, not fantasy hour.*

"Why are you in such a damn good mood?" One of my teammates skates past and heckles me.

I roll my eyes, flipping my mask up and resting it on my head.

"Maybe I'm just happy to be here, fucker—ever thought of that?"

"Since when?" Collins skates around the neck, continuing to taunt me. "Is it that chick on the news?"

DING DING DING.

Bingo.

My mask flips back down and I refocus on the ice, trying to ignore the heat crawling up the back of my neck.

"Don't know what you're talking about."

"Bullshit," he shouts back, skating closer. "That chick is all over social media, and so are you. Your 'brilliant and beautiful' good luck charm? Makes me want to vomit—what's the deal with you two?"

Of course it would make him want to vomit.

From what I know, Collins is relationship adverse and would rather sleep around than settle down. Not that I have room to talk; that's been my track record, too, until the past year of reevaluating my priorities.

"Our deal is none ya business," I snap, crouching back into position as Coach lines up the next drill. "Maybe if you spent more time shooting pucks and less time gossiping like a middle schooler, you'd actually score on me for once."

"Why are you being a bitch about it? I'm just asking."

He feigns left. He feigns right. But I'm already reading him, tracking the puck as he swings left again and goes for a wrist shot.

Not today.

I snap my glove hand out, catching the puck mid-air with a

HIT ME WITH YOUR BEST SHOT

satisfying smack. He groans as I toss the puck back into play, giving myself a mental pat on the back.

"That's all you've got?" I taunt, feeling the rush of adrenaline. "My grandmother could shoot better than that."

She can't—but you get what I'm saying.

The drills continue and my mind keeps wandering. I wonder what Austin is doing right now. Lecturing a class? Telling another poor undergrad they've got no chance of an extension on their paper? Teaching the future of the world while I'm here in a cold rink, chasing pucks and nagging my teammates.

What does a guy like me even have to offer someone like her? She's got degrees on her wall, a sharp wit, and a life filled with intellectual conversations. And me? I've got a stick and a pair of skates. Pads and a face mask.

Big.

Dumb.

Jock.

Who drives a big, dumb, truck.

Eventually, Coach's whistle blows to signal the end of practice; we skate to the bench and I grab my water bottle. The guys are still ribbing me as we head off the ice—I let it roll off my back. Let them talk.

Let them speculate.

Because the truth is, they're not wrong.

And I know the first thing I'm going to do when I'm dressed is send Austin a message because I just cannot fucking resist.

Why should I?

I presented her with a challenge; so by the time I'm dressed and pulling my phone out of my bag, I've already got a message drafted in my head:

> Miss me yet?

Not very clever, but no one has ever accused me of being a poet.

Hitting send before I can overthink it, I shove my phone back in my pocket like it's burning a hole there. The guys are still lingering near the locker room doors, talking about grabbing food, but I wave off their invitations, citing an excuse about needing to head home to help Nova.

Truth is, I've got no plans other than replaying the last two days in my head and wondering how the hell I ended up here: nearly obsessed with a woman completely out of my league.

Me? I've got one foot out the door, my mind already miles away, wondering what kind of witty, sassy, flirty thing Austin is going to say back.

Sliding into my truck, I dig my phone out of my duffle and check for a notification, wondering what kind of witty, sassy, flirty thing Austin is going to respond with.

Nothing.

I don't know why I thought she'd respond immediately—as she so eloquently pointed out, she's got a career. *A life.* Unlike me, who spends his days practicing a sport. Working out. Conditioning. In rehab or recovery.

Sigh.

Finally the phone buzzes. Lights up my cupholder. My pulse kicks up as I grab it, already grinning like a damn fool.

Her reply is short, simple:

> Austin: Don't flatter yourself.
>
> Austin: Are you flirting with me?

Gio: Yes.

Gio: When am I NOT flirting with you?

I glance out the windshield at the now empty parking lot.

It's quiet, save for the occasional car passing on the main road, but my mind is buzzing. I should probably head home, grab something to eat, but the thought of putting the conversation on pause for the next half hour while I drive into the city bums me out.

> Austin: Valid point.

Gio: Have you given any thought to my proposal?

I type another message and delete it.
Twice.

> Austin: I mean—you want me to come to games... but I'm almost always at the games to begin with, so...

Gio: No. In your special seats.

> Austin: Those special seats are your SISTER'S.

Gio: Nova has those seats because of me. Let's not kid ourselves, she's happy to share.

> Austin: So what I hear you saying is—not only do I have to show up, I have to sit in the SAME seat???

Gio: Yes. And bring the sign heckling me, and wear the same outfit.

> Austin: Okay, now you're acting superstitious.

Gio: Not superstitious. Routine.

> Austin: Same thing!!!!

Gio: It's not the same thing! It's science.

> Austin: Science?

Gio: Yes. Cause and effect. You show up in the same spot, wearing the same outfit, holding the same sign, and I win. That's hard data, professor.

Austin:

Gio: Don't roll your eyes at me through the phone. I can feel it.

Austin: Good. Then you can feel me telling you how ridiculous you are.

Gio: You say ridiculous, I say irresistible.

Austin: No comment.

I don't want to come off like some guy who's desperate for attention—but here I am, sitting in my truck like a complete idiot, hanging on every damn word.

Admit it, Gio. You're whipped.

The thought hits hard, and I let out a low laugh. I am, aren't I? Sitting here waiting for her to text back, smiling at my phone like some lovesick teenager.

It's embarrassing.

"Christ," I mutter, running a hand through my damp hair. "What the hell are you doing, man?"

But I know what I'm doing. I'm falling for her—I must be. Austin isn't like anyone else I've met. She's sharp, confident, and unimpressed by all the usual shit that usually impresses the ladies, like my money and clout.

Gio: Alright, let's cut to the chase—are you coming to my game or what? I'm dying here.

Austin: I haven't given it any thought...

The biggest lie I've heard her tell, to date. And I've only known her for a matter of days.

HIT ME WITH YOUR BEST SHOT

Gio: You owe me ten dollars for that little white lie.

Austin: Ten dollars?! Whoa.

Gio: I said what I said. Any time you tell a fib, you pay up.

Austin: What about YOU!?

Gio: I haven't lied to you, but sure—if that will make you feel better, agreed.

Austin: That is the LEAST interesting way to make someone "put their money where their mouth is."

Gio: Did you have something better in mind? Like, every time I catch you in a lie, you owe me _____. Fill in the blank.

Austin: Lap dance?

Austin: KIDDING.

Gio: No take backs!

Austin: I take it back! LOL I was kidding

Gio: It's in writing, sorry.

Austin: I was just providing an example of more interesting ways to win a bet!!!

Gio: We're not betting! Not what that was, but I get what you're saying and I love where your mind went. Keep up the good work. Question: do you plan on lying to me on a regular basis?

Austin: No, no, no not at all, I swear—I am not a liar. I just… don't know how to talk to you yet. I'm figuring it out.

Gio: I'm easy to talk to, what are you talking about?

Austin: You're intimidating as hell!!! Don't pretend you weren't aware.

My fingers are moving a mile a minute, texting faster than I've texted before.

Gio: That is not my goal. The last thing I want is for you to feel uncomfortable with me. If you do, I apologize

Austin: Oh, I TOTALLY feel comfortable with you. All I meant was... I'm still wrapping my brain around the fact that we're friends.

Gio: Friends?

Gio: You're my lucky charm 😊

Austin: 😳

Gio: And.

Gio: You like me. Admit it.

Austin: ADMIT IT?! You're going to be waiting a long time, buddy.

Gio: Shhh... I'm a patient man.

Austin: Tell you what—if I show up, it'll be entirely on my own terms.

Gio: Deal. As long as those terms include you being there. And you sit your sweet little ass in that special seat.

I tap my fingers against the steering wheel, waiting for her reply. The message is delivered, the "read" receipt taunting me like I'm in the net and missed an easy save.

HIT ME WITH YOUR BEST SHOT

I could sit here all night if it meant winning this little back-and-forth with Austin. She's stubborn as hell, but I know she's got a weak spot for me somewhere in there.

The phone buzzes in my hand.

> Austin: You don't give up, do you?

I grin. Victory is mine.

> Gio: Nope.

My thumbs hover over the keyboard. Should I add something flirty? Dirty. Something to make her blush?

No.

Not yet.

Don't want to freak her the fuck out and scare her away.

> Austin: I feel like this deal heavily favors you. Where's my incentive?

> Gio: I told you. You can have WHATEVER you want...

The three dots appear. Then vanish. Appear again. She's typing, erasing, and typing again.

I grin at the thought of her overthinking this.

> Austin: Whatever I want, huh?

> Gio: Yup. Name it.

She likes this game as much as I do.

> Austin: I'll have to think this through to make it worth my while, since I'll be doing all of the work.

Gio: YOU'RE doing all the work?! What about me, I'm busting my balls down on the ice! That seat is cushy!

Austin: Technically, yes. But being your lucky charm is A LOT OF PRESSURE. What if I'm there and you still lose next week??

Gio: We won't.

Austin: You don't know that.

Gio: I'm also not willing to risk finding out.

Gio: So tell me what you want.

10
austin

I cannot force myself to wear a MONTAGALO jersey. I want to.

But I can't.

The man is cocky enough; I'm not about to stroke his ego by showing up to the game wearing his name across my back and his number across my chest.

Nervously, I check my makeup one more time, leaning forward for a closer look as I rub glossy lip stain over my bottom lip with the tip of my pinkie finger.

I slide into my boots, glancing down at Gio.

My dog.

Yes.

My dog's name is Gio—have I failed to mention that?

And I know what you're thinking: *"Austin, there is no way you can tell the man you named your dog after him. He'll think you're a total psycho!"*

Bullshit. Plenty of people name their pets after their favorite players. People get tattoos of their faces, their numbers, their freaking stats! People do far crazier things, and let's be real—there are probably a dozen other animals named after Gio out there.

Mine is just one of many.

So there.

"Listen, buddy." I look down at him. "I'll only be gone for the first period." I pause, reconsidering. "Maybe two." I sigh as he stares up at me, tongue lolling out of the side of his mouth. "Okay, fine—I might stay the whole time. But I won't be late."

I crouch down, scratching behind his ears. "I'll keep an eye on you with the cameras, and if you're having a rough night, I'll have Dolly come check on you. Deal?"

He just keeps gazing up at me with those big, soulful eyes.

"Don't look at me like that. You can't come with me."

He blinks.

I give him more pets.

"Gio, seriously, stop. You had school today, played with all your friends—you should be knocked out in your bed right now, not making me feel bad about leaving."

I stand. "Be good, okay? No guilt trips. No chewing the couch cushions. I mean it this time."

He tilts his head, all innocent and adorable, as if he has no idea what I'm talking about. But he knows: Gio is a chewer and often gets into trouble, hence the cameras throughout my apartment.

Video evidence.

"Alright, I'm going. And I *will* be checking the cameras." I narrow my eyes.

I grab my keys and the sign I made for the last game that screams **GET YOUR SHIT TOGETHER**, and sprinkled in glitter.

Thank God I saved it because I'm too lazy and too busy to make a new one.

Heading for the door, I squeeze through it so Gio the Dog cannot follow, shutting it gently before I can change my mind and stay home.

The crisp night air hits my face as I step outside, my breath puffing in small clouds. The streetlights flicker faintly, and I pull my jacket tighter around me as I make my way to the curb—the Uber I ordered is already waiting to take me to the game.

It's a busy night—most home games are—and I find my seat section as the players are taking the ice. I hold the rail as I take the steps down, making my way to the first row, carefully balancing the beer I bought in one hand and the sign in the other, while navigating the crowd.

People are running up and down the steps to get concessions and pee before the game starts and it's hectic.

Loud.

The energy in the arena is electric, everyone in scarves and jerseys, shouting encouragement before the game has even begun.

When I reach my row, I stop in my tracks. Instead of there being an empty seat next to me, sitting there with an air of practiced coolness is Nova. Gio's sister.

Oh.

My.

God.

She's slouched in the seat, one ankle crossed over her knee, scrolling through her phone like she's got better places to be, but decided to grace the rink with her presence anyway. Her platinum-blonde hair is tucked beneath a knit beanie, and her leather jacket stands out starkly against the sea of team colors.

She doesn't glance up as I awkwardly shuffle closer, gripping my beer like a shield.

I shuffle closer.

Nova glances up.

Raises her gaze.

The moment her eyes land on me, they light up like the alarm above the goalie net.

"Austin!" she exclaims, standing halfway like she's about to pull me into some kind of enthusiastic hug but thinks better of it at the last second. "*Finally*! I thought you'd never show up!"

She looks so happy to see me!

"Oh lord," she continues as I get closer, reaching to flick the sign in my hand. "Is that the sign from last week?" She grabs the bright yellow cardboard and flips it over, inspecting it with a deep frown. "I thought the two of you were getting along!"

"We are!" I laugh, settling into my seat and unwinding the striped scarf around my neck. My hair sticks up in a few directions, and I smooth it with one hand. "He wanted me to bring it again—for good luck."

Nova's face stays blank for a long beat, her mouth slightly parted like she's buffering and can't quite process what I just said. Then, out of nowhere, she bursts into full-blown laughter—the kind that has her doubling over with shaking shoulders.

"Good luck?" she gasps between giggles.

"Yes! I'm supposed to heckle him too. It's motivational?" I shrug, as if questioning the logic of this whole situation. But if there's one thing I understand, it's superstitions and routine and trying to keep my team on a winning streak because as a fan, I have my own pre-game ritual so my team wins.

"Why is he like this?" his sister says. "Why can't he, oh, *I don't know*, wear the same socks like a normal weirdo athlete? No, no—he'd rather be publicly roasted."

Whatever works.

"Do you want to hold the sign instead?" I deadpan, lifting the sign toward her like it's the Olympic torch. "That totally counts, right?"

Her laughter cranks up a notch as she grabs the sign and holds it high, waving it around, glitter sparkling under the bright lights.

The crowd eats it up, erupting in cheers and whistles.

"Yes!" she whoops. "I'm absolutely taking credit for this moment."

"You weren't even here last week!" I shout over the commotion, laughing despite myself as I reach for the sign. "You can't just swoop in and steal your brother's humiliation from me!"

"Correction." Nova's green eyes sparkle mischievously. "It's not humiliating if *I'm* doing it. It's entertainment. You plus me equals the dynamic duo of public embarrassment."

"He was begging for me to bring this." I snort, lunging for the sign again. "Don't be a glory hound."

"Too late," Nova quips, raising the sign even higher and twirling it like she's in a parade. "The crowd loves me."

Before I can retort, my attention shifts.

Out on the ice, a familiar, hulking figure skates toward us. Big, brawny, and unmistakably looking straight in my direction.

He stops right in front of us, his stick tapping against the plexiglass with an audible *thunk* that feels like a scolding all on its own. Even through his face mask, his frown is visible, a stern expression that makes him look like a peeved gladiator.

His gaze darts between Nova and me, as if catching two kids red-handed with a jar of cookies.

Yikes.

"You let her hold the sign?" he shouts, his voice muffled but clear enough for me to catch. His massive shoulders rise in protest, gloves raised as if he's calling foul. "That wasn't part of the deal!"

I squint, doing my best to read his lips and piece together his tone, though the indignation is practically radiating off him.

"She took it!" I shout back, throwing my hands up in mock surrender. "What was I supposed to do, *fight her for it?*"

Nova leans into the exchange and adds her two cents. "I'm scrappy! She wouldn't have stood a chance!"

He huffs, his lips twitching upward like he's trying not to laugh. Then, with exaggerated deliberation, he tips his helmet slightly forward before skating backward with an effortless grace that belies his size, stick tapping once more as he heads toward the goalie box.

God damn he's sexy…

"You're drooling," his sister teases.

I snap out of it, hand reflexively brushing the corner of my mouth—just to check, of course. "Am not."

"Don't bother denying it." Nova plops down into her seat. "I enjoy being the matchmaker for once."

"For once?" I echo, raising a brow as I fold my arms and settle in beside her, gaze affixed to the ice. "Are you saying you usually scare people away?"

She gasps, clutching her chest in mock horror like I've just insulted her honor.

"*Excuse* you, I'm a fantastic wing woman. But," she leans in conspiratorially, lowering into me. "It's rare that I get to sit back and watch the sparks fly all on their own. Gio has never actually chased a woman I told him about—he usually ignores my suggestions. You're a first."

Out on the ice? Her brother is impossible to ignore, all focus and precision as he fields practice shots from his teammates.

"Face-off in two minutes, three seconds," Nova singsongs, glancing at the scoreboard. "Plenty of time for him to score a date."

I shoot her a sidelong look. "Are you ever not meddling?"

"No. I'm his twin, his business is my business."

My head shakes. "I'll keep that in mind."

She freezes for a second, then waves her hands frantically, like she's trying to retract the words. "Wait, that's not what I meant! I mean… his past girlfriends were awful. Total puck bunnies. You know the type—only interested in him for his money or the NHL connections. I didn't mean I'm an impossible pain in the ass to deal with, I swear!"

I arch a brow, folding my arms as I lean back in my chair. "Sounds a little like you're playing hockey mom."

She groans, running a hand through her hair, clearly frustrated with herself. "God, no. I swear, I'm not that bad. I just… okay, maybe I'm a little overprotective, but only because I care, you know?"

I soften, the edge in my tone giving way to understanding. "I get it. You just want the best for him."

"Exactly!" she exclaims, slapping her knees in mock victory, her expression lighting up. "The night I bumped into you at Five Alarm, you were so animated and fun, the first thing I thought to myself was: *Gio has to meet this woman.*"

I smile at that, warmth creeping into my chest despite myself. She flatters me and I'm falling for it.

"And here I am."

She grins, leaning back in her seat like she's basking in her own matchmaking success. "And here we are."

The weight of her words hangs between us for a moment, comfortable and light, and I can't help but laugh softly even though she probably cannot hear it over the noise.

"You really don't take a day off, do you?"

"Never," she says proudly, chin tilting definitely, the beret on top her head tipping with the motion. "Besides. It's working out pretty well so far, wouldn't you say?"

Wow. *She is so much like her brother.*

"Ask me again in a week," I tease, though I can feel my cheeks heat up.

"Oh, I will." Nova nudges me with her elbow, pulling my attention back to her. "Okay, so important question: are you a vocal fan, or do you do the polite golf clap thing?"

"You already know the answer to that." I roll my eyes. "You saw me in action, remember?"

Her response is a burst of laughter as the puck drops in the center of the ice and play begins.

The puck zips from stick to stick, the action quick and relentless. The tension in the air is palpable, every play met with gasps or cheers. Then, Gio intercepts a pass with a sharp flick of his stick, sending the puck flying toward a teammate. The crowd erupts as the play progresses, and Nova jumps to her feet, her voice cutting through the noise.

"Nice save, Gio!" she screams, jumping up from her seat.

The last thing I want is the television cameras finding me and putting me on the ne—

Nova elbows me sharply, cutting off my internal monologue. "Do it."

I blink, confused. "Do what?"

"Say something mean!" she says, as if it's the most obvious thing in the world. "That's part of the deal, remember?"

I stare at her like she's lost her mind. "I am not going to say mean things to him in front of his sister! We just talked about how you don't want anyone dating him who's an asshole!"

She waves a hand dismissively. "Not the same thing. This is heckling. It's tradition. You're doing it out of love."

"No one else knows that!" I gesture to the surrounding crowd. "To them, I'm just some psycho yelling insults at their precious goalie."

Whom I also totally love.

Not love, love—but you get what I'm saying.

He's my favorite.

She laughs, tipping her head toward a guy a few rows down. "Look around you—half the crowd is pissed off at him for those losses." She points at the man's oversized foam finger, which is clearly not being used for supportive purposes. "See that guy? He *hates* Gio. His sign literally says *'GIO EATS SHIT.'*"

I squint at the crude letters painted on the obnoxiously large poster. "He's a Nashville fan, Nova. Of course he wants Gio to eat shit."

"Exactly!" she says triumphantly, throwing her hands in the air. "You'll blend right in! Come on, get up."

I stay firmly planted in my seat, crossing my arms. "This is peer pressure, and I don't appreciate it."

"This is the *reason* you're here," she counters, undeterred. "Do it."

Before I can protest, she gives me a nudge, and somehow, against all better judgment, my ass rises out of my seat. The crowd roars around us as a near miss on the ice draws everyone's attention.

Perfect—*no one will notice me making a fool of myself.*

HIT ME WITH YOUR BEST SHOT

I groan as she hands me the GET IT TOGETHER sign.

Take a deep breath.

Glance around nervously down at the ice. For a second, I wonder if he's even aware of the crowd. Then, with a burst of courage—or insanity—I cup my hands around my mouth and shout, "HEY, GIO! MY GRANDMOTHER HANDLES A PUCK BETTER THAN YOU!"

The words echo loud and clear, slicing through the cheers and whistles.

It feels as if everyone heard it.

On the ice, Gio's head snaps up. Even with his helmet on, I can *feel* the glare he's aiming in our direction. He shakes his head, and I'm pretty sure I see his shoulders shake in a laugh before he refocuses on the game.

"Happy now?" I ask.

My heart is pounding in my throat and I've never had this much unwanted attention before in my life. I hate it. Heat creeps up my neck, pooling in my cheeks, as if everyone in the arena is staring at me (they're not, but it sure *feels* like they are).

"No," his sister demands, straightening up with a mischievous grin. "Do one more."

I gasp. "Absolutely not."

"Now you have stage fright?" She laughs. "Yell one more insult and I'll buy you nachos."

That gets my attention because I could totally eat a snack.

All I have is this measly beer, and drinking on an empty stomach isn't exactly smart. My stomach growls in agreement, making the decision all the more tempting.

I glance back at the ice, where Gio is crouched in the crease, his glove and stick poised, completely in the zone. The opposing team is charging down the rink, and the puck flies from player to player with lightning speed.

It's a tense moment, the crowd leaning forward in collective anticipation.

"Fine," I mutter, gripping my sign tightly. "But if I get booed, I'm holding you personally responsible."

Nova claps her hands together, positively gleeful. "Deal. But make it count!"

I wish she'd stop telling me what to do as I focus my attention on Gio; the puck hurtles toward him. Then. Just as the opposing player winds up for a slapshot, I yell at the top of my lungs, "HEY, GIO! ARE YOU GONNA STOP THAT PUCK OR INVITE IT TO DINNER?"

It's loud.

So much louder than I intended.

So loud in fact, several heads turn my way.

I watch in horror as Gio flinches—*it's enough to throw him off.*

The puck zips past his glove and into the net. The goal horn blares, and the opposing team's fans erupt in cheers. My jaw falls open as he stands, broad shoulders rising and falling with exaggerated breaths.

He turns his head, looking directly at me. Even from here, I can see the glare in his eyes, like he's silently saying, *Really?*

The guy with the GIO EATS SHIT sign raises his foam finger in a salute of approval and waves it at me in solidarity.

Great.

I've joined the ranks of the haters.

Nova is *dying* beside me, doubled over with laughter. Positively. Dying.

"That was perfect." She can barely speak. "You're officially my favorite person."

"I just cost him a goal!" I hiss, sinking back into my seat and hiding my face behind the sign. DON'T LOOK AT ME!

"He's going to kill me."

"No he's not," Nova says, waving me off. "If anything, he's going to play even harder now just to spite you. Watch."

Sure enough, as the game continues, Gio is a brick wall. He deflects every shot with precision and speed, his movements sharper and more aggressive than before. The throng roars with every save, and even I can't help but cheer for him, my earlier embarrassment fading into awe.

I live for this shit!

Between plays, he glances up at the stands and points his stick in my direction, a subtle but unmistakable acknowledgment at my presence. Nova nudges me, her grin so wide it might split her face in two.

"See?" she says smugly. "He loves it. You're his muse."

"His muse?" I repeat, rolling my eyes. "More like his nightmare."

"Same thing." Nova shrugs, stealing a sip of my beer. "Oh hey—you know what this reminds me of?"

"What?"

"Foreplay."

I nearly choke on my breath. *"What?!"*

"You heard me," she says, entirely too pleased with herself. "The insults, the banter, the way he keeps glancing up here? Foreplay. You two are basically stripping each other naked with words." I hear her sigh. "I mean, look at the moron. He's been on *fire* since you started shouting at him. You've unlocked his *passion.*"

"Or his rage," I mutter, sinking lower in my seat, though her words linger in the back of my mind, unwelcome and intrusive.

I can't help it though—can't help but wonder if she has a point. Him coming to my office unannounced, leaning against my desk with that cocky grin. Me lobbing insults. Watching him glare toward my seat. Watching him stop every puck. Him pointing his stick in my direction....

Thinking about it is getting me so hot.

My stomach is a mess of knots, and my face is practically on fire. I take a long sip of my beer, hoping the cold will cool me down, but it doesn't help.

I need water.

A cold shower.

And those nachos I was promised.

11
gio

Steam still clings to the bathroom mirror as I rub a towel through my hair, the faint ache in my muscles a satisfying reminder of tonight's game. The second shower of the night was necessary—post-game adrenaline always leaves me too wired to just crash, and nothing clears my head like scalding water and a moment of silence.

The house is quiet, except for the low hum of the fridge in the kitchen and the occasional creak of the floorboards as I pad barefoot down the hallway.

I grab a bottle of water from the fridge and flop onto the couch, letting my head rest against the cushions as I unlock my phone.

> Gio: Roses are red, violets are blue, that's two in a row... so I feel like I owe you...

> Austin: Wow.
>
> Austin: Just...WOW.

> Gio: I'm a poet and I didn't know it.

There's a pause, and I can practically feel her debating how to respond. When the three dots finally appear, I stare, waiting.

> Austin: Don't do that.

> Gio: Do what?

> Austin: Say you're a poet and didn't even know it. That's horrible. So cheesy.

> Gio: Sorry??

I'm not sorry. Not even the tiniest bit.

> Austin: Okay pal, let's get down to business. What's your excuse for letting that puck past you in the first period?

> Gio: Distracted by a certain loudmouth in the stands.

I hesitate for half a second before adding: *A sexy, little loudmouth.*

> Austin: Oh, please. I'm your biggest motivator. That's why I'm paid the big bucks to be there.

I grin.

> Gio: Thanks for coming.

> Austin: Well, you're welcome. But honestly it's because you made me that offer I couldn't refuse—aka: anything I want, remember?

As if I would forget. She's got a way of keeping me on my toes, always pushing, always challenging. It's addicting.

> Gio: Right. Have you decided what that 'anything' is?

This time, there's a pause. A long one. Long enough that I check my phone twice to make sure the message was actually sent. Finally, the dots appear, and my stomach does this ill-feeling flip I'm not sure I'm okay with.

> Austin: Maybe.

I roll my eyes, already knowing where this is going.

> Gio: Great, you're being cryptic. LOVE that for me.

> Austin: You'll love it when I tell you.

> Gio: You're such a pain in the ass.

It's true—since we met face-to-face she's been a total pain in my ass. *But she's also the reason I've been grinning like an idiot since that day, too.* The reason my heart races every time my phone gets a new notification. The reason I'm sitting here, wondering what it is about her that makes everything feel just a little bit brighter.

I want to see her face, not just see her name.

Without overthinking it, I hit *Video Chat* and settle into the couch cushion, bracing for the possibility that she might not even pick up.

It rings once.

Twice.

On the third ring, the screen shifts, and there she is. Her hair is fanned out across a bright, white pillow, and the annoyed expression on her face is undercut by how utterly gorgeous she looks.

"You are not seriously video chatting me with no advance warning," she grumbles, narrowing her eyes at the screen.

I pat myself on the back for interrupting her with no warning.

"I like surprises."

"I don't," she grumbles some more, adjusting the angle of her phone. "I could've been in the middle of something, you know."

"Like what?" I ask, raising a brow. "You're already in bed."

"Exactly."

My grin is shameless. "I love the sound of that."

Tell me more.

"This is so invasive," she continues complaining.

"Invasive?" I repeat, laughing as I adjust my phone, trying to find a comfortable angle. "You answered, didn't you?"

"Only because I was curious!"

"'Curious?'" I tilt my phone a bit, angling it so I don't have to hold my arm awkwardly. "About what?"

"About why you're calling me at"—she glances at the corner of her screen—"*Eleven*-thirty at night."

I shrug, playing it cool. "Wanted to see your face."

That gives her pause.

Her lips part slightly, and for a moment, she just looks at me, like she's trying to figure out if I'm being serious or if this is just a dumb joke.

It's not.

I'm being dead seri—

"Jesus Christ," I gasp, flinching so hard my phone nearly slips out of my hand. "What the hell is that?"

"Uh. My *dog*."

"That's a dog?" I blurt, unable to mask the horror in my voice.

As if on cue, an animal slinks into the frame, walking across her pillow with all the regal confidence of a creature that has no business being that confident. It's... startling. Hairless except for a tuft of fluff on its head and a scraggly plume of a tail.

Its body is so skinny I can see its ribs, and its big, buggy eyes stare straight into my soul as it gets even more comfortable. It hunkers itself down—like a cat—curling around her head like some kind of ghastly stole.

I swallow hard, trying to process the scene in front of me. "I almost pissed my pants." Gulp. "That dog is the ugliest fucking thing I've ever seen," I say, *because what the hell am I looking at*?

Her jaw drops, and for a split second, she looks like she might actually hang up on me. "Excuse me? He's beautiful!"

"False. That is the ugliest dog in existence."

She can't possibly find that dog adorable.

"First of all," she says, pointing a finger at the screen, "He's not ugly. He's unique."

I snort.

"That's what people say when they can't admit something is ugly." My large palm runs over my face. "No offense. It's an overgrown rat with barely any fur."

She gasps, scandalized, and reaches behind her to cover one of the dog's floppy, tufted ears with her hand like I've just insulted her child and she doesn't want him to hear it.

"Take that back."

"I will not," I say firmly, though my lips twitch as I try not to laugh. "Your dog looks like he belongs in a Tim Burton movie."

Austin narrows her eyes at me, her fingers gently stroking the dog's bony back. "You're lucky Gio is very secure in his identity."

Come again?

"Wait." I hold up a hand, my brain short-circuiting. "You named the ugliest dog in existence after *me?*"

Her lips twitch, the corners threatening to curl into a grin. "Technically, I am not the one who named him."

"What?" I blink, confused. "What does that mean?"

"I inherited him after my dad died," she explains, her voice softening just a little. "Gio was *his* dog and my dad was a fan."

That gives me pause.

For a second, I feel like the world's biggest dickhead—but then I glance at the dog again. He's still staring at me with his bugged-out eyes and his scrawny body, like he knows we're talking about him.

"Okay." I rub the back of my neck. "I get that you didn't

name him, but you kept the name. Which means you're still partially responsible."

"He's too old to have his name changed." Austin gives him a few scratches behind his ugly ears, already laughing. "This is just a happy accident."

Glad she finds this so funny.

"Happy?" I ask, utterly incredulous. "This is an *identity crisis.*"

Her dog has my name.

I have the dog's name.

If my mother were alive, I'd be calling her right now to vent about it.

Austin is laughing so hard, tears are streaming down her face as she says, "I can't believe this is what's breaking you. Not the heckling, not the game pressure—*this. The dog.*"

"That dog is an atrocity," I can only whisper, still shocked and alarmed.

She gasps, as if I've just insulted a family heirloom. "*Atrocity?* You're talking about my dad's *beloved* dog. Do you have no soul?"

Welp, it's official: I'm an asshole.

I just insulted her deceased father's ugly dog.

"It's not my fault he looks like he crawled out of the Underworld!" I practically shout at my screen, throwing up the hand not holding my cell. "I mean, come on—*look* at him."

"Stop it!" she says, though she's still laughing as she strokes the dog's back. "You're going to hurt his feelings."

"Hurt his *feelings?*" I repeat, incredulous. "He doesn't have feelings, Austin. He's too busy plotting world domination."

Look at him!

"You're the worst." *She thinks this is hilarious and nothing can convince me otherwise.* "This wouldn't have happened if you had given me notice that you were going to video call."

I do not believe that for one second. "That is such bullshit."

She would find a way to torture me regardless.

Her laughter has finally subsided, but there's still a bright, infectious smile on her face.

And even with her ridiculous, not-cute dog in the frame, I can't bring myself to look away from her.

"It's not!" she argues, though the grin on her face gives her away.

"If you had texted me first, I could've prepared. Moved Gio off the pillow so you didn't have a full-blown *melt*down."

The fact that she keeps calling the dog Gio is killing me.

Not even softly.

A stab to the heart.

"A meltdown? That is not what this is!" I protest too much, my voice cracking slightly at the end. Great. It's exactly the tone of having a meltdown.

"Oh no?" she teases, tilting her head as she adjusts the dog so he's perched even higher on her pillow, his big, unblinking eyes staring directly into the camera. "You're glad you called, though, aren't you?"

"I'm regretting it more by the second," I moan.

"Stop! You love it," she says smugly, her eyes sparkling with delight. "And don't worry, he'll start loving you, too."

I glance back at the screen, where Gio continues to stare at me with an intensity that could melt steel—or summon demons. I can't decide which.

"I don't want him to love me," I whisper, not wanting the dog to hear me.

"Too late," she says with a soft laugh, scratching the dog's bony back. "You're part of the family now. Gio adopts people whether they like it or not."

Her laugh is so...*cute.*

So fucking adorable and delightful and contagious I find myself joining in, the tension from earlier fading completely. For a moment, it's just us, trading jabs and laughter like we've been doing this forever.

"Admit it; you're just jealous Gio is better looking than you."

I gape at her, utterly aghast. "I *cannot* believe you just said that."

"You're so dramatic," she says, wiping her eyes. "It's like you've never seen a Chinese Crested before."

"I've seen pictures. They burned my eyes."

Austin scowls. "You are officially uninvited to our house."

"I was never planning to visit!" I volley back, though we both know that's not true. *I am totally planning on visiting…*

She smirks, tilting her head like she's daring me to take it back. "We'll see about that."

The thought of stepping into her house and coming face-to-face with that dog sends a shiver down my spine—but not enough to keep me from wanting to see her again.

In person.

Somehow, her ridiculous humor, paired with her obvious affection for her creepy little pet, only makes her more endearing.

Funny – check.

Sexy – check.

Has her own career – check.

Quirky in all the best ways – check, checkity, check, check.

I lean back into the couch, staring at her through the screen as she scratches The Other Gio behind his mangy ears, her laughter softening into a smile that's way too distracting for my own good. My thoughts start to stray, and before I can stop myself, a horrifying scenario pops into my head: *Shit. What if we get to the point where we're having sex and The Other Gio is on the bed?*

The image is so vivid, so *disturbing* I actually grimace.

My shoulders shudder involuntarily, and Austin catches it immediately.

"What was that?" she asks, narrowing her eyes suspiciously. "What's going on in that overactive brain of yours?"

She already knows me so well.

"Nothing," I say quickly, shaking my head. "Absolutely nothing."

Her brow furrows, and she leans closer to the camera, like she's trying to read my mind through the screen.

"Liar. What are you thinking about?"

You.

Me.

Sex.

The dog.

"Nothing important," I insist, though the thought is stuck in my head and I know it's going to haunt me for days.

"Bullshit," she says, grinning as she props her chin on her hand.

"Come on, spill. Is it about Gio? Because if you're still obsessing over him, I think you owe him an apology."

My lips clamp shut.

Lips open. A gust of word vomit spews from my mouth, "*If he ever sets foot on a bed I'm in, I'm leaving. No questions asked.*"

"Oh. My. *God*," she whispers, her voice dripping with amusement. "Are you imagining him watching us do it?"

"No," I lie, far too quickly. "Absolutely not."

"You totally are!" she exclaims, bursting into laughter. "You're picturing us having sex with the dog on the bed!"

I shake my head but it's pointless.

The damage is done.

It's official: she can read my mind.

"I am *not* picturing that," I argue weakly, my face hot enough to fry an egg. "And please stop laughing."

My bruised ego can't take it anymore.

"And let's not get ahead of ourselves," I mutter, rubbing the back of my neck. "We haven't even been on a date yet, so we can't be having sex on your bed."

That finally slows her laughter, though her grin stays firmly in place.

"Are you already planning the logistics of our future?"

I groan, dragging a hand down my face. "Can we please talk about literally anything else?" Please? I'm begging.

"Fine, we can change the subject," Austin allows, tilting her head like she's thinking it over. "But *only* because I'm generous."

"Generous," I repeat, deadpan. "That's definitely the word I'd use."

She ignores my sarcasm, adjusting herself on her bed and pushing her hair over one shoulder in a way that feels completely unintentional—yet I have a feeling it's not. She's sitting this way because she knows she looks hot.

And I get a clearer shot of her tits in that white tank top she has on.

"Okay, new topic: when are you taking me on this date you mentioned?"

I perk up.

This is *exactly* where I was hoping this conversation would lead when I called.

My mind immediately kicks into overdrive, sorting through possibilities—places, times, ways to impress her without coming off like I'm trying too hard. Casual, but not *too* casual. Fun, but not circus-level chaotic.

Romantic, but not painfully so.

"Depends." I keep my tone light. Chill vibes only. "What kind of date we talkin' about? A movie? Something more adventurous, like a tour of Area 51 so Gio can visit his cousins?"

She snorts, covering her mouth with her hand, but it's no use—she thinks I'm hilarious. "Keep it up and Gio and I will go on the date without you."

Keep up that sassy talk.

"Threats. I like it." *I like it a lot.* "Rock climbing? Bounce house? Or dinner and drinks on a rooftop bar with a killer view—you know, so you can get all dressed up?"

Show off the boobs, maybe?

Her lips curve into a sly smile, and she props her chin on her hand. "What makes you think I even own heels?"

Such a brat.

"Oh, you own them," I say confidently, leaning forward like I

can somehow close the distance between us through the screen.
"And you're already planning which ones to wear."
She rolls her eyes.
"And what if I don't?"
Silly girl. She should know better than to try and verbally spar with me.
"Something tells me you'd hate missing the chance to knock me out with how good you look." I pause. "You're dying to try and eat me alive."
Eat me alive.
Please do.

12
austin

I've changed my outfit ninety-two times.

The discarded rejects are draped across every piece of furniture in my bedroom, forming a colorful, chaotic pile that might actually be judging me. A graveyard of "almost" outfits. Too casual. Too dressy.

Too much cleavage.

Not enough cleavage.

I stand here staring at myself in the mirror in what might finally be *the outfit*...but suddenly I'm not sure anymore.

It's the nerves. They're throwing me off.

It's weird because I don't *do* nerves. As a professor I have to be self-assured and fully capable of keeping my composure. I'm cool. Sarcastic. Confident on most days.

Yet here I stand, red-faced and fidgety like a teenager getting ready for her first prom.

I've had to redo my makeup.

Twice.

Mostly because I still cannot figure out how to do a wing-tip at the corner of my eye, and kept smudging the liquid liner and UGH! How hard can it be?!

Apparently, hard enough.

I barely recognize myself. Can't decide if that's a good thing or a bad thing or if I look like a contestant on one of those reality dating shows where they're dolled up to see the love of their life for the first time.

Not that this is *that*, of course. Definitely not.

Grabbing my mascara again, I lean over the counter, squinting at my reflection as I fix the lashes on my left eye. They decided to rebel at the last minute, giving me that uneven, half-hearted look that doesn't match the flawless right side.

Rude.

I carefully swipe it through the stubborn lashes, willing them to cooperate before I accidently smudge something. One wrong move and I'll have to start over, and at this rate, I might combust if I redo my makeup a third time.

Satisfied, I lean back, examining my handiwork. Better. Not perfect, but good enough to make it look like I didn't spend an hour agonizing over every tiny detail.

"Good as it's gonna get," I reason with myself, going to the closet.

This is dinner, not the Oscars, but Gio was right; as soon as he said the words 'date' and 'heels' I immediately began mentally scanning my closet for a dress. And shoes.

The dress I landed on is bodycon—sheer in all the right places, and ombre—from deep brown at the hem fading to a lighter beige shade up top. It screams: *picture me naked*!

It's the kind of dress that demands flesh tone bra and underwear, which I had to dig through a drawer of mismatched options to find.

As a sweatpants on the weekend girlie, tight dresses and high heels aren't normally my thing. Give me oversized hoodies and sneakers any day of the week, and I am *thriving*. But if I'm going to commit to this, I might as well commit all the way.

Go big or stay home.

There's something about the tight fit that makes me stand a little taller (mostly because now that I'm dressed, I can barely breathe), and the sheer panels leave *just enough* to the imagination to make me wonder if I'm actually dressed too sexy.

It's a fine line between looking good and looking like I tried way too hard, and I'm teetering dangerously close to the latter.

I glance down at my shoes. Beige, strappy, and clearly designed by someone who has never had to wear them for longer than ten minutes.

A man, probably.

I'd wobbled slipping them on, already envisioning my future as a meme: "Baddie tries to look cute, twists ankle before appetizer."

I glance at the clock on my phone. Five minutes.

Time to grab my clutch and fill it with all the things I have in my other bag: gloss, ID, credit card, keys.

"Dinner's going to be fine." Gio, who's been lying at my feet napping like the unbothered king he is, cracks one eye open at the sound of my voice. "I'm going to be fine. Worst-case scenario, he sucks at conversation and I can stuff myself with breadsticks."

Love myself some carbs.

Yum.

I take one last look in the full-length mirror that is my closet door. Turn this way and that way so I can give my ass a glance. The dress, the heels, the makeup—I look pretty freaking gorgeous, if I do say so myself.

Damn, girl.

I hop in the Uber that just pulled up and we drive the several blocks to the restaurant; Gio—Human Gio, not the dog—offered to come pick me up, but I politely declined. Not because I don't trust him, but because the idea of him showing up on my doorstep feels… too soon.

Also, there's the matter of Little Gio.

My loyal, judgmental dog is home, probably snoozing in the exact spot where I left him. Introducing Human Gio to his namesake tonight feels like it's going to be a *whole thing* and that can wait.

I giggle at the thought as I stare out the window at the city lights of Houston passing me by—everything feels a little brighter tonight.

A little more alive.

The ride is only a few, short minutes and my brain is already buzzing with what-ifs. What if I trip on the way in? What if I spill something. What if I have to fart?

He's standing outside the restaurant when we pull up, looking so unbelievably handsome it should honestly be illegal. Like, *dang*. The kind of handsome that makes you rethink allll the questionable guys you've dated before and wonder why you *ever* settled for less.

My panties get wet by about 20%.

Gio is leaning casually against the railing for the building, his hands tucked into his pockets, shirt snug enough to hint at the body that spends more time at the gym than I spend watching Netflix. Which is a ton.

His hair looks effortlessly perfect, like he woke up five minutes ago and decided to make the rest of us mere mortals feel inferior.

Smoking hot.

I take one last deep breath, smoothing down my dress and checking my lipstick in my phone's camera.

"Here goes nothing," I mutter to myself as I step out onto the curb. For a second, I think my knees might give out. Or my heels might. Either way, I say a silent prayer that I can walk ten feet to him without face-planting and my life flashes before my eyes.

"Wow," he says, his voice all warm and gooey. "You look." He lets out a low whistle. "Incredible."

And then I notice the flowers.

How did I not see them before?

The bouquet is a mix of soft pinks and whites, with little pops of green that make it look like something out of a Pinterest board. It's not one of those over-the-top, massive arrangements you see in romantic comedies—just thoughtful, simple, perfect.

He holds them toward me. "These are for you."

I take them, bringing them to my nose so I can sniff their delicate fragrance and smile into them, too, before raising my gaze at him.

"Thank you," I say, my voice softer now. "They're beautiful."

"Not as beautiful as you," he replies, his tone so sincere I *almost* roll my eyes but don't have the heart.

Gio surprises me further by leaning down and kissing me—on the cheek, next to my mouth. The contact is fleeting—just a whisper of warmth—but sends a zippy little jolt straight through me.

Straight to my lady parts, to be specific.

Panties = 25%.

Then it occurs to me.

I have a crush on him.

I have a crush on one of the nation's hottest, most eligible hockey players and he's gazing down at me as if I were...

As if...

He has a giant crush on me, too, all starry-eyed; the kind of look that belongs in a romance novel. The kind of look that makes you *forget* you're standing on a city sidewalk clutching a bouquet of flowers while your brain turns to MUSH!

Ugh!

"You smell good." He makes my legs even wobblier with that deep rasp and my brain scrambles for a witty response.

"So do you," I manage, my voice soft and breathless. *Wow, Austin. Bravo. For a college professor who lectures in front of hundreds of people on a weekly basis, you really have a way with words.*

As he opens the door to the building for me, I catch a glimpse of our reflection in the glass—him: tall and effortlessly handsome. Me: sexy and serious and clutching the bouquet in my hand like it's some kind of lifeline.

For a split second, I wonder if I'm dreaming.

Someone pinch me.

My brain scrambles—desperately, hopelessly—for a witty, clever something to say—as we step into the elevator for our climb to the restaurant. When those doors close, the soft hum of motion fills the space as we begin our ascent.

I glance at the glowing numbers above the door—75th floor. Of course it has to be one of the tallest buildings in the city, giving me way too much time to stew in my own thoughts.

Gio leans casually against the wall, hands in his pockets, watching me with a mix of curiosity and amusement.

"Nervous?" he asks, his lips twitching into a teasing smile.

I lift my chin, determined to be nonchalant. "Why would I be nervous?"

He shrugs. "I'm nervous so I thought maybe you might be." He smiles over at me. "Guess I was wrong."

That gets my attention. I glance up at him, arching an eyebrow. "You're nervous?"

"Sure. First date with a smart, beautiful woman? Hell yeah I am."

Moments tick by. We continue to ascend, the soft hum of the elevator the only sound filling the small, enclosed space. The air feels heavier now, charged with something I can't quite put into words. Tension? The space around us *seems smaller and smaller* with each passing second, like the walls are closing in—or maybe it's just him.

I can't decide if I want to step back or step closer.

Turns out, I don't have to decide.

Gio pushes off the wall, closing the distance between us in one smooth, deliberate motion. He stops just short of touching me, his eyes locked on mine, and the tension is so thick it's hard to breathe.

He does not hesitate…

Our mouths meet.

It's not the soft, tentative kind of kiss you'd expect on a first date.

No, this kiss is bold, confident, and completely devastating in the best way possible. His hand brushes against my waist, grazing the fabric of my dress, and I swear I forget how to breathe.

His hands grip my ass.

Squeeze.

The elevator dings, announcing our arrival at the 75th floor and we pull apart. The doors slide open to reveal a stunning view of the city skyline and when we pull away from each other —enough to catch our breath...

I'm left dizzy. Disoriented.

My hands are still resting on his chest as I try to regain some semblance of control.

"We can't make that a habit." I lift my chin and exit the elevator, heels clicking loudly against the polished stone floor. "It's *so* unprofessional."

His laughter booms out behind me.

It follows me as the hostess leads us through the dining area, echoes faintly as we're seated at our table.

And our banter continues—soft and teasing—even after we've ordered drinks and our meal.

The view is stunning, all glittering city lights and endless horizon, but it pales in comparison to the way he's looking at me. His eyes are warm, crinkling at the corners as his laughter finally dies down, though the smirk playing on his lips suggests he's far from done with this topic.

"You're so fucking adorable." He leans forward then, resting his forearms on the table and fixing me with a gaze so penetrating it makes me squirm.

Panties = 33%

"You're the cutest thing I've ever seen."

"Cute," I repeat, unimpressed, though my pulse is betraying me with how fast it's racing. "Cute is for toys and hairstyles and..." I trail off, throwing my hands up in exasperation. "Ugh."

His eyes drop to my neckline—or lack thereof. "Not sure I'd

call that neckline 'cute,'" he rumbles, sending a warm shiver down my spine. He takes a slow pull from his cocktail, a bourbon old fashioned with three cherries, the movement impossibly distracting. "Stunning."

His eyes flick back up to mine.

My chin notches. "I like that description better."

He chuckles softly, the sound vibrating low in his chest. "Don't worry—you can be sexy and cute at the same time. I'm great at multitasking."

I hesitate to ask the next question, but the spark between us is impossible to ignore and curiosity wins out, so here it goes: "What else are you good at? Besides hockey?"

He leans forward at that, his drink still in hand but forgotten for the moment, his eyes darkening just slightly. "You want a list?"

Panties = 50%

Wait, no = 52%

"Depends," I reply, lifting my glass to my lips to cover the slight hitch in my breath. "Is it a *long* list?"

His grin widens, the expression both lazy and predatory. "Very."

God help me he's one sexy motherfucker.

I set my drink down, fingers lightly brushing the rim of the wine glass as I try to hold onto some semblance of control.

"Well," I say, forcing a steady tone. "I guess I'm asking for the highlight reel."

He doesn't respond right away, letting the silence stretch just long enough to make me fidget. Studies me, tilting his head and tapping the side of his cocktail glass with his thumb.

"I'm good with my hands," he says at long last before raising it to his lips again. I can't help but watch the way his Adam's apple moves up and down in his throat as he swallows.

Why is that hot?

My mouth feels suddenly dry, and I grab my wine glass to

take a sip, the cool liquid doing little to steady the racing of my heart.

I shift in my seat, ankles crossing and uncrossing under the table, the fabric of my dress brushing against my skin in a way that only adds to the heat simmering between us.

Squirm some more.

"What else?" I ask, my entire body practically burning up.

Gio takes another swig of his drink before swirling the amber liquid lazily as he studies me, the giant ice cube inside clinking side-to-side.

"Well. I'm good at reading people," he says, the corners of his mouth lifting in a knowing smirk. "Like right now, for example."

I take another sip of my wine, desperately trying to compose myself, but the way he's looking at me, like he knows exactly what he's doing to me, makes it nearly impossible.

He wants me to ask and I oblige, because what else is there for me to say except: "What about me? What am I thinking?"

He tilts his head slightly, studying me with that same penetrating gaze, and for a moment, the silence stretches, thick and heavy, until I'm readjusting myself in my seat.

"You're wondering," he continues, his voice dipping even lower, "if my hands would be as good as I said they are."

My eyes lower to his hands again, still gripping that glass, thumb stroking the side of it.

Up.

Down.

Up...

Down.

The rhythmic motion is maddening. Fascinating. Hypnotic. I can't look away. I can't stop thinking about that thumb running back and forth over my cli—

He knows exactly what he's doing.

"You're staring," he points out, his tone teasing, though there's an unmistakable heat behind it.

"So?" No point in denying it; doing so would only make him more impossible. "Was I not supposed to look?"

Before he can respond—his mouth is literally hanging open to speak—the server appears at the edge of the table, her bright, cheerful voice breaking the tension like a glass shattering on the floor.

"Here we go!" she says brightly, setting a plate in front of me and one in front of Gio. "One medium and one medium well!"

I blink, momentarily disoriented, and murmur a polite "Thank you" as the smell of seared steak and roasted summer vegetables wafts up to greet me.

The silence that follows when she walks away is heavy—still charged with that building sexual tension—hitting play on whatever game we'd been playing.

"Convenient timing." I pick up my fork, stabbing a roasted carrot more aggressively than necessary.

"Was it?" he teases, picking up his knife and fork. "Now it's your turn to give me your list of things you're good at. It's only fair."

"Alright, fine," I say, setting my fork down and leaning back in my chair. "I'm good at teaching, obviously. Debating. Making spreadsheets."

"Spreadsheets?" he repeats, his lips twitching as if he's trying not to laugh.

"Yes, spreadsheets," I tell him firmly, lifting my chin—daring him to judge me. "They're very useful and require a lot of skill."

"I'm sure they do," he says, his eyes gleaming with barely contained laughter.

I narrow my eyes at him. "You're mocking me."

"I mean—it was a pretty fucking nerdy thing to say."

I lift my chin to look affronted, despite the fact I'm trying so desperately not to laugh. "It depends on who you're asking. Some people appreciate organization and efficiency."

God I sound like a prude.

Organization and efficiency?

My vagina dries up a fraction at my own, dull words.

Gio chuckles at me quietly, shaking his head. "Sure, but those people probably aren't sitting across from you right now."

"And what exactly would you prefer I say?" *He wants me to match his energy, to throw it right back at him.* But for some reason, the words feel clunky coming out of my mouth, stiff and awkward like I'm trying too hard.

I have no idea what my problem is—why I sound so stuffy and rigid.

I need to loosen up.

Relax, Austin.

He's flirting with you, and he wants *you* to flirt back.

"Alright, Professor," he says, leaning forward slightly, his voice dropping just enough to make my stomach flip. "What else?"

The heat in his gaze sends a spark of confidence through me, and I decide to stop overthinking.

"I'm good at reading people," I tease, throwing his earlier words back at him with a playful smile.

His grin widens, slow and dangerous, and I can tell he's enjoying this.

"Oh, *are* you?"

"Mm-hmm," I reply, leaning back in my chair with a cocky air, my wine glass dangling loosely between my fingers. "It's a gift. Comes in handy."

"What do you read when you look at me?"

I take a moment, letting the question settle, my eyes drifting over him as if I'm truly analyzing him.

Then.

I meet his gaze, steady and unflinching.

"I see a man who likes to be in control, but not because he's controlling." *It's because he has had to take care of his sister, provide for her, and be a grown-up sooner than anyone should have to.*

His smirk fades entirely, replaced by something quieter, more vulnerable. He doesn't say anything; when his jaw tenses, I'm worried I may have hit a nerve.

"You're good at being the adult," I choose my words carefully. "Stepping in when no one else would. But that doesn't mean you don't feel the weight of responsibility."

For a moment, the playful banter is gone, replaced by a silence that feels heavier, more intimate. He leans back in his chair, his drink forgotten on the table, and just…

Looks at me.

"That's quite the read," he says finally, his voice quieter now, almost thoughtful.

"Did I get it wrong?" I ask softly.

He shakes his head, a faint smile tugging at the corner of his mouth.

"No," he says softly, resting his knife on the edge of his plate. "You didn't get it wrong."

I eat a few more bites, letting the silence stretch and marinate between us, comfortable and unspoken.

"Also," I murmur, glancing up at him under my long lashes. "You *hate* spreadsheets."

That earns me a full laugh, rich and genuine, and I shiver, enjoying the sound of it. Me—I made him laugh like that. A laugh so loud several patrons in the restaurant turned to stare at us.

"I don't hate spreadsheets. I just think there are more exciting things to look at."

"Like *what*?"

"You."

I totally knew he was going to say that.

He walked right into it.

Panties = 80% wet.

He sets his glass down, removing the napkin from his lap. Gio leans forward, resting his elbows on the table as if he were ready to leave. "I have a surprise for you."

"A surprise?" I echo, my eyebrows lifting.

I don't love surprises.

He nods, a small, mischievous smile playing on his lips. "But there's a catch."

"Of course there is." I lean back in my chair. "Hmm, what's the catch?"

"You'll have to give up dessert," he says, his tone light, but his eyes never leave mine.

I narrow my gaze at him, trying to gauge if he's serious. "Give up dessert? Do you know how hard it was not to order the molten lava cake?"

"I promise," he says, leaning closer, his voice dipping just enough to make my stomach flip. "This is better than cake."

Better than cake.

Is it dick? I want to ask, but don't have the nerve. Actually, I wonder what he would say if those were the words that came out of my mouth.

"Do I get a hint?"

"Nope. You just have to trust me."

"Not even a little one?" I press, my curiosity already eating away at me.

He laughs, shaking his head. "Patience is a virtue, Austin."

"Yes, and I have none."

13
gio

*S*preadsheets.

Of all the weird shit you can say on a date, she leads with *that*.

Singing. Running.

Blow jobs.

All better options!

I glance over at her as the car, driven by the hired driver I arranged for tonight, glides smoothly down the nearly empty street, her clutch balanced on her lap, legs crossed at the ankle, the hem of her dress barely brushing her thighs.

The purr of the engine is the only sound, my focus is entirely on her—on the way the streetlights outside catch the soft curves of her profile and the subtle rise and fall of her chest as she breathes.

I slide my hand onto her thigh—absentmindedly, as if it were the natural thing to do—not too high, not too low—just to feel the warmth of her skin through the sheer fabric of that sexy dress.

The fabric is something sheer and shimmery, clinging to her body like it was poured on; her hips. Waist.

Tits.

They're impossible to ignore, framed by a neckline that's low enough to turn me on— but high enough to keep it classy.

Jesus, I can barely keep my eyes off them.

I've already weighed and measured them in my mind, determined they're perfectly full, the kind of size that would fill my palms just right.

They rise and fall with each breath she takes, and I catch myself staring for a split second too long before forcing my eyes back to hers.

Not that it matters.

Austin already caught me looking at least three times tonight, the ghost of a knowing smile playing at her lips every time she catches me peeking.

And honestly? Not sorry.

I am such a boob guy.

She doesn't move my hand when I slide it across the flesh of her leg; rather, shifting her hips in a way that tells me she likes it.

Smooth.

Freshly shaved.

"You good?" I ask, keeping my tone casual, as though my hand isn't resting exactly where it is.

"I am." Her lips curve into a smile when she turns her head away from the window to look at me. "Thank you for dinner."

She's thanked me twice already, but I'll take it.

I let my fingers linger, my thumb brushing lightly against the fabric, just enough to tease, and lean in closer, catching the faintest trace of her perfume—a mix of something sweet and floral that makes my pulse quicken.

Unable to resist, I tilt my head and press a soft, deliberate kiss against the curve of her neck.

She inhales.

Lets out the tiniest groan.

My cock stiffens when she shifts again, lilting her head to the side—it's an invitation to keep going. Keep kissing her neck.

So, I do.

My lips trail lower, brushing against the sensitive parts of her skin, the sound of her breath catching again is enough to make me tighten my grip on her thigh.

God damn, I'm in the mood to fuck.

Maybe I can ask the driver to keep going around the block and—

"Gio," my date murmurs, voice barely rising a fraction.

I raise my head. "Hmm?" My reply is against her skin, the vibration of my voice next to her ear earning me the slightest shiver.

"I think we're here." She taps me on the leg. "We're not driving anymore."

Fuck.

She's right.

The car has indeed come to a stop, the soft idle of the engine now filling the silence.

The timing sucks.

I pull back just enough to glance out the window, catching sight of the private lot outside the arena, illuminated by overhead lights. My jaw tightens, a mix of frustration and anticipation bubbling to the surface.

This moment? Ruined. But the next one will be perfect, I'm sure of it.

Her gaze follows mine, brows furrowing slightly as the wheels in her head start to turn. I can see the questions forming behind those curious eyes.

"Wait—are we at—?" she begins, turning to face me fully.

"C'mon," I cut her off, sliding my hand from her thigh and grabbing hers, giving it a tug. "You'll see."

Her hand tightens around mine when I help her out of the vehicle, though whether it's from excitement or nerves, I can't tell. Maybe both. She steps out gracefully, clutching her bag while her eyes sweep over the building in front of us.

"Oh my God, what are we doing here?"

She sounds like a kid on Christmas morning and I can't help

HIT ME WITH YOUR BEST SHOT

but feel a swelling sense of pride as I lead her toward the private entrance.

"Did you bring me to skate? I'm in heels," she asks, her voice laced with playful suspicion.

I shake my head as I swipe the keycard over the door pad and pull it open, holding it so she can walk in ahead of me.

"Trust," I say, grin widening.

She steps through cautiously, her high heels clacking softly against the concrete floor. Her hand grips my arm, steadying herself as if she doesn't fully trust the shoes she chose for tonight.

The moment we step inside, we're hit by an explosion of cool air, the unmistakable chill from the rink's air conditioning wrapping around us.

Her steps slow almost immediately, and I feel her hand tighten over my bicep.

Austin's eyes widen as the rink comes into view—a massive expanse of pristine, gleaming ice that stretches out endlessly under the glow of the overhead lights.

It's a sight to behold when there's not a single soul around, and even I take a second to appreciate it.

George, the rink manager, leans casually against the Zamboni, his attention fixed on his cell phone. His thick fingers tap at the screen with a slow deliberation that says he's in no hurry.

Her gaze flickers from George to the Zamboni, then back to me, her lips parting in disbelief.

"Stop it right now," she whispers in disbelief. "We are not."

"Oh, but we are," I say, my grin widening as I pull her a little closer to the edge of the ice.

She turns her whole body to me, eyes wide and sparkling with a mix of excitement—and disbelief.

"You're *kidding.*"

"Do I look like I'm kidding?" I reply, gesturing toward the

massive machine at the same time George realizes he's no longer alone and begins lumbering toward us.

"Finally," he grunts, his voice rough and low, like gravel. "I was starting to think you weren't gonna show up."

Burly old shit.

Always a ray of sunshine.

"You know me," I reply, my tone breezy as I keep Austin close to my side. "I like to keep you on your toes."

George snorts, giving me a once-over before shifting his gaze to Austin. His eyes narrow slightly, like he's sizing her up, but there's a faint twitch of amusement in his expression.

"This the reason you've been blowing up my phone all week?" he asks, jerking his chin toward her.

"No comment."

I shoot him a look, but he's already turned back toward the Zamboni, muttering something under his breath about "kids these days," and "no respect."

"You've got twenty minutes," he gripes loudly, throwing the words over his shoulder. "Try not to wreck anything."

George grunts one more time for good measure before trudging off toward the office. His heavy boots stomp against the stairs and he doesn't bother looking back again, already done with us.

Austin bites back a laugh, her lips twitching. "What a delight."

"Don't let it fool you," I whisper back, smirking. "Deep down, he hates everyone equally."

"This is a dream come true," she squeals, clapping her hands and bouncing on her toes. "I'm so excited I can hardly stand it. I don't even care that I'm in a dress and my boobs are falling out."

With zero shame, she adjusts the neckline of her dress, tugging it a little higher, her movements carefree.

"They look fine," I say, fighting the urge to stare. "Better than fine, actually."

Her tits look so great, especially now that they're struggling to stay concealed.

LET THEM BREATHE! I say.

She gives another yip, turning her attention back to the Zamboni. "Alright, what's next? Do we just climb on?"

Climb on...

Images of her on top of me, moaning—riding me—suddenly flood my brain.

Quit being such a fucking pervert.

She beams, bouncing in place, tits jiggling.

"I'm driving first?"

"Uh. Of course," I say, stepping aside to give her space. "Ladies first, right?" I guide her toward the side of the Zamboni, planting my hand on the edge of the small step. "Put your foot here, then you pull yourself up."

She climbs onto the machine carefully, still in her high heels, with more enthusiasm than grace, dress hitching up her thighs, giving me a clear shot of a sliver of thong and her bare ass.

I do not avert my gaze, staring directly at it.

"Stop staring at my ass."

An impossible task when I want to bury my face there...

"You coming?" She's parked in the seat, both hands already gripping the steering wheel.

I clear my throat, forcing my focus back to the moment as I climb up after her and plop into the second seat. "You ready?"

"Ready as I'll ever be." Her hands tighten on the wheel, her excitement almost radiating off her in waves. "We only have twenty minutes, so let's get this show on the road."

Bossy little thing.

I smirk, leaning back slightly and gesturing toward the controls.

"Alright, first things first. We're not going to turn on the board brush or actually shave the ice—or shine it. This is a test drive, not a full-on maintenance job. You're just gonna drive."

Austin nods eagerly, her smile so wide and genuine it's impossible not to get caught up in it. The way her eyes light up, her whole face glowing—it's rare to see someone so unguardedly happy.

And damn if it isn't contagious.

I'm happy she's happy…

"Okay, what do I do?" she asks, glancing at the various levers and buttons like she's sitting in the cockpit of a plane.

"I think you just have to turn the key, put it into drive—and go. Should be like driving a car," I say, recalling George's very brief tutorial. "At least, that's what he told me."

The twenty-minute deadline looms in the back of my mind.

George is clearly depending on me not to screw this up—or let her crash the damn thing—trusting me with only a ten percent margin. Basically I had to bribe him with cash (five hundred dollars) and six rinkside tickets for his family the next time his brother and sister-in-law come to town with their kids.

Fine.

Whatever.

Austin giggles and follows my instructions, nudging the throttle forward enough to make the Zamboni crawl forward.

"Oh my God, look at me!" she shrieks, glancing at me with wide, sparkling eyes. "I'm doing it! I feel like I'm piloting a spaceship!"

She grips the wheel tighter as the Zamboni glides across the ice at an almost comical crawl.

This thing cannot be going faster than five miles per hour, *tops.* The machine crawls across the ice, leaving behind a faint trail where the wheels press against the pristine surface.

"Don't let all this power go to your head," I warn her, teasing. "We've got about thirteen more minutes left."

"Plenty of time," she shoots back, confidence growing with every second. "I could drive this thing with my eyes closed."

"Please don't."

Austin bursts into laughter, the sound echoing across the empty rink. She glances over at me, her cheeks flushed and her eyes sparkling. "You can relax—nothing is going to happen. I'm going at a glacial pace."

"I am so relaxed," I argue, though my shoulders are tense. "I just have no desire to explain to George why there's a Zamboni-shaped hole in the penalty box."

"God you're cute when you're stressed out. This is such a damn turn on." She turns her head to look at me. "Thank you for this—I'm having so much fun."

"I…you're welcome."

"Seriously." Her sigh is blissful. "I want to suck your dick so bad right now."

My gulp is audible, my hands tightening on the edge of the seat.

"We both want the same things."

Her laughter is louder this time, ringing out and echoing off the cold metal walls of the building. It's an unrestrained laugh, full of mischief, and does absolutely nothing to help me regain my composure.

My dick, her mouth.

Lots of suction…

"Truly. I want what you want." *I cannot stress this enough.*

Her grin widens, and she bites her bottom lip, a move that is both innocent and suggestive, I'm seconds away from unzipping my slacks and letting her go at it.

"I can't believe I said that out loud." Her focus is back to the ice in front of her, pretty head shaking back and forth, scolding herself. "But for real. This is hot."

My eyes dart around the area, searching for evidence of any interlopers, specifically, George.

I want to suck your dick so bad right now, I want to suck your dick so bad right now, I want to suck your dick so bad right now…

I can't take it anymore.

I move from my seat, sliding over to her side. Before she can ask what I'm doing, my hands are on her waist, lifting her effortlessly. She lets out a startled laugh, her hands briefly gripping the steering wheel for balance.

"What are you—"

She doesn't finish because I've already settled her in my lap, her back pressed against my chest. My hands instinctively find her hips, holding her steady as I press a kiss to the back of her neck, just below her hairline.

A gasp escapes from her lips. "Are you trying to distract me?" she asks in a whisper, her voice wavering as I trail my kisses lower. Austin's head tips back, resting against my shoulder, and for a moment, I forget where we are or that we're on borrowed time.

My hands slide upward, gliding from her waist to her rib cage, my thumbs grazing the sides of her curves. Her breathing quickens, and she shifts in my lap, hips pressing back against me in a way that makes it nearly impossible to think straight.

Slowly, she begins grinding her ass into my cock, round and round, slowly.

My head lolls back and I moan, gripping her tighter, blood flow leaving my brain and skyrocketing straight to my dick as my teeth graze her skin—not enough to hurt—but enough to make her *gasp* and arch against me.

"I'm going to crash this thing," she moans as my big palms slide further up, cupping her tits through the thin fabric of her dress.

They're soft, *full*, and fit perfectly in my hands, just like I knew they would.

I squeeze gently, earning another gasp from her as she tilts her head to the side, giving me more access. Wanton now, her skin is warm beneath my lips as I nuzzle into her, my nose inhaling the faint scent of her perfume.

It's an intoxicating mix of sweet and spice, *and I can't get enough.*

My thumbs brush against her nipples through the sheer fabric, and her sharp intake of breath sends a shiver down my spine as my fingers move across her collarbone, dipping below her neckline. Like a heat seeking missile, desperate to touch her bare breasts…

I would fuck her now if we were alone.

She needs to stop grinding on me before we both tear our clothes off and get caught by Geo—

"Hey!" a loud voice booms. "Knock that shit off!"

The roaring demand snaps us out of our stupor, and Austin jumps out of my lap, her hands flying to the steering wheel as if to make it seem like nothing inappropriate was happening. My arms drop back to my sides, though I can't wipe the sheepish grin off my face.

George stands at the edge of the rink, hands on his hips, his glare cutting through the distance.

"I said twenty minutes—I didn't say 'turn this ride into soft porn!,'" he hollers, his voice echoing off the empty seats around us. "Get down from there, we have cameras everywhere you fucking moron."

He's grumbling as he ambles forward, determined.

"Oh shit. He looks pissed," I muse, cutting the Zamboni's engine and standing. "Party's over."

Though my *hard-on* isn't.

One at a time, we climb down off the machine and George averts his eyes as Austin adjusts her dress; tugging the neckline, pulling down the hem so it covers her thighs.

George grumbles under his breath as he trudges toward us, keys jangling against his hip, each step punctuated by an over-dramatic huff.

"I should've known better," he gripes, stopping just short of the Zamboni. "Young people can't keep your hormones in check for even five minutes. The ice is sacred! You wanna paw each other like that, rent a goddamn motel room."

Honestly I'm flattered he considers me young people.

Austin, cheeks flaming, ducks her head and adjusts her dress again, the movement quick and flustered. She tugs the neckline higher, muttering something under her breath that sounds like, *"Never wearing this again."*

"Sorry, George," she says, trying to smooth over his ruffled feathers. Her voice is soft, sweet—and entirely *un*convincing.

She's adorable when she's embarrassed.

"Don't 'sorry' me," George snaps, pointing a gnarled finger at me. "You. I trusted you with this."

"Technically," I say, stepping forward, hands raised in a gesture of innocence. "You trusted me with the *Zamboni*."

"You think you're clever?" He huffs again, his face turning a shade darker. "I don't care what you call it, just get the hell off my ice before I call security. And next time you're feeling frisky, take it to a parking lot."

The parking lot?

Er. He obviously knows jack shit about women if that's what he considers a romantic gesture.

We walk in silence for a few moments, the sound of her heels clicking softly against the concrete floor. When we reach the hallway leading to the private entrance, she bursts into laughter, her shoulders shaking as she clutches her stomach.

"Oh my God, I can't believe that just happened. I'm dying, give me a minute," Austin wheezes, barely able to catch a breath.

I lean against the wall to watch, crossing my arms as she does her darndest to compose herself.

It's not working.

Her laughter echoes through the empty corridor, bouncing off the cinder block walls.

"Think he'll let us drive the Zamboni again?" I ask, deadpan.

Austin's laughter somehow manages to kick up a notch, and she starts gasping for air between the peals.

"Stop. Stop making jokes," she chokes out, waving a hand at me. "I'm going to pee my pants, I swear."

I wait her out.

When she finally straightens, her face is flushed and her

mascara is smudged from the tears rolling down her cheeks but she doesn't seem to care.

Her smile hasn't dimmed—not even a little—and she looks up at me, eyes sparkling and full of mischief.

"Oh my God—we got caught fooling around on the Zamboni. If you would have told me that yesterday, I wouldn't have believed you."

I chuckle, pushing myself off the wall and putting my arm around her waist as I guide her toward the exit and our waiting car. "For the record, I'm pretty sure we just broke every rule in George's imaginary handbook."

"He's going to be scarred for life."

I doubt that.

But I am going to have to apologize—probably with an expensive bottle of whiskey that will make him forget this ever happened.

Ha!

We step out into the cool night air, the crisp breeze wrapping around us and making her shiver slightly. Instinctively, I pull her closer, rubbing her arm as I lead her to the car parked at the curb.

We climb in. Buckle up.

Hold hands in the back seat.

"This was so much better than cake," she murmurs, her voice just above a whisper—wistful and content. Her words remind me of the promise I made back at the restaurant, but the look in her eyes now tells me she doesn't feel shortchanged.

Not even close.

I look down at our hands, her fingers warm and snug between mine; I can't help grinning like a damn fool.

Best fucking night ever.

The driver glances at us in the rearview mirror, his expression carefully neutral, though I can tell he's curious. "Home, sir?"

I look at her again, letting the question hang in the air

between us for a moment. Her cheeks flush slightly under my gaze, she doesn't look away. Instead, she raises an eyebrow.

"My place?" I suggest, my tone casual, but laced with anticipation.

She doesn't hesitate. "Only if there's dessert."

The corners of my mouth lift into a slow grin. "Oh, there's dessert."

Austin gives a curt nod.

Bites her lower lip.

And just like that, the dick between my legs is hard again…

14

austin

*H*is apartment is insane.
   No.
Scratch that—this is not an apartment.

Sure, it's in a *building*...but Gio is at the top, in the penthouse, and the view is sick. The moment the elevator doors slide open directly into his penthouse, I'm greeted by floor-to-ceiling windows framing a city view so stunning it takes my breath away. The glittering skyline stretches endlessly, like it was pulled straight out of a social media post.

It's equal to—if not better than—the view from the restaurant.

The open floor plan is sleek but warm, modern without feeling cold. A plush gray sectional dominates the living area, with deep cushions that practically beg to be lounged in. There's a fireplace built into the wall and a massive TV mounted above it —*because of course there is.*

He's a guy, isn't he? They love that shit.

I catch sight of a small bar in the corner, its glass shelves stocked with an impressive collection of liquor bottles. The kitchen, visible off to the side, looks like something out of a cooking show, all stainless steel and glossy countertops.

I feel like I've walked into a magazine spread.

So different from my modest abode.

Gio has a terrace.

An expansive one that wraps around his entire penthouse, dotted with potted plants and sleek lounging chairs that look like they belong in a luxury resort. There's a fire pit on one side and a table with chairs on the other, perfectly set up for late-night dinners or early morning coffee.

It's incredible.

I walk out and go to the railing, leaning to peer over the edge.

"Holy shit," I mutter under my breath, gripping the railing a little tighter than necessary. My heart skips three beats.

We are *so* high up.

Gio steps up behind me, handing me a glass of wine. Before I can even thank him, his arms slide around my waist, pulling me back against him. His nose nuzzles into the crook of my neck—his favorite spot, apparently. And now?

My favorite spot, too.

I feel the warmth of his breath against my skin, and I have to fight the urge to melt completely.

"You live here and get to look at this every day?" I ask, my voice tinged with disbelief as I lift the glass to my lips, taking a small sip.

His grip on my waist tightens slightly, and I feel him smile against my neck.

"Every day."

"That's insane," I murmur, shaking my head, hair whipping around from the wind. "I don't think I'd ever leave if I were you."

He chuckles softly, his chest rumbling against my back.

"You get used to it," he says with a shrug, though there's a softness in his tone that tells me he still appreciates it. But I've followed his career and understand enough to know his opportunities didn't come easy; they came with hard work, lots of injuries, and dedication.

Gio Montagalo had nothing handed to him, not his glossy penthouse or professional hockey career.

I glance up at him, raising an eyebrow. "Do you, though?"

He meets my gaze, and for a moment, there's something unspoken between us that makes my stomach flutter.

He is so hot.

"No," he says as last. "I don't think you ever really get used to it," he admits, voice quieter now as he rests his chin on my shoulder. "Not completely. I mean, sometimes…" He trails off and he clears his throat. "Sometimes it feels like something is missing. Like—there's no point in having all of this if you can't share it with someone."

I have no idea what to say to that honesty.

It's so real.

For a moment, the world feels impossibly small—just me, Gio, and the view stretching out before us.

"Come on," he says suddenly, pulling back and grabbing my hand. "Let's go back inside. Too cold out here."

Curiosity piqued, I allow him to lead me back into the penthouse, his hand warm and steady in mine. The lights are dimmed, casting a warm glow over the space, and I notice how large his hand is compared to mine; how rough and calloused it is as he guides me down a hallway.

"Where are we going?" I ask, my voice breaking the silence.

Because the bedroom would be great.

I'm past the point of pretending—or caring about my own make-believe dating rules so I can fake being a 'Good Girl.' I want more of what we had at the arena; more tension. More flirting. More touching.

I'm addicted to how much fun Gio is.

Le sigh…

The hallway opens into another room—this one darker, with floor-to-ceiling windows lining one side. A massive sectional couch dominates the center, piled high with plush throw pillows and blankets. They look so soft and beg to be touched.

"Okay, wow. This is spectacular," I admit, my eyes scanning the room. "Is this your office?"

He walks to a sleek console table against the wall and picks up a small remote, pressing a button. Instantly, the far wall begins to move, a hidden panel sliding open to reveal a massive screen.

"Technically, yes. But no work gets done in here." He tosses the remote to the couch. "I thought we could watch a movie."

"You have a home theater." I blink in disbelief. "Of course, you do."

"Only for my favorite guests," he teases, plopping down on the couch and patting the spot next to him.

Hesitating for a moment, I take in the cozy setup, imagining him here alone; the blankets draped across the back of the massive sectional, the soft lighting casting a warm glow, and the way the city skyline sparkles in the background through the windows.

It's a space to be enjoyed with a partner.

"Come here," he coaxes. "I don't bite. Unless you want me to."

I have no issues if he did.

Kicking off my heels, I join him on the couch, sinking into the plush cushions. He's already reclined, one arm stretched across the back of the sectional like he owns the world—well, this world, at least.

In his free hand, he's swirling a glass of wine, too, the deep red catching the soft light.

I tuck my feet under me and take a sip from my own glass, savoring the taste. It's smooth, rich, and probably something I'd never buy for myself.

Figures.

"What are we watching?" I ask, setting my glass down on the side table.

"Whatever your little heart desires."

After a bit of scrolling through the apps, we settle on an action movie; I'm only half paying attention, though. *Like who cares about a movie when I'm warm and a little fuzzy and Gio's arm slid from the back of the couch and is now resting on my shoulder?*

Not me.

I melt as his fingers graze my skin, back and forth, in a slow caress.

"Comfy?" he murmurs, glancing down at me.

"*So* comfy," I breathe, unable to find my voice.

My body is hot.

"You're not watching the movie," he teases.

"Neither are you," I shoot back, glass of wine all but forgotten on the side table, the room feeling impossibly hot.

Whew, baby it's warm in here!

"Touché."

For a moment, we say nothing at all, quietly acknowledging one another.

Then.

His hand slips from my shoulder to my collarbone, his thumb brushing lightly against the sensitive skin there. Unhurriedly—almost reverently—Gio's fingers sweep upward, tucking a stray strand of hair behind my ear.

The motion is intimate, as if he's memorizing the curve of my neck.

My pulse spikes, and I lean closer, drawn to him like a magnet. Every nerve in my body is tuned to the moment, the space between us shrinking with every passing second....

"Gio," I whisper, unsure if it's a warning or an invitation.

"Yeah?" His voice is low. Rough.

Hesitant.

So polite...

"I..." Whatever I was about to say vanishes as his lips meet mine.

The kiss is slow at first, teasing, as though he's testing the waters.

My fingers curl against his chest, feeling the steady, reassuring beat of his heart beneath my palm. It's grounding in a way, even as everything else—my thoughts, my breath, my sense of time—*spirals completely out of control.*

I want him so bad.

So sexy.

So masculine.

Gio's hands find my waist, steadying me, pulling me closer, and it's not enough. The angle feels all wrong, the space between us still too much despite the heat radiating off him.

Without a second thought, I shift. Moving onto my knees, I slide one leg over his lap, settling myself astride him. My dress rides higher with the motion, the fabric easing its way to my hips as I settle against him.

His hands instinctively move to my waist, gripping firmly, holding me there as his head tilts back to meet my gaze.

His eyes are dark, intense, the flicker of hesitation from earlier?

Gone.

Gio's palm smacks my ass.

My fingers slide up, curling around the back of his neck as I lower myself against him, bringing our mouths back together.

This kiss is different.

It's heated, *desperate,* our mouths colliding like we're both racing to make up for lost time. His hands tighten on my hips, guiding me as I shift slightly, my thighs pressing against his, my body aligning with his in a way that makes me dizzy.

I shift against him again, and his grip tightens, a groan escaping his lips that makes my stomach flip.

"Keep doing that," he murmurs, his voice rough and low, the words almost lost against my skin. "Don't fucking stop."

I obey, moving against him with more urgency. Every brush, every shift of our bodies stokes the fire that's burning between us, making it harder to focus on anything but the way he feels beneath me.

His hands slide up inside the fabric of my dress...

Palms skimming my bare skin.

Flirts with the clasp of my strapless bra.

Every movement, every slight shift in pressure, ignites a fire that has me leaning into him, desperate for more.

He pulls at my dress until it's up...over my head...tossed to the floor like a rag.

Gio's huge hands find my breasts, tips of his fingers trailing over the lace of my strapless bra, thumbs brushing my already sensitive nipples through the satin fabric.

I watch, spellbound, as he studies my body.

Let him explore.

The corner of his mouth tilts up as he dips his head, pressing a kiss to the swell of my breasts, then lower, nose tracing the edge of my bra. *The heat of his breath against my skin is maddening.*

Large hands slide around to my back again, deftly undoing the clasp of my bra. The hooks give way, the fabric slipping from my body; cool air hits my bare skin before his mouth replaces it.

Gio sucks.

Licks.

A gasp escapes my lips as his tongue flicks over one sensitive peak; he sucks as his other hand kneads the soft curve of my breast. My fingers tangle in his hair, pulling him closer, needing more of him, needing everything.

I arch into him, desperate for more...

Panties = 88%.

"Jesus, Austin," he slurs against my skin, his voice vibrating through me. "You drive me so fucking crazy."

Then.

His hands leave my boobs to cradle my face.

His thumbs brush gently across my cheeks, a contrast to the tension coiling between us, as his eyes search mine. For a moment, time stops.

With a loud grunt, he moves, standing effortlessly with me still in his arms.

Instinctively my legs wrap around his waist as he takes long strides across the room, his focus completely on me.

"Where are we going?" I manage to ask, heart pounding in my chest—and my vagina.

"Somewhere with a fucking headboard."

Oh jeez.

A shiver runs down my spine at the promise in his voice, anticipation coiling in my stomach as he carries me down a long hallway of closed doors.

The last door is ajar and he nudges it with his shoulder and crosses the threshold, his hold on me steady as he turns to push the door shut with his foot.

The soft click of it closing behind us sends a thrill racing through me, my pulse pounding in my ears.

My brain barely has time to register the massive bed before he dumps me on it: white linens. Sleek nightstands.

Gold reading lamps.

The bed beneath me is impossibly soft, the kind of plush luxury you sink into, and if I wasn't in the middle of seducing him I'd pay more attention. *I'm too focused on him to notice the finer details of his bedroom...*

For a moment he goes still as he watches me, his blue eyes burning with intensity—intense and predatory—as if he's committing this moment to memory.

"You look so good here," he murmurs huskily as he leans over me, hands framing my hips. His breath fans across my cheek, warm and teasing. "Right where you belong."

"I—"

Whatever I was going to say is lost when his lips find mine again, the kiss deeper and more insistent this time. He moves closer, his weight sinking onto the mattress, one knee pressing into the bed beside me as his hands explore.

Every touch, every movement, is deliberate, as if he's

savoring the experience as much as I am. His hand skims up my thigh, sliding higher and higher until it brushes against the lace edge of my underwear.

He tugs.

"Not so fast." I shake my head, tsking. "You can't take these off until you remove something. Fair is fair."

I don't have to ask him twice.

"Fair *is* fair," he repeats, eagerly grabbing the hem of his shirt. He pulls it over his head in one fluid motion, revealing a body that is all hard muscle and tanned skin.

My mouth goes dry.

Bone.

Dry.

"Better?" he asks, his tone laced with amusement as he tosses the shirt aside. He crosses his arms, the muscles in his biceps flexing as he watches me watch him.

Show-off.

"It's a start," I manage to say, though my voice betrays just how flustered I am. My attempt at nonchalance falters entirely when my gaze drops to his abs. "Keep going."

"Bossy," he murmurs, taking a step closer, his hands already working the button of his jeans. I watch transfixed as he pops it open, the zipper whirring down agonizingly slow, the denim hanging low on his lean hips.

Gio smirks when he catches the way my eyes follow every movement, as if I weren't going to enjoy the show.

"Now can I take off your panties?" he says, voice dropping to a husky whisper as he steps forward until he's standing right between my knees.

My head nods up and down. "Only if you do it with your teeth."

That's all the invitation he needs.

Gio's smirk deepens, tongue darting out to wet his bottom lip as he sinks to his knees before me.

The sight of him there, *between my thighs*, sends a jolt of heat through my body, my breath catching in my throat.

"Yes, ma'am." His hands trail leisurely up and over my thighs, thumbs skimming the sensitive skin as he leans in, his face just inches away from my—

I hold my breath.

Balancing myself on my elbows so I have a front row seat, my eyes gloss over as they fixate on his mouth; he leaves an open mouth kiss as close to my pussy as he can get without pressing his lips on it.

The tip of his finger teases, hooking on the elastic of my thong…back and forth beneath it.

Gio inhales.

My body is strung tight, every nerve ending alive and begging for his touch. He smirks, clearly relishing my reaction, and leans down once more.

This time, there's no teasing.

His beautiful, white teeth graze the waistband of my thong.

A strangled gasp escapes me as he tugs it down with an infuriating mix of skill and sensuality, taking his time, his breath searing my skin. The lace slides away, leaving me bare and vulnerable, and I'm helpless to do anything but watch as he tosses it aside.

He glances up, his gaze locking with mine, and the hunger in his eyes is enough to make my heart stutter.

"You're so beautiful like this," he murmurs, his voice low and gravelly. "I cannot wait to bury my face in this hot little pussy."

Hot little pussy…

Bury my face…

"Oh God." I gasp as his big hands drag me closer to the edge of the bed—to the brink. Palms spread me wider, holding me open as he lowers his face and licks me. Gio's eyes slide closed as he goes to town on my pussy, lapping and sucking at me as if it were his new full-time job and I moan…

Groan.

Thrash my head, fingers grasping at the white comforter…

"Oh God..."

Gio moans deep in his chest as he eats me out—moaning like he's dining out on the most delicious fucking thing he's ever had and can't get enough of it, his hips grinding against the edge of the bed where he's kneeling to alleviate some of this own tension.

"I want you inside me," I whisper, pushing at his shoulders.

"Not yet," he says as he shakes his head.

"Please..." I want to be on top. Why is he making me beg?!

I want to sink down on top of you and take control so you lose control...

15
gio

She's begging me to fuck her.
Meanwhile I'm basically fucking the mattress.

I mean—twist my arm. What guy wouldn't rather dump his load inside a pretty woman than on the duvet cover of his bed?

I'm flat on my back in the middle of my California king, condom on the pillow next to my head, and Austin's tits beckoning from above.

I cup them and play with her nipples, cock stiff, pressing into her ass crack as she rests on my stomach, pussy slowly gyrating in slow circles.

It's taking every ounce of self-control I possess not to bury myself inside her—*I feel like I'm losing my mind.*

I lower my hands, pressing my thumb into her clit in small circles and she leans back to give me more access…

Her body is perfect for me.

Nice boobs.

Soft stomach.

An ass I want to pump into from behind, knowing I won't snap her like a twig.

Austin leans forward, pressing a hand against my headboard and gripping it, raising herself above me…lining my dick up between her pussy and moving back and forth without taking me inside her.

It's torture.

She's practically panting.

"I could come like this." She lets out a whimper. "I love your dick so much."

Her hair falls over her shoulders, covering her nipples the briefest of moments and my fingers brush it back so I can look my fill.

I toy with her boobs as if they were my playthings…

Her breath hitches when I roll her nipples between my fingers, her hips stuttering in their rhythm.

"Jesus," I rasp, my voice thick with need to thrust. My head falls back against the pillow as I stare up at her, chest heaving. "You're killing me."

Her head rolls to the side.

"I can't stand it anymore."

Neither can I.

The tension snaps, sharp and electric. My hand shoots out, grabbing the condom from the pillow beside me. The wrapper crinkles as I tear it open, my hands shaking just enough to slow me down.

"Hold on," I mutter, reaching around Austin's body to fumble with the condom, my fingers brushing against her soft, warm skin as I try to steady myself. "Shit."

"Here, let me," she whispers, her fingers pushing mine aside to take over. She rolls the condom over me with a deliberate slowness that has my teeth clenching and my vision blurring.

Sex brain.

That's what this is.

Pure, primal, animalistic need overriding every logical thought in my head.

The desperation to fuck her.

Our contact is a spark to dry tinder.

My breath hitches as she sinks down, taking me inch by

agonizing inch. The feeling is indescribable, her warm pussy, the tightness, the way her body molds to mine.

A groan rumbles in my chest, raw and guttural. "Holy fuck."

So good.

Her head tilts back, a soft cry escaping her lips as her body adjusts to mine. For a moment, everything stills—the world narrowing to just this: her warmth surrounding me, her hands braced on my chest.

One gasp.

Another.

Austin lets out a *mew* and it's the most beautiful sound I've ever heard come out of another person and it drives me to the brink.

I moan so loud I'll be embarrassed about it later.

"You like that?" she asks. It's obviously a rhetorical question because obviously I fucking like it.

Am I a man?

"God, yes," I groan, my head falling back against the pillow as I surrender completely. "Don't stop."

I swear to God I'm half in love.

Sex drunk.

That's what this is….

My thighs begin shaking as she rides me, the pressure in my balls building to the point I feel out of control.

My body shakes.

Sweat builds on my forehead.

Her hand pushes against the headboard…bearing down…deeper…I'm buried to the hilt…moans…

For the briefest moment I wish I was back in college, in a cheap double bed with a cheap headboard, so we'd hear the sound of the headboard slamming against the wall—and so neighbors would hear us fucking.

I come to that thought.

My body jolts as a guttural moan tears from my throat, and I come hard, spilling into the condom. The release is blinding, my grip on her hips tightening as I ride the wave, every muscle in my body tensing and then giving way all at once.

Then.

Several seconds later Austin comes, too, lowering herself and burying her face in the crook of my neck. Her breath is warm, her skin slick against mine, and the weight of her feels perfect.

My arms go around her, pulling her close, holding her as her body relaxes into mine.

Neither of us speaks.

We don't need to.

∽

"Are you awake, too?"

Her voice breaks the stillness of the dark, soft and hesitant, carrying across the quiet space between us. My eyes open, and I turn my head toward her.

I shift my arm beneath the covers, sliding it closer until my fingers find hers. Her hand tightens around mine, and the small gesture feels like an invitation. I take it, rolling onto my side to face her.

Raising my other arm, I glance at the watch on my wrist. The faint glow of the dial reads three.

"Yeah," I whisper back, my voice low, barely louder than hers.

"Can't sleep."

The bed shifts as she mirrors my movement, turning onto her side and curling her body toward mine. I feel the faint brush of her breath against my shoulder, warm and steady.

We lie there for a while, our hands tangled beneath the covers. The silence isn't heavy—it feels peaceful, like we're sharing something unspoken. Her breathing slows and deepens, and I wonder if she's drifted off.

Just as my own eyes start to close, her voice breaks the quiet again, soft and unexpected.

"Tonight was the most fun I've had in forever."

I smile into the dark. "Same."

"I still can't believe you talked the guy into letting you drive the Zamboni," she says, and I can hear the smile in her voice.

I chuckle, the memory fresh and vivid. "It wasn't that hard. You just have to find the right bribe."

Cash.

"I've never been in an ice rink with no people. It was surreal."

It was.

"Yeah," I say, my voice softer now. "It's not often we're in there alone. There's always a crowd—teammates, coaches, someone. But tonight..." I trail off, letting the memory fill the space between us.

"Tonight, it was ours," she finishes.

I tilt her chin up with my fingers, just enough to find her lips in the dark. The kiss is slow, tender, the kind that says all the things we don't have to say out loud.

When we pull back, she doesn't move far, her forehead resting against mine. Her breath is warm, mingling with mine, and for a moment, I think the night can't get better.

Then she speaks.

"You know what the best part of tonight was?"

"Obviously the Zamboni," I tease, the corners of my mouth tugging upward.

She laughs, soft and genuine, and her hand playfully smacks against my chest.

"No," she says, her tone light but steady. "The best part was you. Just being with you."

The words hit me harder than I expect, settling deep in a place I don't think I've let anyone reach before. I don't answer right away because I'm not sure I can. So instead, I pull her closer, wrapping my arms around her as though that will somehow show her what I can't quite put into words.

We kiss again, her hands caressing my chest, the light touch skimming my pecs. Fingers trail over my flesh, giving me goosebumps.

I can't help but move, rolling us so I'm over her, bracing myself on my forearms as I lean down. My lips already know the shape of her body in the dark…the curve of her shoulder…the dip of her clavicle.

It's a map I've memorized without even realizing it.

"You're beautiful," I tell the darkness.

And yeah—my cock is stiff, so what?

Her hands slide down my back, fingertips tracing the lines of my thick muscles—when she leans toward the side table, her hands fumbling to find the drawer, I know she's going to thank me for the compliment by fucking me.

A slow…

Lazy…

Fuck.

16
austin

"You cannot keep getting hard." I yawn, rolling the wrong way—of course I do—and it only makes things worse. Gio scoots closer, spooning me tighter, and I swear his dick wedges itself even more firmly between my thighs. "Oh my God, Gio, I won't be able to walk today."

My words are muffled against the pillow, but I know he hears me because his laugh rumbles low and soft against my back.

Thank God I don't have a class.

I would be limping.

His mouth finds the space between my shoulder blades, his lips warm and soft against my skin. The sensation sends a shiver down my spine, and I burrow deeper into the comforter, snuggling down into the mattress.

Most comfortable.

Bed.

Ever.

I could live in here.

I hum, drowsily. "Never leaving."

"Good," he murmurs, his hand slipping under the comforter to rest on my hip.

His fingers are warm, his touch gentle, with the undercurrent of possessiveness in the way he holds me. I don't have to look at him to know he's smiling.

I can feel it, the curve of his grin against the back of my neck.

I try to focus on the warmth of his blankets—they smell like him too—the steady rhythm of his breathing, the way his arms feel like the safest place in the world. Every nerve in my body is tuned into him, into the way he feels against me, into the quiet intensity of his touch.

"Comfortable?" Gio murmurs, his low rasp causes me to shiver despite the warmth of the blankets.

"Mm," I hum, pretending to be unimpressed though my body betrays me with every subtle arch and shiver. "I was until you turned into an octopus."

Honestly, his hands are all over me.

"Octopus?" He chuckles, the sound vibrating through me. "I'm keeping you warm."

"Is that what you call this?" I tease, twisting slightly to glare at him over my shoulder. "I'm pretty sure you're the reason I couldn't sleep."

Not all.

Not even a little.

We had sex three times, which is a record for me.

His lips brush my neck again, just below my ear, and I feel him smirk. "You weren't complaining last night."

I roll my eyes, yawning at the same time. "Last night was different. Last night, I wasn't trying to sleep."

"It's not my fault you're so sexy and irresistible."

I melt into that comment and lie. "Flattery gets you nowhere."

"Are you sure?" he murmurs, hand sliding lower, just above my best bits. "I think it's working."

I let out a dramatic sigh, though it's hard to sound annoyed when his lips are making a trail of fire down my shoulder.

It feels so good.

Best way to wake up…

My eyes flutter shut as I try to resist how good it feels, but I'm losing the battle. I should be annoyed. I should push him away, climb out of this bed and get dressed to reclaim my morning as mine.

Go be productive! *Carpe Diem*, seize the day!

Instead, I tilt my head just slightly, giving him more access 'cause I'm thirsty like that.

"You're way too confident for someone who hogs blankets and snores."

"I don't snore," Gio feigns offense, nipping at my shoulder.

"Oh, you definitely do," I tease, glancing at him over my shoulder. "It's like sleeping next to a bear."

His hair is a mess, the bed head sticking up in a way that should look ridiculous but only makes him more attractive. Gio looks as tired as I feel, but still in a great mood considering how early it is.

He is in no rush to shoo me out of his place.

"You just told me you got no sleep last night."

Busted.

His giant hand squeezes my hip before it begins tracing lazy patterns against my skin. Over my pelvis. Around my belly button.

"You're not running for the hills."

"I'm too tired to run," I whisper with another yawn. "And you're warm. Like a space heater."

I roll onto my back, tilting my head to look up at him fully, and the sight nearly makes me lose my train of thought.

Big smile. Crinkles at the corners of his eyes when he looks at me. A nose that drags itself down the side of my neck, sniffing me like he can't get enough.

"How 'bout I cool you down with a pussy full of my dick?"

A laugh bursts out of my lips and I pull the blanket up further, covering my face.

"Oh my God—you sound like a massive perv."

"Answer the question, Austin." He laughs, tugging the blanket back down, exposing my breasts, his mouth creeping dangerously close to my nipple, his lips pressing hot, warm kisses on the swell of my breasts.

I don't usually sleep naked, but when I do...
I don't mind morning sex.

"You're lucky you're slightly above average at the sex." I can't stop myself from giving him a hard time. The longer we lay here, the more awake I feel, the funnier I become. Ha ha.

"Above average?" he repeats, leaning down until his lips hover over mine. "Is that your final answer?"

"Yup," I pop the 'p' to be a brat, though my smirk falters when his hand slips between my thighs, index finger slipping its way inside my pussy.

Despite myself, my legs part by several inches...

"Still only above average?" he teases, his voice low and rough.

My teeth catch my bottom lip, something I know he likes. I've seen the way his eyes watch my mouth when I do it and I do it now to drive him crazy.

"Will you put another finger inside me if I say yes?"

Gio shakes his head slowly.

No.

That finger inside me begins small circles over my clit and it's not enough...not nearly enough...

I bite back a moan, my fingers tightening in his hair as my head falls back against the pillow.

"If you want my face between your legs, say my name," he whispers next to my ear, voice thick with lust. He's horny, too, kissing the corner of my mouth, hand still working its magic in my pussy, *and I can barely think straight anymore.*

"Gio," I manage to gasp, though it comes out as more of a plea than I intended. I want his face between my legs but I also want another finger inside me.

Decisions, decisions.

He shouldn't make me choose.

"Yeah, baby?" His tone is playful, but his eyes are dark, full of heat and focus as he watches me come undone beneath him.

"Why can't I have both?" I muse out loud, realizing he hasn't heard my inner turmoil. His hand stills, just enough to drive me mad and I wiggle my ass so he gets the message: *keep going*.

Don't stop!

"Are you pouting?"

"No," I reply, though my voice is breathy, and the way my bottom lip juts out, betrays me.

"No?" He tilts his head, pretending to consider my words, though the glint in his eyes tells me he already knows exactly what he's going to do. "Because I think…you want my fingers and my mouth inside you. Unless I'm wrong."

He's not wrong.

I nod, breath hitching as his thumb brushes over my clit, the slightest pressure that leaves me aching for more.

He chuckles, leaning down until his lips are just a whisper away from mine. "Greedy."

I open my mouth to argue, but he cuts me off with a kiss—hot, hungry, and entirely too consuming.

So greedy.

"You can have both, baby," he murmurs against my skin, his voice muffled as he moves lower. Sucks a nipple on his way down. Licks on it. Blows so it puckers. "But only because I can't resist you."

I spread my legs, greedily. Anxiously.

Willing him to hurry.

I want it bad…

I watch, giddy.

He doesn't rush—of course he doesn't.

Gio loves to take his time, to savor every moment, every reaction, every little sound I make.

"You're so impatient," he teases, his lips brushing over the sensitive skin of my inner thigh. His hands grip my hips firmly, holding me in place as his kisses trail lower, each one slow and deliberate. "But I like that about you. Plus, you taste so fucking good."

My fingers tighten in the sheets beneath me as my back arches off the bed, silently begging him to stop teasing and start eating me out.

This is torture!

"Gio," I plead, louder this time, desperate for him to stop tormenting me with his slow, calculated movements. "Please for the love of God."

"I love it when you beg." Then his mouth is on me, warm and insistent, and I can't hold back the moan that escapes my lips. A loud, drawn out moan.

My head falls back against the pillow, my fingers tangling in his hair as he sucks on my clit for breakfast—going at me hard and it doesn't take long for my thighs to start quivering, his tongue moves in maddeningly perfect strokes.

And when his fingers slide inside me, I want to die.

He groans, little noises from his throat that are as erotic as the sight of his bare, broad shoulders glistening between my wet thighs.

The top of his head.

His nose pressed against my mound.

Gio doesn't quit. Doesn't pause.

Doesn't stop until I'm trembling, until I'm left boneless and breathless and utterly spent.

When he finally pulls back, his grin is smug and entirely too self-satisfied, but I can't even bring myself to care.

Then.

He reaches for a condom, which we've left out on the nightstand after fumbling around in the dark one too many times... tears it open, rolls it on, makes the short crawl up my body.

He slides in so easy...

Thrusting slowly, bracing his hands on the headboard, Gio reaches under me to grab my ass so he's buried as deep as he can get. The deep rumble from his chest vibrates through the room as he pumps into me, hips rolling.

God he is in such good shape...

My nails rake down his back, down to his ass and press into his flesh; I can't help but marvel at his body—the tension in his muscles, the way he moves with so much control it makes my head spin.

Slowly and deliberately, his head dips.

He is gorgeous.

Watching him is like watching a piece of art, if art could fuck you.

Then...

Just as I'm about to lose myself in the moment...

This happens:

"*Oh. My. Gawd!*"

The voice is shrill, horrified—and unmistakably female.

I freeze.

Gio freezes.

For a second, time seems to stand still as the sound of footsteps echoes in the room. My head whips around toward the door, and there she is—Nova.

Standing in the doorway, her face contorts into a mix of shock and disgust before her hands fly to her face, to cover her eyes.

"Nova!" Gio roars, his voice full of panic and anger as he scrambles to grab the blanket. He yanks it over us in one swift motion, shielding my body from view. "What the hell are you doing?!"

"What am *I* doing?" Nova screeches, her eyes wide and her hands flying up to cover her face. "What are *you* doing? And why is your door open?!"

"It's MY FUCKING HOUSE!" he roars.

Oh shit.

Eyes still shielded, Nova gestures wildly with one hand in our direction without actually looking at us. "I thought you were here alone!"

I bury my face in Gio's chest, mortified beyond belief. My entire body feels like it's on fire, and I can't bring myself to look at her.

"I want to die," I mumble to no one because no one is listening. "This is a nightmare."

"This is burned into my brain forever," Nova shouts at her brother as if he were the one at fault for barging in, feeling around the air with her hands as if she cannot see. "I'll never recover!"

"Then leave!" Gio barks, picking up a pillow and chucking it toward the door. "Get out and close the goddamn door!"

"I'm going! *Jeez!*" she barks back, spinning on her heel and marching toward the hallway. Still, before she leaves, she whips around one last time, pointing an accusatory finger at him.

Us. "Also, you're paying for my therapist!"

With that, Nova slams the door shut, leaving a stunned silence in her wake.

Gio groans, flopping back onto the bed and dragging me with him. "I'm gonna kill her," he mutters, staring up at the ceiling like he's reevaluating every decision he's ever made.

I can't help it—I start laughing. It bubbles up uncontrollably, breaking through the awkward tension, and soon I'm clutching my stomach, tears pricking the corners of my eyes.

"This isn't funny," Gio grumbles, though the corner of his mouth twitches, betraying his amusement. "She has no boundaries."

I pull the blanket up to cover my face, letting out a muffled laugh despite the mortifying situation.

"She looked horrified."

"She's *so* dramatic," he says dramatically, though his tone softens as he turns to look at me. "And I'm sorry. That should *never* have happened."

No, it shouldn't have.

But it did and there's no point in dwelling. Or freaking out.

I peek out from behind the blanket, meeting his gaze. "It's not your fault. But maybe…lock your *door* next time?"

That seems like the obvious answer here.

"There is no lock. It's a door code and I'm changing it."

We lay there for a moment in awkward silence before I burst out laughing, unable to hold it in any longer. Gio glances over at me, a reluctant grin tugging at his lips.

"I'm glad you think this is funny," he says, though there's a teasing edge to his voice. "I was about to orgasm and now my balls are full of cum."

17
gio

"Remind me to change the door code."

I lean back against Nova's kitchen counter, arms crossed, glaring daggers at her as she goes through the steps of making herself a cappuccino —from the machine I bought her, no less—as if she hadn't fucked up my morning.

The ultimate cock block.

The faint sound of her music plays from a speaker somewhere, but it does nothing to cut the tension I'm radiating in her direction.

"In my defense, I wanted to go for a run." She slurps from the coffee mug. "And ran out of electrolytes to put in my water bottle so I was coming to steal yours.

I stare at Nova, dumbfounded as she continues babbling.

"Then I heard noises and got worried—like, you could have been throwing *up* or whatever."

Those noises were me fucking the woman I'm dating.

I clamp my lips shut because if there's one thing I do not do, it's discuss my sex life with my twin. Unlike Nova, I have boundaries I do not cross.

"When is the last time you heard someone throwing up? What world do you live in?"

My sister laughs, leaning against the counter. "All I'm saying is I'm sorry! I'll never come unannounced ever again—I swear."

Her apology feels more like an afterthought than anything else, but that's my sister for you.

She pokes at the foam on top of her coffee.

"Let's stop talking about you, it's annoying," Nova announces, throwing up her free hand in mock surrender. "Let's talk about me and my sex life. Oh wait. That won't take long, I don't have one."

That piques my interest and I jump at the chance to change the subject. "What do you mean?"

She sighs dramatically, setting the mug down on the counter with a loud clink. "I mean, my love life is a barren wasteland. An endless desert. A desolate void of despair and loneliness."

"Okay, tone it down, Shakespeare," I say, but a pang of guilt tugs at me for finally finding someone I click with on a personal level when Nova struggles to meet someone. "Why? What happened to that guy you were seeing? Uh, Todd, right?"

"Bart," she corrects, expression souring. She sticks out her tongue as she says, "He ghosted me."

Ghosted her?

What the fuck kind of dumbass dumps the sister of a professional hockey player? It comes with perks and Nova is a badass. What reason could he have to stop responding?

"Could it be because his name is *Bart*?" I ask, frowning. Nova doesn't usually seem fazed when a relationship doesn't work out, but the way her shoulders sag tells me she may have liked this one more than the others. "The dude sounded like an idiot."

I'm trying to be supportive, already hating this guy.

She shrugs. "I mean, I thought we were having fun. Good conversation, decent chemistry. And then—poof. Gone. Like he never existed." She snaps her fingers for emphasis.

I tilt my head, studying her. "Guys are such assholes. What a pussy."

She sets down her mug and crosses her arms.

"Honestly, it's fine. I wasn't that into him. It's just...I don't know. Getting ghosted sucks, you know? Seriously, why can't people just be honest and say, 'Hey, I'm not feeling this' instead of disappearing like cowards?"

I nod slowly, watching as she picks at a loose thread on her sweatshirt. "Yeah, I get that. It's not about Bart, it's the principle."

Bart.

What a stupid name.

Can you imagine banging a dude and having to moan *that* name?

I almost laugh, but hide it in the hoodie of my sweatshirt.

"The principle." She nods. "Exactly. I'm over it, you know? Dating. Talking to someone for a day and being unmatched on a dating app. Or having a guy I don't know ask to see my boobs. It's exhausting. Everyone is either playing games or looking for the next best thing. I hate it."

Shit.

That does suck.

I've never had those issues; women slide into my DMs and hit me up after games on a regular basis. But those women are typically puck bunnies or fans, and the last time I got involved with one of those, it ended so poorly the entire break-up was headline news.

So yeahhh...

"Maybe I'm better off alone. At least then I don't have to worry about idiots like Bart."

I stand straighter, not loving her tone.

Or the sadness in her voice.

"You're not better off alone, Nova," I say, my tone more serious now. "You'll find someone. Someone who calls you back and actually deserves you."

She looks up at me, her expression softening for a moment before she smirks. "Aww, look at you, being all supportive and brotherly. Who are you, and what have you done with my real twin?"

"Funny."

She sighs. "I thought it would make me happy setting you up with Austin, but all it's done is make me jealous." Her laugh holds no humor.

"You're jealous?" I ask, trying to keep my tone light, though I can tell this isn't entirely a joke to her.

She rolls her eyes. "Not of *Austin*, you idiot. I'm jealous of...I don't know—the fact that I'm single and you're dating. I've gotten used to barging into your place and having you all to myself. I am happy for you, I *swear*. It's *just* weird seeing you act your age. And it's improved your game."

It has improved my game.

We've won the last two games we played—because Austin was at both.

"Any dude that ghosts you or plays mind games. Or makes you question the relationship is not your guy, Nova. He's not. He's *just* a lesson and sometimes we learn that the hard way."

"Yeah, yeah—I know," she waves me off. "I'm not feeling this way 'cause of Bart. Maybe I'm just not meant to do this whole…" She waves a hand in the air. "Relationship thing."

I narrow my eyes on her. "That's the dumbest thing I've ever heard you say, and you've said some *really* stupid shit."

Her snort is a weak attempt to cover the vulnerability. "Gee, thanks."

I take a step closer, forcing her to look at me.

"I'm *serious*, Nova. You deserve someone who gets you and likes all the dumb shit you do and your weird little quirks. Stop wasting energy on dudes who waste your time." I run a frustrated hand through my hair, feeling like a life coach. "Stop settling for losers."

"They're not losers."

Is she defending these lazy assholes who can't be bothered to text her back?

How hard is it?

I scoff. "Any guy who doesn't at least text you to say he's not interested is a fucking loser." Or lazy at *minimum*.

Her lips twitch, but the sadness in her eyes doesn't fade. "You're annoyingly good at motivational speeches, you know that? Maybe dating someone like Austin is rubbing off on you."

I shrug, letting a smirk creep onto my face. "What can I say? I'm thriving or whatever."

My sister watches me for several seconds, tapping her long nails against the ceramic handle on her mug. Opens her mouth, then closes it.

"It's easy for you to stand there and tell me not to settle for losers when you literally have women trying to get naked in your hotel rooms."

She is not wrong.

That happens on occasion.

"I don't think you can take offense to me telling you to stop settling and maybe raise your standards a little."

Nova wrinkles her nose. "Oh—'cause my standards are so low?

Newsflash: it's not like I go searching for these guys. They find me. Like stray cats, but with worse manners and no social skills."

"Then stop feeding them."

She blinks at me for a moment absorbing my wisdom, then a genuine laugh bursts out of her.

It's the first time she's really laughed all morning, and it's enough to make me grin.

"Can I ask you a question?" Nova asks once she's done giggling. "Why haven't you ever set me up with one of your teammates on like…a date?"

I raise an eyebrow. Never not once has my sister mentioned wanting to be set up with one of the guys on my team.

Never.

Not that I would do it.

"Uh. You mean the guys who think *Taco Bell* is an appropriate pre-game meal and that socks are optional in public?"

No offense to Taco Bell, but you get what I'm saying. Most dudes our age aren't exactly taking women to fancy restaurants and sweeping them off their feet. They take them for coffee.

Or: to the bar then back to their place for a quick fuck.

She smirks, crossing her arms. "But at least *one* of them has to be decent, right? Like, statistically?"

"Statistically, sure," I say, rubbing my chin to make it seem as if I'm seriously mulling the idea over. "But then you realize they're overgrown toddlers with too much testosterone. Jank once missed practice because he "lost track of time" watching videos of cats riding Roombas. Ivan can't remember to pay his phone bill, so he uses everyone else's to order UberEats."

I frown at the idea of her dating either of them.

My sister tilts her head. "Knock it off. Be serious, I've met a bunch of them, they're not terrible. Maybe you're overprotective and it wouldn't kill you to do me the same favor I did you." She hesitates. "Things are going well with Austin, maybe you could…you know. Hook me up."

Hook her up?

Over my dead body.

"What about the new assistant coach?"

"Tyler?"

Nova rolls her eyes at the ceiling. "Yes, Tyler. What is he, like —thirty-five?"

I rear back, *hating* the idea. "How the hell would I know how old Tyler is? The answer is no. He's a fuck boy."

My sister is undeterred. "How do you know he's a fuck boy?"

"He looks like one."

Duh.

Nova snorts, crossing her arms. "He *looks* like one? That's your entire basis for judgment? You can't just slap a label on someone because they have good hair and a decent jawline."

HIT ME WITH YOUR BEST SHOT

She thinks he has a decent jawline?

The man has a beard. "He has a weak upper lip."

"Fine," she says with a dramatic sigh, throwing her hands up in defeat. "Forget Tyler. Forget your teammates. Forget everything. I'll just join a nunnery or something."

"Good call," I say, nodding. "You'd look great in a habit."

"You are such a jackass." Nova's laughter finally fades as she wipes at her eyes, still grinning. "Seriously, though. What's your problem with setting me up? You're acting like I'm asking you to marry me off to one of your idiot teammates."

I cross my arms, leaning against the counter. "It's not that. I just know these guys, Nova. They're my friends, sure, but I've seen what they're like off the field. Half of them don't even know how to do their own laundry."

"So?" she says, arching an eyebrow. "That's why I wouldn't date *half* of them. I just need you to point me to the one with a working brain cell."

"You're assuming one of them *has* a working brain cell." I realize I'm losing my patience and take a deep breath. Let it out. "Look. I'm not saying you can't handle them, but why would you *want* to? Do you know how many times I've had to explain to Jank that you can't put metal in the microwave? Twice, Nova. Twice."

"He is not from America!" my sister shouts in his defense. "He's from Ukraine, of course he doesn't know you can't put metal in the microwave!"

"I'm trying to protect you. You deserve someone who isn't going to make you question all your life choices every time he opens his mouth and a loose tooth falls out."

Nova shakes her head, laughing. "You're such a pain in the ass, but thanks, I guess."

"You're welcome, I guess."

Nova tilts her head, a mischievous glint in her eye. "Maybe Austin knows some single guys."

"No," I say flatly, already regretting where this is going.

She frowns. "Why not?"

"*Because*. The guys Austin knows are college students and too young for you." I am delighted to enlighten her. "She's a professor. You want me to set you up with one of her *students*?"

"Pause." Nova blinks, jaw dropping. "Wait—what? Back up. She's a professor? You're dating a professor?"

My chest swells with pride.

"Yeah," I say, smirking at her stunned expression. "What did you think her job was when you played matchmaker?"

"I wasn't thinking about jobs at all!" Nova admits, throwing her hands up. "You didn't exactly say, 'Hey, I'm dating a genius.'"

"She's not a genius," I say, rolling my eyes. "I mean, maybe she is—I'm still getting to know her. Hard to tell under that sassy mouth."

"Wait. Back up. What does she teach? I'm literally so stunned by this news," Nova presses, still trying to process. "English? Rocket science? Marketing?"

"Sociology."

My sisters rears back. "I have *no* idea what that is."

Yeah, same.

"Me either—I had to google it," I say with a shrug. Sociology is: in a nutshell, *the study of people and how they interact with each other*. Why people do the things they do in groups, how societies form, what influences them. "She's smart, but normal. Unlike the guys you keep chasing."

Instead of letting them chase you.

Nova stares at me for a moment before shaking her head. "Unreal. You're dating a college professor, and I can't even get a guy who knows how to use a dishwasher."

"I have no idea how to use my dishwasher, either."

My sister scoffs. "That's because you have a housekeeper."

As I stand in my sister's apartment my mind begins to wander; now that we're speaking about Austin, I can't stop my brain from going back to my bedroom.

This morning and last night—and all the times in between.

And then another thought enters my brain and before I can stop myself, the question pops out:

"Can I ask you a question—promise you're not going to freak out?"

"Of course I'm not going to freak out," she says earnestly, expression serious. "Just ask."

I rub the back of my neck, feeling the weight of the words before I even say them, already wanting to snatch them back: *"Do you believe in love at first sight?"*

For a moment Nova stares, blinking like she didn't hear me right.

Then she gasps, putting a hand to her lips. "OH MY GOD, are you in love with Austin?"

"NO!" I blurt, a little too loudly. I mean...maybe? "No, I'm just asking if you believe in it. Hypothetically."

Nova takes a few moments to respond.

"I don't know if I believe in love at first sight—I've never seen it." She leans her hip against her counter, shifting her weight as she fiddles with her mug. "I think people can feel a *spark*. But love? I don't believe it's instant, no. I believe love grows. It takes time—don't you agree?"

She's watching me expectantly.

"Yeah. I agree." I nod, pretending like her words don't land a little heavier than they should, because I also don't agree.

My voice sounds hollow even to me, and I know Nova hears it too. I glance away, pretending my phone buzzed and I need to check messages, anything to avoid the intensity of her stare.

"Gio," Nova says, her voice cutting through the silence. "You're such a terrible liar. Just tell me what's going on."

That's certainly true enough.

The truth is that the truth is somewhere between: *I've never felt this way before and I have no idea what the hell I'm doing—or how to begin communicating how I feel to a woman I only just started dating.*

What if she thinks I'm out of my fucking mind?

What if she feels like I'm needy and decides to peace out?

"What I can't believe is that we're having this conversation," my sister echoes what's in my mind, doing that creepy twin thing we used to do when we were younger.

Our mom loved it.

It was one of her favorite things about us.

Mom loved having twins—even dressed us alike, though Nova is a girl and I'm a boy—we coordinated in matching sets until we were ten and I'd get humiliated by it, once throwing a temper tantrum so horrible on an Easter Sunday that spelled the end of the outfits.

What I wouldn't give to go back to those days…

Whatever you want, Mom.

Yes, Mom.

I love you, Mom…

I miss you.

Not to get sappy, but she would have the answers for me. And she would have liked Austin—had this way of making everything feel less complicated, even when it wasn't.

And boy do I need that now.

"What's with the look on your face?" Nova quietly asks.

I shrug, glancing at her. "Thinking about what Mom would tell us about relationships if she was here."

Surely she'd impart wisdom.

My sister goes still a few seconds before her shoulders go back and her spine straightens. "She'd tell you to stop overthinking everything and enjoy dating. She'd tell you life is too short to sit around waiting for the perfect moment."

I swallow hard, the lump in my throat making it impossible to respond. Nova is right.

That's exactly what Mom would've said.

"Maybe we should both take her advice." I sniff, feeling tears welling in my eyes.

"Do *not* make me cry right now, you dick." Nova's laugh is

quiet as she regards me. "Mom would think my love life was a mess, because it is."

"Yes, but you were her favorite."

She rolls her eyes. "Only because I was a girl and she loved buying me outfits and doing girly things with me. Dad did all the hockey shit and I think she probably felt left out sometimes."

I nod my head.

That's true, too.

"She probably did," I say, my voice soft.

"But you know she loved watching you play. She never missed a game." Nova snorts. "She spent half the time asking Dad what was happening. Like, what's a power play? Or, why does Gio keep sitting in the penalty box? I think she secretly hated hockey."

I can't help but laugh at that. "She hated watching me get the crap kicked out of me."

I wasn't always a goalie.

When I started the sport I was shuffled around from position to position and began in the goal box my senior year of high school. Until that point, I'd gotten into tons of fights, many of which were started by *me*.

"She did hate watching you fight," Nova agrees, a smile on her lips. "She *hated* seeing either of us get hurt—but she was so proud of how good you are. She bragged about you all the time."

I raise an eyebrow. "She bragged about you *more*."

"Well, *obviously*. I was her little sidekick," Nova recalls fondly. "Straight A's, her little gymnast. You were a little shit growing up."

"I was not," I protest though we both know it's a damn lie. "Okay I was. But you were annoying as hell."

Nova laughs, shaking her head. "We were *her* little shits and she loved us. Even when we went at each other's throats."

I nod, my chest tight. Nose stinging. "I miss them."

"Me too," she says, just above a whisper, her eyes shining a little too brightly. "Every damn day."

We sit there for a moment, the silence heavy but not uncomfortable. It's one of those rare moments where words aren't necessary—where we both know exactly what the other is feeling.

After a while, Nova nudges me with her foot. "You know she'd kick our asses if she saw us sitting around moping."

"We're not moping. We're bonding over the fact that you busted in on me fucking my girlfriend."

The word slips out before I can stop it.

And I don't hate the sound of it.

My sister's eyes go wide and her mouth makes the surprised shape of an O.

"Pause," she says, drawing out each word. "*Girlfriend*? Did you just say girlfriend?"

Her eyes are wide, and the grin splitting her face is borderline obnoxious. I groan, dragging a hand through my hair, suddenly feeling about ten years younger—like when she used to tease me about crushes in middle school.

"It just slipped out, okay?" I mutter, avoiding her gaze.

Nova's smirk doesn't fade. If anything, it grows fifty sizes wider.

"It *is* a big deal. My brother, the emotionally constipated hockey player, just admitted he has a girlfriend. I feel like this is a milestone—our baby boy is growing up."

"Can we not make this a big deal?"

"I'm not making it a big deal," she says, setting her mug on the counter behind her and holding up her hands in mock surrender. "I'm appreciating the moment. They don't happen often."

"Yeah, well—appreciate it silently."

Nova nods. Pretends to zip her lip.

Sighs.

"So what's next with you and Austin?" She wants to know.

"Another date?"

"I think so. She wants me to watch a movie at her place this weekend, but..."

Nova nods, her brows raised in curiosity. "But?" she repeats, leaning forward like she's already anticipating the drama I'm about to unload.

"She has a dog."

"So? You like dogs."

I shift on my heels. "Not this dog."

That has my sister's attention. "Why? What's wrong with the dog?"

"It's ugly." I pause, dreading this moment. "And its name is Gio."

My sister blinks.

Hand goes to the counter to brace herself as she dissolves into uncontrollable laughter. She's gasping for air, face turning red as she struggles to form words.

"Shut. Up," she coughs. "I'm dying, shut up she does not have a dog named Gio. How? Why?"

This isn't exactly something I want to share, but Nova's relentless stare is like a pry bar, cracking me open. "Her dad died," I tell her quietly, glancing away. "And he was into hockey."

Nova's laughter halts mid-breath. Her head tilts, her expression softening with a bit of regret.

"Oh," she says, her voice dipping sadly. "Wait, so..."

"Yeah," I mutter, running a hand through my hair. "Apparently, he was a huge fan of the Baddies. Came to every game, had season tickets, followed my stats—the whole thing. When he passed, he left the dog to Austin."

"Oh my God," she whispers, covering her mouth with her hand. "That's so sweet. And so awkward." My sister giggles. "You're literally competing with a dog version of yourself for Austin's attention."

"Not helpful," I grumble. "Did I mention it's ugly?"

"There is no such thing as an ugly dog."

I shake my head in disagreement. "False. It's a Chinese Crested and it's the ugliest fucking thing I've ever seen and now she wants me to meet it in person."

"Hey. Listen to me." Nova straightens, putting on her "big sister" face, a trace of amusement in her eyes. "You've got this. It's a *dog*, not a gatekeeper to her heart."

Famous last words.

18
austin

"You be on your best behavior," I tell my father's dog, pointing a finger at him like he actually understands what I'm saying.

Gio tilts his head and blinks at me with his bulging, watery eyes, the tiny tufts of white hair sprouting from his head and ankles.

He is looking undeniably handsome tonight with his underbite on full display, making him look both confused and vaguely threatening at the same time.

I sigh, kneeling down to his level, adjusting the bow tie I clasped around his neck earlier, adding to his charm.

"Listen," I say to him in the soothing tone I reserve for babies and cute animals. "Gio is coming over—the *other* Gio. And I need you to not do that thing where you bark for no reason. Be nice. This is important."

He flops to the floor for belly rubs, completely uninterested in the gravity of the situation.

I give him some pets and continue my lecture.

"You know," I impart. "For once you could help me out by being *cute* and *endearing* instead of looking like the creepy little goblin he's accused you of. Wag your tail when he comes in. Or, I don't know—don't growl at him. At all."

Gio yawns, his long pink tongue curling as he stretches out on the floor.

"I take that as a no."

Shithead.

Ugh, *why am I so nervous!?*

I stand, catching sight of my reflection in the mirror above my living room fireplace and smooth a hand over my hair, which I've spent the last thirty minutes trying to tame into something effortless but pretty. My outfit is casual but flattering—jeans and a mohair sweater that's loose enough without being frumpy.

I've gone back and forth on the makeup, eventually settling on only mascara and lip gloss.

Natural.

Easy.

I pace the living room, glancing around to make sure everything looks tidy. The throw pillows are fluffed, the blankets draped over the back of the couch are arranged *just so*, and there's a candle burning on the coffee table that smells like vanilla and cinnamon—yum—without being overpowering.

I've spent way too much time agonizing over these tiny details, but I can't help it. I want everything to be perfect.

Which means that inevitably it won't be.

As if on cue, there's a knock at the door. My stomach does a little flip again, and I shoot the dog a warning look.

"Behave," I hiss at him, pointing a finger at him before hurrying to the door. "Stay!"

He sits.

I take one last deep breath, plastering on what I hope is a relaxed smile—and open it.

"Hey," he says, his smile easy and warm.

"Hey," I manage, moving aside to let him in. "Come on in."

He steps into my small foyer, glancing around the room as if he were searching for something—or some*one*, aka: Gio—tentatively crossing the threshold.

"Thanks." He kisses me on the lips by way of greeting before stepping further inside. "Is it safe?"

Before I can respond, my dog makes his presence known, trotting into the room with his signature awkward gait. He stops a few feet away from Gio, eyes locked on the human version of Gio, sizing him up.

The dog sniffs the air.

Takes one dinky step forward.

It's like a showdown in the Wild West.

When Gio puts his hand on my waist to pull me in for a hug, the dog freezes, his scraggly body stiff, watery eyes narrowing.

One more step forward…

I half expect tumbleweed to roll across the carpet.

"This is Gio," I tell my date, pointing toward the dog, who tilts his

head, underbite catching the light enough to look menacing, like he's debating whether to make friends or declare war.

Gio kneels down a few feet away, keeping his movements slow and deliberate.

"Hey, buddy," he says, his voice warm and unthreatening. He holds out his hand like a peace offering, palm up so Gio can sniff it. "We're going to be cool, right?"

"No," I mutter to the dog. "Don't you dare start growling."

Jesus, can nothing ever be easy?

My dumb dog rumbles low in his chest, barely audible, and grows in volume that should not be so loud given the size of his body. His lip curls, exposing far too many crooked teeth.

"Great." Gio's laugh sounds nervous as he holds up his hands in mock surrender. "He hates me. Message received."

"He doesn't hate you," I insist, reaching out to scratch Gio behind his silky ears. "I'm so sorry he's growling—I warned him to behave, but he doesn't want to listen."

I give the dog a sharp look. "Gio, knock it off." Then to Gio, "He won't eat you, I swear."

I don't think…

Truth be told, I haven't introduced the dog to a man. I haven't dated anyone since Dad passed away, so this is new to both of us.

The dog and I, I mean.

His scratchy snarl fades to a weak grumble, though his stance remains cautious. His eyes flick to me, then back to the man, almost as if he's waiting for my signal.

Oh for the love of God.

"He's not used to strangers," I explain, embarrassed. "Especially uh, male strangers."

Gio chuckles, the sound warm and surprisingly genuine. "Challenge accepted."

The dog gives a single bark as if to say, *We'll see about that, chump,* and I debate: should I let the dog stay in the living room with us…or put him in the laundry room with his bed and toys?

I bite down on my lower lip, bending to scoop the little pain in the ass up off the floor, carrying him to the other room so I can bond with Gio in peace and quiet without this tiny terror ruining the evening.

He whines for a second, but I give him a firm look. "Don't even start. You'll survive."

He is so spoiled and it's not even my fault.

Gio gloats as I close the laundry room door and turn back toward him. "I feel like I should be flattered that you're locking your guard dog away for me."

Ha ha.

"Don't be. If I thought he'd actually go for your throat, he'd still be out here," I tease, crossing my arms. "Honestly, he's more likely to annoy you to death than to try to eat you."

Gio snaps his jaw like a shark, wanting to take a bite of my arm.

"I can handle him. The jury is still out on you though."

I roll my eyes, heading to the living room. "Big talk for someone who hasn't proven themselves worthy of the remote yet."

While I wouldn't call my living room impressive, it's comfortable, and the big windows offer a decent view of the rooftops of my neighbors and twinkling lights shining in the distance.

I love city living.

"Oh, I'm worthy," he replies, dropping onto the cushion next to me. His knee is plastered against mine and he takes my hand, kissing my palm. "I just haven't gotten the chance to prove it."

"Well, here's your chance." I toss the remote onto his lap. "Pick something. But if it's boring or another action movie, you lose serious brownie points—and don't even think about putting on a documentary."

"*Who hurt you?*" He holds a hand to his chest as if he's been hurt. "Documentaries are great." Gio hums as he channel and app surfs, finally stopping on a movie. "Horror okay with you?"

Not my first choice, but I put him in charge and thus cannot complain.

"Sure, this works." I cozy up next to him, sinking into his side and the cushions.

"You sure you won't chicken out halfway through?"

"Not a chance."

He glances at me, a playful glint in his eyes. "If you get scared, feel free to grab my arm. Or climb on top. Whatever."

I giggle.

The opening credits roll, and for the first fifteen minutes, we actually watch. Well, mostly.

Gio spends them sneaking sidelong glances at me whenever a tense moment builds, clearly waiting for me to flinch or react. I refuse to give him the satisfaction, keeping my expression neutral even when a jump scare is on screen.

He shakes his head. "Remind me not to put on another scary movie during movie night. You're no fun."

That makes me laugh. "Not screaming is a skill."

His grin widens, and before I can process what's happening, he leans in and presses a quick kiss to my cheek. "Thanks for having me over. I was excited."

He was excited.

Awww, I love that.

Tilt my chin up so he can kiss me on the mouth in a proper hello, now that we're settled in.

The kiss is soft, tentative at first, but it doesn't stay that way for long. His hand moves to gently stroke the side of my face, thumb brushing against my cheek as he deepens the kiss. The warmth of his lips, the way he tastes faintly of mint from gum—it's enough to make the rest of the world fade away.

He's smiling, and it's not the cocky grin I've gotten used to—it's softer, genuine, and it sends a warmth straight to my chest.

"How was your day?" he asks, his voice low, like he's afraid to break the moment.

I let out a small laugh, the kind that escapes when you're caught off guard.

"It was fine—nothing exciting, which is always good. What about yours?"

He shrugs, pulling back and leaning into the couch cushions, taking my hand along with him and pressing his thumb into my palm, massaging it.

"Worked out. Had practice." He pauses. "Went down to Nova's after you left my place—she won't be walking in on us any time soon. For the record, she thought it was hilarious."

Great. At least one of us did.

My face immediately flushes at the memory of his sister seeing us having sex.

And before I can reply, Gio's gaze flicks to my coffee table.

"Hold on—is that Connect Four?"

You bet your sweet ass it is.

I follow his line of sight to the game sitting neatly on the table, the red and yellow pieces already half-filled from my last game against myself a while back.

"It is." It's a classic.

Gio untangles himself from me and leans forward to sort the pieces, sliding the tiny blue bar at the bottom, allowing all the chips to land on the table.

"Dude, I haven't played this game in ages."

Same. I like it because it looks cute on the table.

A fun talking point that no one actually plays; not that anyone besides Dolly and my other friends come over.

"I haven't played in forever, either."

Gio separates the yellow and red pieces into piles, his movements methodical. "Let's do it."

Click.

Click.

Click.

He stacks them neatly, sliding the yellow ones closer to my spot on the couch and I nod, moving to the edge of my seat.

"You're on."

"But let's make it interesting." He glances at me, a mischievous grin spreading across his face. "*Strip* Connect Four."

I choke on the laugh that bursts out of me, shaking my head. "Will you stop at nothing to get me naked?"

His head shakes. "Obviously not. Any cheap way to get those pants off. Plus, it's a chance for you to get me naked 'cause I'm an equal opportunity streaker."

I chew on my bottom lip, *pretending* to consider it, knowing I'm game. "Alright, *fine.* But I'm not going easy on you."

Big words considering it's mostly a game of chance.

And luck.

The first few moves are harmless enough, but it doesn't take long before his strategy—or lack thereof—becomes apparent. He's playing more to distract me than to win, making exaggerated moves and muttering fake strategies under his breath.

I roll my eyes.

Gio's grin falters when I drop a piece into the perfect slot, blocking his next move.

"Boom," I say, sitting back with a triumphant smile. "What was that about strategy?"

He mutters something under his breath, peeling off his hoodie to reveal a tightly fitted Blaze tee shirt.

I take a moment to admire his muscles, reaching over to squeeze one.

He flexes.

"So firm," I compliment him. "You must work out."

He flexes some more. "A little here and there. You know, just trying to stay in shape and impress the ladies."

I smack him.

I laugh, sitting back and watching as he makes his move. His focus is clearly divided—half on the game, half on trying to impress me—and it's almost too easy to block his next play.

When I drop my red piece into the grid, cutting off his carefully laid plans, he stares at the board for a long moment, his mouth opening and closing like he's trying to think of a way to recover.

"Wowza," I say, smirking. "You're not great at this."

"This game requires zero talent," he claims, though the sheepish grin on his face says otherwise. "I'm just distracted by the idea of getting you naked."

"And how's that going for you?" I drop my chip into another slot. "Boom, I win again."

He peels off his tee shirt.

I blink, momentarily thrown off by the sight of his bare chest.

Smooth.

Fit.

"My turn since I just lost," he tells me, resetting the board and leaning forward to rest his chin on his hand. "And don't get cocky, you've only won twice. I'm just getting warmed up."

"Sure you are," I say, forcing myself to focus as I take my

turn. But it's harder than I expect with him sitting there, shirtless and smirking like he knows exactly what he's doing to me.

The game continues, and while I'm determined to keep my winning streak alive, Gio seems equally determined to make me lose my focus.

He leans closer every chance he gets, brushes his hand against mine when I reach for the next piece, and tosses compliments my way that are just distracting enough to make me hesitate.

"I have an idea," he murmurs close to my ear, sending a shiver down my spine, straight to my vajajay—it knows what that mouth can do…

"Hmm?" I manage, the proximity of his lips to my ear is enough to short-circuit my brain.

He smells so good…

My mouth waters at the memory of how good his skin tastes.

"I think," Gio murmurs, his voice low and teasing. Tongue flicks my ear. "You're working so hard to win this game. And for what? A shirtless date? How about I reward you with a little…performance?"

A little performance?

What's that supposed to mean?

He leans back against the couch, relaxed and confident, arms going behind his head. Gio has a tattoo on the underside of his bicep and I fixate on it before my eyes go back to his face.

I blink, pulling back slightly to look at him.

"Performance?"

He nods. "A lap dance. Think about it—what better way to celebrate your inevitable victory?"

"I…" I swallow nervously. "I've never had a lap dance."

"Neither have I."

I snort, shaking my head. "You're so full of it. Do not sit there and tell me you haven't been to a strip club."

What a liar.

"Am I?" He leans in closer, his voice dropping to that low,

teasing tone that always sends a shiver down my spine. "Come on, Austin—don't tell me you're not curious."

"I didn't say I wasn't curious." My cheeks are on fire, heating under his penetrating gaze. "I just feel like this is one of those things that *sounds* better in theory."

Before I can think too hard about it, he pushes himself off the couch and steps back, running a hand through his hair like he's actually preparing for this. He's shirtless and the dim light of my living room only makes the sharp lines of his chest and abs more noticeable.

Then, he pushes the coffee table to the other side of the room, clearing the space between us.

Oh, God. *He's serious.*

His phone comes out, and he thumbs through it for several seconds before a sultry beat fills the room. He sets the phone on the now-displaced coffee table.

I sit frozen on the couch, my pulse racing as I watch him. There's a glint of mischief in his eyes, a challenge that has me equal parts intrigued and terrified. His movements are slow, deliberate, as he steps closer to where I'm sitting, the music building around us.

"Relax, babe." He is teasing me. "It's just a dance."

Babe.

"Just a dance," I repeat, my voice coming out a little shakier than I'd like. "Uh huh."

My breath hitches as he unbuttons his pants, sliding the zipper down with maddening patience. The denim clings to him for a moment before he peels them off in one smooth motion, leaving him standing there in nothing but boxer briefs.

Tight. Blue.

Briefs.

The dim light of the living room casts shadows over the sharp planes of his chest and abs, the soft glow making every muscle more pronounced.

Smooth and luminous, as if they were oiled up.

So handsome.
So sexy...
I gulp back a shot of air, nerves on edge, eyes straying to his dick.
It strains against the cotton material.
I want to touch him.
Run my fingers down his abs...
Gio steps closer still, lowering himself onto the couch until he's straddling my lap. His knees press into the cushions on either side of my thighs, body radiating heat as he wraps himself around me like a second skin.
The proximity is the best kind of overwhelming...
...and when his hands rest lightly on my shoulders, *I forget how to breathe.*
The music pulses around us, filling the silence, and for a moment, all I can do is stare up at him.
His confidence is magnetic, intoxicating, and when he starts to move—slow, fluid rolls of his hips perfectly in time with the beat—I can't look away.
How is he so good at this?
Seriously?
Did he practice before he arrived?
Was he an exotic dancer in a former life?
Before I know what's happening, his fingers take my wrists, prying my hands off the couch, guiding them to his rib cage. His skin is ablaze under my touch, and I can feel the ripple of his rock-hard muscles as he moves. He moves with practiced ease, like he knows exactly the effect he's having on me.
"Gio," I whisper, though I'm not entirely sure if it's a plea or a warning.
He lifts my arms, pinning them behind my head.
Leans down, nuzzling my hair so he can kiss my neck.
"You smell amazing," he murmurs, his voice low and husky. "Like vanilla. *Sweet like your pussy.*"
My heart skips thirty beats; my body responding to the way

his words drip with intention. His teeth graze the spot just below my ear, and I can't stop the small gasp that escapes my lips.

He kisses me on the mouth.

"Touch me," he croons against my lips, rough with desire.

I don't hesitate.

My fingers slide down his back, his skin warm and taut under my touch. He takes my hands lower, placing them firmly against the curve of his ass, and I feel the flex of his muscles as his hips continue their maddening rotation.

I can feel his erection against my core.

He knows what he's doing—he has to—because the subtle grind of his hips sends a jolt of heat racing through me.

Every roll of his hips, every brush of his lips against mine, every whispered breath that tickles my skin—it's all-consuming. My fingers grip his waist, pulling him closer as if I could somehow fuse us together, and he lets out a low groan that sends a shiver straight down my spine.

I want to be naked beneath him.

I want…

"You have no idea what you're doing to me, Austin," he murmurs, his voice thick with need as his lips trail down my jawline, finding the curve of my neck. "You're the only thing I can think about."

Gio reaches for the hem of my shirt.

Tugs until it's up and over my head.

On the floor.

He adjusts himself, dick straining toward me, as he unbuttons my pants and pulls down the zipper. When my jeans join my shirt on the floor, he pauses for the briefest of moments, his hands resting on my bare thighs as his gaze flicks up to meet mine. *The look he's giving me is so exciting…*

We're frantic, now.

Heated.

I explore his flesh, hands skimming up his backside.

Down into the waistband of his boxer briefs, tugging them down over his lean hips.

He gives me an assist.

Together, we move his briefs and now it's my turn to be in charge, pushing at his chest so he's on the couch, sitting with his legs spread.

I climb down off the couch…

Settle myself on the carpet, kneeling before him.

His eyes are glassed over already, tongue darting out to lick his lips.

"Austin…"

His cock is as stiff as a cock can be and he watches, mesmerized, as I lean forward to lick up his shaft.

19
gio

*T*his is how I die…
 With my dick in her mouth.
Without two brain cells to rub together.

Every nerve in my body is firing at once, a constant, overwhelming pulse of sensation that makes it impossible to do anything but feel.

And God, do I feel.

My head tilts back against the couch, my hands gripping the edge of the cushion as a loud groan slips out of me.

Guttural.

Austin sucks harder, taking me deeper.

I hear her choke and my cock rushes with more blood.

I have the urge to take her hair in my hands and pull, but I resist, keeping them at my side.

My hips want to thrust.

I resist that urge, too.

Fuck…

Oh fuck….

I want to marry this girl tomorrow.

How is she so good at this?

My pulse pounds in my ears, drowning out the music, the creak of the couch, even my own labored breaths as she sucks my dick.

Austin's hands skim up my thighs, her touch deliberately close to my balls, and my vision blurs for a second.

"Baby," I rasp. "If you keep this up..."

I don't even finish the sentence.

Her response is to grin about my cock as it fills her mouth.

The sight is so fucking hot—so fucking...

So...

The words are swallowed by another wave of sensation, my head tipping back as I fight to hold on to some semblance of control.

My thighs quake.

I try to still them, pelvis wanting to pump.

I moan again.

"Get on my lap."

She shakes her head.

No.

"Please." *Let me fuck you...*

She shakes her head again.

Jesus, *please.*

The wet heat, the pressure in my nutsack, the way she takes me deeper—it's overwhelming, and I feel myself hurtling toward the edge, powerless to stop it.

"Let me fuck you," I beg as my legs shake, every cell in my body about to rocket to the moon.

Arms behind my head.

I close my eyes.

Feel the cum shooting through my veins...

Austin sucks harder, fingers squeezing my balls.

I come.

Moan as I dump my load in her mouth...

...peel my eyes open to watch her swallow it.

She looks so fucking satisfied with herself as she moves away, leaning back on her haunches—my mind is a chaotic mess but one thing cuts through the haze with startling clarity: she's perfect.

And I think I'm in love.

20
austin

*T*he one thing I cannot do is concentrate.
On anything.
Work?
Forget about it. What are students? What is a lecture? What's a syllabus?
Mid-term?
Pfft.
I'm supposed to be finalizing grades, putting together review materials, but my brain is somewhere else entirely. Correction: my brain is somewhere else entirely because of Gio.
The man has taken up permanent residence in my head, living rent-free, making a mess of my carefully organized thoughts.
And the worst part? I don't care!
I like it.
Love it.
Want some more of it…
I stare absentmindedly out my office window at the quad, where students lounge in the grassy knoll, some of them studying but most of them on their phones.
I tap a pen.

Fiddle with a fidget ball.

My laptop screen mocks me, a half-finished email to a faculty advisor sitting there, waiting for me to remember how to function like a professional! I AM A PROFESSIONAL, DAMMIT!

My phone buzzes on the desk beside me, and I glance at it, my heart doing a ridiculous little flip when I see Gio's name on the screen. It's a text. Simple, straightforward, and entirely him.

> Gio: Miss me?

Of course I miss him.

He knows it, too.

And the fact that he's texting me in the middle of the day just to see how my day is? Yeah, that's not helping my ability to be productive and get shit done.

> Me: Not at all. WHO are you again?

His reply comes almost immediately.

> Gio: I see how it is. Guess I'll have to take my lap dances elsewhere.

> Me: We all know where those lap dances lead…

His response is a little slower this time, and I wonder if maybe he's finally run out of ways to torment me.

> Gio: Stop it. We're both at work and I can't afford a boner rn. How would I explain this to the trainer?

I snort, covering my mouth to stifle the laugh that bursts out, fingers hovering over the keyboard, trying to think of something clever to fire back.

> Me: Sounds like a you problem, not a me problem. Maybe don't text me next time you're supposed to be working.

His reply comes faster this time, almost as if he's been waiting for me to call him out.

Or in a rush.

> Gio: Bold of you to assume I can go a whole day without talking to you. Spoiler Alert: I CAN'T.

Awww.

That's literally the sweetest thing he's ever said to me.

Not really, but still—it's amazing dating a man who doesn't leave me guessing. No woman wants to play games—or insecurely navigate their relationship.

> Me: Does that mean you're dying to see me again??

> Gio: DING DING DING... and I don't mean at my game on Thursday, that doesn't count. I need you there, but I want to take you on an actual date.

Another date.

I've seen him twice this week and he's already planning to see me again.

My entire body fills with warmth, the implication that he wants to spend all his free time with me has me giddy.

> Me: WHAT IF... we do something with Little Gio. You two need bonding time.

> Gio: Little Gio cannot be tamed. The dog hates me.

> Me: I know but we have to TRY.

> Gio: So what are you thinking? Dog park? Frisbee showdown?

> Me: How 'bout a walk or a trip to the pet store?? Gio could use a new toy, and you can see what it's like to shop for "kids."

> Gio: Are you trying to scare me off by bringing up future children?

> Me: Scaring you off isn't the right term for it. Maybe…feeling you out??

> Gio: Does this mean you want kids?

Is this the kind of conversation you have over text? Would it be best to have this talk in person, maybe over dinner or when it's quiet at his place or mine?

Not in a casual text thread about taking the dog on a date.

I chew on my lip, my thumbs hovering over the keyboard. What do I even say to that?

Do I want kids?

Yes.

Growing up as an only child, I used to love the quiet and the space to myself. But now, with Dad gone and Mom living out of state—meaning I barely get to see her—I can't help but feel the absence of family in a way I never did before.

A sibling would have been amazing—someone to lean on, to share memories and grief with, to call when life feels too heavy to carry alone. I never realized how much I craved that connection until it wasn't an option.

So when Gio asks, the answer feels clearer than I expected. I do want kids.

Maybe not tomorrow or next year, but someday.

> Me: I do. How about you??

HIT ME WITH YOUR BEST SHOT

> Gio: For sure. Can you imagine how cute a little Gio would be?

> Me: I already HAVE a little Gio ;)

> Gio: WOWwwwww

I laugh to myself, this entire text thread filling me with joy.

I love the way he always leans in, always engages—even when the topic is as heavy as future kids or family or the stress he's feeling at work. He doesn't shy away.

He meets me there, every time.

Gio Montagalo is a walking green flag.

> Gio: Shit, babe. Gotta go. Talk to you later, sweet tits.

Sweet tits?

"Sweet tits," I repeat, muttering under my breath at his audacity. Should I let him get away with that one? Probably not. Will I?

Absolutely.

And just like that, he's gone...

The three text bubbles disappear, leaving me left staring at my phone, grinning like an idiot. I set it down, taking a deep breath as I try to refocus on my work.

Minutes pass, maybe longer, and just as I'm starting to make progress on the stack of tasks in front of me, my phone buzzes again. I glance at it, expecting another message from Gio. Instead, I'm met with a text from an unexpected sender.

> 227-555-0495: Hey Austin, it's Gio's sister.

> Me: Hey Nova! What's up?

> Nova: This is going to sound so awkward—and I should have apologized sooner but getting your number from my brother was an impossible feat.

I wait.

> Nova: Anyway. I've been wanting to apologize for the other morning. I am SO SORRY and it will never happen again. I violated your privacy and feel like an asshole.

I swivel in my desk chair, worrying my bottom lip as I message her back.

> Me: I promise it's not a big deal. Awkward, sure, but we all survived.

> Nova: You're honestly cool about this. I get why Gio is head over heels for you. He won't stop talking about you, by the way. I love seeing him so happy.

Head over heels for me?

I bite my lip, warmth spreading through me at the thought of Gio talking about me like that. It's one thing to hear his flirty one-liners or feel the weight of his attention when we're together, but knowing he talks about me like this to his sister?

It feels like a big deal.

She's the closest person to him.

I haven't met any of his friends or teammates yet, but I've met her, and know how much she means to him. Meeting her feels like having been handed a tiny, fragile piece of his world—something I'm discovering he doesn't share with everyone.

His sister is beautiful, vibrant, and sharp—with this infectious energy that makes me want to get to know her on a more personal level.

Another message comes through.

HIT ME WITH YOUR BEST SHOT

> Nova: You guys are disgustingly cute, and I'm here for it.

I cannot wait to share this with Dolly—wondering if any of my friends have time for a girls' night on such short notice, disappointed when they respond and can't make it for another few weeks.

Dammit.

Everyone is so busy.

> Nova: Do you have any interest in having drinks or something? Tonight or whenever?

My heart stops.

Drinks with his sister?

I mean—we took in a Blaze game but had that to distract us. One on one drinks seems so intimate! What if she asks me personal questions about myself?

What if this is all some elaborate ruse to interrogate me?

Seriously.

She caught me in bed with her brother—screwing him.

I stare at her message for far too long, overthinking every possible scenario. Nova grilling me about Gio. Nova realizing I'm just a person trying to figure things out like everyone else and deciding I'm *not* good enough for her brother.

My phone buzzes again, her follow-up making my stomach twist.

This is so much pressure!

Like a first date.

> Nova: No pressure if you're busy or if it's weird! I just thought it'd be cool to hang out.

I let out a breath, trying to focus on the "no pressure" part. She's being genuine. Normal. Doesn't seem to have an ulterior motive.

I kind of want to say yes. It's not like I don't have time.

I start typing before I can talk myself out of it.

> Me: Drinks sound good! Tonight works!

I have no life.

Just kidding. Now I do, thanks to her brother.

Her response is immediate, as if she was waiting for my reply.

> Nova: YAY! Let's do it. 7 okay?

> Me: Perfect. See you then.

Tonight is going to be a test of my ability to not say something awkward. And knowing me?

I'm going to say something super awkward.

Still, *as nervous as I am*, there's a tiny part of me that's excited. Nova didn't have to reach out, didn't have to try to connect with me—but she did. Perhaps this is a chance to show her who I am outside of the mortifying situation she walked in on, and the psycho hockey fan she's witnessed on two occasions.

The rest of my afternoon drags by.

I sleep-walk through a lecture and have office hours. One short meeting with the TA.

By the time I'm racing home to walk Gio, I'm more than ready to clear my head.

The second I clip his leash onto his collar, Gio is bounding out the door, his stubby tail wagging furiously as if this is the highlight of his day. It probably is, honestly. The cool evening air hits my face as we make our way down the sidewalk, and I finally feel like I can breathe again.

"Well, buddy," I start, glancing down at him as he trots along beside me. "You're the only Gio in my life who isn't making me want to vomit right now."

He has no idea what I'm talking about, but that's what makes him the perfect listener.

"You know your namesake is kind of a big deal, right?" I continue, my voice softer now as we turn down a quieter street.

"Professional hockey player. Famous. Everyone loves him."

He's so hot.

I don't say this part out loud, even though the dog has no idea what the hell I'm saying.

"What if I don't fit into his world?" The thought has been sitting in the back of my mind for a while now, quietly gnawing away at my confidence. Gio's world is big, flashy, full of people who expect him to be perfect all the time.

The world I've created for myself is small, predictable, and comfortable.

Boring, until now.

Safe.

Just me, my dog, and I.

Gio pauses to sniff at a patch of grass, completely oblivious to the mini-spiral happening above him. I tug gently on his leash, and we keep moving.

"I mean, don't get me wrong. He's amazing," I admit, the words tumbling out as if saying them out loud will help me make sense of them. "He's funny and ridiculously good in bed."

The sex is so good.

"That thing he does with his tongue? My God."

Gio barks, snapping me out of my thoughts, and I glance down to see him wagging his tail again, his excitement undeterred by my brooding.

"You're right. Sorry," I say, laughing softly. "Probably not the kind of thing I should be sharing with you, huh?" I go on. "It's not that I don't trust him," I continue, thoughts taking a sharp left turn.

"I do. But dating someone like him? I'm basically just a nerd."

A sexy nerd.

"The weird thing is he loves it. Like—he loves that I'm a

professor. I think it turns him on. Is that weird? Is that a fetish?"

It has to be.

Gio pees on a garbage can.

"You're right, intelligence is sexy."

I shouldn't discount that.

"I worked my ass off to get to where I am the same way he did."

Well. Not exactly the same.

He uses his body, I use my brain.

That's the polite way of putting it, anyway. The man spends his life skating around in full gear, dodging pucks and body checks, while I sit at a desk grading papers about the *cultural hegemony* and *structural functionalism* to students who barely make it to class on time.

Totally not the same.

"But seriously," I say, glancing down at Gio as he trots along beside me, blissfully unaware of the existential crisis happening just a few feet above him. "What do you think he sees in me? Objectively? Because I can't figure it out."

Gio barks, his tail wagging furiously as we turn a corner, and I roll my eyes.

"Yeah, yeah, I know—*you think I'm amazing*. You also eat cat shit and chase your own tail, so excuse me if I give little weight in your opinion of me."

"Gio. His ex-girlfriends all look like runway models and here I am with my cardigan collection and a bad habit of accidentally quoting Jane Austen when I'm flustered." I tug at my baby blue cardigan sweater; it's layered over a white tee shirt.

My dog sneezes.

I shake my head, a reluctant smile tugging at my lips. "No, I get it. You're right. Cardigans are sexy."

Never judge a girl wearing a cardigan.

Damn straight.

"Look, I know I'm not exactly a hockey WAG or a puck bunny, whatever they call them," I say, my voice softer now.

"And I know I'll probably embarrass myself at least a dozen more times before this relationship is over, but..." I trail off, biting my lip as the thought forms. "He chose me, didn't he?" Gio barks.

By the time we circle back to my apartment, I feel a little lighter, a little less trapped in my own head. Gio prances happily inside, pleased with our stroll, and I can't help but smile as I unclip his leash.

Within seconds he's gone, off like a shot to grab a toy.

21
gio

My sister isn't responding to her text messages.
Weird.

Usually, she's glued to her phone, rapid-firing back sarcastic replies or random memes that don't make sense half the time. Tonight though?

Radio silence.

I've called twice, too. Straight to voicemail.

The knot in my stomach tightens as I head down to her apartment. It's probably nothing. Maybe she left her phone at work or went out with friends. Still, I can't shake the feeling that something's off. She's my sister. I know her better than anyone else, and this isn't like her.

While I'm in the elevator, I shoot Austin another message.

Odd that she hasn't gotten back to me, either?

Not that I expect her to be waiting by her cell, but still. We're in that honeymoon phase and can't get enough of each other...

After a long day of practice, my body is beat down and tired. My shoulders ache, my legs feel like lead, and all I want—the *only* thing I want—is to talk to one of the two leading ladies in my life. Is that so wrong?

A quick message. A phone call. Anything to remind me that

the world isn't just weights, drills, and endless team meetings. But no. I get nothing.

Not from my sister, not from Austin.

Fuck. Is this what pouting feels like?

I WANT ATTENTION. IS THAT SO WRONG?

The elevator dings, and I step out into the hallway. Her apartment is all the way at the end of the hall, and with every step I take, my mind spirals. Is she sick? Hurt? God, please don't let this be one of those horror movie scenarios where I walk in and find her body on the— No.

She's probably taking a nap. Or a shower.

She's fine.

When I turn the corner to her apartment, I slow down.

Laughing.

I hear laughing...

It grows louder as I approach Nova's door, muffled but unmistakable. Two voices, both female.

One of them is definitely my sister—her laugh is impossible to mistake, that obnoxious, almost hysterical sound that makes everyone else laugh, too.

Muffled voices.

Snorting.

I stop in my tracks, tilting my head.

I inch closer to the door, their laughter tumbling out in waves now. It's not just polite chuckling—it's full-blown, gasping-for-air kind of laughter. My brow furrows as I stand there, listening, torn between relief and confusion.

Austin?

I try to make sense of what I'm hearing. The two of them are absolutely losing it, laughing so hard it sounds like they're struggling to breathe. I can make out a few words between the gasps, but they're so garbled, it's like listening to an inside joke I'll never understand.

I knock firmly, loud enough to cut through their wheezing. The laughing stops immediately, replaced by the kind of silence that's more suspicious than reassuring.

"It's me," I call out. "Open up."

Nothing.

I knock again, harder this time. "Seriously, I know you're in there. Stop pretending you don't hear me."

A muffled "Shhh!" comes from inside, followed by a burst of barely-contained giggles.

Great.

They're messing with me.

This is so annoying.

I try the door handle and surprisingly, it turns.

I push the door open and step inside. The smell of one of Nova's candles smacks me in the face first, followed by the sound of upbeat tunes from the sound system.

Then I see them.

My sister and Austin, cross-legged on the floor, surrounded by an array of snacks: half-eaten popcorn, an open bag of chips, and what looks like an entire cheese board they didn't even bother putting on plates. A half-empty bottle of wine sits between them, two mismatched glasses perched precariously on the coffee table.

They both look up at me, startled, before dissolving into another fit of giggles.

"Seriously?" I say, crossing my arms as I close the door behind me. "This is what you're doing?"

Nova raises her glass, her face red from laughing so hard. "Welcome to the party."

Before I can respond, Austin lets out a dramatic gasp and jumps to her feet. She rushes toward me, throwing her arms around my neck and kissing me full on the mouth. "Babe! You're here!"

Oh my God—they're drunk.

I carefully untangle Austin's arms from around my neck and hold her at arm's length, looking her over. Her eyes are sparkling, and her smile is so wide it's almost contagious.

"How much have you had to drink?" I ask.

She scrunches up her nose, pretending to think.

"Umm...like...two glasses? Three? But Nova's glasses are really big."

"Two glasses," Nova calls from the floor, still sitting cross-legged among the snacks. "And maybe a little from the bottle. Don't be so uptight."

"Uptight?" I echo, raising an eyebrow. "I came down here because neither of you were answering your phones. I thought something bad happened."

"Something bad *did* happen," Austin says solemnly, gripping my shirt like she's about to deliver earth-shattering news. "We ran out of crackers for our cheese tray."

Nova bursts into another fit of giggles, almost spilling her wine as she leans back against the couch. "It was tragic."

Nova pats the floor beside her, still grinning. "Come on, sit down. Have a drink. We're solving all of life's problems tonight."

"Yes, come sit down." Austin grabs my hand and pulls me toward the living room to join my sister.

I let out a mock sigh, sinking onto the floor between them. "Alright, but I'm warning you now—if you two are trying to drag me into whatever nonsense this is, I'm charging a babysitting fee."

Austin hands me a glass of wine, her eyes twinkling. "Consider this your payment."

She plops unceremoniously down beside me, leaning her head on my shoulder like she's perfectly content with the world.

I can't wait to hear the shit they've been talking about, taking a sip from the glass I've been given.

It's good – surprisingly good – not too sweet, not too dry.

I take another sip from the glass I've been handed, then another, letting the wine settle as I lean back against the couch.

"So," I say, glancing between the pair of them. "What were you yapping about while I was gone?" I pause, raising an eyebrow. "Better yet, could someone please explain how you even ended up here? Together?"

Nova grins, tipping her glass toward me. "Austin was giving me advice."

I turn to Austin, my curiosity piqued. "What kind of advice?"

"About boys." I laugh. "Mostly how horrible dating apps are."

Nova nods emphatically.

"She was lecturing me about not *settling*," Nova replies, swirling her wine like she's about to say something profound. "Deleting guys the second they display red flags instead of waiting to be disappointed." She pauses dramatically, her eyes narrowing as if she's just realized something. "Actually, she sounds freakishly like you."

Austin snickers, nudging me with her elbow. "See? Great minds think alike."

I laugh, leaning back against the couch. "It's not exactly groundbreaking advice, Nova. Red flags are red for a reason."

Taking another drink from my wine glass, I let my gaze drift between the two of them as they dissolve into another round of giggles. They're both so caught up in their own little world of bad dating profiles and half-finished snacks that I almost feel like an outsider just watching them.

And honestly? It's cute.

Nova never had a sister, and for that matter, neither has Austin. Watching them laugh and bond like this, it's hard not to feel a little proud. I'd worried about how this dynamic would play out—my sister and my girlfriend spending time together without me as the buffer.

But seeing them now? They're like two peas in a very chaotic, wine-fueled pod.

"You two are ridiculous," I mutter, but there's no bite to it.

"We're delightful," Nova corrects, raising her glass in mock cheers.

"Delightfully tipsy," I counter, which only makes them giggle harder.

Austin leans her head against my shoulder, still laughing. "You love it."

I do love it.

The thought sneaks up on me, unbidden but undeniably true. Watching them like this—completely at ease with each other, laughing like idiots, their glasses half-empty but their smiles full—it's hard not to feel a little soft about it.

Then Nova catches my eye, her grin shifting into something sly, her brows lifting knowingly.

"Stop it," I blurt out, pointing my wine glass at her as if it were a weapon.

Her grin widens. "Stop what?" she asks, all innocence.

"You know what," I say, narrowing my eyes. "Whatever you're thinking, don't."

I glare at her, silently willing her to shut up.

The last thing I need is for her to start running her mouth about the conversation we had earlier—about love at first sight and whether or she believes in it or not because lately, I feel myself turning into a lovesick idiot.

Austin lifts her head, glancing between the two of us. "What's happening? Did I miss something?"

"No," I say quickly, shooting Nova a warning look. "You missed nothing."

"Gio, *relax*," my sister says slyly. "I'm not going to tell her the things we talk about. I'm not *that* drunk."

"You're drunk enough," I mutter, sinking back against the couch and shooting her one last warning look. She just smirks, clearly enjoying herself way too much.

Austin looks between us, suspicious but amused. "You're both weird."

"However!" Nova says, holding up a finger like she's about to make a grand proclamation. Her gaze lands on Austin, pointed and deliberate. "Do you believe in love at first sight?"

Oh.

My.

God.

The air leaves my lungs in an instant, and my brain short-circuits. Why the hell did I open my mouth and say anything earlier? If I'd just kept my stupid questions to myself, we wouldn't be in this situation. Nova wouldn't have the ammo, and Austin wouldn't be staring at her like she's just sprouted a second head and that head is Wayne Gretzky.

"Nova," I say sharply, sitting up straighter. "Don't."

I chug all the wine in my glass and grab the bottle.

"What?" Nova asks innocently, batting her eyelashes. "I'm just saying—it's interesting, isn't it? Some people believe in it. Some people *wonder* about it."

I am stupid, stupid, *stupid*!

This is why we can't have nice things.

Austin swallows a lump in her throat, setting her wine glass on the coffee table. "For the record, no—I don't believe in love at first sight. Since you brought it up."

Oh.

The word sinks in, heavy and hollow. I shift awkwardly on the floor, reaching for the bottle of wine to pour myself another glass, the act giving me something to do other than meet her eyes. The sting of disappointment is sharp, but I shove it down, covering it with a practiced nonchalance.

"That's fair," I say finally, forcing my tone to stay light. "It's not exactly the most logical concept."

Out of the corner of my eye, Nova freezes. Her grin falters, and she looks at me, her expression tight with something close to regret.

Guilt.

"Exactly," Austin says, relaxing a bit as she settles back into her spot beside me. "Love takes time. It's not something that happens the second you meet someone."

Nova fidgets with her glass, not meeting my eyes.

HIT ME WITH YOUR BEST SHOT

"Right," my sister says softly, her earlier confidence gone. She looks like she wants to say something more, but she bites her lip instead, her shame practically radiating off her.

I nudge her with my toe.

She glances at me, startled, and I give her a look—a silent *it's fine, stop beating yourself up*.

Chaos is practically her default setting.

I don't want her to feel like shit because she's drunk and messing around—this is supposed to be fun.

But just when I think we're about to successfully steer the conversation into safer territory, Nova blurts out, "What about my brother though? Did you fall head over heels for him?"

Again, the room goes silent, except for the music in the background.

Austin freezes mid-reach for a pretzel, her eyes going wide. Nova immediately clamps a hand over her mouth, as if she can take back the words by sheer force of will.

Her gaze flicks to me, panic written all over her face.

I am going to kill her!

"I mean—" Austin stammers after a beat, her voice slightly higher-pitched than usual. "I've been his biggest fan since he was drafted."

She lets out a nervous little laugh, trying to cover her discomfort.

"That's not what I mean," Nova says, lowering her hand. Her tone is softer now, but the damage is already done.

My face burns as I glare at my freaking sister, silently screaming *what the hell are you doing?!* She winces, mouthing a quick "sorry" in my direction, but it's too late to undo her slip.

I clear my throat, desperately trying to salvage the situation.

"Okay, let's just pretend Nova didn't say that," I say quickly, forcing a light laugh. "She's had too much wine and clearly has no filter right now."

"Agreed," Nova says, holding up her glass in a weak toast. "Too much wine. Blame the wine."

Austin chuckles nervously, her cheeks still faintly pink. "Yeah, let's blame the wine."

But as much as I try to focus on the banter, I can't help but feel the weight of Nova's words hanging between us. Because as much as I'd like to believe Austin's answer didn't matter, the truth is, I was holding my breath for it.

We sit here for another several hours, wine bottles empty, charcuterie board dwindling, the laughter coming and going in waves. By the time the conversation finally slows, it's eleven o'clock, and my eyes are starting to feel heavy.

I yawn.

Stretch.

"I should get going," I say, reluctantly pushing myself off the floor. "I have to be up at five."

Both women wrinkle their noses in unison, the distaste on their faces almost comical. "Ew," they say at the same time.

I chuckle. "Yeah, I know."

When I stand, Austin stands too. "Mind if I come with you?"

Of course I don't mind.

I nod, a smile tugging at the corners of my mouth. "Yeah. Let's go."

"Oh, sure. Leave me here all alone!" Nova makes a half-hearted attempt at protesting. "It's fine. I'll just sit here and continue to be lonely."

I chuck a pillow at her. "Drink some water."

"Rude," she mutters, catching the pillow and pulling it into her lap. "But fair."

Austin steps over the remnants of snacks and empty glasses, slipping her hand into mine. The gesture sends a warmth through me I can't ignore. I squeeze her hand lightly, grateful we're leaving together.

When we're back in the elevator, she leans into my side, her arms wrapping loosely around my waist. The faint scent of her shampoo lingers, and I resist the urge to rest my chin on top of her head. Instead, I keep my arm around her shoulders, holding her close.

"What about Gio?" I ask after a moment, my voice low in the quiet hum of the elevator. I might not love her dog—okay, fine, he's kind of a menace—but I don't want the poor little bastard stuck alone overnight.

She tilts her head up to look at me, a soft smile on her lips.

"He was out with the dog walker tonight—but thanks for asking. I'll relay the message."

"Thanks. I need all the help I can get."

She grins, leaning up to press a quick kiss to my jawline. "It's because you're not handing over the treats fast enough. He's a slut for snacks."

22

austin

"What was the first thing going through your mind when I was shit talking you at Five Alarm that night you were sitting at the bar?"

I ask him from out of the dark, holding his hand in mine.

It's pitch black, and we've been laying here in silence since we climbed into his bed, enjoying the kind of comfortable that settles in when you've said everything—but still want to be near each other.

I love this solitude.

And his sheets.

And his bed.

"I loved your sassy mouth," he says softly. "And I thought you were so freaking gorgeous."

I furrow my brow. "You thought I was gorgeous while I was *insulting* you?"

He is so strange, ha ha.

"Absolutely. You were fearless. A little terrifying, actually."

"Terrifying?" I tease, nudging his ankle with my toe.

"Pretty, confident women are always a little intimidating, don't you think?"

I smile into the blanket. "You're so sweet."

"Thanks." He pauses. "You were exactly what I didn't know I was looking for."

I melt into the mattress. "Without prying, I really have to ask what all that nonsense was between you and Nova—the love at first sight stuff."

Gio squeezes my hand. "I thought we agreed we were going to blame the wine for her blurting that out."

"Don't deflect. I want to know."

"Fine. It wasn't about you specifically."

"I wasn't thinking it was." *But that has me wondering…*

"It wasn't about you specifically tonight. But I've been thinking about it more since you came into my life."

"Oh?"

"Yeah. I mean, I didn't really believe in that kind of thing before. Love at first sight. Soulmates. All that Hallmark love stuff."

"And now?"

"Now, I think maybe it's not so impossible. You've got me reconsidering everything."

Wow. I have no idea what to say.

I roll toward him, tucking a hand beneath my chin. "I had no idea what to say so I said I didn't believe in it. When she asked, I panicked. I didn't want to sound naive."

Silence.

"You sounded like someone who's careful about who they let in. I respect that."

"I don't know if I believe in love at first sight," I admit, voice barely above a whisper. "But I do know you gave me butterflies at Five Alarm—and when I saw you, I didn't know it was you. I thought you were just some random, good-looking guy."

"Random and good-looking," he repeats, a teasing edge to his voice. "I'll take it."

I roll my eyes, but a smile tugs at my lips. "You know what I mean."

"So—we got the kid talk and the love at first sight talk out of the way. What are the other big ones we should throw out there now that we're being all deep and honest?"

He can't see my grin. "You mean like marriage? The zombie apocalypse?"

"Sure."

"Marriage—yes, but I have to be sure. Zombies? Hard no. I'm not surviving anything if they're faster than I am and where would I even run?"

He laughs, the sound low and warm in the quiet room. "Noted. I have to save both our asses."

"Facts." Pause. "What about you? Marriage…"

"Yeah, for sure. For the right person."

My face gets even hotter, and I'm grateful he can't see me blushing in the dark.

I can't believe we're discussing this stuff. I feel like such an adult!

"How do you even know when it's the right person?"

"You just know," he says simply. "At least, that's what I've always heard."

"That's scary."

"A little," he agrees, his hand finding mine under the blanket. "But I think it's also kind of amazing." Gio pauses. "Any deal breakers besides someone being a Bruins fan?"

Ha ha. But also, true.

I think for a moment, letting his hand settle warmly over mine.

"Someone who doesn't respect boundaries. Or someone who's rude to waitstaff. That's an automatic no."

"Solid picks," he agrees. "Anyone who mistreats dogs is dead to me."

"Okay, good one!" I admit. "Even if Gio sometimes makes me question my sanity." I go quiet as I think for a few seconds. "Someone who doesn't know how to communicate, which I have to give you kudos for. You're amazing."

"That's a big one. I agree."

HIT ME WITH YOUR BEST SHOT

"Your turn. What are your deal breakers?"

"Hmm." He pretends to think, but I can hear the smile in his voice.

"Well, besides Bruins fans, obviously, I'd say someone who doesn't laugh at my jokes."

"There are women who don't laugh at your jokes?" I repeat, sounding as horrified as I feel. "That's tragic."

"Can you believe it? Crazy," he says. "But, you know, not everyone has good taste."

"Clearly."

"Exactly. So, they're out. Automatic deal breaker."

"Fair enough," I say, nodding into the dark. "What else?"

"I guess someone who doesn't respect my time. Like, if they can't handle that I've got a busy life, it's not gonna work."

"That's fair," I say softly, appreciating the honesty in his tone.

"What about you?" he asks. "Anything else you haven't told me yet?"

I think for a moment, letting the silence stretch out. "Probably someone who isn't kind. Like, I don't care how smart or funny or good-looking you are—if you're not a good person, it's a no."

"Agreed," he says, his voice low and warm. "Kindness is non-negotiable."

The mattress sinks as he rolls toward me, searching for my face in the dark, his lips finding the bridge of my nose and kissing it.

"I love spending time with you."

"I love spending time with you too," I admit, my voice barely above a whisper.

"Good," he says, his hand brushing lightly over my cheek. "Because I don't think I'm ever going to get enough of it."

I'm not sure what he means by that. His words hang between us, heavy and soft, and I feel his breath against my cheek, warm and steady.

"What do you mean?" I ask quietly, my heart thudding in my chest. "You make it sound so simple."

"Maybe it is," he says, his voice low and thoughtful. "Maybe you and I overthink things too much. Now I understand why people complicate things."

"Why?" I ask, my voice barely above a whisper.

"Because they're scared," he says simply. "Scared of how easy it could be if they'd relax and let the universe work its magic."

I stare into the darkness. "That's not how it works though. It can't always be that easy. Relationships are messy and complicated."

"Sure. Sometimes," he says. "But not always. Not every second of every day needs to be hard. If it's right, it should feel good, shouldn't it?"

I'm not certain how to put my thoughts into words.

"I guess I've just always thought love was supposed to be hard. My parents fought a lot when I was younger so that was the example. It's hard to unlearn that, you know?"

"I know," he says quietly into the dark room. "It's like hockey—you practice, you work at it, and yeah, sometimes you lose. But when you're on the right team? The wins outweigh everything else."

I let out a soft laugh, shaking my head. "Only you would compare love to hockey."

"Hey, it's a good metaphor," he says, grinning. "You've got to trust your teammates, be willing to pass the puck, and know when to take the shot."

"And what happens when your team screws up?"

He's silent for a moment. "Then you regroup, figure out what went wrong, and try again. You don't just quit because it gets hard."

I don't have a response, not one that feels big enough for the moment. So instead, I let my head rest against his shoulder, the steady rhythm of his breathing lulling me into a quiet sense of calm.

"You're right. Showing up is half the battle."

He nods, kissing the top of my head.

The simple gesture sends a wave of warmth through me, and I close my eyes.

Gio is such a contradiction. Outwardly, he's everything you'd expect a big jock to be—confident, a little cocky, with a grin that could charm anyone in the room. But moments like this? They reveal something so much deeper.

He's introspective. Polite, but not *too* polite.

Funny.

Considerate. Kind.

Handsome, *obviously*–but so much more.

Thoughtful in ways that constantly surprise me. Sensitive in a way that doesn't feel forced or performative, *but real*.

It's strange, because when I watched him on television, went to his games and followed him on social media, I thought I had him figured out: another athlete with a God complex, a guy who cared more about his stats and image than anything else.

Piece by piece, he's shown me the parts of himself that don't fit that narrative.

The way he talks about his sister and his teammates is with so much care and affection—and the effort he's making to show me he's interested in me as a person, and not just a casual bang...

Gio is the guy willing to admit when he's scared, who wants to know what makes me tick—not just on the surface, but the things that make me *me*.

"You're quiet," he murmurs, his voice low and soft in the dark. "Are you falling asleep on me?"

"Not yet," I whisper. "Just thinking."

"About what?"

I hesitate, wondering how much I should share.

"About you," I admit. "How you're not what I expected."

"*Good* different or bad different?" he asks, his tone teasing but with curiosity.

"Good different," I say quickly, feeling my cheeks warm even though he can't see me. "You're more than what I expected."

"More, huh?" I can hear him grinning. "I like the sound of that."

I laugh, nudging him with my shoulder. "Don't let it go to your head."

"No promises," he says, chuckling. "My head is already super big."

I get the innuendo about his dick and ignore it.

"I noticed," I say dryly, rolling my eyes even though he can't see it.

"It must be exhausting carrying all that ego around."

"It's a burden," he agrees, his voice dripping with mock seriousness. "But someone's gotta do it." Gio pauses a beat. "On a scale of one to ten, how into me are you?"

Whoa. "Where did that question come from?"

"Just asking," he says casually, but I can hear the smirk in his voice. "It's science based."

"Science based?" I repeat, laughing softly.

"Yep. Completely unbiased research," he says. "So? One to ten."

"Hmm—probably a solid six?" I tease.

"A six?" he exclaims loudly, voice filling the room. He is so offended. "That's barely above average!"

I try not to laugh. "What's *my* score?"

"Oh, that's easy," he says without missing a beat. "A twelve."

Somehow I knew he was going to say that.

I squeeze his hand. "I was messing with you." Obviously. "I'd give you an eleven."

He is the most loveable, sweetest guy I've ever dated and it's only been two weeks.

"An eleven? Not even a twelve, like you?"

I laugh softly, shaking my head even though he can't see me. "You have to leave room for improvement."

"Oh, so this is a motivational thing? Got it."

"Exactly." I yawn. "Consider it an incentive to keep being sweet to me."

I squeeze his hand again, my heart swelling at how easy this feels—how easy *he* feels. Somehow he has managed to completely dismantle every wall I've built around myself.

"You're kind of the best," I admit with a quiet whisper as if I'm admitting it to myself.

"You're the best," he murmurs.

I smile, my fingers tracing small patterns against his palm. "You don't have to say that just because I called *you* the best."

"I mean it."

I tilt my head slightly to look up at him, even though the room is dark and I can't make out his expression. "You're really good at this whole relationship thing."

"Thanks," he says, his tone teasing. "I'm trying."

"No, seriously," I say, my voice softening. "You're like—the best communicator I've ever met."

"And you're making it hard not to fall for you."

My breath catches, my chest tightening in the best possible way.

I'm not sure what I was expecting him to say, but it wasn't *that*.

I don't know how to respond, so instead, I let him pull me closer, wrapping me in his arms like he's afraid to let go. His warmth surrounds me, and I let myself sink into it, my head resting against his chest.

"Is that okay?" he asks softly, breaking the silence. "That I'm falling?"

I press my cheek against him, his heartbeat steady and sure beneath my ear.

"Yeah," I whisper, my voice barely audible. "Of course it's okay."

I feel his lips press lightly against the top of my head, a gesture so sweet it makes my chest ache. "You scare me a little," he admits quietly.

"Me?" I ask, tilting my head to look up at him again, even though I can't see his face.

"Yeah," he says, his fingers lightly tracing patterns on my back. "You make me want things I didn't think I'd want this soon." He doesn't say what those things are.

We fall into a comfortable silence after that, the kind that feels full even though no words are spoken. His hand moves to tangle with mine again, our fingers lacing together under the blanket. It's such a simple thing, but it makes me feel grounded—safe.

"You're the easiest person to be around," I murmur, almost to myself.

"So are you," Gio replies, squeezing my hand.

I don't know how long we lay there like that, wrapped up in each other, but my body starts to relax, the weight of the day slipping away. My eyelids grow heavy, my mind finally quiet for the first time in what feels like forever.

"I think I could get used to this," I whisper sleepily, my voice fading.

"Me too," he says, his words soft and full of promise.

The last thing I feel before sleep takes me is the gentle squeeze of his hand, his thumb brushing lightly against mine, as if to say, *I'm here.*

23

Gio: Should we be one of those couples that sexts?

Austin: Do you WANT to be one of those couples that sexts...?

Gio: I wouldn't be opposed to it.

Austin: Of course you wouldn't—you're the one who brought it up!

Gio: I have a quick break before I have to meet with the assistant coach, Tyler, figured it couldn't hurt to ask.

Austin: I mean. I don't think I'd be good at sexting but give it your best shot.

Gio: So that's a yes?

Austin: I don't think most people have a long discussion about texting sexy-time. I think they just DO it. This is cracking me up.

Gio: Well I don't want to offend you by sending you a mirror selfie or by saying something offensive, like 'Thinking bout those sweet tits right now'

Austin: Fair enough.

Austin: Are you asking for a preview?

Gio: Let's call it research.

Austin: Oh right—I know how much you LOVE science.

Austin: "You're so hot, babe."

Austin: There. How was that?

Gio: That's how my grandpa talks dirty.

Austin: How would YOU know? Ha ha.

Gio: Let me show you how it's done.

Austin: Oh, this outta be good...

Gio: If you were there in your office right now, I'd push you up against the wall, kiss you until you couldn't think straight, and hike your skirt up. Then I would...

Austin: ...then you would...???

Gio: That's it.

Austin: That can't be it!

Gio: Nah. Don't want to scare you off.

Austin: OMG.

Austin: You can't just leave me hanging like that.

HIT ME WITH YOUR BEST SHOT

Gio: Damn right I can. That's how you build suspense.

Austin: You asshole.

Gio: LOL

Austin: You know—I didn't wear panties to work today...

Gio: Is that so?

Austin: Nope. Was hoping you'd drop in on me today and...

Gio: ...

Gio: AND?????

Austin: That's it. Don't want to scare you off.

Gio: OMFG.

Austin: LOL I am laughing so hard right now.

Gio: You're mean.

Austin: Or am I hilarious?

Gio: Yes.

Austin: Admit it—you kind of love it.

Gio: I mean, yeah, but you can't just stop there. What am I supposed to do with that information?

Austin: Suffer, I guess?

Gio: Wow. You're unbelievable.

Austin: You knew this when you started dating me.

Gio: Yeah, but I didn't realize you'd be this good at torture.

Austin: You're welcome.

Gio: I'm coming by after practice.

Austin: Oh, are you now?

Gio: Tell little Gio to stay the fuck out of my way.

Austin: You still have to take him on a walk so he can bond with you.

Gio: Oh jeez—stop reminding me. Maybe after I fuck you against your living window.

Austin: Oooooo

Gio: Bare ass pressed against the glass. Mmmm...

Austin: Oh, you're confident today

Gio: I'm full of adrenaline—just got done working out.

Austin: Alright. Keep talking.

Gio: Fine. Picture this: your bare ass pressed against the glass, my hands on your hips, and your moans echoing through the room.

Austin: Uh huh...

Austin: Then what?

Gio: Then I'd turn you around, lift you up, and make sure the neighbors in the other building get a full show.

Austin: My neighbors would probably call the cops.

HIT ME WITH YOUR BEST SHOT

Gio: Not my problem.

Gio: It's always been my fantasy to fuck in a spot where people can see but unable to identify me.

Austin: Oh. Bit of a exhibitionist fetish have you? You've got my full attention....

Gio: Enough to leave work early?

Austin: Not a chance.

Gio: My mouth on your neck, my hands sliding down your waist, gripping your hips. Every move designed to make you beg for more...

Austin: I don't beg.

Gio: Yes you do.

Austin: Fine, I do. But so do you.

Gio: I like begging. It gives you the false sense of being in control.

Austin: I swear, the ego on you is unreal.

Gio: Says the woman who was practically drooling watching me in the goal box last night.

Austin: I wasn't drooling.

Gio: Sure you weren't.

Austin: Fine, maybe I was a little. You're hard to ignore when you're in your zone.

Gio: Go on. Daddy is listening.

Gio: Tell me more about how hot I looked out there.

Austin: So fucking hot...

> Austin: I was squirming in my seat and couldn't wait to get back to your place and tear your clothes off.

> Gio: Knowing I got you all worked up watching me play is enough to fuel my ego for days.

> Austin: Days, huh? You might want to pace yourself.

> Gio: Why? I've got plenty of stamina.

> Austin: Oh, I'm aware.

> Gio: Good. Coz I plan on showing you exactly how much I've got left…

> Austin: Say more.

> Gio: Imagine this—you walk through the door, and I'm already waiting for you. I don't even let you set your stuff down before I've got you pressed against the wall.

> Austin: I'm listening…

> Gio: My hands in your hair, your legs wrapped around my waist. I kiss you like I've been starving for it all day.

> Austin: You're off to a strong start.

> Gio: I carry you to the couch, strip off whatever you're wearing, and make sure you forget every stressful thing that happened today.

> Austin: What if I don't want it on the couch?

> Gio: Then I take you wherever you want. Bed, kitchen counter, shower…

> Austin: Shower. Now there's an idea.

HIT ME WITH YOUR BEST SHOT

Gio: Stop it.

Austin: Stop what?

Gio: You, soaking wet? I just got hard.

Austin: YOU ARE AT WORK.

Gio: What are you saying—I can't get hard at work?

Austin: I didn't make you think about me in the shower.

Gio: You planted the idea and now I won't be able to stop thinking about it.

Austin: Well I have office hours today and you have to meet with Tyler.

Gio: When are your office hours?

Austin: Technically they're right now.

Gio: I'm skipping Tyler. I'm dirty and need a shower.

Austin: LOL you are not dirty.

Gio: I AM.

Austin: You're not skipping Tyler.

Gio: Watch me.

Austin: Gio.

Gio: Austin. Meet me at my place in 40 minutes.

Austin: This feels so wrong. I never skipped school a day in my life.

Gio: Okay nerd.

Gio: Tell me you don't want the wettest, hottest orgasm of your life. From behind.

Austin: From behind you say?

Gio: I have that lovely tile bench in there…and 8 jets…

Austin: 8???????

Gio: Have I not mentioned that?

Austin: NO. YOU FAILED TO MENTION YOUR SPA SHOWER.

Gio: My bad. I thought it was implied when I said I wanted to take you in the shower.

Austin: This is information I could have used earlier to make an informed decision.

Gio: So what's the consensus?

Austin: If I'm skipping work, this better be worth it.

Gio: ABSOLUTELY FUCK YES THIS WILL BE WORTH IT.

Austin: You're ruining my resolve.

Gio: I'll worship at your feet while the water gets your body slippery—before I make you scream

Austin: I'm packing up my shit.

Gio: Hurry

Austin: I'm not speeding for you. I can probably be there in 25.

HIT ME WITH YOUR BEST SHOT

Gio: 24 minutes and 59 seconds too long.

Austin: Don't make me regret this.

Gio: Get ready for the best shower of your life.

24
gio

The second the door shuts behind us, it's game on. Austin's hands are already tugging at my hoodie, her fingers slipping beneath the hem to find bare skin. I yank it over my head and toss it somewhere—I don't care where. She's laughing, breathless, as I cup her face and kiss her, backing her toward the hall.

"Impatient much?" she teases against my lips, but her hands betray her, already working at the button of my jeans.

"You started this," I growl, nipping at her bottom lip before dragging my mouth down to her neck. She lets out a soft moan, her nails scraping lightly down my chest as my jeans hit the floor.

"That is a lie—you did when you started sexting me."

My fingers are on the zipper of her conservative pencil skirt, and she's kicking off her heels, the clatter against the hardwood mingling with the sound of our heavy breathing.

By the time we make it to the bathroom, there's a trail of clothes leading back to the door—a chaotic breadcrumb trail we'll probably trip over later.

Not that I'm thinking about that right now.

Who gives a shit about the mess?

Austin stands in front of me in her lace bra and panties, cheeks flushed and hair slightly mussed as she spins around. I catch the soft gasp she tries to stifle when she sees the stone-enclosed spa shower with its slate tile, jets on every wall, and the wide bench in the corner.

A rainfall showerhead is mounted in the center.

"Holy smokes, you weren't kidding," she says, turning back to me. "How did I not notice this?"

"Because," I say, my hands finding her hips. "You've never showered here before."

My dick strains against her ass crack, body presses against hers, and I feel the heat between us ignite.

My lips find the curve of her shoulder, trailing kisses along her bare skin, and her soft sigh is all the encouragement I need.

I step around her slowly, letting my fingers brush her waist as I move. Her eyes follow my every movement, dark with anticipation, as I reach for the sleek faucet handles. One twist, then another, and the shower bursts to life.

Water cascades from the showerhead in the ceiling, its sound echoing softly in the spacious enclosure.

Steam begins to rise, curling around us like an invitation, and the room grows warmer by the second.

Sexy.

As.

Fuck.

Her lips curl into a smirk; there's no mistaking the spark in her eyes. "I'm so ready for this."

Off come her panties.

Off comes her bra.

Honestly, part of me wouldn't have minded seeing those delicate pieces of lace clinging to her skin, soaked and plastered to her curves. But I'm not going to complain about her standing there completely naked, water droplets already beginning to kiss her bare body.

Her confidence is intoxicating, the way she stands there unabashed, owning every inch of herself.

My hands itch to touch her, to explore every curve, every line, but for a moment, all I can do is take her in.

"You're staring," she says.

"You're worth staring *at*," I reply, my voice rougher than I intended.

Dick.

So.

Hard.

She doesn't look away, her eyes locked with mine as her fingers trail down my chest. The featherlight touch sends a shiver through me despite the heat.

And then her hands find the waistband of my boxers.

"Your turn," she murmurs.

In one swift motion, the last barrier between us is gone, and the cool air hits my skin before the heat of her body replaces it.

"Happy now?" I ask, stepping forward and closing the distance between us completely.

Her smirk is the only answer I get before I press my lips to hers and push her toward the stream of water, stealing whatever witty remark was about to leave her mouth.

"Beyond."

Austin gasps as the first spray of hot water hits her skin, her head tilting back, hair slicking against her shoulders as water trails down her body. Every drop seems to highlight her curves, making her glow in the dim light of the bathroom.

So fucking sexy.

My fantasies come to life.

"Mmm," she mutters, spinning slowly under the water, taking it all in. "This is insane."

The water sprays around us, steam rising, but nothing feels as hot as the way she melts into me. My hands explore her wet skin, her body fitting against mine like it was made to.

Every sigh, every touch feels amplified by the water

cascading around us, and I can't help but think bailing on Tyler was the best decision I've made all week.

He was pissed, but he'll get over it.

"This feels amazing," Austin moans. "Imagine how good it feels when it's freezing outside."

I already know how it feels when it's freezing out.

Like heaven.

She points to the handheld showerhead resting in its cradle on the wall.

"What does this one do?"

I grin. We both know what the handheld one can do.

"Shower toy."

Her brow arches, curiosity dancing in her expression as I unhook it and adjust the settings. Water sprays lightly from the nozzle, and I guide it across her shoulder, letting the warm stream trace a path down her arm.

"You could get creative with this," I say, my voice low and teasing.

She bites down on her bottom lip, gaze locking with mine.

"Show me."

Tilting the showerhead, I trail it down her stomach, the spray splashing gently against her skin. Her breath catches, her body leaning back against me as I move the showerhead lower, closer to the apex of her thighs.

"This is strictly scientific, right?"

"Of course," I murmur, shifting the nozzle slightly so the water teases the inside of her thigh. "Shower math. Head plus pussy equals—"

Her gasp is audible, her hips tilting instinctively toward the sensation.

"Science my ass," she mutters, breath hitching in excitement.

I chuckle, the sound reverberating against her skin as I slowly move the stream of water upward. The warmth caresses her in a way that makes her legs tremble, and her grip on my hair tightens.

"Mmm, Gio," she whispers. "I like that."

"I've got you."

Her head falls back against the tile, her chest rising and falling with shallow breaths as the handheld jet does its work. I alternate between light sprays and more focused streams, watching the way her body responds to every shift.

Eventually Austin grabs my wrist, pulling the showerhead away, her breath coming in short gasps. "Okay, okay," she says, her voice trembling. "I can't feel my legs."

I lean down.

Slide my hands over her hips, around to her ass, bracing myself firm and steady as I heft her up. Press her against the wall and demand, "Put your legs around my waist."

"You're not going to drop me, are you?" she teases again, her voice softer this time, her lips brushing against mine with each word. "It's slippery."

I chuckle, leaning in close until my lips brush her ear. "I'm insulted you think I'd drop you. Do you have any idea how strong my legs are?"

Fit and thick like a motherfucker.

The heat of the water cascades over us as I press her gently against the wall, my hands firm but careful as I support her weight.

I grip her tighter, the pressure of her body fitting so perfectly against mine with her thighs locked around my waist. Her arms loop around my shoulders, nails lightly grazing my back, sending little jolts of electricity down my spine.

"I wasn't questioning your strength," she murmurs, her lips brushing my jawline. "Just concerned about the physics of this situation."

I laugh, the sound deep and rumbling in my chest as I lean in to kiss her neck. "Physics is on our side, babe. You're not going anywhere."

Her breath hitches as I press my hips against her, the slickness of the water only making the contact between us more tantalizing. Her hands tighten in my hair, pulling slightly, and I groan in response, tilting my head to give her more access.

"You're good at this," she teases, her voice shaky but playful.

"Good at what?"

"Making me forget to be scared."

I pull back just enough to meet her eyes, water dripping between us. "That's because you trust me, babe."

Her lips part, but no words come out. Instead, she pulls me closer, her mouth finding mine in a kiss so deep it leaves me breathless. The heat of the shower is nothing compared to the fire building between us, each kiss more urgent, more consuming.

I turn, the slick tiles steady beneath my feet as I move toward the bench, lowering myself onto it with her still wrapped around me.

Straddling my lap, she smirks, her wet hair clinging to her shoulders.

"This feels safer," Austin jokes, her tone light. Relieved.

"Safer?" I echo, sliding my hands up her thighs and letting them rest on her rib cage, thumbs stroking her side-boob. "You think sitting on top of me is safer?"

"Well, I don't have to worry about you *dropping* me now."

Our mouths fuse together.

She melts into me, her hands cupping my jaw as she kisses me like she's claiming every part of me.

The heat builds between us, intensifying with every touch, every kiss, every soft gasp that escapes her lips as she lifts her ass...lines herself up with my rock hard cock...seats herself on top of me, completely impaled.

I groan.

Tilt my head back against the wall.

"This isn't as easy as it looks," Austin complains. "I don't think I'm flexible enough for this."

I laugh, adjusting my hips.

Thrusting up, doing most of the work.

"Just be still then and relax. I'll do the work."

All of it.

I grip her hips tightly, guiding her rhythm, feeling every inch of her as I move; Austin clings to my shoulders, nails digging into my skin, a perfect mix of pleasure and desperation in her movements.

The bench beneath me feels solid, but it's her—the heat of her body, the way I fit inside her—that grounds me.

She throws her head back, exposing her neck, and I lean forward, kissing the curve of her throat. "You feel incredible," I murmur against her skin. "Every part of you. You're so—"

"Stop talking," she interrupts, her fingers threading through my hair, pulling me closer. "Just stop talking and fuck me."

Yes, ma'am.

"I fucking love it when you boss me around."

She doesn't respond with words—just a sound, half-moan, half-whimper, that spurs me on. I press my back against the wall, leveraging my hips to meet hers, my hands sliding from her waist to the curve of her ass, guiding her movements.

Austin's breath catches and her rhythm falters for a moment. "I—oh G-God," she stammers, with a trembling stutter.

"Come for me, babe," I growl out a demand, driving into her harder, deeper, pulling her closer until her entire body tenses in my arms.

Fuck yeah….

The loud echo of her orgasm vibrates off the tile walls, her fingers raking up the back of my neck as she unravels around me. The sight of her like this—wet tits, hard nipples, water dripping all over her body—sends me over the edge.

My grip tightens, and I thrust inside her one last time, groaning as the release takes me, the intensity stealing my breath.

For a moment, the only sound is the water cascading around us, and the heavy, shared rhythm of our breathing. She slumps forward, resting her forehead against my shoulder, her body trembling slightly.

"I am so lucky you're an athlete. Few men have this kind of stamina."

I nod.

Smack her ass.

As the heat of the moment subsides, Austin lets out a small laugh, her breath warm against my neck. "We're going to end up pruned if we stay like this much longer."

I grin, running a hand up her back and gently nudging her to sit upright. "Alright, let's make good use of this shower as it was intended."

Carefully, I help her off my lap, holding her steady as her feet find the tile. She glances at me, her cheeks flushed, water glistening on her skin, and I swear I've never seen her look more beautiful.

"Pass me the body wash," she says, her tone light and teasing as she scans the nooks built into the tile interior. "I have to say, for a dude you have a great selection."

I grab the bottle from the shelf and squeeze some of the gel into my palm before handing it to her, lathering it between my hands. The cherry almond scent fills the steam-filled air as I start with her shoulders, hands gliding over her skin in slow, deliberate movements.

"This feels suspiciously like a massage," she murmurs, tilting her head to the side to give me better access.

"Yup." My thumbs dig gently into the muscles along her neck, kneading gently.

Austin's shoulders relax under my touch, and a low hum escapes her lips.

She raises her arms above her head, and I don't hesitate. My hands move lower, running over her chest, fingers splaying as I spread the foam across her curves. My hands glide over her tits, firm and full, taking my time as the water rinses the suds away, only for me to lather her up again.

Her skin is impossibly slippery under my palms.

I smirk, sliding my hands down her sides, tracing the curve of her waist, before stepping back. "Turn around."

She obeys, wet hair clinging to her back, a dark, gleaming waterfall that I can't help but reach for. I gather it up in one hand and drape it over her shoulder, exposing the elegant line of her spine.

Lathering my hands—this time with shampoo—I work the gel into her hair, fingers threading through the thick strands as I massage her scalp.

She sighs, leaning slightly into my touch.

Closes her eyes.

"This is nice," she says softly, voice almost drowned out by the rhythm of the water.

"Yeah," I agree, my voice low. "It is."

She shifts slightly, glancing at me over her shoulder, her lips curling into a small, content smile.

"Your turn," she says suddenly, turning to face me, her hands now reaching for the same bottle of body wash. "Don't move."

Her hands find my chest, gliding over the hard planes with deliberate precision. Her touch is firm but teasing, and when her fingers skim down to my stomach, she bites her lip, suppressing a grin.

"I could lick these abs." Her hands dip lower as her palms smooth over my skin, over my stomach.

I lift my arms. "Be my guest."

Flattery will get you everywhere.

And everything.

Her hands slide lower, and my breath catches. She's thorough, taking her time with each stroke, each movement of her hands a tantalizing mix of playful and seductive.

"Careful," I warn, my voice rough.

Dick tingling.

Blood rushing.

HIT ME WITH YOUR BEST SHOT

We just had sex, but I watch as my cock stiffens again.
Watch as Austin drops to her knees…

25
austin

"You look like a woman in love."

Dolly is at the end of my couch, stroking Gio as he sits on her lap, lounging like a tiny emperor on his throne.

"Do I?" I ask, sinking into the cushions and tucking my feet under me.

"Yes. You're glowing."

Am I?

I press my hands to my face and smile, but the second I feel how warm my cheeks are, I drop them, trying to downplay it. "I think it's just the lighting in here."

"Or maybe you've had too much wine."

That can't be it because I haven't had any. I glance down at the wine glass sitting on the coffee table in front of me, the deep red liquid untouched.

None of it has passed my lips.

"I love the two of you together." My best friend goes on. "It's so fucking great seeing you happy—it's about damn time."

A warmth spreads through my chest, replacing the slight embarrassment with a feeling I can't quite name. "Thanks, D. That means a lot."

She sighs dramatically, leaning her head back against the couch. "Men suck."

And just like that, the moment is over. I laugh, shaking my head at her ability to switch gears so quickly. "Not all men suck."

"Most men suck," she amends, lifting her head to glare at me. "Gio is clearly an exception. But the rest of them? Bottom of the barrel."

I tilt my head, considering her words. She's not wrong—Dolly has had her fair share of disastrous dates and flaky guys.

"You know," I say slowly, "I seriously have to introduce you to Nova. The pair of you are basically the same person. Single, looking, and totally over dating apps."

Her eyes light up. "The sister, Nova?"

"Yep. She's hilarious, and honestly, you'd love her. She's not afraid to call people out on their bullshit, and she's got this infectious energy. Plus, she's a great drinking buddy."

I make a mental note to text Nova later. The idea of introducing the two of them feels like one of those things that could either be brilliant or an absolute disaster—there's no in-between.

Not that I want Dolly to replace me with Gio's sister, but the more the merrier—and I haven't been giving her as much of my time since he and I started dating. And sleeping together. And all the things...

"Speaking of modern dating," Dolly continues, her tone turning more serious, "how's it going with Gio? I mean, really going. Any red flags I should be concerned about?"

I shake my head. "No red flags. Honestly, it's kind of surreal how easy it feels with him. Like, I keep waiting for the other shoe to drop, but it hasn't."

"Good." She nods, her expression softening again. "You deserve someone who makes it easy. Relationships shouldn't feel like a constant uphill battle."

"I think I might actually be in love with him," I blurt out before I can stop myself.

Dolly freezes, her hand hovering mid-scratch on Gio's back.

"Holy shit, Austin. Say that again."

"I said I think I might be in love with him." I repeat it slower this time, the weight of the words settling over me. "Is that crazy? It feels crazy."

"No, it's not crazy," she says quickly, her eyes wide. "It's amazing."

I pick at the blanket folded across my lap and fail to meet Dolly's eyes.

"What's that look?"

My head shakes. "Nothing."

Dolly's eyes narrow, her no-nonsense expression settling in. "Austin," she says firmly. "I've known you too long for that 'it's nothing' bullshit. Spill."

Gio shifts in her lap, grunting softly, but even he seems to be waiting for my response.

I sigh, my shoulders sagging under the weight of what I've been holding in.

"I'm sure it's nothing," I repeat, softer this time, finally glancing up to meet her gaze. "But I haven't gotten my period yet."

The words hang in the air, heavy and terrifying, and for a moment, Dolly stares at me, her mouth slightly open.

"You mean you're late?"

I nod, a lump forming in my throat. "Yeah. By a few days."

Her eyes widen. "Austin! Why are you just now saying something?"

"Cause! There are no other symptoms. And why would I be pregnant, we've only had sex like…" I try to add up all the times we've had sex in my head, but the math isn't mathing.

"*Girl*." She stares at me like I'm an idiot. "Have you taken a test?"

I shake my head quickly. "No. I mean, it's probably just stress or something, right? I've been busy with work and… Gio." My voice falters at his name, and I grip the blanket tighter.

HIT ME WITH YOUR BEST SHOT

Dolly's expression softens, but her concern doesn't fade. "Okay, first of all, stressing isn't going to help. Second, it might be nothing—but it also might *not* be nothing, so you need to know for sure. Have you told him?"

My stomach twists at the thought.

"No," I confess. "I don't even know how to bring it up. It's just a missed period? It happens, right? So what if I say something and that makes things awkward and they didn't have to be?"

Dolly sets Gio the dog gently on the floor and slides closer to me on the couch.

"Listen to me," she says, her voice steady and calm. "You're not doing this alone, okay? Whatever happens, we'll figure it out."

Gio has never given me a reason to doubt him—if anything, he's shown me time and time again that he's solid, dependable, and, most importantly, all in. But this feels different.

This is serious!

"What if he's not ready for something like this?" I ask, my voice barely audible.

Dolly squeezes my shoulder. "Then he'll have to get ready. That's what grown-ups do. And from everything you've told me about him, I think he'll step up."

I take a deep breath, trying to calm the storm of emotions swirling inside me.

"I'll tell him. *After* I take a test."

"But you won't know until you're sure," Dolly says, her tone firm but kind. "Do you have a test laying around?"

I blink at her. "*No*, why would I just have pregnancy tests laying around?"

"Uh—cause I do? Just in case?" Dolly whips out her phone with determination. "I'll DoorDash us some."

"You can DoorDash pregnancy tests?" I ask, eyebrows shooting up.

"You can DoorDash pretty much anything," she replies, her

thumbs flying across the screen. "This is what convenience is all about, babe."

I bite my lip, watching her with a mix of gratitude and nerves as she scrolls through the app. "I feel so weird about this. Like, what if the driver judges me?"

Dolly snorts. "Trust me, they've seen weirder. Besides, they don't know you. For all they know, I'm the one taking the test." She flashes me a cheeky grin before holding up her phone. "Okay, I've got three different brands in the cart. Extra sensitive, digital, and one of those fancy ones that tells you how many weeks along you are. Anything else?"

"More snacks?"

She grins. "Oh look at you, pregnancy munchies already."

I'm not amused. "That's not funny."

"Sorry."

Forty-five minutes later, and Dolly springs to her feet like it's Christmas morning.

"I'll get it!" she announces, dashing toward the door. Gio barks excitedly, spinning in circles as if he knows something monumental is happening.

I sit frozen on the couch, my stomach churning as the reality of the situation sets in. Pregnancy tests. Three of them. My entire future could change with one tiny little plastic stick. My hands are clammy, and I rub them on the blanket draped across my lap, trying to ground myself.

Dolly returns triumphantly, holding up the discreet brown paper bag like it's a trophy.

"Voilà! Our DoorDash hero didn't bat an eye. Now," she says, dropping the bag onto the coffee table. "Let's get down to business."

I stare at the bag as if it might bite me.

"I don't know if I can do this."

Correction: I don't want to do this.

I'm scared shitless.

Dolly sits beside me, her tone gentle but firm. "You can. Whatever the result is, we'll deal with it. Together. You're not alone, okay?"

I nod, swallowing hard. "I know."

She pulls out the tests one by one, lining them up on the coffee table like some sort of bizarre science experiment. "Alright, we've got options. The digital one is probably the easiest—no deciphering faint lines. Or we can go old school with this one. Your call."

I hesitate, staring at the tests. My voice feels distant when I finally speak. "The digital one, I guess."

"Good choice," she says, tearing open the box with precision. "Go do your thing, and don't overthink it. It's just pee."

"Just pee," I echo, though it feels like so much more than that. My legs feel wobbly as I stand, and I clutch the test in one hand like it's a ticking time bomb.

Dolly gives me an encouraging smile. "You've got this."

The bathroom feels like the smallest, quietest room in the world as I close the door behind me. The instructions on the box are straightforward, but my hands shake as I follow them: Pee on the stick, try not to make a mess, set the test on the counter when I'm done.

Now comes the hard part: waiting.

I pace the tiny space, my mind racing with possibilities.

What if it's positive?

What if it's negative?

My stomach flips as I glance at the timer on my phone, the seconds ticking down like an ominous drumbeat.

Finally, the timer goes off and I freeze, my heart pounding. For a moment, I can't bring myself to look. What if this changes everything?

A knock on the door startles me. "You okay in there?"

I take a deep breath and open the door, holding the test out to her without looking at it. "You check."

Her eyes widen. "Are you sure?"

I nod, my voice barely a whisper. "I can't."

She takes the test gingerly, her expression unreadable as she glances down. Seconds feel like hours as I search her face for any clue. Then she looks up at me, her lips parting as if to speak.

"Well?" I ask, my voice cracking.

"It's…" She pauses, her expression softening. "Austin, it's positive."

When the room tilts, I grip the doorframe to steady myself.

I feel like I'm going to pass out.

Faint.

Literally topple over.

Dolly is at my side in an instant, wrapping me in a hug. "It's okay—you can take another one to be sure."

I nod, filling with dread.

Dolly hands me another small, white box, her hands trembling enough that I notice. I take the second test, removing the plastic stick from its plastic wrapper.

"It's going to be fine," Dolly says softly, but her voice wavers, betraying her own uncertainty.

I force myself to breathe, even though my chest feels tight. The walls seem closer, the air thicker. I lean over the sink for a moment, gripping its edge, trying to ground myself.

You can do this.

Just take the test.

I pee on another stick.

Wait.

My heart is pounding so hard it feels like it's trying to climb up my throat. I pick up the test and force myself to look at the screen.

The digital screen says one word: PREGNANT

Again.

Dolly lingers in the doorway.

I hold up the test wordlessly; her eyes dart to it, and then to my face. She doesn't say anything at first, but then she reaches for my hand, threading her fingers through mine.

"It's real," I say, my voice breaking on the last word. "This is happening."

Dolly exhales shakily and nods, a faint smile flickering on her lips before fading. "We'll figure it out," she says, squeezing my hand.

"It's going to be okay," she tells me confidently. "You're going to be okay. Gio is going to be okay."

Tears prick my eyes as I nod against her shoulder, the weight of the news settling over me.

"What am I going to tell him?" I croak out. "Oh my God, Dolly—what if he thinks I'm trapping him for money?"

"He's not going to think you're trapping him. He slept with you *clearly* without protection." Her lips purse. "It's as much his responsibility as yours."

My mind goes back to the day he came to my apartment, unannounced, and we had sex on the table in my entryway.

And the time we banged in the shower with no condom.

Still. Nothing is foolproof.

"Hey." Dolly's hand squeezes my shoulder. "Do you want to celebrate with ice cream or cry into it?"

I laugh, the sound shaky but real. "Both?"

This is kind of a nightmare.

I can't eat.

Can't sleep.

The next morning, after Dolly has gone because she had to go to work—I act weird when Gio texts, unable to be my normal, upbeat self.

> Gio: Everything okay babe?

I stare at his message, stomach curling.

I press a hand there.

> Austin: Yeah, just tired. Long day.

I hate myself for lying, but what am I supposed to do? Spill my guts and admit the truth? That I'm not okay, that my thoughts are tangled in knots, that I don't even know how to explain this overwhelming unease?

I have to figure this out before I self-sabotage.

> Gio: Are you sure? You seem off.

Of course I seem off!

I'M PREGNANT!

I let out a shaky breath. How does he always know? It's like he has a sixth sense for when I'm not being completely honest. My fingers hover over the keyboard, but I can't type anything. What do I even say?

Instead, I toss the phone again and flop backward on the bed, staring up at the ceiling. The faint smell of Dolly's vanilla-scented perfume lingers in the air. I miss her already—her calm presence, her ability to make even the worst situations feel manageable.

Another buzz.

I groan and pick up my phone.

> Gio: I can come over if you need me.

My chest tightens.

He would drop everything he's doing to come to my place.

The idea of seeing him now—having to look him in the eye and pretend everything is hunky-dory feels unbearable. But so does pushing him away. I type out a quick reply before I can overthink it:

> Austin: Just need some time to myself.

Tears sting my eyes as I read his words. He's being so understanding, so patient, and it makes me feel even worse for keeping this from him.

I clutch the phone to my chest and close my eyes, letting the tears spill over.

I need to tell him—OBVIOUSLY.

I can't keep this to myself for long, I don't have it in me to keep secrets. And I can't lie to him.

But how do you tell the person you're just learning to love that everything is about to change?

26
gio

I've been traveling for the past two games, both back-to-back WINS.

The guys are hyped, Coach is finally *not* up my asshole every five minutes, and our backup goalie stopped crying in the locker room after practice. Life is good.

Or it should be.

I'm crammed into the middle seat of the plane—because apparently, being hockey players doesn't warrant first-class treatment unless you're the Coach—which is fine because I'm preoccupied anyway.

I can't stop thinking about Austin.

The teammate next to me has been snoring like a chainsaw, and the guy on the *other* side keeps elbowing me for clues because he's working on a Wordle but all I can focus on is her last text.

> **Austin:** Just need some time to myself.

Time to herself?

We only see one another a few times a week!

Tops!

In fact, I would kill to see her everyday.

I'm totally hard for her, twenty-three hours of the day.

Don't know if it's something I did or she's just being stubborn, but she's been dodging my FaceTime calls. Not to mention, her messages have been lacking those cute little emojis she sneaks into her messages.

Something is definitely up.

The plane lands, and I practically sprint to baggage claim, which is pointless because my bag is *always* the last one off the carousel. I stand watching my teammates grab their duffles and leave, while I'm stuck waiting for my poor, beat-up bag to tumble out like a drunk toddler.

By the time I get to my car, it's late, and I'm starving.

I contemplate hitting up a drive-thru but decide against it. My nutritionist would strangle me if I showed up to practice tomorrow smelling like a bacon cheeseburger and large fries, so instead, I scrounge around my center console and unearth a protein bar.

Gnaw on it as if it's the best meal I've had all week.

I debate going home.

I should.

I'm beat.

Sore.

Tired.

Glance at the clock in my truck: ten after ten PM.

Just need some time to myself.

Her message plays on a loop in my brain and before I can think better of it, I'm hanging a right instead of turning onto my street. Within a few short minutes I'm pulling into the parking garage in Austin's complex. Search for a spot—one where my truck will fit—and cut the engine.

Dropping by unannounced has never been my thing, but I'm feeling neglected and for all that talk she's done about good communication, hers sucks right now.

Something is wrong and I want to know what that something is.

The elevator dings as I step inside, and I hit the button for her floor. The ride up feels longer than it should, and I spend the entire time rehearing in my head what I'll say. *Hey, passing by... thought I'd check in... totally not because I'm spiraling and imagining every worst-case scenario possible.*

Are you breaking up with me?

By the time the doors slide open, my palms are sweating.

I wipe them on my jeans and make my way down the hall, stopping in front of her door.

I hesitate a moment, wondering if this is a terrible idea. But then I hear her voice in my head: *I love the way you communicate. More men should be like you...*

Yeah, well—that works both ways, doesn't it?

I knock twice and step back.

Stuff my hands in my pockets.

Bounce on the balls of my feet, anxious.

The dog barks; it's a sharp bark erupting on the other side of the door—one of those small-dog yaps that sounds more like an alarm system than a greeting.

There's a pause, followed by shuffling on the other side of the door. Her hair's up in a messy bun, and she's clutching Gio, the dog, in one arm like he's her tiny bodyguard.

His ridiculous fur mohawk bristles, and he stares me down with his wide, slightly unhinged eyes.

"Gio?" Her eyebrows shoot up in surprise. "What are you doing here?"

I shift on my feet, suddenly overcome with the urge to wrap her in a hug and squish her.

"I was on my way home from the airport and I'm hungry, so..." I say, holding up my protein bar wrapper. "I thought I'd stop by."

"You stopped by because you're hungry?"

"No. I stopped by because I'm worried about you," I say,

stepping inside the apartment. It's warm, cozy, and *the last time I was here we played strip Connect Four and I gave her a lap dance.*

Good times I'd love to repeat.

"So?" I say, tossing the protein bar wrapper into the trash. "Are you going to tell me what's going on, or are we going to play another round of 'Austin avoids my questions while your dog waits for an opportunity to strike.'"

Austin laughs. "He's not going to bite you."

I'm not so sure about that.

I follow her into the living room, taking a seat on the couch.

She joins me—and instead of sitting on the other side like I expect her to—she lays, her head resting in my lap.

My hands go to her hair.

Her hair is soft under my fingers, and I start running them through it without thinking. It's a habit by now—something I do when she's stressed, even if she pretends she doesn't need it. Gio trots over, leaps up onto the armrest, beady eyes locking on me.

Fine.

Whatever.

Austin sighs, and for a second, it feels like the whole world slows down.

She doesn't say anything, just stares up at me with those wide, tired eyes. It's enough to make me forget how much my left shoulder still aches from getting slammed into the boards last night and how hungry I am.

I ignore the growling in my stomach.

"How do you feel?" she asks, resting her head against the back of the couch.

"Glad we won. Glad to be back." Her long lashes flutter at me. "Couple of highlight saves. No big deal."

Her lips twitch. "No big deal? That's the most humble thing I've ever heard you say."

"Don't get used to it," I say with a shrug. "I'm just saying, it's not every day you stonewall their best shooter in a breakaway with five seconds left on the clock."

"Ah, there it is," she teases, smirking. "The humility was fun while it lasted."

"Come on, admit it—you're impressed."

She rolls her eyes, but her smirk softens into a smile. "I'm always impressed. I'd be more impressed if you weren't still scared of my dog."

"That's different," I argue, pointing at Gio, who yaps in protest. "He wants to bite me, I can see it in his eyes."

The dog's ears twitch.

She shakes her head, a small, tired smile on her face.

I brush a few loose strands out of her face, leaning down to kiss her forehead.

"What about you? Did the students survive today, Professor?"

"Barely." She sighs, rubbing her temples. "I had to explain to two different students why Wikipedia isn't a credible source of information. One of them argued that if it's on the internet, it's basically fact."

"It's not?" I tease.

Her lips twitch, but she narrows her eyes at me. "Don't you start. I get enough of that from my students."

I hold up my hands in surrender, grinning. "Hey, all I'm saying is— if Wikipedia says I'm the best goalie in the league, would you argue?"

She rolls her eyes, but the corner of her mouth twitches like she's trying not to smile. "You're ridiculous. Wikipedia would probably say you're a unicorn if the right someone edited the page."

"I'd take that as a compliment."

For a moment, the conversation pauses, the room settling into an easy quiet. Gio, the dog, gets up. Stretches. Without missing a beat, he crawls onto her lap and curls into a skinny ball, glaring at me like he's daring me to even think about petting him.

She strokes his body absentmindedly, her gaze drifting to the window. Her fingers move in slow, comforting circles, and I can tell she's lost in her thoughts.

"Thanks for coming over," she says softly.

"Want to order food and watch a movie?" I ask, keeping my tone light, worried she's going to reject my offer.

Austin sighs, leaning back into the couch. "I was watching one of those housewife shows before you showed up."

I nod. No surprise there—she loves reality TV, especially the messy kind that involves arguments over champagne and passive-aggressive party invites.

"Sounds good to me."

Her head tilts, her lips quirking into a small smile. "You hate those shows."

"I don't hate them," I say. "I just don't understand how they're always fighting. But hey—if you're into it, I'm into it."

The smile grows, and for a second, I feel like I've won the Stanley Cup.

"That was easy." She's happy so I'm happy.

"True," I admit, leaning back and crossing my arms. "I seriously couldn't care less what we watch. I just want to be here with you."

She looks at me then, really looks at me, and something shifts in her expression. The tenderness in her eyes is enough to make my chest tighten, and for a brief moment, I forget about the game, the travel, and even the dog's continued silent loathing.

"Okay," she says, her voice quiet but steady. "Let's order food."

And just like that, the world feels a little bit lighter.

"What are you in the mood for?" I ask, pulling out my phone to scroll through the delivery apps. "Pizza? Thai? Or do we just go all in and order burgers with fries and milkshakes?"

Silently, I apologize to my nutritionist for pre-smelling like bacon burger, tapping away at my screen while Austin continues to stroke Gio's naked body.

"Burgers sound good," she says. "Can we get sweet potato fries?"

"On it," I reply, pulling up the menu for our favorite burger place.

"Oh. And extra pickles," she says, giving me a playful nudge with her foot. "And lots of secret sauce packets."

"Got it."

After placing the order, I set the phone down on the coffee table and lean back into the couch. "Food's on the way." I sigh, looking forward to our late night snack. "Have you seen Nova lately?"

Austin's face lights up at the mention of my sister. "I ran into her at the coffee shop yesterday. She was bitching about the date she was on Tuesday night."

"Sounds about right," I say, grinning.

Austin's eyes widen. "Did she tell you he spent half the night talking about his 'crypto empire.' I thought she was going to lose it."

"She told me the same thing. I have no idea why she's going to dinner with these dudes." I shake my head. "Apparently, he called her 'babe' within five minutes of sitting down. Who does that?"

"It's called Love Bombing and it's a thing," Austin informs me, fingers plucking at the tufts on Gio's head.

I frown, shaking my head. "So basically, it's manipulation with extra steps?"

"Pretty much," she says, nodding. "Classic red flag behavior. Nova probably realized that right after he called her 'babe.'"

"She did," I say, chuckling. "She told me she almost walked out when he tried signing her up for his multi-level marketing scheme."

"People are still signing up for those?"

Dang.

Austin's laugh is warm and soft, her shoulders shaking just

enough to make Gio lift his head and glare at me for disrupting his peace.

Austin nods. "I don't think Nova falls for it because she's naive. I think she's just looking for someone to love her."

That hits me square in the chest. I sit there, processing her words as Gio shifts on Austin's lap, curling into a ball. "Yeah," I say finally, my voice quieter now. "I know."

"She told me a little about that," Austin says gently. "How hard it's been since your mom passed. How it feels like she's been trying to fill a void."

I glance away, my jaw tightening. "She doesn't talk to me about that stuff. She just jokes around, acts like she's fine."

"She doesn't want to worry you. You're busy and she looks up to you even though you're the same age," Austin says softly, her fingers still stroking Gio. "But she's trying, Gio. She's putting herself out there, even if she picks the wrong guys sometimes. She just... wants to feel wanted."

The knot in my chest tightens. "I hate that she feels like she has to do that. Like she has to chase after these idiots who don't deserve her."

"I think she'll figure it out," Austin says, her voice steady. "She's smart. She's just learning what she deserves—and that takes time."

"She's been through enough already. I just want her to be happy."

Austin smiles at me, a warm, understanding look that makes me feel like I'm doing at least one thing right. For a moment, we sit there in the quiet, the weight of the conversation settling around us.

"Next time she goes on a date," Austin snorts. "Maybe we should double-team it," she says with a grin. "I'll vet him, and you can glare at him from across the room."

That is a great fucking idea. "I love it. In fact, we should take her phone and do the swiping for her."

Austin bursts out laughing, shaking her head. "You think

Nova's going to hand over her phone and let us play matchmaker? You're bonkers."

"No seriously. This is an amazing idea…"

"I have a question," she says. "Why haven't you ever set Nova up with one of your teammates? There are so many single guys on your team."

I groan. "Now you sound like her."

Austin's eyes widen with delight. "Wait, she's actually asked you to set her up with one of your teammates?"

"Teammates. Assistant coaches…" I admit, shaking my head humorously. "'Gio, aren't there any decent single guys on your team?'"

"And your answer is always no?" Austin asks, raising an eyebrow.

"Of course," I say, shrugging.

"Why?"

"Have you *met* my teammates?" She hasn't—but she will. "They're great on the ice, but off? Half of them think microwaving ramen counts as cooking. Nova deserves better than a guy who forgets his laundry in the washer for three days and walks around smelling like mold."

Austin laughs, leaning into the couch. "So, you've never even considered it? Not once?"

"No."

She seems to give this some thought. "Question: if you had to choose one guy to set her up with, who would it be?"

I shake my head. "No one."

"This is a game—you have to play."

I shake my head again. "Don't want to. The last thing I want to do is visualize her banging Jank or Tyler or whatever dipshit she dates."

Not happening.

She pretends to think this over, tapping her chin. "What about your captain, Wes? He's got that whole 'strong and silent leader' thing going on. Girls love a broody guy."

I glare at her. "Wes? He drinks pickle juice straight from the jar."

"So? I drink pickle juice straight from the jar." She tilts her head, her eyes gleaming with mischief. "Ooh, I've got it! The manager, Fitz. He's tall. Cute."

"He's allergic to peanut butter," I deadpan.

"Oh my God, so?"

"*So.* Nova loves peanut butter. That's a deal breaker."

Austin stares at me like I've lost my mind. "You are seriously a cock blocker. These are the dumbest reasons not to date someone I've ever heard." Pause. "Give me one guy."

I have to think long and hard about this.

Austin stops petting Gio to nudge me. "Well? I'm waiting. One guy. Give me *one*."

I exhale slowly, racking my brain. "Fine. If I *had* to pick someone…" I pause for dramatic effect. "Luca."

"Luca?" Austin's eyes widen. "The backup goalie?"

"Sure, why not?" I shrug, trying to sound casual. "He's decent."

She bursts out laughing so hard she startles Gio into jumping off her lap and onto the floor.

"Decent? Luca is a human golden retriever. Your sister would eat him alive."

Fun Fact: I love that Austin knows so much about hockey… until she knows too much about the players and who may or may not make a good match for my sister.

"At least he's polite," I argue. "He says thank you to his elders, aka, me. Which is more than I can say for half the idiots she's dated."

Austin calls the dog back up to her lap. "Do we honestly think Nova would get a lady boner for a guy who apologizes every time someone bumps into *him*?"

I roll my eyes. "You asked for a name—I gave you one. Take it or leave it."

"You're right. This is great," she says, grinning like she's just figured something out. "However, I personally think you picked Luca because he's harmless. Nova would never, in a million years, go for him."

"That's not true," I lie.

He's not her type.

My sister enjoys an Alpha male—like me, kind of—and Luca Babineaux is not one.

"You can't stand the idea of her dating anyone, can you? Admit it—you're the ultimate overprotective brother."

"I'm not overprotective," I grumble. "I just don't want her with some moron."

"Right." Her eyes roll. "So, basically everyone you've ever met."

"Exactly."

She laughs again, shaking her head. "Poor Nova. Good thing she doesn't let you vet her boyfriends, or she'd be single forever."

I shake my head to argue. "I don't want her to be single forever. I want her to be happy, the same way we are."

"You know, if these guys knew you were talking about them this way, they would die. Luca would die…"

She's not wrong.

Luca would shit his pants.

"I just hope," Austin reaches up to stroke the bottom of my chin, "your plan isn't to gatekeep every guy on the team until Nova gives up and focuses on her knitting career?"

"She doesn't knit," I snap, and Austin dissolves into laughter again.

"Relax, I'm kidding," she says, grinning as she wipes a tear from her eye. "But seriously, if Luca's just a hypothetical and the rest are idiots, what kind of guy do we want her to date?"

I hesitate, shifting uncomfortably. "I don't know. Someone… decent. Dependable. Kind. Someone who treats her right."

Austin softens, her teasing grin fading into something more

thoughtful. "You know, for all your big brother bear energy, that's very sweet."

I shrug, avoiding her gaze and fixating on the TV. "She deserves the best. That's all."

Austin smiles, tickling my neck. "Don't worry. Nova's got a good head on her shoulders. She can handle herself. Probably better than you give her credit for."

I sigh, knowing she's right but still unable to shake the instinct to protect. "Yeah, well, I'm still keeping an eye on her."

I lean down, kissing the tip of her nose.

There's a knock at the door and Gio scrambles toward the door, barking like he's auditioning for a guard dog gig. "Guess dinner's here," she says, untangling herself from the couch.

I follow, pulling Gio back by his collar before he can launch himself at the delivery guy and to both of our surprise, he lets me.

"Relax, buddy. It's just food."

Opening the door, I'm greeted by a guy holding a takeout bag and wearing the world's most unimpressed expression as he holds it toward me, blue ball cap pulled low over his eyes.

"Thanks, man." It smells so fucking delicious and my stomach agrees. "Tip is in the app."

"Sure," the delivery guy mutters, barely sparing me a glance as he turns and goes to stride back down the hall.

Stops in his tracks.

Looks over his shoulder.

"Are you…" His head gives a shake. "Montagalo?"

I grin, hand still curled around little Gio's collar as he does his best to break free and tear the man to shreds, all false bravado and posturing.

Meanwhile, the delivery guy drops his act completely, replacing it with a wide grin that looks out of place under the shadow of his cap. He takes a half step back, looking me up and down like he's trying to match the face in front of him with the one he's seen on game highlights or the roster page.

He can't believe it.

"Damn, man, I knew it," he says, pointing a finger at me like I've just won a game in overtime. "Man, you have no idea how much I love you, holy shit," he continues, vibrating with excitement. "That double save in OT last night? The *glove snag*, and then the pad stack? I rewound that three times."

"Well it's good to meet you."

"I've delivered here before," he says. "Never seen you."

"I'm new here," I laugh.

Gio barks sharply, trying once again to launch himself at the guy's legs, his tiny frame full of unnecessary aggression. I tighten my grip on his collar and hold him back. "Dude, chill. He's a fan."

The delivery guy laughs, stepping back again like Gio might actually take him down—all ten pounds of him. "I mean, I'd probably be barking too if I got to live with you!"

"Thanks man, I appreciate it."

The guy hesitates. "Could I...I hate to ask. Can I get a picture?"

"Yeah—sure, no problem." Austin sneaks up behind me and takes her dog, carrying him out of the doorway and into the living room while the young fan takes a selfie.

"Man, my buddies are gonna freak when they see this," he says, holding up his phone like it's a trophy. "You're their favorite player. Hell, you're my favorite player."

I laugh, rubbing the back of my neck.

My stomach protests. "Thanks, that means a lot. Glad I could make your day."

The guy laughs again nervously, clearly not wanting to leave but aware he's pushing his luck. "Alright, I'll let you eat. Thanks again, man. Seriously. Highlight of my week."

"No problem," I say, giving him a wave as he finally turns to head back down the hallway. His footsteps echo away, but his excitement lingers in the air like static.

I close the door.

Austin lets Gio loose.

He scampers into the kitchen. Sits.

Stares up at me expectantly, whip of a tail wagging.

"That's a first," I say to him, rummaging through the food to unearth a fry. "Is this all it takes to win you over?" He's been growling at me nonstop!

Unreal.

I toss him a sweet potato fry, and bend over.

Behind me, I hear Austin's soft footsteps, and then her arms slide around my waist, warm and steady. Her chin comes to rest lightly against my shoulder as she leans into me, her body fitting perfectly against my back.

"Looks like you've won him over," she murmurs, her voice low and teasing. Her breath brushes my ear, sending a faint, pleasant shiver down my spine. "Guess you're not so bad with small, feisty creatures after all."

I smirk, tossing another fry into my mouth. "Feisty creatures like you?"

"Ha ha," she says dryly, but I can feel her smile against my shoulder. "But yes."

27
austin

> Me: You should come up to your brother's place. He's at practice and I'm here with my dog...

> Nova: You brought your DOG?! OMG I love dogs, be right there.

I'm hunkered down in his living room, the massive windows offering me a view of the entire city as I lay wrapped in a faux fur blanket, little Gio burrowed near my feet.

So warm.

So cozy.

Moments later, Nova bursts into the penthouse, her excitement practically bouncing off the walls as she slips out of her sneakers by the door.

"Where is he? Where's the dog?!" she demands, eyes scanning the room with the determination of someone on a mission.

I lift the edge of the blanket I'm wrapped in, revealing Gio, nestled comfortably by my feet. His big ears twitch at the sound of her voice, and his nearly hairless head peeks out from under the throw.

Nova gasps like she's just seen the most precious creature on the planet. "Oh my God, *look* at him! He's so *weird*—but so *perfect*! Come here, little guy! Come to Auntie Nova."

Auntie Nova...

Her words hang in the air, a casual comment on the surface, but to me, they land with a heavy reminder: she's going to be a real aunt soon.

To an actual, living, breathing baby.

For a second, the thought clouds the moment, pulling me out of the warm, cozy cocoon I'd created in her brother's living room. I shift slightly, adjusting the blanket around me.

Nova doesn't seem to notice my lapse, too busy letting Gio climb into her lap and paw at her sweater like he's decided she's his new favorite human. She laughs, scratching his neck.

"You've got the best taste in pets." She loudly kisses his snout.

Gio narrows his eyes in that suspicious way he does with strangers, but seems to decide she's acceptable.

"Are you playing hard to get?" she whispers as he sniffs her hand before nuzzling it. "Are you?" Without hesitation, she cradles him gently. "Oh, I love you. I'm taking you home."

"Good luck with that," I say, smirking. "He's picky. He barely even likes *me*."

I move, making room for her to stretch out beside me.

"Having a lazy day?" she says.

"Yeah—I am so run down that I decided to leave school early and not do office hours." My yawn punctuates the sentence. "It feels so good to camp out here."

So quiet.

Serene.

The cleaning ladies came in briefly, emptying trash cans and making Gio's bed, going through the fridge for expired food.

Surreal, this life he has...

"I don't blame you. If I had this setup, I'd never want to leave either."

Gio snuggles against her, his tiny body fitting perfectly into the crook of her arm. He closes his eyes, fully trusting her already.

"It's a little weird, though," I confess, my voice soft. "Cleaning ladies who know his routine better than I do. A fridge that somehow always restocks itself. It's like he's living on autopilot."

Nova raises an eyebrow, her fingers absentmindedly stroking Gio's nearly hairless back.

"Sounds convenient, not weird."

"Yeah, but it's not *real*, you know? It's like a curated version of life. He's barely here to enjoy it, and when he is, everything's already done for him. It's more like he's staying in a fancy hotel than living in a home."

She's quiet for a moment, her gaze drifting to the floor-to-ceiling windows and the breathtaking city view beyond them. The skyline sparkles against the afternoon sun, a constant reminder of the privilege and distance that comes with this kind of lifestyle.

"I get it," she says finally. "It doesn't feel personal sometimes. Probably why he's always down at my place."

"Exactly." I lean back, pulling the blanket tighter around me. "It's kind of lonely, honestly."

Nova turns her head to look at me, her expression softening.

"Well, he's not alone right now," she says simply, her voice warm.

I smile, grateful for her presence. "No, I guess he's not."

"You have each other."

That warms me on the inside and I debate if I should tell her about…well. You know. Being pregnant. How she'll react.

Too soon.

She just got here.

"I had an interesting conversation with your brother last night," I say. "He was at my place and we started talking 'bout you—as usual—and dating came up."

Nova rolls her eyes. "I'm sure it did."

"Interestingly enough, I got him to give me a name."

This perks her up. "What do you mean, a name? A name for who?"

"Someone on the team he'd be cool with you dating."

Nova narrows her eyes, shifting slightly so she's facing me fully. "Wait—hold on. You're telling me my brother, *Mister Overprotective,* actually gave you a name? Like—willingly?"

I grin, leaning back against the cushions and enjoying her skepticism. "I was just as surprised as you are. I figured he'd shut it down completely, but nope. He thought about it for a good, solid minute."

I'm exaggerating of course, finding pleasure in her shocked expression.

"Who is it?" she presses, her tone a mix of curiosity and suspicion.

I raise an eyebrow, dragging out the moment.

"You really want to know?"

"Obviously!"

"Alright," I say, drawing out the word. "He said, and I quote, 'If I *had* to pick someone on the team, I guess I wouldn't hate it if Nova went out with—'"

"Stop stalling!" she screeches. "Spit it out!"

"—Luca."

"As in, Babineaux?" Nova seems to rear back. "Seriously?"

I nod. "What's wrong with him—he's so cute."

"Yeah he's cute but he's so…" Her hand waves aimlessly in the air as she searches for an adjective to describe the nice, low-key forward on the Baddies. "Boring?"

I smirk. "Ah, so what I'm hearing is you'd rather date someone your brother *wouldn't* approve of?"

"No. I'm saying I need someone who's more fun."

"Poor bastard," I laugh, shaking my head with mock sympathy. "The guy doesn't know we're over here dismantling his *entire* personality."

Nova grins, already reaching for her phone. "Let's see how boring he really is."

"Wait, you're seriously gonna stalk him right now?" I ask, laughing.

"Of course," she says, as if it's the most obvious thing in the world. Her fingers fly over the screen as she types his name into the search bar. "If I'm gonna reject him in my head, I might as well have receipts to back up my claims."

I lean over, peering at her screen as she pulls up Luca Babineaux's profile. His profile picture is exactly what I expect—him in his Blaze jersey, smiling at the camera like he's uncomfortable even being photographed.

"Classic," I comment. "The humble athlete pose."

"Let's dig deeper," Nova says, clicking on his tagged photos. The first few are standard fare—team pictures, action shots on the court, and group photos at what looks like team dinners.

But then she scrolls past a photo of Luca holding a black lab retriever puppy that was posted four days ago, his smile wide and genuine.

"Oh, come on," I groan. "He has a *puppy*? That's an automatic ten points. You can't hate on him for that."

Nova narrows her eyes. "He's *too* perfect. Of course he has a puppy." She scoffs. "I bet he volunteers at an animal shelter on the weekends."

"Would that *really* be so bad?" I tease. "You could be the one to turn him into a bad boy—like not returning library books on time."

She snorts, scrolling further. "Fine. Maybe he's not *that* terrible, but look at this." She pauses on a photo of Luca at what looks like a team charity event.

He's wearing a Santa hat and holding a plate of cookies while surrounded by kids.

"Aww. Santa Luca," I say, stifling a laugh. "Too nice, too wholesome. He'd probably text you good morning *and* good night. What a jerk."

"Nope." Nova groans dramatically, tossing her phone onto the couch. "Can't do it. I'd suffocate under all the kindness."

"*Or,*" I counter. "You'd *finally* meet someone who doesn't ghost you after three dates."

Her lips twitch, but she doesn't say anything, blue gaze drifting to the large windows.

"You know," I say softly. "Your brother makes a valid point. A guy like Luca, who is less exciting than your last dating app match, may not be the worst thing."

Nova doesn't respond right away, and for a moment, the room is quiet except for the faint hum of the city outside. Then she sighs, picking up her phone again.

"I dunno." She taps on the puppy photo again. "I'll give him this—the dog is cute. But I'm not sold on the whole package."

I laugh, nudging her with my elbow. "You're impossible, you know that?"

"And proud of it," she replies, her grin returning as she sets her phone down. "Maybe a boyfriend and kids aren't in the cards for me."

I roll my eyes. She is twenty-six years old.

"You make it sound like you're seventy years old."

"I feel seventy—like I've been at this for years." Gio's sister heaves out a massive sigh. "My ovaries are drying up."

This is it.

The perfect window of opportunity.

I suck in a breath.

"You know whose ovaries aren't drying up?" I quip. "Mine."

She laughs like I'm kidding, petting the dog.

"Yeah, okay. Like you're over here bursting with fertility or something. What are you even talking about?"

I hesitate, my fingers fidgeting with the edge of the faux fur blanket. *The joke had been a test*—a way to gauge how she might react. But now that the moment's here, my throat tightens, and the words feel impossible to say.

"Well..." I trail off, forcing a casual tone. "I was being serious."

Nova's hand freezes mid-pet. She glances up at me, her brows knitting together in confusion.

"Wait. *What?*"

"I'm serious," I say, my voice quieter now. "I'm... pregnant."

For a moment, she just stares at me, her mouth slightly open. Then, as if to break the tension, Gio lets out a laborious yawn, and she blinks, sitting up straighter.

"Wait, wait, wait," she says, holding up a hand. "You're telling me—like, right now, this second—you're *preg*nant?"

Unfortunately I can do nothing but nod my head. "I just found out. I have no idea how far along I am or anything..."

"Holy. Shit." She shakes her head, a slow smile spreading across her face. "I mean... wow. Okay. This is huge. Are you okay? How do you feel? Wait—does my brother know?"

"Not yet," I say quickly. "Dolly was there when I took the test and now I'm telling you." I nibble at my thumbnail. "I honestly have no idea how I'm going to tell him."

Or when.

"Wow," she finally says, her tone softer now. "Okay. First of all, I'm honored you told me. Second..." She lets out a long breath, leaning back against the couch. "We need a plan. You can't just wing something like this with *him*. He'll probably short-circuit."

Not probably. He is.

I groan, sinking further into the blanket. "You think I don't know that? That's why I haven't said anything yet. I mean, how do I start a conversation like this?"

"Something casual like, 'Hey, remember that one night we banged? Turns out we made a person.'" Nova shifts, pulling her legs up onto the couch and cradling Gio in her lap like the tiny, spoiled prince that he is. "Seriously, though, you've got to tell him soon. He deserves to know. Plus, the longer you wait, the more lonely and isolated you're going to feel."

True.

I hadn't thought of my feelings at all.

Only his reaction to it.

"I know," I admit, running a hand through my hair. "I don't want to freak him out. Or make things more complicated than they already are."

"Complicated how?" she asks, raising an eyebrow.

I hesitate, my stomach twisting. "We're not *together*, together," I say slowly. "We're dating. I don't even know what his favorite ice cream flavor is."

"Vanilla." She yawns. "He's dull—but that's not the point. The point is: you don't have to know his favorite ice cream flavor to know how he'll handle this. If he's worth anything, he'll step up. And if he doesn't..." She shrugs, her tone light but her expression serious. "Then you know exactly what kind of person he is."

I sigh, leaning back into the couch. "I guess you're right."

"Of course I am," she replies, grinning. "Don't worry, though. You'll be fine. You're stronger than you think, and this kid's gonna have the coolest mom ever."

"Thanks." A relieved smile tugs at my lips.

"And the coolest aunt," she adds, winking. "Obviously."

"Obviously," I say, rolling my eyes.

I'm glad she doesn't hate me. And I'm glad she doesn't think I trapped her brother into a lifelong commitment before he's ready.

Nova leans back, stroking Gio absentmindedly. "So, how are you actually going to tell him? Can I help?"

"I hadn't thought about it. I've only worried about it," I tell her honestly with a laugh.

She gets animated. "Oooh! I have an idea! How about this: you get a onesie printed that says, 'Daddy's Little Teammate,' and hand it to him."

I pause, chewing on my lip. "I don't know. Maybe I should sit him down and tell him—the old fashioned way. No frills, no gimmicks. Just honesty."

Nova pulls a face, not loving that idea. "Or—hear me out—you get a puck and write, 'You're gonna be a dad' on it, take him to the arena. Get him in the box and chuck it at him. Very on-brand, right?"

I groan. "Nova, I'm not trying to give the poor guy a heart attack."

"Lame," she pouts. "What about balloons? Everyone loves balloons. You could fill one with confetti and pop it, and the confetti spells out the news. Super dramatic."

"Super messy," I point out, shaking my head. "Besides, I don't think he's the kind of guy who needs theatrics."

"Pfft. My brother loves drama, what are you talking about? If you hadn't noticed, one of the reasons he's so into you is because you're willing to make an ass of yourself in public."

I take offense to that. "When do I make an ass of myself?!"

"Uh—at every home game? The signs? The tauntin—" She stops speaking and looks at me. "That's it. That's the idea!"

"What is?"

"A sign! At the game!" Nova's eyes light up as she scoots closer, clearly excited by her latest brainwave. "Think about it! You're already his number one fan—literally. You could hold up a sign during the game that says something like, 'You're Gonna Be a Dad!'"

He would die.

I gape at her, absolutely horrified. "Nova, no. Absolutely not. Do you know how mortifying that would be? For both of us?"

She cackles, clearly enjoying my discomfort. "Oh, *come on*. It's perfect! Public, dramatic, and completely on-brand for you two. Less of a heckle, more of an announcement. So Khloe Kardash of you."

I groan, throwing a pillow at her. "First of all, I am nothing like Khloe Kardashian. Second of all, no. Absolutely not. I'm not announcing this like it's a gender reveal party on steroids."

Nova catches the pillow, her grin widening. "You are no fun. Admit it, it'd be unforgettable! For everyone! The fans would eat that shit up!"

They seriously would.

The announcement would likely go viral and plastered on every major news network across the country.

The more she talks the *less* I hate the idea.

It would be Classic Austin.

"Oh my God, Nova. He would shit his pants."

For so many reasons.

Nova hoots, clapping her hands together. "It's perfect. Public enough to make it memorable, but not so over-the-top that it's a complete shit-show."

I shake my head with another laugh. "What if Gio gets distracted and they lose which could lose The Baddies, the championship, and then the Cup and suddenly I'm the reason they had a horrible season."

Not to mention, being highlighted in all the Sports Fail reels.

"You are *way* overthinking this."

"Am I?" I ask. "I'm just making sure Gio lets a puck through his glove 'cause he's too busy reading my sign?"

She ignores my question and continues making arguments for the sign. "...Or are you bringing your entire relationship full-circle? It's perfect."

"I can't argue with that, I guess," I continue chewing my nail nervously. "Ugh, why is this so hard?"

"Because this baby is going to be life changing–in a good way!" Nova says optimistically. "You're not dropping this massive bomb on his life and hoping he doesn't explode."

I sigh, staring up at the ceiling. "That's exactly what I'm doing."

Dropping a bomb.

"Right. So why not make it funny?" Nova reaches over and grabs a throw pillow, hugging it to her chest. "For what it's worth, I think he's going to handle it better than you think. I think he'll be excited. You may not have known him long but he's already shown you he's a decent guy."

Decent guy.

"High praise," I say dryly.

She laughs. "Hey, you're the one who picked him."

I roll my eyes, but the truth of her words settles in. She's right—he is a decent dude and I did pick him—*with her help*.

Looking over, my eyes narrow playfully as I say, "You practically shoved us in each other's way."

Nova shrugs, a smirk playing on her lips. "You're welcome, by the way. Don't I have impeccable taste?"

I bite my lip, thinking it over.

Nova has a point. And the more I picture the idea, the more it makes sense. Maybe surprising him at one of his games is perfect. I can already see it—me, sitting front row with a sign that reads, *Congrats, Daddy!*

Yes.

I like this idea more and more.

"Impeccable taste? If by 'impeccable taste' you mean meddling to the point of no return," I tease. "I mean—you meddled *so* hard that your brother is going to be a dad. So really, this is on you."

"Meddling? How *dareee* you." Nova clutches her chest in mock offense. "This is slander, which I prefer to think of as divine intervention." She smirks but then leans in, curiosity sparking in her eyes. "*Seriously* though—how are you feeling? Like, is anything happening yet? You're super early, right?"

I nod, pulling the blanket tighter around me. "I'm two or three weeks along, tops. I barely feel anything. No nausea. Boobs are normal. Just tired. Like, I could nap anywhere, anytime."

But that's also nothing new.

I'm always down for a nap.

Ha!

Nova raises an eyebrow. "Tired already? That's wild. Your

HIT ME WITH YOUR BEST SHOT

body's, like, 'Hey, girl, we're gonna make a human, so shut everything else down.'"

I laugh softly. "Pretty much. It's weird—I feel fine one minute, and then the next, I'm totally wiped out."

She tilts her head, studying me like I'm a science experiment. "No cravings or weird stuff yet?"

"Not really," I say, shrugging. "I did devour a whole bag of salt-and-vinegar chips yesterday, but that's just me being a snack monster."

She shifts closer, her expression softening. "What about emotionally? Are you okay? Excited? All of the above?"

I exhale, my shoulders sinking into the couch. "Yeah. All of the above. It doesn't feel real. Half the time, I'm like, 'What if this is a mistake?' and the other half, I'm scared. My mom doesn't know I'm dating someone so I have to break that news, plus the news about a baby?"

Nova's smile fades slightly, and she reaches over to squeeze my hand. "You're literally weeks in—it's okay to feel like this. We've got this."

We.

Me + Dolly + Nova

What more do I need?

"Thanks, Nova," I murmur, her words settling into me.

She brightens again. "So, I need to know—are we gonna find out what the gender is? Or are you going to wait until you give birth?"

I stare at her, deadpan. "Nova, I don't even know how far along I am. Can I get through the part where I break the news to Gio?"

She laughs, throwing her head back. "Fine, fine. But when you're ready, I'm here for the gender reveal brainstorming. Glitter bombs, confetti, maybe a piñata full of baby socks—"

I cut her off with a laugh. "Stop. You're too much."

"And you love me for it," she quips, grinning as she grabs

the remote. "Now, do you want to keep overthinking, or should we put on something dumb and distracting?"

"Dumb and distracting, please."

"Perfect," she says, pulling up a reality dating show. "Let's watch people mess up their own love lives so we can stop stressing about ours."

28

Gio: You planning on coming to the game tonight?

Austin: Yup. Me and Nova will be in the special seats.

Gio: YOUR seats, you mean?

Austin: Sure, ha ha. If that's what you want to call them, who am I to object.

Gio: How was your day babe? You looked so cute when I left this morning, all snuggled in my bed with that beast of yours.

Austin: I was. And so was Gio.

Gio: He sure did get used to my place pretty darn quick.

Austin: He's a leech. As long as you're feeding him...

Gio: He's the dog version of a gold digger.

Austin: OBVIOUSLY. Can't have him settling for less.

Austin: You say that like you're not completely smitten with him already. Admit it, he's got you wrapped around his paw.

Gio: Lies. I'm just trying to keep the peace. Can't have your dog hating me.

Austin: Don't worry, you're winning him over. He didn't even growl at you last night.

Austin: That's progress.

Gio: He only growls at me when you're not looking.

Austin: STOP IT HE DOES NOT!

Austin: Does he? Oh God…

Gio: It's fine. No one can take him seriously with that mohawk.

Austin: What he needs is a cute Blaze sweater. It's getting cold out, he's going to need one.

Gio: A Blaze sweater for your dog? You realize I'm the one on the ice, right? Not him.

Austin: He's basically your mascot now.

Gio: Pretty sure the team's ACTUAL mascot would have an issue with that.

Austin: That giant flame can fight him for the title. Gio would win.

Gio: With that attitude, he might.

Gio: Switching gears: how was work today?

Austin: The usual.

HIT ME WITH YOUR BEST SHOT

Austin: Oh! That's a lie—your fan club was in my office today asking about you.

Gio: Fan club? Be more specific, I have like, 50 of them.

Austin: Cute.

Austin: I mean my students. Remember Fanboy Paul? He's obsessed with finding out details about our relationship and sent Logan (the TA) in to fish around. Everrrryyyyone has a big ol' crush on you.

Gio: I respect the dedication.

Austin: He's relentless. Logan tried to act casual, but I could tell he had a list of questions.

Gio: Like what?

Austin: Oh, you know, the usual. How long we've been dating, what your favorite food is, whether you're single (again, YOU ARE NOT), and if you've ever fought a bear.

Gio: A bear?

Austin: Apparently, he thinks you're some kind of Canadian action hero.

Gio: I mean, I do play hockey. Basically the same.

Austin: Sure, if skating really fast counts as "fighting a bear."

Gio: I'd totally take a bear down if it meant impressing you.

Austin: You've already won me over. No need to get your face torn off to impress me.

Gio: Good to know. But if Paul asks again, I can invite him to a game.

Austin: You'd make his year. His face would melt off.

Gio: That's the point.

Austin: How soon do you have to be in your uniform?

Gio: Little bit yet, I'm about to get tapped up by the trainer. My shoulder's been bothering me so he's gonna take a look at it.

Austin: Why didn't you tell me you were hurt?!

Gio: I'm not HURT. It's just sore. The usual

Gio: You worried about me, babe?

Austin: I'm worried about the win.

Gio: Wow.

Gio: What would you do to make me feel better if I were hurt?

Austin: Oh, you know. Soup or something.

Gio: SOUP? That's it?

Austin: What else were you hoping for?

Gio: Something more hands-on…if you catch my drift.

Austin: Hands-on, huh? Like helping you stretch?

Gio: Probably something lower.

Austin: Lower? You mean, like tying your skates?

HIT ME WITH YOUR BEST SHOT

Gio: Not what I had in mind.

Austin: Oh?

Gio: Let's just say my idea involves a different kind of stroke.

Austin: You're really going there?

Gio: My shoulder's not the only thing that could use some attention.

Austin: What if we make a little wager?

Gio: Can we make it interesting?

Austin: You lose the game and you have to go down on me.

Gio: And if I win, you suck my dick?

Austin: Exactly.

Gio: I like those odds. Babe, you've officially made this the most important game of my life.

Austin: It's DEFINITELY going to be the most important game of your life—I guarantee it.

29
gio

*L*ife is good.
    Damn good.
    The sex is amazing. Austin and I have so much fun together.

She and my sister get along. The dog has stopped growling at me and has now started letting me pet him.

Work is great.

Finally—we're fucking winning and it's all thanks to my good luck charm.

I home in on the forward as he skates toward me, the puck bouncing back and forth between his stick as he skillfully maneuvers through my defensemen. His movements are sharp, fluid—too damn smooth. My muscles tighten, every nerve in my body screaming to react.

Focus.

That word beats in my head like a war drum. I shift my weight slightly, my stick angled down, blocking the tiniest opening. The crowd roars as the forward gets closer, cutting sharply left. My heart pounds in time with their chants.

He shoots.

Instinct kicks in.

My glove snaps up, catching the puck mid-air like it's second nature. The play ends, and the horn blares, signaling the end of the period.

I skate out of the goal box, chest heaving as adrenaline courses through me. The crowd goes wild!

I glance over to the spot in the front row, where Austin and my sister will be sitting tonight, setting it in my sights.

Already distracted.

I love seeing Austin so damn much.

Can't get enough of her…

When we're done warming up I follow my teammates to the bench, skates cutting sharp lines into the ice. Coach is already shouting, clipboard in hand, giving orders about tightening up defense.

Yeah, yeah, yeah—I've heard it all before, not to get cocky.

I nod along but the truth is, I'm riding a high straight into the first period.

My reflexes are sharp.

My confidence is soaring.

We're up by two, and *I'll be damned if I let anyone close that gap.*

I sit on the bench alongside my teammates, pulling a water bottle and taking a long sip, letting the cool water wash away the heat building under my mask.

Coach is yapping away.

As he does, my mind drifts back to those empty seats.

I trust Austin to show—she said she was coming—but the nagging thought that something might have held them up eats at me. It's not like her to miss the start of a game, not when she's been so consistent about showing up, screaming her lungs out every time I make a save.

The buzzer sounds, signaling the end of the timeout.

We're back on the ice, the energy electric as we take our positions; gloves are secure, mask snug.

I block out the noise of the crowd, everything except the puck and the players surrounding it…

My heart pounds as I track the puck—*left, right, left.* The forward winds up, *and I know what's coming.*

The slap shot is hard and fast, but I'm faster. I drop low, my pads taking the brunt of the hit as the puck bounces off and ricochets into the corner. The crowd roars, and I hear my teammates shouting through the thunder.

And then I see them.

My sister and Austin, sidestepping people as they make their way to their seats, bright blue and yellow jerseys on—I couldn't miss them if I tried.

I grin. "It's about fucking time."

I'm fighting for my life here!

Zing!

A puck nearly flies past me, snapping me out of my daydream.

Another forward barrels toward me, stick angled, looking for a rebound shot.

"*Not today, motherfucker.*"

My mind clears in an instant, instincts taking over. I crouch low, scanning every movement like a hawk, ready for the next play.

My eyes dart, tracking the puck like a pinball machine.

Twenty feet…

Ten…

Two.

I slide into position just as the puck ricochets off my blocker, bouncing harmlessly into the corner. My teammates swarm it, battling to clear the zone. The crowd roars, but all I hear is my own heartbeat thundering in my ears.

Another period goes by.

Then the beginning of the third.

Austin stands, clapping, and from here I can see her face lighting up; her fingers go in her mouth, whistling. Next to her, my sister's holding up a ridiculous sign that reads, **GIO = BRICK WALL!** in giant letters.

"Brick wall?" *Goddamn right I am.*

My chest puffs out with importance.

The opposing team pulls their goalie for the extra attacker, desperation dripping from every move they make. My defense holds strong, throwing their bodies in front of shots, clearing the puck every chance they get. But it always comes back. Always.

Thirty seconds.

A scramble in front of the net sends the puck flying toward me. I drop low, my pads sealing off the bottom of the net as the shot deflects off my leg and bounces out. My stick lashes out, sending it toward the boards.

Ten seconds.

The puck clears the zone, and time seems to slow as it slides, untouched, toward their empty net. The buzzer blares before it even crosses the line.

We've won.

Fuck yeah, we did—my good luck charm is here.

As the team rushes toward me in celebration, sticks clattering against the ice, helmets knocking into mine, I glance up at the stands, starting my skate over to my sister and Austin and two things happen at once:

1. She's holding a sign, but it's not the sign Nova had.

2. She is *not* smiling.

My momentum slows, the elation of the win crashing into confusion as I focus on her. The bright yellow poster in her hands has big, blocky letters that I can just make out as she lowers it slightly.

GIO.

I AM PREGNANT.

The words hit me like a slap shot straight to the chest. My skates falter for a moment, and I nearly lose my balance. My stick drops to the ice, forgotten, as my eyes dart from the sign to Austin's face.

She isn't smiling.

Not even a little.

The team is still swarming around me, celebrating, shouting, patting my back, but it all feels distant, muffled, like I'm underwater. I can't look away from her. From the sign. From the sheer seriousness etched across her face.

"Gio, you good?" one of my teammates asks, smacking me on the back of the helmet.

"Yeah, I…" My voice trails off as I glance at him, then back at the stands. "I need a second."

I skate toward the boards, my legs heavy, my heart pounding in my chest. Austin doesn't move. She stands there, gripping the sign like it's the only thing keeping her grounded. Nova looks as if she's trying not to laugh, arms crossed as she stands next to Austin like a mama bear.

Daring me to skate away.

Clearly, she knew about this.

When I reach them, Austin's eyes meet mine—I can see the fear hidden behind her usual self-assurance.

I unhook my helmet, pulling it up so she can see my face. "Austin," I breathe. "Is this for real?"

I know she can't hear the words coming out of my mouth, but I'm certain she can understand me.

She nods.

Yes.

The air feels like it's been knocked out of me. My grip tightens on the boards as I try to steady myself, my heart pounding so hard it feels like it might explode. She doesn't break eye contact, her usual confidence flickering just beneath the surface of her fear.

Nova leans toward her, muttering something I can't hear, and Austin's grip on the sign falters before she clutches it tighter.

I AM PREGNANT.

HIT ME WITH YOUR BEST SHOT

Bold. Bright.

Not a joke…

PREGNANT.

Holy shit.

I can't get to her.

Can't do anything.

My brain is short-circuiting, the enormity of her words crashing over me like a wave. But my body knows what it needs to do, even if my head doesn't. My glove goes up, instinctive, pressing against the plexiglass between us.

Austin's eyes soften, and for a moment, everything else falls away—the noise, the crowd, the game, even Nova's soft smile.

It's just us.

Her hand hesitates, then rises to meet mine on the other side of the glass.

I want to say something, to do something, but all I can manage is a single word that barely escapes my lips: "Okay."

She nods, understanding more than my voice can convey.

We're okay.

The moment is over in a nanosecond.

My teammates are already skating toward the center of the ice, the coach shouting something about sportsmanship from the bench. *I know I have to go.*

If I don't, I'll catch hell for it later.

I glance back at Austin one more time. Her hand lingers on the glass as I drop mine and skate backward, keeping my eyes on her as long as I can.

Nova is saying something to her now, enveloping her in a side hug, both of them watching me; the fear in Austin's expression is replaced by something softer.

Hope?

Shit, I don't know.

At the center of the ice, I shake hands with the opposing goalie, who's saying something about a great game. I nod, moving my lips to say the words but nothing comes out—I am miles away.

My glove feels heavy where it touched the glass, like her touch is still there, singeing my fingers.

We're okay.

As the formalities wrap up and I head back to the locker room, my thoughts are racing, my pulse pounding in my ears. What happens next?

I'm not running from this. From her.

Holy fuck.

A baby?

My mind is fucking mush as I step off the ice…

My legs feel unsteady—not from the game—but the weight of what just happened. This is insane!

A baby.

The thought is as overwhelming as it is exhilarating, and I can't keep my feet from moving faster.

Shoving past my teammates, most of whom are trying to slap my back in congratulations, I ignore the chatter in the locker room as I head straight through it.

Still on my skates, I don't bother unstrapping anything, don't bother stopping.

Some of them start yelling.

They think I've lost my goddamn mind but I have one destination in my sights:

Austin.

I have to get to her.

I can't leave her sitting there alone—after a normal game I could be here for hours, post-game massage, ice plunges, all that shit…

The heavy metal door slams open as I burst into the corridor leading toward the stands.

My chest heaves, my breath catches in the tight space of my throat.

I'm moving fast, the blades of my skates scraping against the concrete, but I couldn't give a shit.

Everyone is watching in stunned silence. Out of my peripheral view I notice several fans beginning to get their phones out, holding them to film me...

I move toward section 107.

Lingering fans part like the sea, stepping aside as I barrel through without slowing down. The yellow glow of the sign still lingers like a ghost in my mind, bold and bright, impossible to forget. **I AM PREGNANT.** It flashes behind my eyes with every step, like a neon warning light.

When I reach her section, *Austin is exactly where I left her*—still standing, still clutching the crumpled sign in her hands. Her face is flushed, and her eyes widen as she sees me approach, a mix of relief and anxiety flickering across her features.

Nova's saying something to her, her hand resting lightly on Austin's arm, but Austin's focus is completely on me.

The moment I'm close enough, I reach out, pulling her down the last couple of steps and into my arms.

"I can't believe you came out here," she breathes, her voice shaking.

"Of course I did," I say, my voice rough with emotion. "What the hell did you expect me to do?"

Go about my business like she didn't drop a bomb?

Her hands grip the collar of my jersey as she stares up at me, the noise of the arena fading into the background. People are gathering around.

Murmuring.

Cheering, even.

"I don't know," she admits, her voice barely above a whisper. "I wasn't sure what you'd do."

I glance down at the crumpled sign still clutched in her hand, shaking my head with a disbelieving laugh.

"You weren't sure?" I ask. "Austin, you put it on a damn poster."

Typical.

Her lips twitch, but she doesn't smile. "I didn't know how to tell you."

"This will do it." I just can't fucking believe it. It's on the tip of my tongue to say *"how can you be pregnant? It's only been a few weeks..."* but I'm not an idiot. Instead I say, "Leave it to you to make it a public roasting."

"Would you have preferred a text?" she shoots back, the smallest flicker of her usual sarcasm cutting through the tension.

That makes me smile, despite everything. "No. This was on brand."

I brush a strand of hair from her face, my gloved hand awkward but careful. "You're so fucking lucky I didn't have a heart attack in the middle of the ice."

The crowd around us is growing exponentially.

Someone yells, *"Get a room!"* and I shoot them a glare, ready to snap back, but someone beats me to it.

"Go fuck yourself, she's pregnant!" a voice shouts from somewhere behind me, sharp and unapologetic. The comment earns a ripple of laughter and cheers from the gathering fans, and I can't help the stunned snort that escapes me.

I grab the sign. "She's pregnant!"

Hold it up over my head, much to the delight of the fans.

"My girlfriend is pregnant!"

The arena erupts.

Applause, whistles, and chants of "Gio! Gio! Gio!" ring out from the growing crowd. People are standing on the seats now, desperate for a decent view of us—clapping and stomping their feet like I've just scored the game-winning goal in overtime.

Phones are out everywhere, capturing this moment that's bound to go viral in minutes.

Everyone is so bloody stoked.

Austin covers her face with both hands, shoulders shaking—not from tears, but from embarrassed laughter.

"Oh my God," she groans through her fingers. "This is insane."

I turn to the fans and wave the sign one last time for good measure. The cheers grow louder, a deafening roar that reverberates through the arena.

Ha ha. "Get used to it."

She's wearing a jersey over a blue hoodie, all of it three sizes too big on her...but that doesn't stop my eyes from trailing downward, to her stomach.

It's instinctive, automatic, like my brain is trying to catch up with the reality of what's happening. There's no bump yet—of course, there isn't—but knowing what's coming... it's enough to send another shock wave through my chest.

My kid is in there.

My kid.

Holy shit.

Austin peeks through her fingers, catching the direction of my gaze. Her embarrassed laughter softens, her hands falling to her sides.

"What?" she asks, her voice quieter now, uncertain.

"Nothing," I say quickly, shaking my head and meeting her eyes again. "Just a lot to take in."

Her lips curve into a small, understanding smile. "Tell me about it."

Yeah—I'm sure she was as surprised as I am.

Maybe even more so.

The crowd is still buzzing around us, voices blending into a dull roar, but I don't hear them anymore. All I can focus on is her—on the way her hands fidget with the hem of her hoodie, on the way she's looking at me like she's waiting for the other shoe to drop.

It doesn't.

I step closer, leaning down until our foreheads almost touch.

"We've got this," I tell her, my voice steady despite the chaos swirling around us. "Okay?"

Her eyes search mine, and after a moment, she nods. "Okay."

My hands move to her face and I cup her chin, tilting it up.

Press my lips against her lips…

Her hands grip the front of my jersey, holding me close as if the world might pull us apart. Her lips are soft and warm, and for a moment, everything—every doubt, every fear—melts away. It's just her, just me, and the quiet promise in this kiss.

When I finally pull back, her eyes flutter open, her cheeks flushed and her breath shaky. "What was that for?" she whispers, her voice barely audible over the distant murmur of the crowd.

I grin, my forehead still resting against hers. "For being amazing," I say. "And for being brave enough to do this tonight." In this way.

Seriously.

Wow.

She has serious lady balls.

Behind us, Nova claps loudly, breaking the moment. "Finally!" she says, her voice dripping with sarcasm. "I was starting to think you'd never kiss her."

I ignore my sister.

Roll my eyes, stepping back just enough to lace my fingers with Austin's. "You ready to get out of here?"

"Yes," she says, exasperated but smiling now. "Please."

I slide my arm around her waist, and before she can utter a single word of protest, I sweep her off her feet—literally. In full hockey gear, skates scraping against the concrete, I lift her like she weighs nothing, cradling her against my chest.

Austin lets out a startled squeak, her hands flying to grip my shoulders as I hold her securely.

"Gio!" she shrieks, her voice half-laugh, half-protest. "What are you doing? You're going to drop me!"

"Are you kidding me? You've seen my arms," I boast as I shift her closer, holding her tightly against me. "This is the safest place you could be."

HIT ME WITH YOUR BEST SHOT

What am I doing?!

"Put me down!" She laughs. "I can walk."

"Hell no. I'm carrying my pregnant girlfriend to the car!" I holler to everyone as my skates scrape against the concrete steps, the sound like nails on a chalkboard. "You've had enough excitement for one night. Let me take care of you."

Austin, on the other hand, buries her face in my neck, groaning.

"This is so embarrassing!"

"Embarrassing?" I echo, my tone teasing. "This is *romantic*! This is the kind of thing people write love stories about."

"This is the kind of thing that goes viral," she counters, though the faint smile tugging at her mouth tells me she's not as mad as she's pretending to be.

Austin looks pretty pleased with herself.

"So what if it does?" I say, my voice dropping to something softer, something *for her ears only*. "Let the whole world see how much I'm falling in love with you."

Through the commotion I don't miss the intake of her breath, her eyes widening as the words hang between us. I see the shift in her expression, the way her defenses crumble piece by piece until all that's left is the raw, unfiltered connection between us.

"*What did you just say to me in front of all these people?*"

Okay. Now I can't tell if she's horrified or stunned.

"Yeah!" Nova's voice booms over the noise, entirely too amused. "What did you just say?! Say it louder!"

Nova is such a pain in the ass sometimes.

But the fans are familiar with her and the crowd around us cheers louder at her pronouncement, egging her on. I shake my head but don't break eye contact with Austin, not even for a second.

I dip my head, brushing my lips against her temple in the briefest, gentlest kiss.

"She heard me," I murmur softly, just for her, finally at the top of the steps.

Austin's eyes close for a moment, her shoulders sagging as her grip on my jersey tightens.

Nova, of course, can't let a moment this good slip away.

"Say it louder for those in the back!" she hollers, clapping her hands. "Give us what we want!"

The crowd loves her.

A woman wearing a Seattle jersey—the opposing team tonight— shouts, "This is the most romantic thing I've ever seen!" at the same time another voice yells, "Kiss her!"

Austin lets out a breathy laugh, shaking her head. "Your sister is going to haunt me for the rest of my life, isn't she?"

"I mean. You're stuck with us both now," I say, grinning as I tilt her chin up to meet my gaze.

Stuck?

I don't think so.

I *want* to be with her—from the second she sat her pretty little ass on that barstool at Five Alarm and started running her mouth at me.

I knew.

"For at least the next eighteen years," she teases.

At least.

30
austin

Five months later...

Welp.
 I'm still pregnant.
 I know that's what you were wondering and the answer is yes, Gio is *still* the father. And everyone in the free world knows it because he insists on telling every single person we meet, as if he deserves a medal.
 Everyone: "Oh, you're pregnant? Congratulations!"
 Him: "Thanks, it's mine."
 Proud Zaddy vibes.
 Anyway, pregnancy has been a wild ride.
 I'm a hormonal time-bomb wrapped in stretchy leggings, oversized hoodies, oversized Blaze jerseys, messy buns...
 ...and Gio?
 Obviously feeling way cuter than I am and living his best life. He loves my pregnant stomach, loves my changing body, loves how crabby I've become—BECAUSE HE IS SO ANNOYING.
 Seriously.
 He's starting to drive me nuts.
 He narrates everything. *EVERYTHING.*
 "Captain's Log: *bae is going for her third pickle of the day. Her third. Let's see how this plays out in the bathroom....*"

"Ladies and gentlemen, the baby demands nachos at 2 a.m. Will I survive this grocery store run? Stay tuned!"

And do *not* get me started on the names he's choosing.

This week? He's taken to calling the baby *Giovanni Dangerous*. Not Gio, Junior. Not Dangerous. *Giovanni Dangerous*. Like he's naming a damn Bond villain.

The worst part is he's completely serious. I tried to veto his suggestion—obviously—but then he started googling, "How to legally file a baby name without the mother's consent," and now I'm watching him closely—*just* in case.

Worse, still?

Gio has also decided that pregnancy is the perfect time to become a "cool dad influencer." He bought an adventure camera and strapped it to his chest to capture "authentic dad moments." Which thus far includes: footage of him folding laundry, giving pep talks before doctor's appointments, and ordering all available French fry varieties (curly, regular, and sweet potato) because I was craving potatoes.

The thing is…

As ridiculous as he's behaving, I love him.

There.

I said it.

I love Gio Montagalo and if you would have told me six months ago, I wouldn't have believed you. Never, not in a million years.

Gio has been showing up in a big way. Like, *really* showing up.

And I love the way he talks to my stomach, telling the baby about all the places they're going to go and the games they're going to play and the things they're going to learn.

I love how he holds my hand during every single ultrasound.

He's been the best. When I couldn't reach my toes to paint my nails, Gio sat on the bathroom floor with a tiny bottle of pink polish in his giant hand and painted them for me. Granted, it looked like a toddler slopped the paint on wearing a blindfold, but the effort?

A+

The other day, I caught him trying to assemble the crib we ordered online. He had the instructions upside down and was using a wrench on the wrong screw, but the look of sheer determination on his face? Nearly made me cry.

Confession: *It did make me cry, but to be fair, I cry at insurance commercials these days.*

And don't even get me started on the prenatal classes. Gio goes *all in*. While the other dads are quietly nodding along to the instructor, Gio is taking notes like he's cramming for the SATs. He asks questions—*so many questions*.

"What if the baby's first word is in Italian? Is that okay?"

"Can I be in charge of the lullabies? I've been working on a playlist."

"Hypothetically speaking, if the baby looks exactly like me, how do we handle jealousy?"

He's ridiculous.

He's exhausting.

He's *mine*.

"Babe? Are you ready? The realtor is going to meet us at the house in half an hour, and I don't want to hit traffic," his voice calls out from the kitchen, where I'm sure he's pacing in that dramatic way of his.

I walk into the room with an eye roll as I grab my purse from his glossy counter. "It's Sunday, Gio. We're not going to hit traffic—the city is still sleeping."

We're heading to look at houses—can you believe that shit?

Me.

In a house.

Together, we decided we'd rather not be in a high-rise penthouse or an apartment when the baby arrives, and we came to the agreement—after several debates and a pros-and-cons list on his whiteboard—that maybe we should live together.

It makes sense, right?

He doesn't want to miss everything, and quite honestly, I'd love to share the responsibility. And so here we are, scoping out houses just outside the city limits, in a small suburb close to my college and the ice rink—a win-win for both of us.

I'm still trying to wrap my head around it. The idea of waking up every day and seeing Gio—*all of Gio*—with his messy bedhead, his wide-eyed morning enthusiasm, and his inability to properly load a dishwasher.

It's a lot.

"Babe, I think you're really gonna love this one," he says, breaking into my thoughts as he leans against the doorframe, looking way too proud of himself for someone who probably picked this house based on how large the garage was. "The listing said it's got hardwood floors and a pot filler above the kitchen—whatever that is—but most importantly, *a fenced yard.*"

"A yard for what?" I ask, arching a brow. "I don't think Gio will want to wander." He won't even want to go outside.

He hates it out there.

"You know, in the winter. I can build a rink in the backyard so the baby can learn to skate."

"Gio, the baby isn't even born yet, and you're already planning their skating career?"

"Hey, we gotta start 'em early if we're raising the next hockey superstar—this place has two acres of side yard. That's enormous."

I blink at him, trying to decide whether to laugh, cry, or just get back in bed and pretend this conversation never happened. "You can hardly build Ikea furniture without YouTube tutorials, and now you think you can build an ice rink?"

"Totally different skill set," he insists, sounding completely unbothered. "I bookmarked some tutorials on my phone. It's gonna be amazing. Trust me."

We make our way toward the parking garage.

"Gio, just so we're clear—this imaginary rink of yours?

Who's going to maintain it? Because I'm not waking up at five in the morning to scrape ice or whatever it is hockey parents do."

"Oh, don't worry, babe," he says, pulling out the car keys with a flourish. "I've got it all figured out. I'll get one of those Zamboni machines. You know, the mini ones. I'll just drive it around the yard."

I stop dead in my tracks. "A *Zamboni?*"

He nods like this is the most reasonable idea he's ever had. "Yeah. I've already been looking at used ones online. They're not that expensive if you find one from, like, 1998."

I stare at him, waiting for the punchline, but of course—there isn't one.

This man is dead serious.

"Let me get this straight. You want to buy a house, build an ice rink, and then...drive a Zamboni in our backyard?"

"Exactly," he says, grinning like he's just nailed the best pitch of his life.

"Dude, no."

As we pull out of the garage, I glance over at him, his face lit up with excitement. It's ridiculous, honestly—this whole ice rink idea, the Zamboni, everything—but it's also kind of adorable. Because underneath all the chaos and the questionable plans, Gio is trying.

And as much as I hate to admit it, I wouldn't trade this insanity for anything.

"Know what I'm gonna do when we get back to my place?"

"Hmm?" I hum, scrolling through podcasts to listen to on our drive. "What are you going to do when we get back to your place?"

"Go down on you," he announces, grinning at the oncoming traffic like he's just declared he's going to make a grilled cheese.

My brows shoot up at his pronouncement.

He's said it as if he just told me the sky is blue, or that I'm having a baby: matter-of-fact and to the point. No room for argument.

I blink at him, momentarily forgetting how to form coherent words.

"Excuse me?"

He shrugs, still grinning. "What? You deserve it. House hunting is stressful. You're carrying my child. Least I can do."

"Oh, the *least* you can do?" I repeat, torn between laughing, rolling my eyes, and blushing furiously. Still, he is not wrong. It's been a few weeks since he's gone down on me and I wouldn't shove him out of bed for crawling down between my legs. "It's not like we haven't been having sex."

"I realize that. But oral is like a Hallmark card—when you care enough to send the very best."

He slides his big bear paw over my thigh and squeezes. "Sex is great, don't get me wrong, but there's something about oral. I think it's a thoughtful gesture, don't you?"

"A thoughtful gesture," I repeat, staring at him in disbelief, podcast forgotten.

"Exactly," he says, nodding confidently. "Like, '*Hey babe, I see you, I appreciate you, and I want to make you feel amazing.*' That's the message."

His fingers slide up my black leggings, slow and deliberate, and my heart stutters in my chest.

"Gio," I say, my voice a little breathier than I'd like, "we're literally on our way to meet a realtor. Can you not?"

"Why not?" he teases, his hand lingering above my knee, thumb making lazy circles that send a shiver up my spine.

I press my lips together, trying to ignore the heat pooling low in my belly.

"I can't with you," I mutter, crossing my arms in what I hope looks like indignation and not a desperate attempt to keep myself from grabbing him.

Panties = 100%

"You look so fucking sexy when you're hot and bothered."

"Gio," I warn, though my voice doesn't have nearly as much bite as I'd hoped.

"What?" he asks, all innocence, but the glint in his eye tells me he knows exactly what he's doing. His hand shifts ever so slightly, the barest movement, but it's enough to make my breath hitch.

"We're meeting a realtor in twenty minutes," I remind him, tone sharp but my resolve weakening.

"*Plenty* of time to fuck," he murmurs, gaze flicking briefly to my face before returning to the road, far too casual for someone wreaking absolute havoc on my self-control.

My fingers twitch in my lap, and I squeeze my thighs together in a futile attempt to regain composure.

"You are *ridiculous*."

"You love it," he says, his smirk widening. "Admit it, babe—you like when I rile you up."

I do like it when he riles me up.

"Just say the word," he says, his rumbling voice always makes my stomach flip. "I'll pull over, and we'll be late to the showing. Totally worth it."

Despite myself, I giggle.

I love it when he flirts.

And I love that he finds me sexy even though I am five months pregnant, with a round belly and big boobs.

Ugh!

For a moment, we fall into a comfortable silence, the kind that feels warm and safe and easy. The kind that makes me think maybe, just maybe, we've got this whole "starting a family together" thing figured out.

"You know," he says suddenly, his tone softer now, "I can't wait to see you in that backyard with the baby."

I glance at him, my heart squeezing at the shift in his voice. "Oh yeah? What am I doing in this fantasy of yours?"

"Everything," he says, like it's obvious. "Teaching them how to skate, chasing them around, sitting on the porch with a hot chocolate while I scrape the ice because you're mad at me for forgetting to clean it the day before."

I shoot him an irritated look. "Why does everything have to revolve around ice skating and hockey? Did it ever occur to you that I don't even know how to ice skate?"

Gio's head snaps toward me so fast I'm mildly concerned for his neck. Then, with dramatic flair, he pretends to lose control of the car, jerking the wheel slightly. "What? WHAT? Don't know how to ska—"

"Gio!" I yell, clutching the door in mock panic.

He straightens the car, glancing at me with wide, exaggerated eyes. "You've got to be kidding me. Babe, I didn't know. I'm so sorry."

He is dead serious—or at least pretending to be. I can see the corners of his mouth twitching, but his tone?

Heartfelt.

I roll my eyes. "Oh, stop it. It's not like I told you I've never seen *Game of Thrones* or something."

"This is worse," he says solemnly, gripping the wheel like he's delivering bad news. "This is catastrophic. My pregnant girlfriend doesn't know how to ice skate. What have I done?"

"You've impregnated someone with no athletic skill," I deadpan.

Gio shakes his head slowly, muttering under his breath. "This changes everything."

"Does it, though?" I tease, crossing my arms.

"Yes. Because now, not only do I have to teach our kid to skate, I've got to teach *you* too." He glances over, his face lit with a kind of childlike excitement that makes it impossible to stay annoyed. "It's okay. Don't worry. *I've got this.* I'll teach you the basics first—balance, gliding, stopping. We'll take it slow. I'll even hold your hand the whole time."

I burst out laughing. "Thanks."

"You can't be a hockey mom and not know how to skate." He lets me know. "It's, like, the first rule."

"Gio, I never agreed to be a hockey mom," I tease, though the mental image of him teaching me to skate is admittedly kind of sweet. And the thought of our kid being on a hockey team.... Adorable.

"You will," he says with a confident smirk. "Wait until you see me coaching from the bench. You won't be able to resist."

If my ovaries weren't currently otherwise occupied, they'd be exploding from the cuteness. The idea of Gio shouting at tiny humans to "skate faster" while our kid looks up at him with awe?

It's a recipe for emotional overload.

"You've really thought this through, eh?" I say, my voice softening despite my best efforts to stay teasing.

"I'll make sure to keep it fun. No crazy coach dad energy—just hot dad energy."

He already is a hot dad.

Looking at him has me practically drooling.

Swoon!

"So, what happens if the baby doesn't *like* hockey?" I ask, raising an eyebrow at him because it is entirely possible our kid won't have a single, athletic bone in their body—like their mama.

He gasps dramatically.

"Impossible. It's in their DNA."

"Gio," I deadpan. "The baby could just as easily *hate* ice and decide they want to do ballet or play chess. What then?"

He scoffs. "Obviously I'll learn how to be the best damn chess dad ever," he says without missing a beat. "I'll build a life-size chess set in the backyard

Good God.

No.

I laugh again, the kind of laugh that bubbles up uncontrollably.

"I love you," I say, my head leaning back against the headrest, one hand resting protectively on my baby bump.

He reaches over, his hand warm and steady as he places it over mine, giving my bump a soft pat.

"I love you, too," he says in a way that makes my chest ache in the best way. "Both of you."

I let my eyes close for just a moment, a soft smile playing on my lips.

He's a goofball.

A big, hot, sexy goofball.

My goofball.

For *forever*, maybe.

Even if it does mean I'll probably end up with a Zamboni parked in my backyard.

epilogue
Nova

My brother has officially left the building.
Literally.

It's depressing knowing he's no longer going to be three floors above; I can no longer surprise him with visits, can't steal food from his fridge, can't interrupt him and his girlfriend in any tender moments. He's been my built-in safety net, my loud, annoying, overprotective safety net.

And now? He's gone.

Packed up his things, kissed me on the forehead, and drove off into suburbia with his very pregnant girlfriend.

He's moving on with his life and creating a family.

I am so happy for him!

I love him so much—you all know that.

But…

It still leaves me empty inside, not having him in the same building.

Call it habit, call it codependency, call it whatever you want —but it feels like I'm losing my partner in crime.

Partner in crime? Ugh. I hate when people say that, especially men on dating apps. *Ha ha, looking for my partner in crime!* No,

Chad, you're looking for someone to split your Netflix subscription and swipe their ex's password for Hulu.

Let's call it what it is.

With a miserable groan, I throw myself onto the couch, the weight of my sudden loneliness hitting me square in the chest.

"You get it, don't you, Gio?" I ask, scratching Austin's dog behind his weird ears. He glares at me, letting out a dramatic sigh as if to say, *Can you keep it down, lady? I'm trying to nap.*

Jeez.

"Glad someone's thriving," I mutter, pulling out my phone and opening the dating apps. Because when your brother moves out and your couch buddy is a dog that resents you for being a shitty dog sitter, there's no better time for emotional self-sabotage.

Let the games begin!

The first guy? Shirtless mirror selfie.

Swipe left.

The second guy? Holding a fish.

"Why is it always a fish?" Are they trying to prove they can provide sustenance in a post-apocalyptic world?

Swipe left.

The third? Another traveler, every photo in a different exotic location, including Machu Picchu and the Canary Islands.

"Sir, I can't afford a latte right now."

Swipe left.

"Little dude, why are men like this?" I ask the dog, turning the phone toward him. He squints at the screen, unimpressed. Sniffs the air. "Want to move in with me permanently? Wouldn't that be fun? Huh?"

I go to give him more pets but he lets out a soft sneeze and hops off the couch—*clearly* over my pity party. Gio trots to the other end of the room, his bald stick legs barely making a sound, before flopping onto his blanket.

"Never mind. I take that back." *I didn't need a dog's support anyway.*

I glance back at my phone, debating whether to swipe on another profile or just delete the app altogether.

Curiosity wins out and I continue scrolling; mindlessly, thumb hovering over a man's profile named Blake. Five years older, well-dressed, and posing with a golden retriever in front of a hiking trail.

"Hmm," I mumble, narrowing my eyes at the screen. "Are you really outdoorsy, Blake, or did you borrow your cousin's dog for the photo?"

I tap on his bio.

It goes on and on, *blah blah blah*, "lover of coffee, live music, and spontaneous road trips."

Okay, Blake.

A little generic, but nothing offensive. No shirtless selfies, no fish photos—already an improvement!

I glance over at Gio, who is now snoring softly on his blanket.

"What do you think?" I say to no one. "Swipe right or no?"

The dog's ears don't even twitch.

"Fine. Swipe left," I say, swiping past Blake and moving on to the next profile.

It's a guy holding a sword. Not, like, a fencing sword—an actual sword. In his living room.

"Jesus Christ," I mutter, swiping left so fast I nearly drop my phone.

The next guy is a little better: a cute smile, some pictures with friends, and no immediate red flags.

The bio? *Looking for my queen. Must love adventure and tacos.*

I groan. "Must love tacos? What does that even mean? Everyone loves tacos, Kevin. You're not special!"

Left.

My thumb freezes over the next profile, though, because the guy looks... *familiar*? No, not familiar. He looks exactly like my childhood dentist. Same slightly unnerving smile, same weirdly perfect hair, but grayer than the last time I had a cavity, which was over ten years ago.

"Nope," I say aloud. "You are a creep!"

I flop back on the couch, staring at the ceiling as Gio lets out a tiny snort in his sleep.

"This is it," I tell him. "This is my life now. Me, you, and a never-ending stream of weirdos on the internet."

I'm doomed.

Swipe.

Swipe.

Then.

I see another profile that looks familiar.

I freeze, holding the phone closer to my face than necessary, my heart skipping a beat as I stare at the bio of Luca—as in Luca Babineaux, my brother's teammate and the guy Austin and I had been gossiping about months ago...

"No way," I whisper, my brows furrowing as I study his profile.

Luca's profile picture is exactly what you'd expect from a good-looking athlete: standing on a beach, shirtless, with a volleyball tucked under one arm and a smug grin that could rival Gio's on a good day. His bio? *Goal-oriented. Literally. Bonus points if you like dogs and can handle trash-talking during game night.*

Well.

That's snarkier and more clever than I would've given him credit for, considering I've always considered Luca Babineaux boring as fuck.

I squint at the screen; something about it doesn't sit right.

Where are the hockey pictures? The gear? The action shots from their games?

Not a single one.

Instead, I'm greeted with more photos of Luca on a beach or on a catamaran, laughing with his arm slung around Paulie Osborne—a famous comedian, of all people.

"Okay, *what?*" I mutter, flipping to the next photo.

There's one of him in a flannel, holding a coffee cup during what looks like the holidays. A random mountain range looms out the living room window, majestic and snowy and gorgeous.

Then there's Luca on a motorcycle, looking like he just strolled out of a movie poster.

"*Who the hell is this guy?*" I ask no one, my voice dripping with suspicion.

I keep scrolling.

I'm so fascinated.

Him standing with two young women that resemble him—sisters? Cousins? Another photo of him snorkeling, his face half-hidden behind goggles and a snorkel tube.

And then there's a selfie of him hiking with that black lab puppy he had six months ago—only now, the dog's mostly grown, its floppy ears framing an adorably derpy face.

I set my phone down for a moment, rubbing my temples.

It doesn't make sense. Luca's life isn't this…glamorous. *Is it?* I mean, he plays hockey, hangs out with my brother and his teammates, and from what I know—goes home and sleeps. None of this beach-and-motorcycle nonsense fits the image I have of him.

Unless…

I glance back at the screen, narrowing my eyes.

Could someone be pretending to be him? It wouldn't be hard—there are hundreds of photos of him on the internet and he has a face only a mother could love.

"What do you think, Gio?" I say to the dog, asking for his advice. "Is this him, or is someone out there pretending to be Luca freaking Babineaux?"

Gio yawns, showing off his tiny, uneven teeth, and turns his head away, clearly over my dramatics.

"Thanks for your input," I mutter, picking my phone back up.

I hesitate, thumb hovering over the screen.

Do I swipe right and investigate? Or do I swipe left and pretend I never saw it?

Because if it's him…it's going to be super awkward.

But if it's not him…it could be *hilarious*.

I hold my breath.

Close my eyes.

Before I can stop myself, I swipe right, heart pounding for reasons I'd rather not analyze.

I toss my phone onto the coffee table like it's made of lava and cross my arms.

"Oh my God!" NO I DID NOT!

"No way he swipes back," I reason aloud, sending those vibes into the universe. *Oh my God this is so embarrassing*! "There is no freaking way."

A few seconds pass. Then my phone pings.

One new match!

My stomach twists as I grab the phone, my pulse quickening. Sure enough, there it is: **Luca has matched with you.**

"Oh, shit," I whisper, staring at the screen. My chest tightens as I glance over at Gio again, hoping he'll wake up and offer some kind of moral support. He doesn't. Of course.

"What do I do, what do I do?!" I groan, flopping back against the couch cushions. My mind races as I imagine every possible outcome of this—most of them ending in complete and utter humiliation.

Panic at the disco. Full-blown freak-out mode.

Holy *shit*.

I sit up abruptly, clutching my phone like it's my lifeline. "Okay, Nova. Calm down. It's probably not even him. It's probably just some random dude using his pictures."

The phone pings again.

Luca has sent you a note!

"I can't look."

Yes you can. Stop being a wuss.

HIT ME WITH YOUR BEST SHOT

I take a deep breath and peek at the screen, through my fingers.

> Luca: Does Gio know you're swiping on me?

Well. That solves that mystery. This is one-hundred percent my brother's teammate.

Grinning despite myself, I tap out a cheeky response.

> Me: Gio is not the boss of me.

> Luca: Good to know.

I stare at that sentence, my heart doing a stupid little flip; something about the brevity of it feels deliberately careful, like he's testing the waters.

Another message immediately pops up.

> Luca: But I'm sure he'd have opinions.

I snort, rolling my eyes

> Me: Gio always has opinions.

The dots appear again, and I find myself leaning forward, waiting for whatever he's going to say next.

> Luca: Fair. But just so we're clear, this conversation doesn't leave the app. I like my face the way it is—unbroken.

> Me: You want this to stay a secret?

Interesting.
I like it.

> Luca: No need for drama over nothing.

Nothing?

I laugh, a full, belly-deep laugh, not sure if I should be insulted by his insinuation that matching with me amounts to, well–nothing. The dog glances over at me, ears twitching, before deciding he's not interested in whatever has me so amused.

> Me: NOTHING? Wow. I'm SO flattered.

The dots pop up again, and I can practically feel his hesitation through the screen.

> Luca: That's not what I meant. You know that.

> Me: Do I? Because it kinda feels like you're saying matching with me is no big deal.

Another pause, longer this time.
Then,

> Luca: It's a big enough deal that I'm risking Gio's wrath to talk to you behind his back. How's that for flattery?

I bite my lip, trying not to smile too hard. Damn him for being smooth.

> Me: Not bad. But you're still on thin ice.

> Luca: Good thing I'm used to skating on it.

I groan, equal parts annoyed and charmed. "Terrible," I mutter under my breath, shaking my head.

So why is flirting with him making me tingle all over?
Guh!

> Luca: Honestly, I'm surprised to see you on here. You're way too pretty to be single.

> Me: What makes you think I'm single?

> Luca: You're on a fucking dating app?

Oh. Good point.

And that mouth of his...

Who would've known? Luca looks like a choir boy—clean-cut, polite, the kind of guy who probably thanks the refs after every game—but apparently, there's a little edge to him.

He follows up his previous text with:

> Are you on this app to flirt or to find a serious relationship?

I blink at the question, taken aback by how straightforward it is. I nibble on the inside of my cheek.

> Me: For a relationship. I'm tired of being single. You?

> Luca: I want kids and a family and I'm not getting any younger.

I exit out of our chat to give his profile another glance—gawking at his shirtless photograph, seeing him as if seeing him for the first time.

Who even *is* this version of Luca?

The Luca I know is quiet, always polite, with a vaguely broody vibe that makes you forget he's ridiculously attractive. But this? This is something else. The smirk, the shiny washboard abs, the *everything*.

> Me: You look like the kind of guy that wants kids.

I smirk as I hit send, picturing his reaction.

The dots pop up again, and my pulse quickens.

> Luca: What does that mean? That I look boring?

> Me: I did NOT say that...

> Luca: You implied it.

> Me: Okay, fine. You're not boring. Happy now?

The pause is longer this time, and I start to wonder if I've actually annoyed him. But then his message pops up:

> Luca: I'll let it slide. For now. But only because you're cute.

> Me: CUTE?

> Luca: Sorry. I meant smoking hot. You're a real smoke show, Nova Montagalo.

My stomach does a stupid little flip, and I glance over at Gio the dog, who's now awake and staring at me like he can sense my internal chaos.

"Don't look at me like that," I mutter, setting the phone down on the couch for a second. "Stop judging me, Gio is not going to find out about this."

This...

Is dangerous.

Luca is way too easy to talk to. And way too *good* for my peace of mind.

I pick the phone back up, staring at the chat. Should I keep going? Let this conversation turn into something, even though it'll probably end in disaster? Or should I delete the chat right now and save myself the headache?

Gio yawns as if to say, *You're overthinking this, idiot.*

I glance at Luca's profile again, lingering on the easy smile in one of his photos. This doesn't have to mean anything, right? It's harmless flirting.

But now I know he thinks I'm smoking hot.

I bite back a grin, my thumb hovering over the keyboard. Flirting with Luca Babineaux feels like walking into a trap I can totally see coming—and yet, here I am, taking another step forward.

> Me: You think I'm a smoke show? Sounds like you're starting to have a thing for me, Babineaux.

I tease.

Okay FINE.

I'll admit it, I'm fishing for compliments. Are you happy now?!

> Luca: Starting to? You're funny. I've had a thing for you for years...

My jaw drops.

"WHAT?" I blurt out, scaring the shit out of the dog, settling back onto his blanket with a huff. He hates me.

The dog, not Luca.

Apparently.

I stare at the screen, reading and rereading the message at least three times to make sure I didn't hallucinate it.

Years?

Since when!?

My thumbs hover over the keyboard, but for the first time all night, I have no idea what to say. My brain is too busy replaying every interaction I've ever had with Luca, searching for clues I clearly didn't pick up on.

Did he flirt with me at that team dinner last year? Was he staring at me too long during Gio's birthday party?

No. Surely not.

Right?

My stomach does a somersault, and I press a hand to my chest, trying to calm the sudden thudding of my heart, this new revelation sending me.

My phone pings again, pulling me out of my spiral.

> Luca: Still there? Or did I scare you off?

> Me: Scared? Please. It takes more than that to scare me.

The dots pop up immediately, and I swear my heart skips a beat.

> Luca: Good. Coz I've got plenty more to say…

Oh, God.

I glance at Gio the dog, who's now staring at me with those big, judgmental eyes. "What do I do?" I whisper, holding the phone up for guidance. "Little dude, help!"

> Me: More to say? Do go on.

Sorry. I had to ask.
I'm a thirsty bitch, what can I say…
This is bad. Dangerous. Completely reckless.
But damn if it isn't fun.

> Luca: I have 8 words for you, Nova.

He makes me wait, not giving them to me.

> Me: What 8 words?

I am holding my breath.

> Luca: I want you, if only for one night.

have you read the pucker next door?

Available in KU

Chapter 1
Lizzy

"We have *what* in our attic?"

"Squirrels."

I stare blankly at one of my roommates. "So?"

"So," Bethany deadpans. "I'm not staying here with squirrels running around the attic. What if one chews through the light fixture and falls into my room while I'm sleeping?" She shudders. "And what if it's not squirrels. Do I want to be here to find out? No. It's a *no* from me."

There are squirrels all over campus. Obviously, they're going to infiltrate the living quarters of those of us living in crappy, off-campus housing. Also, they're cute. I don't get weirded out by their presence like some of my girlfriends do—and I don't agree they have beady little eyes.

My roommate swears they're going to pounce or worse—attack—and won't look in their direction. She says their little brown eyeballs bore into her soul when she sees one (or five or fifteen) when she's walking to class.

"What's your plan, then?" I stare at the small bookshelf in

our living room, trying to decide on a book to read. It's Friday night, but I have no desire to get cute and go out.

Plus, it's cold.

"My plan?"

"Yeah. Your plan."

"I'm going to stay with Jon until our freaking landlord gets pest control and removes them. I swear there's an entire family up there. It's probably raccoons." She's quiet for a few seconds while she worst-case scenarios all the horrible critters that could be living in our house. "Bats. Opossums. Rats."

Another shudder.

"What's Jill going to do?"

Bethany lets out a puff of air, moving to the kitchen.

"She's going to her parents. Their lake house is like, forty minutes from campus and she doesn't want her face eaten off, either. Her mom said they carry diseases, and Jill doesn't want animal pox."

I have no idea what that even is.

Does she mean rabies?

Ew.

"You're being so dramatic about this." Like *so* dramatic.

"You're not being dramatic *enough*!" she announces theatrically. "You're not staying in this house when there are rodents ready to revolt. You can't."

"I haven't heard a single sound." I shrug. "No animals."

"That's because you snore. If you were in my room, you'd hear it. The door for the crawl space is literally in my closet."

That's probably true that I snore, but I'm still not overly concerned.

"So what I hear you saying is that I'm going to be home alone for the next few days?" I hate being alone, which is the reason I have roommates. That and splitting the rent. "Why do I have to be here by myself?"

What if something is actually going to maim me?

"Go stay with Keesha or Marie. I told them we have an infestation and they offered to let me stay on their couch."

We do not have an infestation. Is that what she's telling her friends?

"I like them both but I'm not staying with your sorority sisters."

It would be weird being there without Bethany, wouldn't it?

"What about Danika and Michelle's place?"

"Are you kidding me? They had a friggin bat in their living room last month, and Paul had to catch it with a lacrosse stick." The words fly out of my mouth, and I immediately regret them, clamping my mouth shut to prevent more verbal diarrhea. Maybe I shouldn't be reminding her when the subject of pests in our own attic is so sensitive.

"Then go next door." Bethany is clearly frustrated with my rebuttal to all her suggestions—and rightly so. "The guys already offered to come over and handle it, but when I told the landlord, he said if anyone came over and went into the attic, it had to be a professional because if there was any damage, we'd have to pay for it."

Of course he did.

"That guy is such an asshole," I groan because our landlord is such an asshole.

We're not sure what his deal is, but it takes him forever to respond to our messages. God forbid there's an emergency, like a pipe bursting and water leaking through the ceilings around the lights. Once, the light fixture in our living room was crackling and buzzing, and we were afraid it would start an electrical fire. You'd think he would want to buzz right over and assess the situation? Protect his investment?

Did the man bother to call us back after we'd frantically left voicemail after voicemail?

Negative, ghost rider.

It took him days.

Why? Because!

Have you read The Pucker Next Door?

He.
Is.
A.
Dick.

So. I'm not sure why he'd give a shit about the alleged critter in our attic, but if he's going to handle it when he gets around to it and not a moment sooner.

I'll believe it when I see it.

My bedroom is on the first floor, which could be a reason I haven't so much as heard a peep from any unwanted houseguests—but that's just a guess.

"Come on, Lizzy, let's be honest," Bethany laments. "Those morons next door would probably actually cause damage if they came here to fight squirrels, let alone more bats."

The neighbors in question?

Four hockey players on the university's team, each and every one of them massive, rough-around-the-edges dudes.

I haven't had much interaction with them. There has been no reason for me to go over there, and I don't count the occasional head nod when one happens to be walking to his front porch at the same time, and we make accidental eye contact.

We were baking once, and I didn't check for ingredients before starting. We needed one egg for brownies, and none of us had wanted to run to the grocery store or pay for delivery, so Bethany waltzed over and knocked on the door.

A life-size Elmo answered the door, or rather...it was a dude in an Elmo costume—we're not sure if it was a kink thing or a costume party thing, but Bethany hadn't known where to look or what to say and long story short: they didn't have eggs either.

Yeah.

Bethany and Jill might know their names, but I do not.

Why would I?

Athletes intimidate me.

I see them headed in my direction, and I turn the other way. What would I do if I made purposeful eye contact with one, let

Have you read The Pucker Next Door?

alone had to talk to one? And these guys next door? They look like action heroes come to life. I'm positive they probably grunt instead of talk...

"Anyway..." Bethany is cramming clothes into an overnight bag, not bothering to neatly fold them. "There should be someone here tomorrow to handle it. Assuming the asshole does actually call pest control."

"I'm still convinced you're overreacting."

My roommate rolls her eyes. "And I'm sure it's only a matter of time before an animal attacks me in the middle of the night while I'm sleeping. I'd rather not take my chances."

"What time do I have to be here to let the guy in?"

"No idea." My roommate shrugs. "Asshole has a key, and asshole has to call the pest dude." She leaves the room and bounds up the stairs, returning with an overnight kit. Toothbrush. Toothpaste. "My guess is he'll text and only give us a ten-minute notice, so hopefully, we're in class. I don't want to have to talk to him. He can figure this out by himself. It's like, a health hazard or something if he doesn't."

Is it, though?

Bethany takes one last glance at me before zipping her bag shut.

"Honestly, I think you're using this as an excuse to go to your boyfriend's house for a few days. There is no need to leave."

It's a rodent, not a bomb.

"I don't need an excuse to stay with Jon for a few days." She tilts her head. "Still not taking any chances."

It's moments like this that I'm reminded how high maintenance my roommates are compared to me, who is willing to stay in the house and gamble that a man-eating squirrel won't come bursting through my bedroom wall.

I mean, what are the actual odds?

"Alright. You know where to find me if you need anything."

Like I'm going to need anything?

Puh-lease.

"I think I'll manage with you down the road, like, a whole block." I'm exaggerating. He lives farther down than a block but it still wouldn't take me that much time to scuttle myself to his house. "I'll be fine." *In fact.* "It'll be nice having the house all to myself. Have I ever been here alone before?"

There are three of us.

Jill and Bethany share a room. I have the luxury of being in my own room thanks to the random drawing we had before moving in. That's what decided for us who was in which room.

Once Bethany has left, I don't know what to do first!

Jump on the couch?

Run from room to room naked?

Eat all the food labeled 'JILL'?

Instead, I run the bath, pouring a healthy dose of oils into the water while watching the steam rise. It's not often I'm able to hog the bathroom. Someone always "needs" it, wants to do their hair, needs to do their skin care routine, take a shower, brush their teeth, or use the toilet.

This is going to feel so good.

I find a romance novel in the living room that Bethany brought home recently, flipping it over so I can read the blurb.

A hockey romance?

I scoff.

Of course, she'd be reading a hockey romance when we have a house full of hockey players next door. Coincidence?

I think not.

I pluck it off the coffee table and take it to the bathroom along with my bathrobe, a fresh towel, and slippers. I test the water with the tip of my toe before stepping into it and push back the shower curtain so it's not dragging in the water.

I lower myself down.

I sigh when I'm submerged up to my boobs, then dip in lower so it covers my shoulders, and close my eyes.

"Ahhh."

This is the life.

No roommates, no exams to study for, and a fridge full of food that no one can yell at me for eating.

I'm winning.

Idly, I lie here a few minutes, enjoying the silence before removing my hands from the suds, drying them off with the terry cloth towel I placed next to the tub, and pick up the paperback that's been chilling on the toilet seat cover.

What the hell was that?

I pause with the remote control pointed at the TV.

Scratch, scratch.

I listen.

Tilt my head to hear better, hitting MUTE on the remote.

Thump.

I sit up, arranging myself into a sitting position, still in my robe after my bath because I don't feel entirely comfortable lying around naked, and it's cozy—like a hug I'm giving myself without all the effort.

I remain frozen on the bed as the scratching noise persists, as if something were gnawing at the wall. Or the wires in the wall? Or...

It sounds like it's in my closet.

There is no way.

Can't be.

I would have heard it before now, yeah?

Bethany and Jill heard it, and you made fun of them for being dramatic.

My roommates, who I may remind you, are both safely out of the house until the landlord comes with his pest control dude.

Shit.

How am I going to sleep with that critter—whatever it is—gnawing away at the drywall?

Scratch, scratch...

I hit mute on the TV to listen, this time getting up off the bed and going to the scene of the action. Pushing the shirts neatly hanging on the rack aside, I stick my arm through them and give the wall a hard thump.

"Take that, you little dickhead."

I pause when it stops scratching, relieved.

"Be quiet." I tell the sound. "You're stressing me out."

I put a hand to my chest and find my heart thumping wildly. Then.

Just as I'm about to turn and leave the closet to walk back to the bed, I see a set of eyes.

Small, beady brown eyes stare back at me from the flannel shirts hanging on the top rack. I open my mouth to let out a bloodcurdling scream when the squirrel squeezes itself through the tiny hole it made and launches onto my dresser, knocking a perfume bottle to the floor.

"OH MY GOD!"

Oh my god, oh my god, oh my god.

I beeline it to the door, slamming the door closed behind me, and holy shit, THERE IS A SQUIRREL TRAPPED INSIDE MY ROOM.

Oh my god, oh my god, oh my god.

What do I do?

"What do I do?" I'm shouting, arms flailing, twirling in frantic circles. "Where's my phone, where's my phone?!"

Frantically, with trembling hands, I find Bethany's contact in my phone and hit CALL BETHANY, and of course it immediately goes to voicemail.

Oh my god, oh my god, oh my god.

What do I do?

I'm going to die in here at the hands of a rabid squirrel.

I dash to the kitchen and desperately search for the Post-it Note with our landlord's cell phone number. I'm unable to locate it anywhere, so I drop my phone because my hands are shaking so bad.

"Calm down, Lizzy. The squirrel can't get you."

No.

It can't *get* me, but it can shit all over my bedroom and tear apart everything inside of it and build a nest while the damn thing is locked in my room, and oh my god, what if he brings his friends to his little party?

There have to be more where this came from. Don't they travel in packs?

What do I do?

Bethany hasn't gotten my call. No doubt she's at a bar somewhere whooping it up, carefree and shit, with bad cell service. Meanwhile, I can't find the landlord's phone number anywhere because my roommates have it, and my parents live too far away for my dad to help.

I worry my bottom lip.

I wish I had the window in my bedroom open because maybe the tiny brown heathen would take a hint and hit the road.

The light goes on next door.

The front door opens.

A big dude walks out and plops down on the wooden porch swing, eating something out of a white takeout container I cannot identify from here, leaving me with no option but to take myself next door and beg for his help.

Him.

He is my only hope.

I pull my robe tighter, cinching the belt securely so my cleavage isn't showing, slide into a pair of flip-flops, and adjust the towel on my head. I keep the towel on because it's cold outside, and also, the last thing I need is to look like total shit when I go to the house next door because I look like total shit when my hair is damp.

Whatever.

Not the point!

Taking a deep breath, I open our front door and step through it. The wind whips my robe, opening it so my lady business is showing and I almost lose the towel wrapped around my damp hair.

The guy hasn't noticed me come outside the way I noticed him, and I hope he's a decent dude and not an insensitive asshole with no interest in my survival.

I have one eye on him as I move down the front porch steps, trying not to trip and kill myself, given that I'm basically stuck wearing a robe with nothing beneath it. Perhaps, he won't even notice?

I'm on a mission: desperate times call for desperate measures…

Down the steps I go, shouting, "Help!" for good measure. "Help!"

I don't know when the guy finally notices I'm in the yard because he doesn't look up right away from whatever it is he's eating, but when he does look up, his eyes widen.

He stops chewing, a white plastic fork halfway to his mouth.

"What," he deadpans with a lack of greeting, and for a second, I'm taken aback. I at least expect him to say hello…

"Hi." I get closer, panting as if I had just run a mile. "My name is Lizzy, and I live next door—"

I throw a thumb over my shoulder to point back at our house for good measure.

He cuts me off. "I know who you are."

He does?

How does he know who I am?

I've never been introduced to this guy before. I would absolutely remember if I had. They don't really throw parties, and neither do we, so I wouldn't have had a reason to go into their house. We don't barbecue or talk in the backyards, which is strange, considering these guys seem to grill out a lot.

Anyway.

He's massive.

And bearded.

And has a really deep voice. He's basically a man? But probably my age, so it's strange reconciling the appearance and age, knowing that he's not a full-fledged adult but looks like one.

"I am so sorry I'm in my robe. I ran out of the house. I'm sort of in the middle of an emergency?" I ramble, causing his eyes to widen, especially when I pull my robe tighter across my chest. "My roommates aren't home, and our landlord isn't calling us back, so I didn't know where else to go."

He abruptly stands, porch swing flying back and hitting the guardrails with a loud thud.

"I hope you're not here because you need help."

Yes, I need help! I was literally shouting 'help! help!' when I ran over!

"I'm sorry, what is your name? There's a squirrel in my bedroom," I blurt out. "It flew out of the wall and scared the shit out of me."

"Brodie. It's in your *bed*room? That flew out of your wall?" He sounds appropriately horrified. "A live squirrel? With fur and stuff?"

"Yes, locked in my bedroom." I can hardly get the story out fast enough. "I heard scratching—lots of scratching. Was just lying there in my robe minding my business when I heard it again."

My neighbor dude is hanging on my every word even though they're the details he did not ask for and probably did not want.

"So I go into the closet, right? Just to see if I was losing my mind or not—and I follow the sound, pushing back all my clothes, and there he is! Staring back at me."

"What'd you do?" His food is long forgotten, and so are the formalities. I still have no idea who this guy is or what his name is.

"I screamed! He's in my bedroom as we speak, probably shitting on all my stuff and building nests and…" I shudder. "Can you please come help me? I have no idea what to do and I don't want to be in there alone."

Have you read The Pucker Next Door?

Chapter 2
Brody

"Can you please help me? I don't know what to do..."

Lizzy Campbell is on *my* porch, asking for *my* help. It's textbook damsel in distress bullshit that I hadn't asked for.

Granted, I think she's hot, and I'd be lying if I said I haven't had a hard-on for her since she and her roommates moved into the house next door at the beginning of the semester, not that I'll be declaring my love to her anytime soon.

But as soon as I saw her on moving day, carrying those cardboard boxes up the front porch steps of their house with her long dark hair, short denim shorts, white tank top, Converse sneakers... yeah.

She's good-looking, big deal.

Plenty of people are.

But no fucking way would I ever go over there, crossing the property line that separates her yard and ours—not that I'm too chickenshit to do it. Yes, I could have helped them on moving day, but moving them in was not a me problem.

And don't think I'm stupid enough to tell my own idiot roommates about my dumb little crush...pfft. It's not a crush. I just think she's cute, so what?

Why wouldn't I say something to them? 'Cause they're the type of guys who call dibs on women, and the less attention I draw to her, the better—not that I ever plan on asking her out myself. Plus, they'd bust my nuts about it the first chance they got, and the last thing I want is for them to embarrass me in front of her. Because they would, because they're assholes and get off on shit like that. Public humiliation is guy speak for showing that he cares.

Considering she lives directly next door, the chances of being embarrassed by my dick roommates are highly probable.

Don't need that kind of drama, and therefore, I would never

say anything. *I do just fine embarrassing myself on my own without anyone's help.*

Besides, just because I think someone is cute doesn't mean I'm interested. Lots of things are cute—puppies, kittens, babies. That doesn't mean I have to think about them all the time.

So I put it out of my mind the way I do with everything else and moved on.

"*Can you please help me, I don't know what to do...*"

Can I help her? Sure.

Do I want to?

No.

Am I gonna?

Yeah. Probably.

Why? Don't ask, I have no idea. I'm feeling generous, I guess, and there is no one else home who she can con into going over there to look at her place. It's just me. And even if I wasn't the only one home, I'm curious enough to help her anyway.

"Have you tried calling your landlord?"

She rolls her eyes at me. "Obviously, we've called our landlord. He's useless."

They always are.

I'm quiet for a few seconds so I can think. Squinting down at her, I scratch at the back of my skull. "You said it's in your bedroom?

Duh, you fucking idiot. She's mentioned that it's in her bedroom like, four times.

Sorry, but Lizzy, the neighbor girl, is standing on my front porch in a bathrobe, and I can see the outline of her tits and a decent shot of skin, and the fact that she's obviously not wearing a bra is throwing me off.

I can barely concentrate.

The wind kicks up, and I catch a whiff of her that I didn't know I wanted or needed.

Goddamn, she smells good.

"Yes." I can see her patience wearing thin. "He's probably

losing his tiny little mind and wrecking all my shit because he can't get outside."

"Yeah, probably," I muse, then regret my choice of words when I see her face fall. "Although I'm not sure how squirrels operate inside a house?" More like it'll be nesting. "We should try to get your bedroom window open." I scratch my chin. "You have a bedroom window, right?"

Lizzy rolls her eyes. "Of course, I have a bedroom window."

I lift my shoulders in a shrug. "Hey, I was just askin' because not everyone does. You know how these landlords operate, cramming as many people into one house as possible to make the most money."

Shady fuckers.

My sophomore year, I lived in a house with two bedrooms, and we had five people living in it. We all paid rent, and the landlord knew we were above max capacity, but he let us lie on our application, knowing full well we were breaking the building code.

Lizzy nods. "Good point."

She shivers, pulling the robe tighter, not dressed for the cooling afternoon temperatures. It's not hot, and it's not cold, but it's going to be dark soon, and along with that comes a dip in the weather.

I set my takeout container on the ground by the door, wiping my hands on the legs of my jogging pants.

"I guess I could assess the situation." So magnanimous of me, wouldn't you say, considering I'm putting myself in harm's way?

The least I can do is crack open one of her windows to see if we can prompt that furry little mongrel to evacuate the premises on his own accord if he hasn't already.

"Aren't you going to bring a hockey stick or something?" Lizzy shivers again, but all I can focus on now is the fact that she knows I play hockey.

My mouth gapes. She wants me to bring one of my precious hockey sticks to combat an animal? Is she out of her damn mind?

Have you read The Pucker Next Door?

1. They're expensive
2. It takes me forever to wrap it to my liking and get it just so. I'm not about to undo all that work by fighting off whatever lurks in her bedroom.
3. Hockey sticks are not weapons. They're gear.

"Uh, no?" I clutch my chest, affronted. "What do you want me to do with it? Take a swing at the squirrel with one of my precious sticks? My stick is my moneymaker." Not to mention how cruel it would be trying to bonk some little dude on the noggin.

I get what she's saying, even if I'm not going to do it.

She wants that fucker gone, and it's not like she's going to grab him with her bare hands. And most people don't have nets lying around or whatever.

I'm no goalie, so I don't have goalie gloves, either.

"I wasn't sure how you wanted to catch him," she tells me.

Keyword: you.

Keyword: catch him.

"Catch him with what? Like with my *hands*? Fuck no."

She's cute but delusional if she thinks I'm going to march inside that house and try to lure or go at him with any athletic equipment.

Or fight the mangy little thing.

"Let's just go see what the lil' dude's been up to."

She scrunches up her face. "Is calling him a lil' dude supposed to make me feel better about the situation?"

She sounds irritated, and I laugh.

"No, I'm just making conversation." I follow her down the steps, padding barefoot across our grassy yard to hers.

Why is she the one racing around the yard barefoot, in a robe, handling this business by herself? Is there no sense of camaraderie between girls?

"If my roommates were home I would have never come over, I promise. I would have had Bethany's boyfriend handle the situation." She considers what she would have done for a few seconds. "Actually, he's a wimp, so I have no idea what we would have done." She sighs loudly.

"Bethany has been listening to the squirrel in her wall for the past few days and was freaking the frick out, so she took off and went to a Jon's house. My other roommate took off, too."

I know Jill.

She dated Charlie, one of my teammates, for a hot minute last semester when they all moved in. Actually, that's not true—dating isn't the accurate term for it.

Fucking. She was fucking one of my roommates, Charlie, for a hot minute last semester.

Several large, mature oak trees are between her house and ours, and acorns are scattered on the ground like confetti—one of the reasons the squirrel population in this town is so high, according to my own theories.

Lizzy's house doesn't have a front porch like ours does.

In fact, it doesn't have a front porch at all, so she leads me to the side of the house, down their short driveway, and to the side door with its tiny awning and small stoop. It's facing our house, and when we step inside, we're automatically in the kitchen—a kitchen I can see inside at night when the girls have all their lights on or are standing at the sink.

Not that I spy.

I'm merely saying we can see them walking around inside sometimes.

The first thing I notice about the inside of the house is its smell. Apples and caramel?

Food?

Baked goods?

Smells a whole hell of a lot better than ours, that's for damn sure. Our house smells like wet gym socks and farts and dirty duffel bags that haven't been cleaned out in years.

The second thing I notice?

How tidy everything seems to be.

Blankets in the small living room are folded into neat squares and stacked on one end of the couch. The kitchen isn't full of dirty cups and plates piled by the sink in the same way they are at our place. Also, the girls hung decorations. And they have throw pillows—and curtains.

And cute pictures of themselves stuck with cute magnets to the refrigerator door.

There isn't clutter anywhere, and I marvel at the differences between chicks and dudes and rubberneck, almost walking into a doorframe while I take it all in, gawking my entire way through the house until we're standing in front of a closed bedroom door on the first floor.

"Well. This is me. This is it." She sounds gloomy and foreboding, as if dark things lurk behind the door.

Furry, demonic things.

"Moment of truth," I joke, not wanting to open the door myself.

Goddamn, I wish one of my roommates were here. I hate this feeling of not knowing what the hell to expect when I turn the knob, cursing toxic masculinity and that it dictates I go through the door first and that I don't make *her* do it despite this being her house.

I hate the unknown.

Even in games, after the puck drop, my gut is usually unsettled. In knots. Occasionally, depending on who our opponent is, I feel the urge to vomit. So standing here on the right side of this door and not knowing what that little fucker is up to on the other side? Not knowing what the squirrel is going to do when he sees us?

It's making me ill.

Is he still in there? *Is he listening to us talk?*

I don't have anything to defend myself.

Do I face palm him with my hand? Deflect him with my mighty palm?

Maybe I should have brought a hockey stick.

Shit.

Lizzy clears her throat, then nudges me with an elbow. Subtly, but it was still a nudge nonetheless, as she steps aside, presumably so she can stand safely in the hallway while I step inside.

Alone.

Unprotected.

I don't like this.

I don't like this at all.

"Do I actually have to go in there?" I can feel my entire face lifted, brows in my hairline, mouth frowning, the space between my brows pulled tight.

I figured I'd ask before cracking the door open and getting my first glance into the fiery abyss of the upcoming battle with an unknown enemy.

Lizzy isn't amused, her jaw dropping. She stomps her feet.

"Are you being serious right now?"

NEWS FLASH, LIZZY: YES, I'M BEING SERIOUS RIGHT NOW!

Here I am, standing at death's door while she clutches her robe—the way one would clutch a string of pearls, tightly and to her bosom like a fucking virgin in an 80s teen movie. Except this isn't a movie, and she probably isn't a virgin—not with tits and a body like that...no way, no how.

My point is, how dare she act as if she's the one who has to step foot behind the door.

'Cause she doesn't.

I do.

Me.

"I don't know what's going to come flying out at me from behind this door, do you? The last time something came flying at my face, it was a puck, and I knew it was going to come flying at my face so I was prepared."

The second last thing that came flying toward my face was a fist, attached to the arm of a dude on an opposing team. He took a cheap shot at me after one of his teammates started throwing punches at Charlie—my roommate—and probably wanted to liven the play.

Fists > squirrel talons.

"Wait. I can't tell if you're being serious or not."

"Yes, I'm being serious about not wanting to go into your room!" Am I pouting? It's hard to tell with my voice this high-pitched all of a sudden. Panic has set in, ha ha. "Cut me some slack, would ya? Five minutes ago, I was shoving dinner into my face and enjoying what promises to be a lovely sunset. Now I'm standing outside the door of someone I just met, ready to be attacked by a squirrel."

I'm sore. Tired.

Oh—and I bit my bottom lip during practice, so that was fun. Sue me for not wanting to fight a squirrel and for wanting to relax instead.

I clear my throat to dial it down a notch. "I don't need my face gnawed off by a rodent. I have a game this weekend."

That makes Lizzy laugh, and she rolls her eyes again, pulling her robe taut across her chest. "It's not going to gnaw your face off."

"You do not know that for a fact."

I don't see why she's laughing or what's so damn funny about my predicament. My hand clutches the doorknob, though I'm somehow unable to turn it.

"And if you were so confident in him being a friendly squirrel, you wouldn't need me here." Boom, roasted.

She laughs harder as if I'd said the funniest thing ever, holding a hand to her mouth as if to stifle the loud giggling.

God, if only she weren't so fucking cute.

"I'm not facing a wild animal on my own." She laughs. "I have *seen* these things lurking on campus, and they are *not* our friends."

Her head shakes, and I think this is the perfect opportunity to let her in on my "Squirrels are here to take over the world" theory.

"Wild animal?" That's a bit of a stretch. But still. "They *are* trying to take over the world. Agree. Way too many of those creepy little fucks."

Lizzy nods at my hard truths. "Those are facts."

I inhale a deep breath—the kind of breath I take during a hockey game when the ref drops the puck onto the ice to begin the game.

"Here goes nothing." My mouth twists into a sardonic smile. "It's been nice knowing you, Lizzy."

Sure would have been nice to see those tits, Lizzy Campbell.

C'est la vie. *That's life.*

With one glance back at her, I give the doorknob a turn and push the door open, one inch—then two. Three inches.

Four.

"My heart is racing so fast," she whispers behind me, voice getting closer, her front pressed against my back as if she were trying to look over my shoulder.

"Mine too," I whisper despite not wanting to sound like a total pussy.

Stepping gingerly—*very fucking gingerly*—into her bedroom, creeping inch by inch, I scan the perimeter for the squirrel, unable to spot the bastard within my first few steps.

I glance around again, scanning.

Wanting to find it but not wanting to find it.

Dresser. Mirror.

Open closet with the clothes moved to one side.

Desk. Lamp.

Bed.

My eyes take it all in.

No squirrel.

"Do you see it?" Lizzy whispers behind me, her boobs pressed into my back as if we were walking through a haunted house during Halloween. It's completely unnecessary—plus, I don't need her latched to my back if I have to make an emergency exit. I'd look like a giant asshole shoving her out of the way to escape.

"Do you think it went back inside the hole?" She's still whispering.

She said hole.

I want to laugh because deep down inside, I'm a twelve-year-old idiot.

"Doubtful." Most likely, it's hiding in plain sight, and we just haven't been able to locate the damn thing because we're looking too hard. Plus, she has a few stuffed animals, and it could be lurking behind those—hard to tell.

Lizzy is on her tiptoes behind me, peering over my shoulder. Breathing heavily, she grips my biceps as if our lives depended on me for survival. In reality, she doesn't stand a chance if I'm her deciding factor. I'm so out of here if that thing pounces.

Her nails dig into my arm, but I don't exactly hate it. I've always liked it a little rough. Ha!

"You can let go of me any day now," I tell her even though it doesn't bother me one bit that her tits stay pressed into my back.

"But I don't see it."

"Neither do I." *It has to be here somewhere.*

Waiting.

We step back out of the bedroom, and I pull the door closed a bit so the squirrel can't hear our discussion. I don't need it hearing our plan because I don't need him trying to outsmart us.

"What should we do?" Lizzy's lips say quietly.

"I have no idea. I'm not sure he's even in there." Okay. There is no plan.

"He has to be in there," she says with conviction. "Can you go in—all the way in, I mean. To make sure?"

Is she out of her damn mind?

"You want me to go all the way into your room, *without* protection, and do what? Wait him out?" I ask slowly so there's no confusing the question. "I have no pads with me."

Pads would be nice. Chest plate, face mask.

Gloves.

"Please?"

Oh god, is she begging me?

I've never had a girl do that before let alone one that is half dressed, in her pretty pink bathrobe, towel turban wrapped around her hair.

Her quiet little plea is enough for me, and I nod like the idiot I am, large and in charge—squaring my shoulders—ready for what awaits me when I go farther into the room.

Turning around to face her, I say, "Wait here," I say somberly, as if I were about to embark on a solo mission to Armageddon. "And close the door behind me. Just in case."

Lizzy nods, hands back on her robe, pulling it closed.

"Okay."

"Stand clear of the door—you know, in case."

"In case what?" Her doe eyes go wide.

"You know," I say it mysteriously. "In case I have to come charging back through it. I don't know what that little bastard is capable of." I growl it the way I imagine someone in the military would growl it, fierce and determined as they head into battle.

"Okay." Lizzy gulps, touching my bicep to reassure me. "Be careful. And good luck."

It's on the tip of my tongue to theatrically say, "Maybe you should kiss me for good luck," but I don't have the balls. Instead, I simply dip my invisible hat. I turn the doorknob, push it open again slowly, then stick my head through before stepping all the way inside her room.

The door closes behind me.

I immediately forget what I'm here for, eyes surveying the landscape now that she's not pressing her boobs into my back, distracting me.

It's pink.

Not the walls, but her quilt. The bed has been made, and everything is as tidy as the rest of the house.

Flowers. Florals.

Girly.

A perfume collection sits on the desk atop a mirrored tray. A flat iron and blow dryer hang on a little rack that's been affixed to the wall.

There's a peg board or whatever you call it next to her mirror, with ribbons and a calendar. A photo of Lizzy holding a furry gray cat. One of Lizzy and a young boy. Lizzy in a triangle bikini swimsuit and three other girls her age, on the pier at a lake.

She's dripping wet.

Laughing.

I peel my eyes off that photo and continue scanning, feet rooted to the floor, not making any sudden movements.

Curtains hang where a closet door would normally be. Dresser nestled away inside, and above it? A squirrel size hole.

"Ah. The scene of the crime," I muse.

I search for the squirrel with my eyes, staying close to the door, legs braced for an attack—the same way I brace myself on the ice during a game or when my teammates are coming to check me in practice.

"Come on, dude—where you at? Help me out here."

I mean, I could actually live without him suddenly appearing. The last thing I need is an assault from a rodent because he's freaking the fuck out, trapped inside this room the same way I am.

Surprisingly enough, I spot a lacrosse stick leaning against the desk and decide to grab it—just in case—with no intention to use it if the thing decides to—

"HOLY SHIT!" I scream as the squirrel appears out of fucking nowhere, leaping to the curtain rod above the closet door, beady black eyes staring into me, whiskers twitching. His tiny little chest heaves in and out.

My heart thumps inside my chest.

His heart thumps inside *his* chest.

We watch each other, both of us calculating.

I hold perfectly still, hands shaking.

"Stay where you are," I tell it, trying to remain calm. "Don't move."

Then from outside in the hallway: "Brodie, are you okay?"

"I'm fine," I say even though I'm afraid to make noise—the last thing I want is the squirrel getting scared of my voice and pouncing from his perch above the window. "Found him."

"What's it doing?"

"Staring at me. He's over the closet." Perched. Like a squirrel.

"Are you going to open the window?"

"Hell no I'm not opening it," I hiss.

At least not from inside the room. No fucking way.

"Why not?"

BECAUSE I'M SCARED, THAT'S WHY!

What I actually say, through clenched teeth, is, "I don't want to move."

Lizzy is silent for a few seconds. "Brodie, you're going to have to. You can't stand there all night." Then she asks, "Should I come in?"

I shake my head. "No."

SAVE YOURSELF!

In a calm, measured voice, I add, "The good news is, he hasn't destroyed anything."

"That's good." Pause. "We really should try to open the window though."

And by *we* she means *me*.

I shake my head again, vigorously. "Nuh-uh. He's right there."

"If he's sitting near the window, that makes it the perfect time to open it."

I wish she would stop talking.

No fucking way am I getting any closer.

No way am I going to—

Chapter 3

Have you read The Pucker Next Door?

Lizzy

From inside my bedroom, Brodie lets out a bloodcurdling scream that could wake the dead. The kind you'd hear coming out of a teenage girl in a horror movie.

One who's being murdered.

Then he comes bursting through the door, his large body almost plowing me down as he dramatically slams the door closed behind him, collapsing against the wall.

"I-it...it...almost..." He huffs and puffs and puffs some more, like someone seriously out of shape that's just run up twenty flights of stairs, and I know he's not out of shape because he's on the hockey team of a division one university.

"Almost what, Brodie?" I patronizingly ask, crossing my arms because he has been blowing this situation out of proportion since the second he walked into the house.

"A-almost...got...me."

Oh, brother. He's being so dramatic.

I put a hand on his shoulder, patting him like a child. "What happened?"

He clutches a hand to his chest. Honestly, he does. "It lunged at me."

"Did it lunge at you, or was it just jumping to a different spot?"

"*At* me."

"How do you know?"

"Because. One second, he was c-chilling there, looking at me with his tiny beady eyes, and the next, he was jumping at my fucking face like MacGyver."

Who the hell is MacGyver?

I don't ask.

He is so worked up.

I try not to laugh. "Did he get you?"

Brodie cocks an eyebrow as if he's insulted I'd even have to ask. "No, but he could have."

"But he didn't."

"But he could have."

"Well." I pause. "Where did he go when he landed?"

"I didn't look." He huffs some more. "I was too busy screaming."

Yeah, I heard.

The whole neighborhood probably heard. "So he didn't touch you, he didn't eat you, and you didn't see where he went after he lunged."

Not helpful.

Not at all.

"Correct."

When Brodie stands to his full height, I finally notice how much larger he is than I am.

How tall.

How broad.

How *good* he smells.

Even though the situation is serious, I can't help noticing all these things about him because I'm a warm-blooded female, and that's what I do.

"What do we do now?" I can feel myself worrying my bottom lip. "My landlord isn't scheduled to be here with the pest control guy until tomorrow, and I can't get ahold of anyone."

He considers this for a few seconds. "We'll open the window and hope he hops out at some point tonight."

Brodie shoulders his way past me, elbow brushing against my right boob as he heads toward the front door.

I follow, trudging behind until we're both standing outside my bedroom window, side-by-side, staring up at it. It's not as low to the ground as it seems from the inside, and I scratch my head, debating our options.

Ladder.

Stool.

"You're gonna have to climb up on my shoulders. There's no

other way we can reach it," he announces, the exact opposite of what I would have suggested as a solution.

I've seen cheerleaders' stunt teams, but I'm not bendy or flexible and cannot imagine myself climbing on this guy, let alone being able to balance and not fall off.

"That's never going to work…"

"You're tiny. It'll be easy."

My girly insides get a little mushy when he calls me tiny because I'm not tiny in the least. He's just massive.

"Well," he says impatiently. "Do you have a ladder?"

"No." I pause. "Do you?"

He shakes his head. "Just get up on my shoulders and push on it if you can. The window is unlocked, thank god."

He gives instructions as if it were going to be easy to hop onto his shoulders and jack a window open—as if I do it every day.

"But I'm…" Naked.

Not wearing underwear.

No bra. *Just this robe.* Because I thought it would be a good idea to lounge around after my shower and not put clothes on. Because I did not think anyone would see me, let alone need to boost me up on their shoulders.

N – A – K – E – D.

My unfinished sentence lingers, and I know that he knows I'm not wearing anything beneath this pink wrap.

"I won't look."

Honestly? *I wouldn't mind if you did.*

Brodie isn't classically good-looking, but he's big, and he has that ridiculous deep voice that has the potential to make a girl cream her shorts with very little effort. I imagine he'd make a great radio DJ if the hockey gig doesn't work out for him.

He is lumbersexual personified, complete with the beard.

"…Just get up on my shoulders, Lizzy. I promise I won't peek," he says, and I snap my attention back to his mouth.

…won't peek, his mouth is saying.

Won't peek, won't peek, won't peek.

"Trust me."

Very tentatively, I step forward.

Brodie squats down as low as he can go to make it easier to climb on. But I'm not coordinated and have no desire to straddle his shoulders, so I start whining about how difficult this is, how I'm not a gymnast, how I'm not bendy, how he's too tall, *blah blah blah*. Complain, complain, complain.

"Fine," he relents. "How 'bout I lift you by the waist. You okay with that?"

Am I okay with that?

"We gotta get this window open so that tiny asshole sees his way out of your room." He hesitates. "Unless you want to leave him inside until your landlord gets there."

He makes a strong argument.

I give my head a little nod. "Okay. This just feels awkward because we just met, and now you want me to climb on top of you while I'm naked." I drop the reminder again because like I said, I'm a warm-blooded female, and now I'm playing a new game—get a reaction out of Mr. Serious and Professional.

"I hadn't even noticed."

Hadn't noticed?

I actually believe him.

"Be careful when you lift me, 'kay? I have sensitive skin." The wind kicks up, and I feel a draft hit my tush, reminding me exactly how naked I am, *fully aware* that I could easily march back inside and borrow pants from one of my roommates so I'm not outside half naked.

I tell him I'm naked as a joke, but the expression on his face falls, and suddenly, Brodie looks miserable.

"Let's get this over with, yeah?" His voice is gruff. Stern.

I step in front of him, bracing to have his hands on my hips, my body, my—

"Ready?"

"I was born ready," I deadpan 'cause I'm totally not ready.

Have you read The Pucker Next Door?

"On three."
One.
Two.
"Three." Brodie lifts me, and when he does, I swear my robe hikes up, exposing my bare bum, the breeze hitting my bare flesh in a way that has me glancing down. I angle to get a glimpse of my own ass but get a glimpse of his face instead.

He's horrified.

"Oh my god, is my ass in your face?" It's the one and only thing I care about right now. The squirrel inside my room is suddenly forgotten as I teeter high above the ground, ass end not far from Brodie's face.

He neither confirms nor denies it. "Just push the window open, please," he grumbles. "We have a job to do."

Right.

A job to do.

Window to open and all that jazz because: squirrels.

If I'm too heavy for him to lift or he's having a difficult time keeping me steady, he doesn't show it. His arms don't tremble, and he doesn't waver.

My *god*, he's so strong.

It's sexy as all hell, and he's right in my backyard...

Then again, with his hands on my waist and the breeze on my skin, it's kind of getting me tingling in places I don't want to think about, considering there's a fucking *squirrel* terrorizing my room.

Leave it to me to be thinking about sex at a time like this.

Read the rest of The Puck Next Door now on Amazon - Available in KU!

about sara ney

Sara Ney is the USA Today Bestselling Author of the How to Date a Douchebag series, best known for her sexy, laugh-out-loud sports and contemporary romances. Among her favorite vices, she includes: traveling, historical architecture and nerding out on all things Victorian. She's a "cool mom" living in the Midwest who loves antique malls, resale clothing shops, and once carried a vintage copper sink through the airport as her carry-on because it didn't fit in her suitcase.

also by sara ney

Biggest Player releasing July 29th

Not Your Biggest Fan

The Pucker Next Door

Campus Legends

How To Lose At Love

How To Win The Girl

How To Score Off Field

Accidentally in Love Series

The Player Hater

The Mrs. Degree

The Make Out Artist

Jock Hard Series

Switch Hitter

Jock Row

Jock Rule

Switch Bidder

Jock Road

Jock Royal

Jock Reign

Jock Romeo

Trophy Boyfriends Series

Hard Pass

Hard Fall

Hard Love

Hard Luck

The Bachelors Club Series

Bachelor Society

Bachelor Boss

How to Date a Douchebag Series

The Studying Hours

The Failing Hours

The Learning Hours

The Coaching Hours

The Lying Hours

The Teaching Hours

#ThreeLittleLies Series

Things Liars Say

Things Liars Hide

Things Liars Fake

All The Right Moves Series

All The Sweet Moves

All The Bold Moves

All The Right Moves

The Bachelor Society Duet: The Bachelors Club

Jock Hard Box Set: Books 1-3